One Quiet Woman

Also by Anna Jacobs

THE RIVENSHAW SAGA
A Time to Remember
A Time for Renewal
A Time to Rejoice
Gifts For Our Time

THE TRADERS
The Trader's Wife
The Trader's Sister
The Trader's Dream
The Trader's Gift
The Trader's Reward

THE SWAN RIVER SAGA
Farewell to Lancashire
Beyond the Sunset
Destiny's Path

THE GIBSON FAMILY
Salem Street
High Street
Ridge Hill
Hallam Square
Spinners Lake

THE IRISH SISTERS
A Pennyworth of Sunshine
Twopenny Rainbows
Threepenny Dreams

THE STALEYS
Down Weavers Lane
Calico Road

THE KERSHAW SISTERS
Our Lizzie
Our Polly
Our Eva
Our Mary Ann

THE SETTLERS
Lancashire Lass
Lancashire Legacy

THE PRESTON FAMILY
Pride of Lancashire
Star of the North
Bright Day Dawning
Heart of the Town

LADY BINGRAM'S AIDES
Tomorrow's Promises
Yesterday's Girl

STANDALONE NOVELS
Jessie
Like No Other
Freedom's Land

ANNA JACOBS

One Quiet Woman

Ellindale Saga Book One

HODDER

First published in Great Britain in 2017 by Hodder & Stoughton
An Hachette UK company

1

First published in paperback in 2017

Copyright © Anna Jacobs 2017

A CIP catalogue record for this title is available from the British Library

ISBN 978 1 473 63080 2

Typeset in Plantin Light by Palimpsest Book Production Ltd, Falkirk, Stirlingshire

Printed and bound by Clays Ltd, St Ives plc

Hodder & Stoughton policy is to use papers that are natural, renewable
and recyclable products and made from wood grown in sustainable forests. The logging
and manufacturing processes are expected to conform to the environmental
regulations of the country of origin.

Hodder & Stoughton Ltd
Carmelite House
50 Victoria Embankment
London EC4Y 0DZ

www.hodder.co.uk

Dear Reader

I hope you enjoy my new story. When I finished the Rivenshaw series, I wanted to stay 'in the area' so I mentally walked through my imaginary valley. At the top, on the very edge of the moors, I 'found' the village of Ellindale.

If you look at the opening credits in the TV series *Last of the Summer Wine*, you'll see what my imaginary village looks like, though Ellindale is smaller: grey stone houses, some three storeys high, perched along the edge of the moors.

I grew up in Rochdale and we used to visit relatives near Todmorden by bus, driving through similar countryside. We lived in a terraced house, typical two-up, two-down. As a child I fell in love with the wide open spaces of the moors and that love has never left me. I still go back up 'on the tops' when we visit England and have introduced my 'southern' husband to the beauties of the north, which are very different from the softer beauty of his childhood surroundings.

For my new series I wanted to stay in my favourite period of history, 1900–1950, so chose the thirties. Yes, there was a depression and people were having it tough, but they were also helping one another, finding ways to carry on. There must have been innumerable small acts of heroism, as there are in daily life today. My granddad actually did go 'on the tramp' looking for work and never failed to send money home.

I enjoyed doing the research and one of my favourite books was J. B. Priestley's *English Journey*, memoirs of a trip round England he made in the thirties. He was very complimentary about the northern spirit in these times. So am I.

Come and meet Leah, a quiet woman who might not be able to change the world but who can make a big difference to her struggling neighbours' lives.

Anna

N.B.: You can see some photos from my childhood at the back of the book.

PART ONE
Lancashire: Autumn 1930

I

Leah Turner saw her little sister off to school, then tipped her purse upside down on the kitchen table. A penny and a halfpenny coin fell out. After staring at them in despair she had a weep into her apron. But not for long. If she let herself continue crying, her eyes would betray her.

'Oh, Dad,' she murmured, 'why did you have to be the one standing in the wrong place?' He'd been killed, her lovely kind father, by a flying piece of metal as one of the machines at the laundry was being repaired and tested.

Since then she'd tried in vain to find a job, eking out every penny and walking for miles, not only around the large village of Birch End where they lived, but going right down into the nearby town of Rivenshaw, at the lower end of the valley. But jobs were scarce in these hard times, had been for years, and anyway, they paid women less than men. She and her little sister Rosa would have to move to a room in a lodging house soon, because she'd not be able to afford the rent.

Mr Harris, the owner of the laundry, had paid for a cheap funeral and given her a month's pay to make up for her father being killed. He'd said she and her sister could live rent-free in this house for six months, but Sam Griggs, the rent man, had come round the following week and told her she'd misunderstood and it was only two months. After that, she must pay the normal rent or get out.

No one dared protest or argue with him.

She went to stand at the front door for a breath of fresh air. The other women in the street had been out already, each scrubbing her doorstep and the flagstones on the nearby pavement, then giving them a creamy colour by scrubbing them with holystones. She couldn't afford a holystone now or the fuel to heat water, but she could still scrub the door-step, couldn't she? She prided herself on being clean.

Bringing out the mat, she knelt on it and began scrubbing. Her fingers were cold because it was a chilly day, even if the sun was shining. Her heart felt even colder.

What were she and Rosa going to do next week when the two months ran out? The government might have abolished workhouses in April – she'd read about it in the newspaper at the library – but they still put people who were destitute in the same building, whatever they called it.

She heard a car approaching and sat up, easing her back and staring round. Like everyone else, Leah knew the car by sight. It belonged to the wife of the owner of the laundry. Mrs Harris owned a lot of houses in Birch End, the poorer sort of house, and kept them in bad repair.

To her surprise, the vehicle stopped in front of her house.

Mrs Harris opened the rear door and got out to stare at what Leah was doing. She looked at the bucket and dipped one fingertip in the cold, dirty water. 'Don't you know any better than that? You need soap and hot water to do a proper job, young woman! I want my houses keeping cleaner than this.'

Leah could feel herself stiffening in outrage at this criti-cism. She dropped the scrubbing brush into the bucket and stood up, trying to speak calmly, 'I know the best way to scrub a doorstep but—'

'Then why are you doing it so sloppily? Go and boil the kettle, you stupid girl.' She turned and walked back to the car.

It was the final straw. Leah took the three steps that brought her next to the open car door and yelled, 'My father was killed six weeks ago at your husband's laundry, so we don't have the money for soap now, or any coal to heat water. We have one slice of bread left and I'm saving it for my little sister's tea tonight. I'll be going hungry.'

She would have to go to the pawnshop, something she'd been dreading. She'd never pawned anything in her life before.

Silence. A passer-by had stopped to listen and stare. Mrs Harris scowled at him and he hurried on. She looked at the person in the car, then fumbled in her big black leather handbag and held something out. 'Here. And don't waste it.'

Automatically Leah took what was offered: a shilling.

Then she saw that it wasn't Sam Griggs sitting behind the driving wheel, but Mr Harris, who normally drove his own car. He nodded to her and it seemed, it really did, that his quick half-smile was genuinely sympathetic.

But he wouldn't intervene. Everyone knew he was hen-pecked, because the laundry had been in trouble when he inherited it from his father and his wife's money had saved it. But he'd paid a terrible price because she was a vicious woman. No one liked her, especially her tenants.

Leah's father had said the laundry was doing a lot better now, but Mr Harris would be stuck with the same nagging wife for the rest of his life, poor man. Leah had never had to accept charity before, but it meant food for Rosa, so she forced herself to say politely, 'Thank you, Mrs Harris.'

The lady pulled the car door shut, saying loudly, 'Drive on, Adam. What are you waiting for?'

As she watched the car go down the street and turn the corner, Leah wondered briefly why Mr Harris was driving his wife round the village on a working day instead of Sam Griggs.

Oh, who cared about them? There were far more important things to worry about.

The bitter taste of charity lingered in Leah's mouth all

morning, but when she came back from the shops, she had a loaf of day-old bread which cost half the usual price, and a pound of carrots. There were even a few pennies left in her purse.

But she'd still have to go to the pawnshop tomorrow and find out what prices they gave before deciding which pieces of furniture to offer them first.

She had one little treasure she was saving: her mother's wedding ring. Surely she'd be able to find some way of earning a living before that had to go?

The following morning, as Leah was about to set off for the pawnshop, there was a knock on the door. She opened it to see Jim Banks, the deputy manager from the laundry.

'Have you got a minute, lass?'

'Yes. Come in.' She held the door open, aware of the shadowy figure of Mrs Foster from across the street standing behind her net curtains watching, looking for something to gossip about.

'Come into the kitchen, Mr Banks. We're not using the front room at the moment.'

He sat down and she told him the bald truth. 'I can't offer you a cup of tea, because we've none in the house.'

'That bad, eh?'

'What did you expect, with Dad gone? There are no jobs going or I'd be out working. And any jobs that come up are given to men.'

'It was a bad do, that accident. We still miss Stan. Your father was a good worker.'

She blinked to clear the tears that would well in her eyes when anyone mentioned her father. 'How can I help you, Mr Banks?'

'I think it's me who can help you, lass. I've come to offer you a job at the laundry.'

'I thought there was nothing going.'

'Janet Green's husband's lost his job. They're moving to Barnsley to live with her aunt. So you'll be doing her job, helping with the bedding and towels, putting dirty clothes in the washing machines, feeding them through the wringers, then rinsing them and using the wringers again before hanging them in the drying room. You know the sort of thing.'

She nodded. She knew what it was like in the laundry from taking her father's lunch in when he forgot it, and from a short stint of trying to work there and not coping with the steamy atmosphere. Once the clothes were dry, the women had to feed sheet after sheet through the big ironing rollers. Tedious work, but she'd welcome anything. There was just one problem now, a big one.

'Will I be able to stay in this house, Mr Banks, do you think? Could Mr Harris speak to his wife about it? I've nowhere else to live, only I can't afford the present rent on a woman's wages.'

'I'm sorry. You'll have to find a room for yourself and your sister. Mr Harris tried, but his wife insists on her houses making a profit.'

Leah didn't allow herself to protest or even sigh. Beggars couldn't be choosers. 'I'll take the job. Thank you very much for offering it.'

'Thank Mr Harris. It was his idea, though I agreed with it.' He stood up and patted her on the shoulder. 'You'll start at six o'clock sharp on Monday morning. I've got to get back now.' Then he stopped and added, 'I'm afraid the other women won't like you getting the job and they might not be very helpful at first. They've daughters looking for work too, you see.'

'I'll manage. Please thank Mr Harris for me.'

'You can thank him yourself on Monday. He doesn't just

sit in the office all day. He knows everyone at the laundry by name.'

When she went back into the kitchen she found a sixpence on the table. 'Thank you, Mr Banks!' she said out loud, even though he could no longer hear her.

She would wait till tomorrow to visit the pawnshop, she decided. Or even the day after. She had enough money for food now, thank goodness. She might buy some potatoes and a bundle of sticks for fuel to boil them.

In the old days she'd have gone out gathering bits of wood, but these days the countryside at the lower end of the valley had been scoured clean of fallen branches and even twigs by others in need. There was no wood to be found on the moors, just peace and freedom. She loved walking there.

She looked at the clock. She might as well sweep the pavement in front of her house. That cost nothing.

Just after she started work, a man came striding along the street, tall, thin and well dressed in a showy way: Charlie Willcox who owned the pawnshop. He stopped beside her and took off his hat. 'Leah Turner.'

It was a statement not a question, so he clearly knew who she was. How strange. She'd been thinking of going to visit his shop. 'Yes.' She leaned on her sweeping brush and waited to see what he wanted.

He studied her thoroughly, his eyes going from top to toe, then back again. They were sharp eyes that saw every darned patch in her clothes, she was sure.

She drew herself up to her full height, which was nearly the same as his. 'I'm busy. What do you want, Mr Willcox? If you're trying to sell me something, I've no money.'

He chuckled. 'It just shows you don't use the pawnshops if you think I go out selling stuff to people. I own one here in Birch End and another in Rivenshaw, you know.'

'Yes. So I've heard.' She'd been going to visit his shop because people said he gave you fairer prices than Ma Baker did. There were two pawnshops in Birch End now, two! That was a sign of the hard times that had hit Lancashire since the Great War.

'No need to look at me like that. People need pawnshops in times like these, Miss Turner, and some need them at other times too.'

She shrugged.

'Can we go somewhere private to talk?'

That surprised her. 'Why?'

'You need a job. I might be able to help you.'

It wouldn't hurt to find out what he was offering. Working in a pawnshop wouldn't be any worse than working in the laundry, especially if it paid more. She set the bucket to one side and gestured to the front door. 'Come inside, then.'

He gestured to her to go first. He was polite, at least. She had to give him that. She led the way down the corridor, hearing his steps behind her.

It was strange. Some men made you feel uncomfortable walking behind you, but he didn't. He might have looked her up and down, but it hadn't been in that rude way Sam Griggs had with women.

'Please sit down, Mr Willcox.'

He took the chair she indicated at the kitchen table and she said it again, 'I can't offer you a cup of tea, I'm afraid, because I've none in the house.'

For the second time that day a man said, 'That bad, eh?' in a sympathetic tone of voice, which surprised her. Pawnshop owners weren't usually known for being sympathetic towards people in trouble. That was how they made their money, after all.

He was studying the room now. 'You keep the place clean.'

'Of course I do. Now tell me what you want. I'm sure you're a busy man.'

For the first time he looked less confident. 'Um, you'll have heard that I have a brother who got gassed in the war?'

'I don't know much about you and your family because I don't waste my time gossiping. All I know is that you've got an invalid brother.'

'His name's Jonah. He used to be a big, strong fellow, but he doesn't breathe very well these days so he isn't able to work full-time, especially not physical work. He helps out in the shop, though, does the accounts for me. He's really good with figures.'

He paused, seemed to be fumbling for words. 'Jonah's been living with me, but I'm about to get married and my fiancée doesn't want him sharing the house. So I'm looking for a wife for Jonah as well. I'm told you're a good housewife and I can see for myself how clean you keep this place, even now.'

She looked at him in puzzlement. Had she misheard him? Surely he didn't mean that he wanted her to marry his brother?

He ran his fingertip round his collar as if it had suddenly become too tight. 'I um, think you might make a good wife for Jonah.'

He *had* meant it! 'Why me?'

'Women gossip in the shop and when your father was killed, I heard about you being left to bring up your little sister. I'm sorry about your father, by the way. Everyone seemed to think well of you, and it made me think. So I checked out a few things. You did really well at school.'

'Why does it matter how well I did at school?'

Mr Willcox grinned at her. 'Our Jonah always has his head in a book. He'd not be happy married to someone who didn't read and take an interest in the world.'

'Oh.'

'So . . . I thought we might make a bargain about you marrying Jonah.'

'If he can't hold down a job, how can he support a wife?'

'He has independent means. He's not rich or anything, but he inherited a few bits and pieces from his mother's side that bring in enough money for him to live on. He's my stepbrother actually, same father, different mothers, you see.'

She wasn't going to accept such a ridiculous offer, but she might as well get to the bottom of things. Perhaps his brother might like a housekeeper instead? 'That means he's above my station in life.'

'He won't care about that, and I don't, either. It's whether you can take care of him, look after the house and so on.' Again, he looked round the room and nodded. 'I want him to be happy, though, and he couldn't be with a stupid wife. His happiness matters a lot to me.'

'Well, I don't want to marry anyone for his money, thank you very much, Mr Willcox. Anyway, a marriage of convenience is a ridiculous idea in this day and age. We're not living in the Middle Ages now, you know. It's 1930, not 1330!'

He leaned back and grinned at her. 'They said you'd read half the books in the library. Sounds as if they were right. You use a lot of break-teeth words like Jonah does. And it's not such a ridiculous idea if the bargain suits us all. It'd surely be better than working in the laundry? I asked a woman who works for me about you as well. Vi said the steaminess in the laundry made you wheeze when you were younger and you had to stop working there. It didn't suit her, either, which is how she wound up working for me.'

He stared at her thoughtfully. 'She said you did so well at school your mother wanted you to become a teacher but she died suddenly, so you had to take over the house and raise your little sister. Am I right?'

'Yes, but I can't see what—' Leah glanced down, noticed her reddened hands and clasped them in her lap to hide their ugliness. 'But I still don't see why you think it'd suit me to marry your brother. Or him to marry me. Does he even know about this?'

'He knows I think it's a good idea and he's prepared to meet you. So I'm only offering you a chance, not a certain thing, till he's approved of you. Look, he gave up a lot in the service of his country, our Jonah did. He's a great talker as well as a great reader. I'm sure you two would get on. I'm told you go to the library every week. Is that right?'

'Yes, because it's free. But reading books doesn't bring in money. I don't think—'

'Don't say no till you've heard me out. Let me tell you more about him. Jonah is three years older than me. His mother died bearing him, which is why my father called him Jonah. But she came from a better family than *my* mother and she left him a small cottage out in Ellindale, as well as a few other things . . . '

'Which suggests that your brother needs someone of his own kind to marry.'

'Bear with me. The tenant of the cottage moved out last quarter day and I told Jonah not to put anyone else in because I was going to get married and he'd need somewhere to live.'

'Why can't this Jonah of yours find his own wife?'

'He's a quiet sort of fellow, a bit shy with the ladies.'

'Well, don't bother to pursue this. I'm not selling myself into slavery for life. I'd rather work at the laundry.'

'No, you wouldn't. No one would.'

She stared defiantly back at his confident smile, but was beginning to realise he was right. She had been dreading working in the laundry, absolutely dreading it.

She supposed his offer was a compliment, sort of. But

how could she possibly marry a complete stranger? This man's brother might be cruel or – or anything. And then she'd be stuck with him. Like that nice Mr Harris was stuck with his horrible wife.

'Look, why don't you come and meet Jonah, Miss Turner, see how you get on? It'll be much easier to decide when you know what he's like. It's not just you, you know. If *he* doesn't want to marry you, I won't push him into anything. And if you're against marrying him after you've met, well, I don't want to give Jonah a wife who resents him. But it wouldn't hurt to give it some consideration. I'm usually quite good at planning and making sure things work out all right.'

She opened her mouth to refuse, then looked down and caught sight of her worn, nearly empty purse. Should she do that? Meet this Jonah Willcox? 'I suppose that's a sensible thing to do. Meet him, I mean. But I'm making no promises.'

'Good. We'll go and see him now.'

'*Now?*' It came out as a squeak. 'With me looking my worst?'

He chuckled. 'I'll give you ten minutes to change while I go and call a taxi. We live just outside Birch End, so it'll be better for us to drive out there. I can't drive, so I don't have a car of my own.'

'I—you—oh, very well!'

She saw him out, then ran up the stairs. Once in her bedroom she moved rapidly round, changing into her Sunday best and tidying her hair. 'You're an idiot,' she muttered to her reflection in the dressing-table mirror.

She was quite pleased with her appearance, though. These clothes weren't shabby, at least. She wasn't a beauty, not with her straight brown hair and blue-grey eyes, but she wasn't ugly, either.

No one had ever come courting her, not in these hard times, because she had her father and sister to care for. She'd got used to the idea of remaining a spinster. Didn't like it, would have preferred to marry and have children, but there you were. Life hadn't given her the chance.

Now . . . it occurred to her she might have a chance if she accepted this offer. She swallowed hard, but already it was beginning to sound a possibility, a better solution than the laundry.

When she thought about it, she realised she'd been wrong to say people didn't marry for convenience these days. Men who were widowed usually married within a few weeks, because they needed someone to look after their house and children. Women who were widowed married to find another breadwinner.

For her, it would all depend on what this Jonah Willcox was like. She wasn't marrying an unkind man, whatever anyone said, because there was Rosa to think about as well as herself.

2

Jonah Willcox woke from his nap with a start that set his heart pounding. It took him a few moments to realise it was only a fever dream, the usual nightmare where he was back in the trenches, slipping desperately in the mud, struggling to keep up with the man in front of him.

Thank heaven! He was at home in the sitting room of his brother's house, and the damned war had happened over a decade ago. He patted his chest a few times and his heart gradually stopped fluttering. He was missing his stroll today. He might not be able to walk fast but he enjoyed the fresh air and always felt it did him good to get out and breathe deeply. He especially liked this time of year, with the leaves starting to fall and the air crisp and invigorating.

Today he'd planned to walk up the lower slopes of the moors, but unfortunately his brother Charlie had phoned to say he was hoping to bring a woman home to meet him about 'you know what', so he had to stay at home.

Charlie might not have come out with any details of why he was pushing Jonah to marry, but he had overheard things. Marion had told Charlie more than once that she didn't intend to start their married life caring for an invalid, thank you very much, especially when it wasn't even necessary. His brother could perfectly well find himself a wife to do that.

Actually, Jonah didn't want to live with Marion either. She

was far too sharp and bossy. He couldn't understand what Charlie saw in her. A slim body and pretty doll-like face might look good, but a selfish nature and scornful attitude towards those below her in the world spoiled a woman's suitability for marriage as far as he was concerned.

Jonah had long fancied living out at Ellindale, but Charlie had got it into his head that if his older brother went to live there, he would need a wife. So as usual Charlie had rushed into arranging all this like a bull at a gate.

The trouble was, when his brother rushed into things so enthusiastically, they had a tendency to go well, even when you didn't expect them to. Charlie was a clever chap, no doubt about that, clever in business especially. He had a gift for making money, even in such economically depressed times.

Jonah sighed. There was something else that worried him about Charlie's idea, something he hadn't been able to say out loud. He wasn't at all sure he could manage the husbandly duties in bed these days.

He'd discuss the whole thing again with Charlie after he'd met this woman. It'd be stupid to refuse to meet her, but a housekeeper would do just as well for his purposes. And not even a live-in one, by preference. He was thirty-four and had got used to his own company because Charlie was out all day and often in the evening too.

The coming changes were a good thing, because they'd made him start to take more control of his life. It was so easy to leave everything to his more forceful brother.

He might even buy himself a car, just a little runabout. Charlie kept telling him to use taxis, but you had to wait around for them. Yes, a car would be nice. He'd seen photos of a rather smart little saloon, an Austin Swallow. Not too expensive, just under £200. He could afford that easily. Even Charlie didn't realise how much Jonah had in the savings bank. He hadn't only been left the cottage at Ellindale but a trust fund and some other bits and pieces too. The fund didn't bring in a lot of money, but there was more than enough to live on and he had been careful with it, so had added to the savings and even made one or two small investments that had paid off. He might not be as pushy as Charlie but he had a similar flair for making money.

As for driving a car, Charlie didn't want to learn because he was short-sighted and hated the idea of wearing spectacles. But there was nothing wrong with Jonah's eyes and he had driven vehicles of all shapes and sizes during the war. He was sure the modern ones would be even easier with their electric starter motors and easier gear changing. He didn't think he'd have the strength to hand crank an engine to start it, not now.

He began pacing up and down the hall, into the kitchen and out again, suddenly feeling nervous and wishing Charlie hadn't got him into this. There was no *point* in him marrying because he doubted he'd make old bones. He had his books, was thinking of taking up oil painting, because he was quite good at drawing, and if he had a car he could go out for drives on fine days.

That would be enough. It had to be. What couldn't be cured must be endured. There was never a truer saying when it came to the results of being gassed.

He heard footsteps coming up the garden path and braced himself to meet the woman prepared to marry a cripple for money. She'd probably be a hard-faced harpy.

He also braced himself to refuse to do what his brother wanted, for once. Some things you had to decide for yourself.

Leah was surprised at how big Charlie's house was, detached, modern and in the best street in the village. Pawnshops must bring in more money than she'd thought if he could afford this.

'This way.' He opened the gate and led the way up the path.

There was a sign on the wall next to the front door saying *Redgate Cottage*, and indeed the gate and door had both been painted a dark red. But this was no cottage. She'd seen places like this advertised for sale in magazines and newspapers and they always called them 'residences'.

As Charlie opened the front door, he called, 'It's me. I've brought someone to meet you, Jonah lad.' He gestured to her to go into the hall.

She could feel herself blushing even before the man walked slowly out of a room at the rear of the house. Jonah bore a strong resemblance to his brother, though he was better looking in a gentler way.

He stared back at her openly, looking stiff and unwelcoming. Her heart sank. He didn't seem any happier about this meeting than she was. She didn't intend to allow herself to be forced on a man who was reluctant. What sort of life would that lead to?

He was taller than her, with a thin, intelligent face, dark hair and that slightly gasping way of breathing she'd heard from other men gassed during the war.

'We'll go into the sitting room.' Charlie led the way, indicating seats and waiting until they'd sat down to introduce his two companions to one another properly.

'Miss Turner, this is my brother, Jonah. Jonah, this is Leah Turner, whose father was killed in that accident at the laundry a few weeks ago.'

She saw Jonah's stiff expression change suddenly into compassion. 'I'm sorry. That must have been very difficult for you.'

'Thank you. He was a good father.'

Silence fell, heavy and awkward. She couldn't think what to say so kept her eye on Charlie for clues about what to do next.

He waited a moment or two, looking from one to the other, then laughed and stood up again. 'You two both know why you're here and you need to have a chat if you're to get to know one another. You won't do that easily with me sitting between you like Piggy in the Middle. I'll come back in an hour or so to drive you home, Miss Turner.'

'Charlie, don't—' Jonah began.

But Charlie was out of the room before either of them could stop him. The front door slammed and footsteps ran lightly down the path.

Leah felt frozen with embarrassment and it was a while before she even dared look at her companion. He appeared to be as embarrassed as she was, which made her feel a little better.

'This is a difficult situation,' he said abruptly. 'Typical of Charlie, don't you think?'

'I'd never met him until today, only seen him in the street, so I don't know. He just turned up at my house and . . . and swept me away.'

'He does that sort of thing. I'd never even heard your name until just now.'

'Did you know he wanted to find you a wife?'

'Yes. But he'd only talked about it in vague terms and I wasn't at all sure I was going to let him. Um, would you like a cup of tea?'

'I'd love one.'

'Let's go into the kitchen, then.' He stared round the room as if he didn't really like it. She didn't either. There was just too much of everything.

'Charlie's fiancée has been decorating in here. There's a little sun room off the kitchen, which I much prefer to sit in.'

At the kitchen door, Leah stopped, staring round avidly. 'Oh, how lovely and modern!'

She'd studied the photos of kitchens in women's magazines, because she enjoyed cooking – when she had anything to cook. She read nearly all the magazines in the library and sometimes copied out recipes. Not that she could afford to try most of them, but still, one day she might.

'It's the sort of kitchen women dream of, with a gas cooker and matching kitchen units. Oh, and there's even a refrigerator. Fancy that! I've never even seen one, let alone used one.'

He was smiling now.

'Come and hold your hand in front of it when I open the refrigerator door.'

She did that. 'It's so cold inside! How do they do it? I bet it keeps food fresh for far longer.' She always thought it wasn't fair of the magazines to show such luxurious dwellings when most women would never get a home half as nice. No one in her street had a house with an indoor bathroom, let alone a fancy kitchen.

Jonah spread his hands in a helpless gesture. 'Nothing but the best for our Charlie!'

She glanced sideways at him. 'He must have worked hard to get all this.'

'He works hard, yes, but he also works clever. That's what makes the most difference.' Jonah poured boiling water into the pot and brought it across to the table to brew. 'What would we do without our cups of tea?'

It was out before she could stop it and her voice was sharp. 'We'd manage.'

He looked at her thoughtfully. 'Is that what you've been doing?'

'I haven't had any choice. Dad was the breadwinner and there's only me to look after my younger sister now. The trouble is, I've been keeping house for my family since my mother died of the influenza, so I've never gone out to work.'

'What's your sister called?'

'Rosa.'

'Pretty name.' He put out a large plate, tipped some shop-bought biscuits on it from a biscuit barrel and carried it out to the sun room, gesturing to a rattan chair. 'We'll wait to let the tea brew.' He sat down opposite her. 'And your name's Leah. That's unusual. I don't think I've ever met anyone called Leah before.'

'I haven't either, so I looked it up in a book at the library. It's an Old Testament name and means "weary".'

'Jonah's from the Old Testament too. He was apparently swallowed by a whale.' He gave a wry smile. 'The name's also used for people who bring bad luck. My brother's fiancée, Marion, told me I should change it to something nicer, because she doesn't like introducing me as Jonah.'

It was out before she could stop herself. 'What a silly thing to say!'

'She can be silly but she can also manage Charlie better than anyone else and her family's well-connected in the valley.' He leaned forward 'I'll just bring the teapot. It must have brewed by now. How do you like it?'

'Milk, no sugar.' It had been one of her little economies before her father died not to have sugar in their tea. You couldn't economise if you had nothing to economise with, though.

'Have a biscuit.'

She wasn't stupid enough to refuse food. Her mouth had been watering at the sight of them and she'd been praying that her empty stomach wouldn't rumble.

When they were settled again, Jonah said abruptly, 'Charlie worries about turning me out of my home here, but I wouldn't want to live with them after he gets married.'

'Well, newly-weds usually do like to be alone till the children come. He must be very fond of her.'

'Charlie doesn't believe in falling in love. If he's in love with anything, it's money. He believes you should marry for sensible reasons. I was engaged to a woman I loved during the war, but she didn't wait for me to return.'

'Do you still think about her?'

He grinned suddenly, surprising her. 'Yes. I see her when I go into Rivenshaw and I think what a lucky escape I had. She's got six children now and always looks harassed. She's stopped caring how she looks and she's rather stupid. I didn't notice that when I was seventeen and enchanted by a pretty face.'

He looked younger when he smiled, but his next words were so blunt she was shocked and couldn't think what to say in response.

'Do you really want to marry a cripple like me, Miss Turner?'

If he could be bluntly truthful, so could she. 'I never thought of getting married to anyone till Charlie came to see me today, so I haven't had time to think it through.'

'How old are you?'

'Twenty-two.'

'I'm thirty-four, a lot older than you.'

He didn't go on so she kept silent too. Well, she didn't know what to say. When she saw Charlie Willcox again, she'd tell him what she thought of him for walking out and leaving them in this awkward situation.

'What sort of books do you read, besides books of names?' he asked.

It was much easier to talk about books than themselves. They were both regular users of the library and it was a wonder she hadn't seen him there. But once she got her head in a book or magazine, she was lost to the world.

* * *

There was the sound of a car outside. Jonah stood up and peered down the hall. 'Charlie's come back for you.'

She looked at a little clock sitting on a small bookcase. 'I can't believe an hour's passed already.'

'Nor can I.' He hesitated, then said, 'If I haven't frightened you off, why don't I send Charlie away and you can have a bite to eat with me? Or do you have to get home for your sister?'

'I left a note saying I was going out about a job and told Rosa to go to our auntie's.'

'So you'll stay a while longer?'

'Why not?' It didn't commit her to anything, after all. And . . . it was rather a compliment really, because he clearly hadn't wanted to meet her at first.

'Right then.' He walked outside to catch Charlie before he came in to join them and a couple of minutes later the taxi drove away.

Jonah came back into the sun room. 'Charlie has to go out to tea with Marion's parents later. He says to phone for a taxi when you're ready to go home and tell them to put it on his account.'

'I'd never ridden in a taxi before today.'

He stopped to stare at that, then shrugged. 'They're just cars.'

'I hadn't ridden in a car, either.'

'Let's go and sort out some food.' He opened the pantry door, revealing shelves full of tins and packets. She had never seen so much food in a pantry. That was real riches, to her.

He took out a jar of pickled cauliflower and the butter dish, then got a loaf out of an enamel bread bin. From the refrigerator he took some celery and a tomato, as well as a cheese dish. It had a wedge-shaped lid like the one at home, but it was china not earthenware, and much prettier.

He studied the table, then went back to the pantry and

pulled out a jar with a bright, cheerful label. 'Do you like pickled beetroot? If so, I'll open this as well.'

'I love it.' She wasn't going to say no to anything. She hadn't had food like this for weeks. 'What can I do to help?'

'Nothing. It's just a simple meal. I can cook, too, but I only found out Charlie was bringing you when he phoned me up this morning so all I have to offer is what I was going to have for my own lunch.'

'It seems like a feast to me.' She'd have called the meal dinner at this time of day, not lunch.

He was a bit breathless by the time he'd set the food out. She didn't comment and when he didn't try to go on chatting, she sat quietly, waiting for him to catch his breath.

He'd put the breadboard on the table and after a few moments he cut some slices off a crusty new loaf. 'Right. I think that's everything. Can I pass you some bread? Do you like the crust?'

'Yes, please.' She was annoyed with herself when she realised she'd licked her lips at the mere thought of that.

'You've been going hungry for a while, haven't you?' he said as he passed things to her one after the other.

'How did you know?'

'I recognise the hunger look. I see it on the faces of men in the street who can't find work. They aren't all as lucky as I am.'

'Lucky! You were injured.'

'Gassed,' he corrected. 'But I still have both arms and legs, and I wasn't blinded. We didn't live in this posh house then, but I never went hungry at home.'

She nodded but her mouth was full of wonderful crusty bread and butter, so she didn't try to speak.

Jonah wasn't eating much; he seemed more interested in chatting. 'Since the Wall Street Crash in the United States, things have got even worse. It upsets me to read about it in the newspapers. Sorry. I don't know why I'm talking about such miserable things. Do get on with your meal.'

'I've read about that in the papers too. I don't always understand the details, though.' She continued to eat slowly, relishing every mouthful.

When he pressed her to have second helpings, she told him the truth: 'I couldn't after managing on so little for the past few weeks.'

'I'll wrap some food up for you then.'

She felt shame flood through her and knew she'd gone red.

His voice became very gentle, such a lovely voice. 'Let me do that for you. I'm so lucky to have a little money and it makes me feel less useless to do something good with it. Your sister must have been going hungry too.'

'You're a kind man, Jonah Willcox. Very well. Thank you.' She'd do it for Rosa.

He gave her another of his lovely, warm smiles and concentrated on finishing his food.

'I'll clear the table and wash up,' she said when he'd finished eating. 'You look tired now.'

He didn't pretend. 'Thank you. I am. That would be a big help.'

As she was finishing the washing-up, with her back to him, he said, 'I'm not promising anything, not yet, but would you like to come and see my cottage at Ellindale tomorrow?'

She didn't turn round. 'Yes, I would. What Charlie suggested is . . . well, too important to rush into, so I'm not committing myself to anything, either. We should get to know one another before we think seriously about . . . it.'

Then she started putting away the cups and plates, remembering where he'd got them from.

He sat and watched her with a half-smile still lingering on his face. 'I'm glad you're not one of those women who natter non-stop, Leah.'

After she'd cleared everything away, he stood up. 'I'll telephone for your taxi now and arrange for the driver to pick you up tomorrow morning. He can call in for me on the way up to Ellindale.'

He stared into the distance for a few seconds. 'I'm really looking forward to living there. The cottage is quite big with several acres of land and it's very peaceful, right on the edge of the moors. My grandparents used to have a big kitchen garden on the sheltered side of the house and they kept chickens.'

'I'll look forward to seeing it.' She found, to her surprise, that this was the simple truth.

Jonah was much nicer than she'd expected. That made a difference.

She wondered what he thought of her.

When Leah turned up in a taxi, Rosa had just got back from afternoon school. She and Hilda, the woman they called 'auntie' because she'd been a friend of their mother's, wanted to know where she'd been. She told them she'd been after a job out on the far side of Birch End and her employers had insisted on paying for the taxi because they considered it a long way for her to walk back.

'They'd have done better giving you the taxi money and letting you walk,' Hilda grumbled. 'Did you get the job? What is it?'

'I'd be working for Charlie Willcox's brother. Sort of a housekeeper. I have to see him again tomorrow.'

'Well, there will be a lot of applicants in times like this. I'll keep my fingers crossed for you.'

'You've got that look on your face,' Rosa said as they walked home. 'What really happened today?'

At ten her sister was a clever little thing and it was such a pity she wouldn't be able to go on to the grammar school.

We've both lost out where schooling is concerned, Leah thought. Her steps faltered as she suddenly realised that if she married Jonah, Rosa might not lose out on a good education.

'I'll tell you when we get home but you have to promise not to tell anyone else, anyone at all.'

Rosa listened open-mouthed and when Leah finished her explanation, she exclaimed, 'Charlie Willcox said you should marry his brother! Oh, Leah, that'd be the best thing of all for you.'

'Would it?'

'Yes. For us both.' She looked round with tears in her eyes. 'I don't like living here without Dad. I keep expecting him to come home from work. And I don't like seeing you so worried all the time.' She pushed her plate across the table. 'We both need to eat, so I'm *not* taking all the food.'

'I had a big meal at the Willcoxes' house and Jonah packed some food to bring home, so that's all for you.'

Leah watched Rosa brighten and take the plate back. She was growing fast and always hungry, but hadn't complained about the lack of food. She understood only too well how short of money they were. If I married Jonah, Leah thought later as she got into bed, my sister need never go hungry again. And he does seem . . . nice.

But she had to find out more about him first. And find out what this Ellindale place was like, too.

Marriage was such a big step to take. Her thoughts were in turmoil and she tossed and turned for half the night.

3

The next morning Rosa refused to eat anything unless she could see Leah sharing the food Jonah had given them. He'd been more generous than Leah had at first realised when he thrust the paper carrier bag into her hands, so she cut herself some bread and buttered it sparingly.

'If he's as kind as he sounds,' her sister's words came out thickly through a mouthful of bread and cheese, 'you should definitely marry him.'

'He is kind but he hasn't actually asked me to marry him yet. He's still thinking about it. Good heavens, Rosa, he and I only met yesterday.'

'Well, if he does ask you, be sure you say yes. You're too shy sometimes, especially with men.'

No one could accuse Rosa of being shy, Leah thought in amusement.

When her sister had run off to meet her friends at the corner of the street for the walk to school, Leah went upstairs to put on her best and only decent clothes for the second day running.

He'd probably notice she was wearing the same clothes. He seemed the sort of man who was aware of details.

She stared at her face in the mirror for longer than usual and gave her hair a hundred brush strokes, trying to make it shine as it used to. But it remained dull: the result of not eating well, she supposed, and not having any shampoo left to wash it with, only cold tap water.

She wondered what Jonah thought of her appearance. She wasn't ugly or anything like that, but an old woman had once told her she'd make a handsome woman one day, when she grew into her face. Whatever that meant. Oh, she was being silly today.

The taxi arrived promptly at half past nine. Leah locked the front door and got into it, ignoring the group of women neighbours staring at her. They'd be speculating about where she'd gone all day, she was sure.

The taxi driver wasn't a chatty sort, which was a relief. It felt strange to be driven through the village for the second day running.

When they got to Redgate Cottage, she could feel herself growing tense. Would she even like Jonah today? She'd found him very pleasant yesterday, which was why she'd agreed to go to Ellindale. But that was just first impressions. People weren't always what they seemed once you got to know them.

He came out as soon as the taxi stopped and when he got into the back with her, she could smell soap and see how shiny and clean his skin was.

She hadn't had any soap for a week now, or any warm water, but she'd used a facecloth to wash all her body, which was the best she could do at the moment.

As Jonah eased his long legs into a more comfortable position, he said, 'Morning, Robert. We're going to Spring Cottage again. We'll stop and look at the village as we go through it. *You* know where I like to stop.'

'Yes, Mr Willcox.'

'I've always been Jonah to you before.'

'Your brother said I should call my clients Mister.'

'Well, I prefer you to keep using my first name, Robert. After all, we were at junior school together.'

'All right, lad.'

As the taxi set off, Jonah turned to Leah. 'Did you sleep well?'

'Yes, thank you. And you?'

'I rarely sleep well. And last night I had a lot to think about. Did you really sleep well?'

'No. Of course not.'

'If you've changed your mind about today . . . ' He let the words trail away.

'I haven't changed my mind about . . . seeing how things go,' she said carefully.

'Good, because I haven't either. I'm looking forward to showing my house and the village to you. I'm going to live there whatever happens between you and me today.'

'I walked up to Ellindale once with my father when I was younger, but I don't remember much about it.'

'It's a pretty little place. I'd call it a hamlet rather than a village.'

'I remember it was a long, narrow place and some of the houses seemed to be clinging to the slopes.'

'Yes, they do. The top end of the valley's like a finger poking into the lower slopes of the moors. The village is mostly sheltered from the worst of the winter weather.'

'And your house?'

'It's called Spring Cottage because it was built where a natural spring gushes out of the side of the hill. There used to be two small labourers' cottages there. When my grandfather bought them, he intended to make them into one eventually. He needed the rent from the other cottage at first, though, because he'd spent his life savings buying another piece of land.'

'There's a piece of land as well as a house?'

'Yes, several acres. The cottages have been there for as long as anyone can remember. They're among the oldest dwellings in the valley. The owner has water rights for the spring in return for keeping the water clean, because it provides drinking water for the whole village, you see. After that the excess water runs away into the stream which runs down the hill as Ellin Brook. But they're forbidden to put their waste water back into it. You must have seen the brook. It passes through Birch End and goes right into Rivenshaw.'

'Of course I have! Fancy our stream starting at your cottage! It's more like a small river by the time it reaches Birch End, and even bigger when it gets into the town.'

'That's because it collects a few smaller streams on the way to your village, and a few more on the way into Rivenshaw. Eventually it runs into the River Ribble and westward to the sea.'

They entered Ellindale just then and the car slowed down to avoid an old lady with a sacking shopping bag, who hadn't even looked before she started crossing the road.

'Some people aren't used to cars, especially older folk,' he said. 'That's one reason there are so many motoring accidents. I was reading an article about it last week in the newspaper.'

The driver didn't move on, so perhaps this was one of the places where Jonah liked to stop and have a look round.

She watched the old lady walk into the nearest building. 'I see there's a village shop now. I don't remember that when I came here before. It must be convenient for people because it's a long walk into Birch End.'

'Mrs Buckley opened a little general store in her front room after her husband was killed in the war. She used his pay entitlements and her widow's pension at first to support herself. She doesn't stock anything fancy but as long as people in the village buy their staples from her, she gets by. Even people on the dole have to buy some food.

'In the summer, people go walking across the moors at

weekends, so she puts two small tables outside and sells the hikers tea and scones.'

'How enterprising of her! Which one is your cottage?'

'You can't see it yet. It's at the upper end, about two hundred yards beyond The Shepherd's Rest.'

Robert had moved on again, but obligingly slowed down outside the pub when he heard it mentioned.

'It's only a small pub but it's somewhere for the men to go in the evenings. Robert can wait there for me today and get a glass of shandy or he can get a pot of tea from Mrs Buckley and then add the cost to the bill. I can walk down the hill more easily than I can walk up it.'

'You seem to know a lot about Ellindale.'

He shrugged. 'I used to come here as a boy to visit my maternal grandparents. I still come here on fine days some-times and I used to collect the rent myself every month so that I could see that everything was all right. I usually make an outing of coming up here, buy a pot of tea for myself and Robert, and take my time. There are always people going in and out of Mrs Buckley's to chat to. I nearly moved back here a couple of years ago, but Charlie made such a fuss, I dropped the idea.'

'Does your brother ever come here with you?'

'What, Charlie? No. He prefers towns to the countryside. He's far too busy to come out to Ellindale. There's no profit for him here.'

'Are these the only houses? There only seem to be about twenty,' she commented, glancing through the back window at the untidy straggle of little dwellings.

'The nearby farms just about double that number. They're small places, eking out a living on the moors with sheep mostly, and whatever else they can find to bring in a shilling or two. Most of them are down nearer to Birch End. The land on the moors isn't much good for farming.'

The taxi stopped outside a large house, which stood sentinel to the left of the road.

'Is this your house?'

'No. It used to belong to the Deardens. Their only son was about my age when he was killed in the war and then a few years ago they themselves were killed in a road accident, so the house went to a cousin. I forget his name, but he hasn't lived here.' He made a faint noise, sounding annoyed. 'You'd think he'd take care of it, though. The place looks more neglected every year and it used to have such a pretty garden.'

'It looks a sad old place.'

'Yes. You'd think the cousin would rent it out to somebody, but it's been left empty for years. I did see two men working on the roof last year, but when someone from the village asked them, they didn't seem to know anything about the owner or what was going to happen to the house. Carry on, Robert.'

The taxi bumped slowly along the road, only a dirt track now, for another hundred yards or so.

'That's Spring Cottage, Leah!'

There was love in Jonah's voice and he leaned forward eagerly, not seeming to notice that he'd taken hold of her hand. His fingers felt warm and firm, rather nice, really. She decided it'd be more embarrassing to pull her hand away and draw attention to what he'd done, so just left it in his as she peered through the car windows.

'Why didn't you come to live here after the war, Jonah?'

'I was quite ill when I came home in '17, so I lived with my father and stepmother. She looked after me till I made a bit more sense. She was wonderful, but it was months before I stopped hearing the guns in my head at night and screaming at them to stop blowing people to pieces. If you never sleep properly, you can't seem to think straight in the daytime. At least, I couldn't.'

Leah had heard tales of other men coming back from the fighting and suffering from severe nightmares. Her father hadn't passed the medical to go into the army, thank goodness.

'Sorry. I shouldn't talk about such things to you,' Jonah said.

'Yes, you should. People ought never to forget what we owe to our soldiers. Please go on.'

'Charlie had just been called up into the Army when I was injured and our parents were worried sick about him, with so many lads being killed. But he came through unscathed, thankfully, and after that we all lived together very happily in a smaller house while he was making his first pots of money. My stepmother was like a mother to me. She's a lovely woman.'

'He's done well for himself.'

'Yes. I really admire him. He'd been buying objects cheaply and sending them home even during the war. We used to have some fun, he and I, so I didn't want to move out, but when he persuaded Mum and Dad to sell their house and helped them make their dream come true – a boarding house in Blackpool – he had to move. He bought Redgate Cottage at the same time and hired Mrs Thwaite to come in daily for us.'

'It was kind of him to look after his parents like that.'

Jonah laughed so heartily it turned into a fit of coughing. Once that was over, he explained, 'Charlie always looks after his family, yes definitely. But he's kind to us in his own way, which means he always has an eye to the money side of things as well. He'll get back what the boarding house cost one day with a good profit on his outlay, because once the Depression is over and our parents retire, it'll sell for far more than he paid for it. He has a good eye for a bargain, for all sorts of bargains, my dear brother does.'

'Sometimes it feels as if the hard times will never end.'

'I think that'll happen in a year or two. It's not nearly as bad down south. I just wish the government would be a little kinder to the north. That Means Test is . . . well, mean.'

'I agree. I've seen people having to sell nearly all their furniture before they could be given any relief. That's not right.'

'I find politics fascinating, but most women don't always care about that sort of thing. If I'd been in better health . . . and richer . . . I'd like to have gone into politics or travelled.'

For a moment his expression was so bleak that her heart went out to him, but she didn't know what to say and was glad when the taxi driver intervened.

'Here we are, Jonah lad.'

They'd stopped at a gate with the words Spring Cottage painted on it; on a few of the letters the paint was peeling. This was the end of the dirt track. It widened out into a turning space, but led nowhere else.

Leah got out of the car and joined Jonah who had gone to lean on the gate as if this was something he always did when he arrived. There was just enough space for the taxi to turn round in a tight circle before it drove slowly away.

She stared round eagerly Above them were the rolling blue-green slopes of the moors with cloud shadows chasing one another across the tops and outcrops of rocks looking as if they were propping up the edges of a few higher, steeper parts here and there.

There seemed to be quite a lot of land next to the house, with a drystone wall around it. She'd had no idea what 'a few acres' looked like. Did all this belong to Jonah? She didn't like to question him too closely because she didn't want to sound mercenary.

To one side, about a hundred yards away and directly opposite the gate, was the house itself. It still looked like two cottages from the outside.

About fifty yards away to their left was another building, with some outhouses straggling behind it as if added on piecemeal.

'What's that building?'

'It's an old barn. I don't use it now, of course. One end's been partitioned off inside because the far end is a bit tumble-down, but it's not worth repairing because I've no use for it. Don't go inside without me. Some parts are dangerous. I'll have to get them attended to.'

'If you repaired it, couldn't you rent it to someone?'

'Who'd need it? No one up here, that's for sure. They're all struggling to survive. There's no spare produce of any sort.'

He pointed up to the land on the gentle slope above them. 'The first wall marks the original boundary of the land that went with the cottages. The field beyond it is ours now. My grandfather bought it. He never used it himself but it's rented out to a nearby farmer because it's a sheltered spot and he can run some of his sheep there in the winter. But I won't sell it to him because my grandparents saved hard to buy it and it'd seem like betraying their trust. Anyway, it brings in regular money.'

'I can't imagine having so much land around a house. It must be very peaceful here.'

'It is. My mother was born in the lower cottage and my grandparents lived here till they died. They grew vegetables and my grandmother sold any spare produce, but their main income came from my grandfather's job and the rent on the field. He was assistant to the local vet, very good with animals, everyone said.'

'If they were your mother's parents, Charlie can't take after *them* in being enterprising. What were his mother's family like?'

'My stepmother won't talk about them, says they're no good. I think Dad knows about them, but he won't say anything. He married my stepmother quite suddenly. Anyway, to continue the tale of Spring Cottage, my grandfather died when he was only fifty, just keeled over dead one day, and that was it. My grandmother's youngest brother came to live with her. He was a shepherd and more at home on the moors than inside a house, but he liked building things, so over the years, especially during the winters, he did the work necessary to combine the two cottages into one, as my grandfather had always planned.'

'I see. Go on.'

'I think people in the village must have been using the spring to supply their drinking water for several centuries, if not longer. There are pipes under the ground, earthenware ones. I think they were put in last century. I saw them once when I was a lad and one needed mending so they had to dig up the road.'

'Where does the water come from?'

'From the moors, rainfall filtering through the ground. It's our good luck that this spring wells out of the hillside summer and winter alike. It's never been known to fail, even in the driest summers, and it's always pure. Ellindale village is lucky to have it. Some of the moorland springs are salty or contain too much iron, then people can't use them.'

As he paused, she said again, 'Go on!'

'Well, if I'm not boring you—'

'You're not. I like to learn things.'

'Great-uncle Thomas said the spring would taste even nicer if it could be kept absolutely clean, so he built a proper basin for where it comes out of the hill and tiled around it. It was the tenants' job to keep an eye on the basin and clean it out, if necessary, though that isn't often needed. There's no water tastes half as good. You must try it before we leave. Now, let me show you inside the cottage.'

He eased away from the gate and opened it, offering his arm and escorting her along a wide crazy paving pathway leading to the front door of the cottage. There he took down a huge old-fashioned key from above the lintel and opened the door with a flourish.

'Do you just leave the key there? Aren't you worried someone will break in?'

'No one in Ellindale would steal from their neighbours.'

She couldn't even imagine feeling so safe.

'This way, *mademoiselle.*'

She felt as if he should go first, but he was standing back, waiting for her, so she led the way into the dim interior.

'I'd better open up or you'll not see anything.' He folded back the tall wooden shutters that closed across the inside of the windows like curtains. Light flooded in, to show a large room that must have formed the whole of the ground floor of one cottage at some stage. It was partly furnished with a scrubbed wooden table and a couple of benches but there was no other furniture.

A kitchen range stood on the side wall. On the rear wall was a big square slop stone, instead of a modern white ceramic sink. There was an old-fashioned tap jutting out over the slop stone and a battered enamel washbasin standing upside down on the wooden draining board.

'We get hot water from the kitchen range because they haven't run the gas pipes out to Ellindale, let alone electricity, though I believe it's being planned for. This table and the benches were heavy and old-fashioned, so were left behind after my grandmother died.'

He pointed. 'That door leads to the ground floor of what used to be the other cottage. My uncle took the kitchen out and made the space into a sort of bathroom instead. The front part is now the best parlour.' He chuckled softly. 'They never used it but my grandmother was very proud of it and used to dust it every two days.

'This is the bathroom. The tap is connected to the spring

so you get running cold water, but there's no hot water in here, so you still have to heat water on the kitchen stove and carry it through in a bucket if you want a bath. But there is a sort of lavatory, thanks to my great-uncle's ingenuity in setting up a system to dispose of the waste, and you can empty the bathwater into it.'

She walked into the bathroom, then came back. 'This is more of a bathroom than I've ever had before. Your great-uncle must have been a clever man with his hands.'

'He was. He turned the staircase of one cottage into big store cupboards, one on the ground floor, one at the top.' Jonah took a key down from the top of a picture rail and opened the door next to the bathroom to show her. 'Oh! I'd forgotten that there were some of my grandparents' belongings left in here. I'll have to go through them. I wasn't in a suitable state to clear it out when I left the army and afterwards, it slipped my mind.'

He grimaced at the jumble of bits and pieces, not bothering to lock the door again. 'Would you like to go upstairs now? Or . . . have you seen enough?'

She could guess what he was really asking. 'I'd like to see it all, if you don't mind. It's a nice house.' That was as much encouragement as she could manage. It was up to him now to decide whether he liked her enough. She could feel herself blushing so said hastily, 'You go first. It's a bit dark.'

He smiled at her and gave a little nod, as if he understood what she hadn't dared say aloud. She hoped she wasn't misunderstanding that.

'Give me a few seconds, Leah, and I'll open some of the shutters upstairs so you can see where you're going.'

But she couldn't help noticing that he walked up the stairs slowly, as if he was an old man.

As light flooded down the staircase she went up to join him. 'This is the main bedroom.'

Her breath caught in her throat; it was spacious and had two windows, one at the front of the house looking across the moors and another at the side, with a wonderful view right down the valley and far beyond.

Ellindale was spread out below Spring Cottage like a living map, with her own village of Birch End in the middle distance. The day was bright enough for her to see all the way to the blur of tiny houses that must be Rivenshaw, well, the part of the town on the eastern side anyway.

'What a wonderful view! I'd be spending half my time staring out if I lived here.'

He came to join her and they stood in silence for a few moments before he stepped back. 'I'd be just as bad. My grandmother used to tell me off for wasting my time staring at the world like an idiot at a fair.'

Leah quoted one of her favourite poems:

> 'What is this life if, full of care,
> 'We have no time to stand and stare.
> 'No time to stand beneath the boughs
> 'And stare as long as sheep or cows.'

'Say that again.'

She repeated the verse.

'That's lovely. Who wrote it?'

'W.H. Davies. I borrowed a book of poetry from the library once and this was my favourite. I was working very hard learning how to run a house at the time and it seemed to echo my feelings perfectly.'

'It must have been difficult taking over from your mother at only fourteen.'

'It was. I missed her so much, but the other women helped me when I was struggling. When you lose someone you love, all you can do is carry on. You can't bring them back.'

'They live on in your memories, though. I envy you that, because I have no memories of my mother. I was only a baby when she died.'

For a short time longer they stood there, then he showed her the other three bedrooms, the next one on this side being rather small, the two from the other cottage almost exactly equal in size.

She'd use the small bedroom as a sewing room if she lived here, she decided. Then realised what thinking that meant.

What was he planning to do now they'd spent some more time together? Was he . . . interested?

He seemed a kind man and she enjoyed chatting to him. Was that enough to base a marriage on? How could you ever tell? People weren't allowed to try out a possible husband or wife beforehand.

Jonah locked the front door then took her further up the slope to show her the spring house, which was tucked into an angle of the lower perimeter wall. Clear water welled gently up into a big tiled hollow and ran away down the conduit. He scooped up some water in his hand and drank it thirstily, so she did the same.

'You're right. It's lovely and fresh.'

'Do you want to bother looking at the inside of the barn, Leah?'

'I wouldn't mind a peep if that's all right?'

'Of course it is.'

Again, he took a key from the lintel and opened one of the double doors at the left end if you looked at it from the house. The door creaked loudly as he pulled it back. Sunlight streamed in, showing dusty pieces of wood, tools and equipment whose use wasn't clear. Everything was piled up any old how, it seemed.

'They used to store the hay up there.' He pointed to a

sort of balcony that ran across the rear half. 'I ought to clear this place out.'

She couldn't believe he'd just left everything lying around like that for all these years, but it said something about his state of mind after the war, and his physical frailty.

'Shall we throw ourselves on Mrs Buckley's mercy now and ask her for a pot of tea? She hasn't got her tables outside today, only does that on fine weekends at this time of year, but she lets me sit in her parlour to enjoy some refreshments.'

'That sounds like an excellent idea.'

After closing the gate, he stopped and took a deep breath, speaking quickly and looking as if he was bracing himself for a refusal. 'Before we leave, I wanted to ask you . . . Leah, would you consider marrying me and making a life here in Ellindale?'

Her heart thumped in her chest and she had to clutch the top of the gate to steady herself. She hadn't expected him to propose yet, if ever.

Jonah saw the shocked expression on her face, then noted the anxious way she studied him after his clumsy proposal. He hadn't expected to make up his mind about her today, but she was so easy to get on with, had such an elegant face and expressive eyes, that he'd suddenly decided to take a chance. He could see she was thinking about it, so didn't press her for an answer.

Eventually she said, 'I don't know, Jonah. It's hard to decide something as important as that so quickly.'

'But you're not saying no?'

She flushed. 'No. I'm not. I'm . . . inclined to accept, actually.'

'I'm glad. If it helps, even though it would be useful for me to have a wife, I wouldn't have asked you if I hadn't liked you.'

'I like you, too, Jonah. What I've seen of you.' She spread her hands in a gesture that said more than words could have done.

'I've not lied to you about anything, Leah, but I need to move out of that house quite quickly because Charlie is getting married in a couple of weeks, so if you could give it your . . . your urgent consideration, I'd be grateful.'

He waited again, watching the slight frown wrinkle her forehead. 'I think *you* need to move out of your present house even more quickly than I do. Am I right?'

'Yes. I've been having trouble thinking where we could go, even. I've been offered a job at the laundry but they don't pay women enough to live on and I have Rosa to think about.'

She looked at him and he saw her frown deepen. 'Tell me what's making you hesitate, Leah, and I'll see if I can help resolve it.'

'I'm worried that you're being pushed into it by your brother and you don't really want a wife, whether it's me or someone else.'

'Charlie did push me into considering it, I admit. And I suspect he pushed you, too, from the expression on your face yesterday. I'd not have dared take the initiative without a firm nudge because, well, I know I'm not a good catch as a husband.'

He patted his chest as if drawing attention to his breathing difficulties. 'But I asked you because I wanted to, not because Charlie is forcing me. I can say no to him when I have to, I promise you. I asked you because I've enjoyed spending time with you and I think you and I could build a very pleasant life together.'

'What about Rosa?'

He smiled. 'Your sister would live with us, naturally. I'm not like Marion! I'd enjoy being part of a family again. Oh, and there's a school bus morning and evening into Birch End from Ellindale and back again. Is Rosa a good scholar?'

'Yes, very. We'd been hoping she'd win a scholarship to the Girls' Grammar School in Rivenshaw, even perhaps the Esherwood Bequest. Winning that would have been the only way we could have afforded to let her go to the grammar school. When Dad was killed, I knew I couldn't afford it however hard I worked, not even if she got the Bequest.'

'If you marry me, I'll be more than happy to pay for her education and I'll support her for as long as she wants to stay at school. I believe in education, for girls just as much as for boys. The one I was given led me to love books, which have been my salvation during the past decade. I don't know what I'd have done without them.'

He waited and when Leah looked up at him, he held his breath, hoping she'd say yes.

'All right. I'll be honoured to marry you, Jonah Willcox.'

He took her hand. 'That makes me feel very happy.' And to his surprise it was the simple truth. What's more, her frown had vanished so she mustn't feel too bad about it, either. 'So, we're engaged to be married, Leah.'

'Yes. How strange!'

'Strange?'

'Yes, very. Yesterday morning I had no money and no food in the house, and I'd been convinced for years that I'd spend my life as a spinster. Today I feel I've been given the chance of a far better life.'

She looked at him with a very solemn expression on her face. 'I'll do my best to be a good wife to you, Jonah. My very best.'

'That should be a double agreement, don't you think? I'll do my very best to be a good husband to you, as well.'

Then he dared take her hand and even kiss her cheek. She was still looking uncertain, so he didn't press his luck and kiss her properly on the lips. But to his surprise, he wanted to. Oh, yes, he did. There was something so fresh and attractive about her that was missing in Marion, for all her prettiness and fine clothes.

Trust Charlie to find a suitable woman for him. His brother had a magic touch sometimes.

Jonah offered her his arm again. As they began walking slowly down the hill into the village, he felt happiness tingle through him, real happiness. Since the war it was as if he'd been wrapped up in cotton wool, first by his stepmother, then by Charlie, as if he wasn't quite touching the world around him.

Why had he let them smother him like that? He should have got out and about, done more with his life.

At the village shop Mrs Buckley greeted them with a beaming smile. 'Lovely to see you again, Mr Jonah. When your tenants were given notice to leave, we wondered if that meant you'd be moving in.'

'Yes, it does. In fact, I've been showing my young lady the house. Mrs Buckley, this is my fiancée Leah Turner.'

'Well, bless my soul!' She dragged Leah against her and planted a smacking kiss on each of her cheeks in turn. 'Congratulations, my dear. You've got yourself a good man here.'

'Thank you.' She was allowed to step back and watched Jonah being hugged just as ruthlessly. Mrs Buckley's delight and friendliness made Leah feel better about coming to live here, as well as marrying him.

When Jonah emerged from the embrace, he was laughing, and for a moment Leah could see the carefree young man he must once have been. Then he grew gentle and quiet again.

'We wondered if you could make us a pot of tea and perhaps find a biscuit or two to celebrate with, Mrs Buckley?'

'I'm still getting the occasional hiker, so I baked some of my special parkin this morning. Would you like some?'

He glanced enquiringly at Leah and when she nodded, he said, 'We'd love a piece. The parkin at the bakery in Birch End is a pale imitation of yours.' He licked his lips.

'Take your young lady through to the parlour – you know the way – and I'll bring the tea in when it's ready.'

Leah stopped in the doorway, staring at Mrs Buckley's front parlour with its myriad ornaments and knick-knacks. 'It'd drive me mad dusting so many ornaments,' she whispered.

He looked quickly over his shoulder and said in a low voice, 'And it'd drive me mad to have to look at such a jumble of figures and animals and Toby jugs. I like just a few beautiful things. Charlie has too many as well.'

'Thank goodness we agree about that.'

As soon as they'd sat down, he asked, 'How soon can we be married?'

'You want to do it quickly?'

'Yes. What is there to wait for?'

She found she was quite happy with that. 'I have to be out of the house by the end of next week.'

'And I'm longing for a home of my own, so the sooner the better as far as I'm concerned. But we'll have to buy some furniture before we can move in.'

'I already have some furniture. It's not fancy or new but it's clean and comfortable. We could start with that and see what else we need once we've settled in.'

His face lit up. 'Excellent. It exhausts me to go shopping in Rivenshaw, I must admit.'

It felt good to bring something to the marriage. Indeed, she hadn't felt so good for a long time, not even before her father died. She really did feel she had a hope of a much better life now, and a happy one.

But she felt a bit apprehensive, too, which was only natural. What would the private side of marriage be like? She'd heard other women grumbling about their husbands' 'demands' and had found a book in the library to tell her the facts of life, since she didn't have a mother to do that. Unfortunately, the book didn't explain anything except the biology of the human body, and she found it hard to relate the diagrams to real people's bodies and lives, let alone their emotions.

But she didn't think Jonah would treat her roughly, unless she'd much mistaken his nature.

No, she trusted him and had done from the first.

4

In the morning Leah went down to the laundry to tell them she wouldn't be taking up the job there. She'd hoped to have a quick word with Jim Banks, but to her dismay she was shown into the owner's office.

Mr Harris nodded to the secretary. 'I shan't need you for this, Jenny.'

The woman cast a speculative look in Leah's direction and went back to her desk outside, closing the door quietly.

'Please sit down. Now, how are you managing, Miss Turner? Do you have enough food for the weekend?'

His concern surprised her. 'Yes, thank you.'

'You're sure?'

'Yes.'

'Then what can I do for you today?'

'I came to say I shan't need the job you so kindly offered me. I didn't want to wait till Monday to tell you, because you'll need to find someone else.'

'Have you found a better job?'

'Not a job exactly. I'm going to marry Jonah Willcox.'

'Ah. Right. This is rather sudden, isn't it?'

'Yes, I suppose it is. But he's moving out to live in Ellindale when his brother gets married, so he needs a wife. And I couldn't really have managed at the laundry, because a woman's wages are so low.' She decided to embroider the truth to stop people making this a seven-day wonder. 'I've known Jonah for a while and we get on well, so it suits us both.'

She couldn't pretend she was madly in love with Jonah and wasn't good at telling lies, but the way people gossiped she had to say something.

'Congratulations, my dear. When will this be happening?'

'We haven't set the date yet, but as soon as we can. Only . . . if I pay rent, can I stay on in the house for an extra week or so?'

'Yes, of course. No need to pay rent, either. My wife shouldn't have been so harsh with you when you lost your father. I was rather busy just then and I didn't hear about it for a while. If necessary I'll pay your rent.'

'I couldn't ask you to do that.'

'Think of it as a thank you to your father for his years of hard work.'

How kind of him to put it that way! It was both her father and this man's kindness which convinced her that she'd ask him for help if she needed it. She stood up to leave. 'Thank you.'

He stood up too. 'I think it's all worked out well for you, after all. I'm so glad.'

'Yes. Thank you for everything, Mr Harris.' She would let the rent man know as soon as she found out when exactly she'd be leaving. She'd better. Sam Griggs didn't like you keeping anything from him.

Mr Harris walked to the door of his office with her and before he opened it, he said quietly, 'I wish you every happiness in your marriage, my dear.'

She walked away trying to reconcile the thought of his kindness with the harsh way his wife and her rent man treated their tenants. Your children could be hungry and Sam Griggs would still take your last penny.

The Harrises must have an uncomfortable life at home. She was sure Jonah wouldn't prove difficult to live with. Well, almost sure. Nothing was utterly certain in this life.

*   *   *

Leah's next errand wouldn't be nearly as pleasant. She had to see Charlie and ask if she could pawn her mother's wedding ring so that she could buy a new dress for her wedding, perhaps other clothes too if the ring was worth enough. It was real gold, after all. Most of her clothes were so worn and shabby that in better times she'd have torn them up for rags.

So far Jonah had only seen her in her Sunday best, a dress and jacket that had once belonged to her mother. The outfit wasn't very smart and was old-fashioned.

To her relief, she could see Charlie through the window of the pawnshop, so she dragged the shreds of her courage together and walked through the door, setting a very loud bell clanging.

He looked up, saw her and seemed surprised. 'I'll deal with Miss Turner, Vi. Come into my office, Leah.'

The woman with him nodded.

When they were in the small room at the back, he said, 'I didn't expect to see you here, Leah. Is something wrong?'

She could feel herself blushing. 'Jonah will have told you that we're going to get married.'

'Yes. I'm very pleased about that.'

'I need an outfit to get married in, so I thought I'd pawn my mother's wedding ring. I won't ask Jonah to buy my wedding clothes. It wouldn't be right. Only, will you please keep the ring safe, because I shall want to buy it back later? It's all I have left of her.'

'Ah. I should have thought of that.'

She waited, feeling miserably uncomfortable.

'I've got the better quality clothes in my Rivenshaw shop because I can get higher prices for them there. Even though most of the mills have closed down, there are still people gainfully employed.'

He looked at her thoughtfully. 'You'll have to come there

with me to find something suitable. But you'll need a woman with you or people will talk about us going off in my car together. They saw us in the taxi when I took you to meet my brother and a few of them put two and two together and got six.'

He looked angry and she suddenly realised that might be why her neighbours had been staring at her and it made her feel angry as well. If they looked at her like that again, she'd march up to them and tell them what she thought.

'How about I ask Marion to come and help you choose something?'

'Um. I don't really know your fiancée and I don't want to trouble her. My Auntie Hilda would come, I'm sure.'

He looked surprised. 'When I checked your family out, there were no close relatives.'

'Checked my family out!'

'Yes, of course. You can't be too careful when you're thinking of asking someone to marry your brother.'

A small huff of annoyance escaped her before she could stop it. 'Well, Hilda's not a blood relative, but we've always called her auntie and we're very close to her. She was my mother's best friend.'

'Why didn't you plan to live with her, then?'

'She hasn't much money either because she's a widow, and she's already got two lodgers, so she can't take me and Rosa in except in an emergency.'

'I see. Well, bring her with you, then. But don't let her talk you into buying something dowdy or cheap looking. See if she's free this afternoon and we'll go into Rivenshaw together by taxi. I was going anyway, so you don't have to worry about it being an extra cost to me.'

'That'd be lovely. Thank you.' She fumbled in her scuffed leather handbag for the little velvet bag containing the ring. He took it out and studied it. 'It's pretty with that twist to it, though it's only nine carat gold. Look! I've got a better idea than pawning it. Come and choose some clothes from the Rivenshaw shop. You can tell Jonah you want to use your mother's wedding ring and that'll save him buying you one, and save me all the bookwork on pawning and redeeming this.'

She didn't argue because she'd love to wear her mother's ring. 'Thank you. That's very kind of you.'

He looked at her indignantly. '*Kind?* I'm not kind! I'm just finding a practical way of saving my brother money. Now, be ready for us to pick you up at one o'clock.'

But she knew he had been kind, even though he didn't want to admit it.

She walked out of the shop, feeling a load lift from her shoulders, and went straight round to Auntie Hilda's house, walking in as usual through the back door. She was about to call, 'It's only me!' when she heard voices.

The speakers didn't hear her come in and she stopped dead when she heard her neighbour from across the street saying very clearly, 'And there she was going into the pawnshop, bold as brass. Now why would she need to do that? She's never been there before. *And* she was seen driving off in a taxi with that Charlie Willcox. *On her own with him.* People are saying he's keeping her as his mistress.'

Leah didn't often lose her temper but she did now. How could someone who'd known her since she was a child think that of her? She burst into the front room, shouting, 'How dare you say such terrible things about me?' She turned to Auntie Hilda. 'And how could you let her say them?'

Hilda grabbed her arm to stop her turning and marching straight out again. 'I was waiting to see what poison she was spreading this time, so I could put a stop to it.' She kept hold of Leah's arm and turned to her visitor. 'You can ask her yourself what she was doing at the pawnshop, Ada Varley. I'm sure she had a very good reason for the visit.'

She gave Leah's arm a little shake as if to nudge her to explain, but Leah was so upset, she could only say, 'It's none of your business, Mrs Varley. And I don't have to deny your fairy tales because everyone knows I don't go with men in the way you're insinuating. I never have done and I never will.'

Then she shook off Hilda's hand, burst into tears and ran out, not caring who saw her as she stumbled down the back alley behind the street and through the back gate of her own home.

Two minutes later, Hilda walked in after her. 'Well, you did make a spectacle of yourself, my girl. What on earth got into you? That fool is now convinced there's something in the story that you and Charlie Willcox are having an affair.'

'Well, there isn't.'

'*I* know that. But you have been seen with him, so how about you tell me what's going on? Aw, come here, love.'

Leah flung herself into Auntie Hilda's kind embrace, sobbing out her shame at being thought a fallen woman.

She was comforted by Auntie Hilda's support and soon pulled herself together, explaining what was really going on.

Hilda stared at her in shock. 'You're going to marry Jonah Willcox?'

'Yes. He's a very nice man.'

'How long have you known him?'

'Two days. Only I'm telling people I've known him for longer.'

'My goodness! Still, it's just the thing you need, a husband to support you, and I'm very pleased for you. Very pleased indeed.'

Leah sagged in relief. 'I'm glad you think it's the right thing to do. Can you come with me this afternoon to choose some clothes for the wedding?'

'I certainly can. And we'll make sure everyone in the street sees me getting into the taxi with you.'

When the taxi arrived, not only was Charlie sitting in it, but his fiancée as well. And he was looking annoyed.

He got out and opened the back door of the taxi for them. 'Move up, Marion. I told you she was bringing her auntie, didn't I?'

'Yes.'

'This is my auntie, Mrs Gordon.'

Hilda received a bare sniff and nod from Marion in acknowledgement, but a genuine smile from Charlie.

A couple of women down the street were staring. Let them stare. They wouldn't know what to make of this outing, but they wouldn't be able to say she was having an affair with Charlie. She sniffed. The cheek of it. She still felt angry.

The taxi wound its way down the hill to the pawnshop in Rivenshaw and Charlie took them upstairs. 'I keep the better clothes up here. The ones on that side are the ones you'll need to go through, Leah. They won't be claimed back because I bought them outright. You can choose any you like.'

He turned to Marion. 'Make sure you help her get something smart, love. I don't want our Jonah walking round with a dowdy woman on his arm.'

Hilda waited for Leah to speak and when she didn't, turned to Marion and eyed her up and down. 'He's right. You'll know better than either of us what to choose. You certainly dress well.'

Marion relaxed visibly and stole a smug glance at herself in the mirror.

Leah wished for the umpteenth time that she had her auntie's ability to set people at ease.

'What exactly do you need?' Marion asked.

'Something smart to wear for the wedding, if possible.' Leah gestured at herself. 'This is the best I have at the moment.'

'Well, you're nice and slim which makes it easier.' Marion turned to the rack and began flicking through the clothes on it, pulling out several items and laying them over the backs of two chairs. 'Those would be the best for the wedding outfit, and you'll need one or two decent frocks for day wear as well.'

'I have some things I can wear round the house.'

She looked down her nose at Leah. 'If that's your best, I'd hate to see your other things. You're going to need a lot of new clothes, even for wearing round the house. How are you for underclothes?'

Leah could feel herself blushing. 'I can make my own if I buy some material. I'm quite handy with a needle, actually. And if I could buy a second-hand sewing machine, I could make clothes for me and my sister. My mother taught me to sew, only Dad gave her sewing machine away to one of her cousins before she died before I could stop him.' He had been generous to a fault, her lovely dad.

'Look, someone has to be frank with you. I am *not* saying this to be rude. You'll be marrying Charlie Willcox's brother, and he has a position to uphold in Birch End, so *you* will need to keep up appearances too, wherever you are, at home or out and about.'

'Who's going to see me on the far side of Ellindale?'

'People in the village will see you every time you go shopping. Your scrubbing woman will see you.' She saw Leah's shock at this and rolled her eyes. 'You won't be expected to do your own rough work, for heaven's sake. And if you think Charlie won't want to visit his brother regularly, you can think again. They're very close, those two. He'll be popping in regularly.'

She let that sink in and finished, 'And *I* don't want to be seen with a sister-in-law who looks as if her clothes came out of a ragbag.'

'I hadn't thought about it like that.'

'So it's a good thing Charlie asked me to help. Now, he and I have an appointment later, so let's get on with this, before he comes up and forces you to buy something unsuitable. Men have no idea about clothes.'

'She's right. Do as she asks, love,' Hilda put in.

Leah felt humiliated but she did need clothes. Desperately. And her husband would see her underwear, so she couldn't just make do even out of sight underneath the new garments. She closed her mouth firmly and went to finger the dresses and skirts, holding them up against her.

She hadn't really considered how her appearance would reflect on her husband and his family, hadn't had time to think anything through, because she'd never expected to be getting married, let alone be doing it so abruptly.

In the end, Marion found her a knitted jumper suit for day wear in a soft shade of lilac with darker lilac trimmings, and a smart frock in dark blue for the wedding. It had a blue silk scarf that slotted through loops at the neckline, and a matching jacket.

'If you can let the hems down without it showing, you should do that,' Marion advised. 'Fashionable ladies are wearing their frocks and skirts longer this year.'

'Those outfits really suit you, love.' Hilda ran one fingertip over the soft material of the blue dress.

Marion tossed a couple of skirts on to the chairs, and some blouses, then two petticoats. 'Oops! I nearly forgot about hats.' She went over to the corner and opened a trunk, lifting hats out and sneering at most of them. 'Ugh! Old-fashioned. Dowdy. Ugly.'

Then she pounced. 'Ah! This one. Beret caps are very

popular at the moment. You shouldn't try to be too fancy. You don't have a frilly sort of face.' She held the hat out, navy with a narrow pink ribbon round it and one matching pink silk flower. 'Try this on.'

Leah couldn't resist doing that, staring in amazement at her reflection in the full-length mirror speckled with age at the edges. She didn't think she'd ever looked this smart in her whole life.

'You're much better at choosing clothes than me,' she admitted.

Marion preened herself. 'Yes, I am. If I say so myself, I have excellent taste in clothes. You must always take me with you when you go out shopping for clothes.'

There were footsteps on the stairs.

'Are you decent?' Charlie called.

'Yes. Come and look.'

He came in, signalling with a twirl of his forefinger for Leah to turn round. 'Good. There's no one like Marion for knowing how to dress.' He plonked a careless kiss on his fiancée's cheek. 'Right then, I've done my business and we need to get back, so hurry up.'

'I need to find something for Rosa as well,' Leah said. 'She's grown out of her best clothes.'

'Marion?' he prompted.

'How old is your sister?'

'Ten and quite tall for her age.'

'What colour is her hair?'

'She looks like a younger version of Leah,' Hilda said. 'Just starting to get interested in clothes.'

'The children's clothes are downstairs,' Charlie said.

'I know where they are. I'll bring some up.' Marion had started down the stairs before Leah could say anything. She came back five minutes later with an armful of clothes. 'These should do.'

'She won't need all those.'

'Of course she will. She'll need to look decent, just as you will. And let her choose which outfit to wear for the wedding. Girls that age like to have a say in their clothes.'

'Thank you. It's, um, extremely kind of you,' Leah said. But she was fed up of being the object of kindness and charity, preferring to sort her own life out. And would do once she was married. Well, with Jonah's help.

Marion shrugged. 'I can remember what it's like to be ten. My mother bought me an *awful* dress and I was mortified to be seen in it. I had to climb a wall and jump off to rip it convincingly before she'd stop forcing me to wear it. Here. Put the clothes in this.' She held out a large paper carrier bag, the sort fancy shops put clothes in when you bought things from them.

Leah took it. The carrier bag had clearly been used already, but that didn't matter. It would still impress her neighbours.

She turned to Charlie. 'You'll have to tell me how much I owe you.'

'Nothing. You're providing the ring. *And* the furniture, I hear. That's a bonus I didn't expect. Now all you need to do is make my brother happy. That'll more than pay the family back.'

He grinned and flourished another slightly crumpled paper bag as big as a suitcase. It too bore the label of a famous London store. 'Pack the rest of your clothes in this, Leah. That'll make your damned gossiping neighbours stare.'

She smiled reluctantly. It would cause talk. Then she wondered how he knew about her neighbours.

'Best if you get married quickly by special licence, I think. We'll arrange it all on Monday and do the deed on Wednesday. We'll have to go into Manchester to get the licence, but we can go by train and taxi, so Jonah won't get too tired.'

A steamroller would be easier to stop than Charlie Willcox, Leah thought, as they got back into a taxi.

And his fiancée was as bad.

The two of them were very suited to one another in that way.

And while she didn't intend to let them run her whole life for her, at the moment she needed their help and could learn a lot from them.

Hilda went back into the house with Leah and the taxi took the other two away. 'Let's look at the clothes and see if they need ironing, then we'll hang them up.'

Leah nodded, staring in bemusement as the garments were pulled out of the bags and spread out in the front room. 'I can't believe this is happening.'

'I'm glad for you. You deserve some happiness.'

'I know you think I'm doing the right thing, but I'm not so sure. I hardly know Jonah and that worries me.'

In truth it felt as if she'd got into a train that was moving faster and faster, and she had no control over where it went. She was having moments of near panic and hoped she'd never again feel so helpless.

Even if Jonah turned out to be the kindest man in Lancashire, she wasn't going to live her life as a doormat. Nor was she going to encourage him to sit around reading books and staring into space. That couldn't be good for anyone. No wonder he had that faintly sad air. Other men with damaged lungs had to carry on working to look after their families. He just did a few hours of bookkeeping.

It seemed to her that his family had mollycoddled him, and he might have needed it at first, but surely not now?

Not unless his lungs were more badly damaged than she'd realised. She wished she could talk to a doctor about him. After all, it was over ten years since the war had ended and Jonah didn't look to be at death's door to her.

★　　★　　★

Two days later, on the Saturday afternoon, Leah's packing was interrupted by someone hammering on the door. Annoyed at the way the person was continuing to thump without giving her time to get to the door, she marched through the house and flung it open. 'Where's the fire?'

Sam Griggs the rent man was leaning against the door frame. He ignored her remark. 'I've come for the rent.'

'Mr Harris told me I didn't need to pay it for this last week. He said he'd pay it if necessary.'

'Well, it's *Mrs* Harris as I answer to and she didn't tell me any such thing. So I'll have my eight shillings or you can get out within the hour.'

'You only have to ask Mr Harris and—'

'I don't have to do anything of the sort. Are you deaf or summat? *Mrs* Harris is in charge of rents and the rule is you pay your rent or I throw you out straight away.'

Leah didn't have eight shillings in the world, not even one shilling, because she'd just bought some food. She'd have to ask Charlie for a loan. 'I'll have to go and see a friend. I'll get the money for you but it may take more than an hour.'

'Rules is rules. Pay within the hour or you and your furniture will be thrown out into the street. And I'm staying here till you pay.'

'Go out the back way and fetch Charlie,' she whispered to Rosa, who was standing behind her. Then she turned and put one arm across the doorway as Sam Griggs tried to push inside. 'An hour, you said. Till then, you can stay outside.'

He leaned forward till his head was too close to her for comfort. 'I hear you give favours for money these days.' The way he looked her up and down made her feel sick.

'Then you hear wrongly.'

'I could pay the rent for you if you gave me an hour alone.'

Fear shivered through her at the way he was staring at her. 'I would *never* do that with anyone.'

He shoved her backwards so hard she fell over and he came quickly inside, slamming the door behind him. 'Maybe you need a little persuading. Some women like that, as well.'

She tried to get up but he shoved her down, so she began to scream for help. But would anyone come when this man was involved?

He stood looking at her for a moment, leering, then bent over her to grasp the bottom of her skirt.

At that moment the door burst open and Hilda came in. 'Get off her, you.'

'You mind your own business, missus, or you'll be in trouble too.'

'She *is* my business. She's as close to me as a daughter.'

Outside someone began banging on a saucepan with a spoon, the traditional signal that a neighbour was in trouble. Doors opened down the street and people peered out.

'It's Sam Griggs,' someone called.

Some went back into their houses again, but enough women and a couple of men came hurrying up to Leah's house.

'Get off her!' one man yelled. 'She's a decent lass.'

'Not as I hear it and she invited me in, didn't you?' He dragged Leah to her feet, keeping her arm twisted behind her back.

'No, I didn't. Ow! You pushed your way in.'

'Because you haven't got the rent money.'

'Mr Harris said he'd pay the rent if I needed it, because of my father working for him, but if he's changed his mind, I told you: I can get the rent money from Charlie Willcox.'

He pulled out his pocket watch. 'I gave her an hour. She has forty minutes left before I throw her out.'

But it wasn't Charlie who came running up the street ten

minutes later: it was Vi, the woman in charge of the day-to-day running of the Birch End pawnshop.

Vi glared at Sam. 'Are you causing trouble again?'

'I'm just doing my job, collecting the rent money.'

'How much does she owe?'

'Eight shillings.'

Vi fumbled in a pouch strapped to her waist. 'Here.'

He took the money from her, muttered something and tried to leave.

'Hoy! You need to sign the rent book first to say I paid,' Leah called.

'Well, get it out then. You should have had it waiting for me.'

She went into the kitchen and took it out of the drawer, feeling tears of humiliation welling in her eyes. Why had Mr Harris changed his mind about helping with the rent? And why hadn't he told her? Or hadn't he known? Yes, that might be it. His wife had arranged this without telling him. She wiped her tears away with the tea towel and went back to get his signature.

Griggs scrawled his initials but if looks could kill, she'd be dead. She'd made an enemy, that was for sure. Thank goodness she was moving away. She hoped he didn't collect from any of the houses in Ellindale because there would be no neighbours close enough there to rescue her.

She and Vi went to the door to watch him lumber off down the street with his heavy tread.

'There goes a piece of muck,' Vi said. 'He didn't hurt you, did he?'

'No. My friend came in time.' She looked back down the hall to smile at Hilda.

'Your little lass came running into the shop like all the devils in hell were after her.'

'Where is she?'

'I told her to stay with Don and help him keep an eye on the shop. He's a nice old fellow, Don is. He'll make sure she's all right. Charlie was out so I came.'

'How can I ever thank you?'

She shrugged. 'I'm always happy to stop Sam Griggs hurting someone. Will you be all right now?'

'Yes.'

'Charlie Willcox is sharp with money, and there's none sharper, but he doesn't pester women, no, nor bully people for no reason, women or men, I can promise you that.'

She started to leave, then turned round again. 'Your Jonah's a good man but he should stop letting Charlie tell him what to do.'

'I've been wondering about that. Do you know Jonah well?'

'I helped look after him when his mother died. I was newly married then. He was a clever little chap. Just as clever as Charlie but gentler. Eh, that damned war destroyed a lot of good men, my husband included.'

'I'm sorry. You haven't married again?'

'There weren't enough men left to go round after the war, and I'm not pretty, so I found a job. I'm doing all right. Charlie pays me a living wage. He says he pays for the job done not whether it's a woman or man doing it.'

She obviously respected Charlie, which Leah hadn't expected. 'Well, thanks again, and if you're ever out at Ellindale, call in for a cup of tea.'

Vi looked at her in surprise. 'All right. Thanks. Maybe I will. I do go out walking on the tops sometimes. Clears the head, it does, that moorland air. I'd have to bring my friend Mary with me, though. She and I share a house and we knock around together at weekends.'

'You're welcome to bring her.'

As Vi left, Leah went to join Hilda, who was sitting in the kitchen looking tired.

'Good thing the Harrises don't own my house, eh?' Hilda
said. 'Or that Griggs would find an excuse to turn me out
of it.'

'Who is your landlord?'

'Me, now my Frank's dead.'

'Why did you never say? I just thought you paid rent to
a landlord yourself.'

'And that's the way I want to keep it. I don't want the
other women to think I'm different from them.'

'How did you manage to buy it?'

'After the war, before he married that woman, Mr Harris
was a bit short of money, so he sold off a few houses. I'd
been left a bit of money an' Frank borrowed twenty pounds
from the bank to make up the rest. Eh, we were that excited
to own our own house. We paid off the twenty pounds as
quick as we could to make sure the bank couldn't take the
house off us. You were too young to notice or care in those
days, and like I said, we didn't go blabbing our business to
the world.'

She sighed. 'Now my Frank's dead, poor love, but I've still
got the house and with taking in lodgers I manage all right,
better than I let on to other folk actually. The house will come
to you and Rosa when I die, because I've no close relatives.'

'Don't talk about that, Auntie Hilda. I'd be happy if you
lived for ever.'

Hilda patted her hand as it lay on the table. 'I know. But
we have to be practical. I'll give you a copy of my will when
you're settled in Ellindale.'

That evening, Adam Harris came home early from the club
and stormed into his wife's sitting room.

As she looked up from her book, he snatched it out of
her hands and threw it across the room, yelling, 'How could
you do it, Ethel?'

She smiled, the nasty little curve of her lips showing she was enjoying his rage. But for once he didn't back off.

'You not only tried to force that poor young woman into paying rent after I'd told you I'd pay anything else necessary, but you set Sam Griggs on to attack her.'

'If he attacked her, it was only because she was asking for it. That sort will do anything to get a man's interest. Or to pay their debts the easy way.'

He looked at her as if he'd never seen her before. 'Don't play me for stupid. You know as well as I do that she's a decent young woman who's getting wed next week. You were just trying to mess up her life. You can't bear anyone to be happy.'

'I know no such thing. *You* should pay more attention to what people are saying about her, then you'd see what she's like and stop doting on her.'

'I should stop *what*?'

'Doting on her. There have been others over the years. Do you think I don't notice the signs.'

He stared at her in bafflement. 'I have never doted on any woman in that way. I've always been true to my marriage vows to you. I was simply trying to be kind to a lass who lost her father because of our fault.'

'It was an accident at the laundry, *not* your fault. And certainly not mine, so don't include me in this.'

'You were the one who said we should go on using the old machinery. You didn't tell me that one had been reported as unstable and dangerous.'

'It was too expensive to replace.'

'Instead it cost a man's life. That's far more expensive as far as I'm concerned. I've let you persuade me to delay replacing things, but not any longer. I don't want you poking your nose in the laundry again. In fact, stay right out of it.'

At that she fell into one of her blind rages, hurling anything that came to hand at him, even expensive ornaments she'd bought for herself. One caught him a glancing blow on the forehead and he felt the warmth of blood trickling down his face.

'You're beyond ridiculous, Ethel.' He ducked just in time to get out of the way of a large piece of pottery and left the room hastily as it smashed against the piano. There was never any reasoning with her in this mood.

When he looked at himself in the hall mirror, he whistled softly in surprise at how heavily his injury was bleeding. The cut was far bigger than he'd thought.

He got out a handkerchief and pressed it to the wound. He'd have to get the doctor to stitch it. He left the house by way of the kitchen.

Minnie, the live-in maid, exclaimed in shock. He paused to look her in the eyes. 'I'm not hiding who's done this, Minnie. You live here too and you know what she's like. If anyone asks me I'll tell them the truth. I'm done with pretence. You'd better keep out of her way till she calms down, if you can. I'm going to the doctor. The cut needs stitching.'

At the doctor's he told the truth about how he'd been injured.

Dr Mitchell gaped at him for a moment.

'It's happened before and I've tried to hide what Ethel is like, but I'm done with that now.'

'But Mrs Harris said—' He broke off, flushing slightly.

'She probably said I beat her or I was "acting strangely" or something to that effect.'

'Well, yes.'

'The violence runs in *her* family not mine. Check the records of your predecessor and find out what happened to her aunt – Miriam Bailey.'

'Give me a few minutes.'

The doctor left the consulting room, returning ten minutes

later with a card in his hand. 'You're right. They had to lock your wife's aunt away.'

'You can check the Harris records and you won't find anyone in my family being locked away for wild mood swings and irrational behaviour.'

'I just checked them. You'd better be careful. Your wife can be very convincing.'

'Yes. And she can be as sweet as sugar when she wants something.'

'I can't do anything to help you keep her calm, I'm afraid, unless she asks me for help, but I will bear witness that you're sane and competent if it's ever needed.'

'Thank you.'

'Come back in eight to ten days to have the stitches removed. I've done quite a few small stitches and I'm a neat sewer, so I don't think the scar will be very obvious. Um . . . and take care.'

Adam went home reluctantly, glad he no longer shared a bedroom with Ethel. Glad there were bolts on the inside of his bedroom door that he never forgot to slide into place before he went to bed.

He was so unhappy with her, he wondered sometimes if he should leave. He could go and live in the colonies, make a new life there. He was only thirty-seven, after all, and though he'd failed his Army medical, due to a foot problem, that didn't interfere with his normal life.

The main thing that was keeping him here was his love of Lancashire and the difficulty he'd have selling the laundry in a depression. And he cared about his employees. If he left, the person who bought the laundry might treat the workers harshly. One man had already been killed because he'd been too timid to step in. He wasn't going to let that sort of thing happen again.

He had a sudden horrified thought that she might even

get that damned Sam Griggs to kill him. He wouldn't put anything past the pair of them. Ah hell, he didn't know what to do, only that he couldn't spend the rest of his life living like this; he just could not bear it.

He found his wife sitting peacefully in the front parlour, which had been swept clean of shards of pottery. She looked up and smiled sweetly, but he stared back at her without speaking, at which she flushed slightly.

But she didn't apologise or even mention the incident, she never did.

He didn't want to talk to her, so went upstairs to his own room, unlocking the door then locking it again carefully, before flinging himself down on the bed.

Thank goodness they hadn't had children to pass on this tainted inheritance from the Baileys.

The main thing he was sure of was that he wasn't going to continue to be a coward. Stan Turner had paid the penalty for that. No one else was going to.

5

As arranged, they went into Manchester on the Monday to get the special licence. Leah would have liked to stroll round the city centre and shops, because she'd never been there before. Charlie, however, was in a hurry to get back. He was always in a hurry to go somewhere.

Why he'd come with them today, she couldn't figure, unless he didn't trust them to get the licence unless he was supervising.

The hours seemed to whizz past as she finished clearing out the house for the removers.

'I can't believe I'll never come back here again,' she said as she and Rosa ate a final meal there.

'We've neither of us lived anywhere else, have we?' Her sister looked round. 'But without Dad, it's not been the same. And I love my new bedroom in Ellindale. I'm so glad you and Jonah made the time to take me up there. It'd have felt awful not to know where I was going.'

On the Wednesday morning, Leah was so nervous she couldn't do more than force down one piece of bread with a thin scrape of jam. Today she was going to marry Jonah Willcox, change her name, change her whole life.

She was terrified.

Rosa came down to join her a few minutes later and ate her breakfast with her usual hearty child's appetite.

'I'm looking forward to dressing in those lovely clothes, aren't you, Leah?'

'I suppose so.'

Rosa looked at her in surprise. 'You sound nervous.'

'Yes.'

'You don't usually worry this much about things.'

'I don't usually get married.'

'Well, I'm glad you're doing it. I like Jonah. Mind you, I like Charlie better. He's always so cheerful. Pity it isn't him you're marrying.'

'He's already got a fiancée.'

'Well, I still think it's a pity.' She looked at the clock. 'I'm glad it's happening in the morning, so we won't be hanging about for hours waiting.'

There was the sound of a vehicle stopping outside.

Leah jumped up and ran to peer out of the front-room window. 'It's the removal men. They said it'd only take them an hour or so to load our furniture and boxes on to the lorry. Have you pinned the label to your mattress?'

'Yes. And tied the labels to the other bits and pieces in my room.'

'Then our things should be put into the right rooms at Spring Cottage. We can sort the smaller bits and pieces out later, but it'd be impossible for us to carry the big pieces of furniture upstairs.'

'I'll clear up the breakfast things and put them in your shopping bag, shall I?'

'Thanks, love. And make sure they don't take our suitcases with the wedding clothes in.'

'Yes, Mrs Fusspot.'

Leah went to open the front door. Anyone would fuss if they were moving house on the same day as they were getting married.

'Ah, come in, Mr Brown. The bedrooms are all ready for you to clear and everything's labelled, as we agreed.'

'Right you are, Miss Turner. And all the best for your wedding.'

'Thank you.'

As he and his son clumped up the stairs Leah wandered round the ground floor, feeling sad. It was only a small house and very shabby these days, but she had some lovely memories of her mother – standing at the sink, chatting away as they did the dishes, or changing the bed sheets with her and laughing as she told the tale of something that had happened in the street while Leah was at school.

Rosa came to join her. 'After they've cleared the house, we can go and change into the wedding clothes at Auntie Hilda's. Won't we feel posh?' She did a little skip for sheer excitement. 'And Charlie's sending a taxi for us. *A taxi!* It'll be the second time in a week that I've ridden in one.'

She put her arm round her sister's waist and gave her a quick squeeze. 'You're very quiet. Aren't you even a tiny bit excited?'

Leah shrugged. 'Not really. I'm too tired. I was packing things till after midnight and cleaning up where furniture's stood.' Numb was the best word to describe how she felt today, she decided. And nervous. Very nervous.

Even if the wedding and removal went perfectly, she'd be giving her body to a husband in bed tonight. That prospect continued to worry her and it wasn't something she could share with anyone.

A small group was waiting for them outside the parish church, whose minister had agreed to marry the couple. Charlie and Jonah both looked very smart in dark suits and white shirts. They were flanked by Marion in a gorgeous pink frock and jacket with bias cut frills placed diagonally on the skirt. Beside her stood a well-dressed older couple who, Leah later discovered, were her parents.

Taking a deep breath, Leah walked forward, flanked by Auntie Hilda and Rosa. And oh, she was so glad she was smartly dressed because they all looked perfectly turned out!

After introductions to Marion's parents, everyone went inside and the minister, whom Leah had only ever seen at a distance before, moved forward to conduct the brief marriage ceremony in a loud, plummy voice.

'I now pronounce you man and wife.'

Jonah turned and kissed her gently on the cheek. 'Hello, Mrs Willcox.'

His smile cheered her up. 'Hello, Mr Willcox.'

When the church business was finished, they walked out and found a photographer waiting for them.

'There wasn't time to ask you, but I was sure you'd want a memento of the occasion,' Jonah murmured.

She didn't know what she wanted. 'I hope he does a good job on me.'

'You'll look lovely.'

He squeezed her hand and again, his touch made her less nervous, so she reached out to clutch his hand properly. That helped a lot.

Then they strolled the short distance to the Green Man Hotel, where Charlie had ordered a luncheon for everyone.

This was another first for Leah, who had never eaten a meal in a hotel before.

'Don't be nervous,' Jonah whispered. 'We're paying customers and they'll fuss over us like mad.'

'I don't know why I'm so nervous,' she muttered. 'Only, I'm not used to being the centre of attention.'

'Neither am I. Good thing we didn't have a big, fancy wedding, eh? We'll get through this small one together.'

That was when it really sank in that she was no longer alone, that she really did have someone on her side now. All of a sudden she felt much happier. 'Yes, of course. Together. That's a lovely thought.'

Their group had a separate room to eat in and were served

a three-course meal. Pea and ham soup, then roast chicken and potatoes, and finally a wedding cake iced in white with *Leah and Jonah* written on it in pale pink.

The photographer appeared again suddenly and took a photo of it, and another one of them pretending to cut it.

Rosa's eyes were wide with wonder at all this food. Well, she'd been born in 1920, so the poor girl had known nothing but hard times, which were hardest of all in the north of England, people said.

Still, as today's display showed, not everyone was struggling to get by. Leah didn't think Charlie would ever have difficulty making a living.

He was a very confident man altogether, and kept the conversation going with such skill that Leah tried to work out how he did it, how he pulled such a disparate group of people together. He asked a lot of questions, she decided, which made people join in the conversation. But how did you think of suitable questions to ask? That was what puzzled her.

Then the waiter brought in a bottle of champagne and everyone went, 'Oooh!' The photographer came to take another photo.

They were each given a glass of it; even Rosa was allowed a tiny amount.

Charlie stood up and proposed a toast to 'The bride and groom'.

Leah raised her glass in return, then savoured her first taste of champagne. It wasn't sweet and sickly like fizzy drinks often were, but astringent with a faint flavour of fruit. If only they did fizzy drinks like this.

'It's lovely!' she exclaimed. 'I've never tasted champagne before, or even wine.'

Charlie looked pleased at that, then Marion claimed his attention. Auntie Hilda was talking to Marion's parents and Rosa was listening to them.

In that rare moment of near privacy, Jonah raised his glass and clinked it against hers. 'A private toast now: to us, my dear wife.'

'To us,' she echoed. But she only took a sip to spin out the lovely taste.

When the cake and a cup of coffee had been served, they made their way down to the foyer.

As they waited for their coats to be brought, Leah found herself next to Charlie. 'Thank you for making this such a special occasion.'

He grinned. 'Nothing but the best for us Willcoxes. How did you like the champagne?'

'I loved it.'

'Not too dry?'

'How can a liquid be called dry?'

'It's the opposite of sweet when it comes to wine,' he explained.

'Oh, I see. No, it wasn't too dry. Usually fizzy drinks are too sugary for my taste. They even make ginger beer sickly sweet when you buy it at the shop. My mum used to make it with a touch of lemon juice. I've never tasted any quite as nice as hers.'

'You'll have to make a batch sometime and give me a bottle. I'm fond of an occasional ginger beer.'

'I'll make it regularly once we're settled in.' She was only just beginning to realise that she'd have the money to do things like that, or to buy something just for a treat. Tears came into her eyes.

'What's wrong?' He moved to stand between her and the others.

'Nothing's wrong. I'm just . . . happy.'

He chuckled and spoke a little more loudly than usual. 'Trust a woman to cry when she's happy as well as when she's sad.'

She realised suddenly that the others had been staring at her. He'd defused that situation and made everyone laugh.

She turned as Jonah joined them and put an arm round her shoulders. 'Sorry. I always cry when I'm particularly happy.'

'Well, until I know you better, you'll have to tell me any time you cry whether they're happy tears or sad ones. They all look the same from the outside. But I'll do my best to keep yours happy. Now, our taxi is waiting. Are you ready?'

They went outside. Charlie tossed confetti over them as they got into the taxi, laughing at their exclamations of surprise.

Rosa tried to catch some of the little pieces before she joined them in the taxi. 'I'm going to put them in my scrapbook.'

Marion stayed back, rolling her eyes and murmuring something to her mother, something scornful about such vulgar behaviour no doubt. Leah was beginning to wonder if Marion always felt *she* should be the one in the limelight. Well, she was welcome to it.

Anyway, the fuss was over now and they'd got through it without any hitches. Hilda had offered to let Rosa stay with her for a day or two, but Leah had refused. She wanted her sister to feel at home in Ellindale, not there on sufferance.

As they drove past the laundry, with its smoking chimney, she felt a bubble of happiness, the first real one that day.

How wonderful it would be to live out at Ellindale, in the peace and fresh air!

Rosa sat in the front seat next to the taxi driver, chatting to him about the wedding and asking questions about places they passed.

'I think your sister has enjoyed the wedding more than anyone,' Jonah commented.

'Didn't you enjoy it?'

'I was rather nervous.'

'So was I.' Leah studied him. 'You look tired now.'

'I am a little. It's not only the getting married that's tired me out, but packing all my things ready for the movers. I didn't want to leave that to anyone else.'

'And when we get there we'll have to unpack everything again. We'll have to change out of our best clothes before we start.' She smoothed her skirt. 'I don't want anything to happen to this frock. It's the nicest thing I've ever owned.'

'You look lovely in it. Marion chose well.'

Leah looked at him. 'You didn't mind me getting it from Charlie? There were no signs of wear and tear on it.'

'Of course not. He told me about you trying to pawn your mother's wedding ring. I'd have given you some money if I'd known how little you had.'

'I didn't want you to pay for my wedding outfit. Anyway, it all worked out well and I love having her ring.' She held her hand out to study it, then turned the attention on to him. 'You look very smart in your dark suit.'

'I confess that Charlie had to do my tie for me. I was all fingers and thumbs.'

'He provided a lovely meal. We won't need much tea after that, will we?'

'No. And I forgot to tell you, my parents sent a hamper of food as a wedding present. They were sorry they couldn't come but they have a full house of holidaymakers this week.'

'That's very kind of them. I bought some ham yesterday and a loaf.'

'One day we'll go to Blackpool and you can meet my stepmum and dad and enjoy a little holiday by the sea. But we can't do that till the end or beginning of the season when they've got no holiday guests staying. They were booked out this summer in spite of the Depression, though mostly it's been southerners.'

'I've never been to Blackpool or even seen the sea.'

'It's the most amazing place. The air is very bracing and I always feel better there, just as I do in Ellindale. Look! We're here.'

They'd passed through the village without her even noticing and were stopping at the gate of Spring Cottage. It felt like home to her already, it really did.

Rosa was out of the car before they'd even opened their door, standing on the gate crossbar to stare round.

'I'll bring the luggage in, Jonah lad,' the taxi driver said.

'I'll carry my bag of clothes. Rosa! Don't go in empty-handed!'

She noticed that Jonah didn't offer to carry anything. He was rather pale and walking more slowly now. She'd make sure he had a good rest before he started any of his unpacking. Or perhaps he'd let her do that for him. It was a wife's job, after all.

'You're welcome to go and explore the house,' she whispered to Rosa. 'You know which is your bedroom.'

As Rosa ran up the wooden stairs, Jonah looked across at Leah apologetically. 'I'm sorry, love. I'm afraid I need a rest. I can only do so much physically, then I get short of breath.'

'You did better than I'd expected. I want to start by making up the beds, so I'll leave you down here. Rosa will be able to help me with that.'

He sat down with a sigh in her father's old armchair, wriggled a bit and nodded. 'This is very comfortable.'

'Dad often used to fall asleep in it.'

'I'll probably do the same.'

When all the bags were unloaded, Jonah paid Robert then gave in to temptation, leaning his head back and closing his eyes.

★ ★ ★

Leah went upstairs to join Rosa, who was staring out of her bedroom window at the moors.

'Isn't it lovely here, Leah? You can see for miles. I can't believe this is my room now. It's much bigger than the one in Birch End. All that one looked out at was backyards.'

'It'll look even nicer after we've sorted everything out. We'll get you a proper bookcase, for one thing, and a table to do your homework on. Have you been into our bedroom and the other rooms up here?'

'No, not yet.'

'Well, two of them will be empty for a while, except for my old bed.' She blushed. 'Jonah and I will be sleeping in Dad's double bed, of course. Anyway, let's sort out the bedding and make the beds up. That job's always easier with two pairs of hands. We should change into our everyday clothes first. Did you bring yours upstairs?'

'Of course I did. I'll only be a minute.' Rosa ran into her sister's bedroom for a quick look, then came back to change, so Leah followed suit.

It took a while to find all the bedding because the movers hadn't paid proper attention to the labels and had left the bundle of sheets in the front parlour downstairs.

'It wouldn't have taken much more effort for them to get it right,' Leah grumbled when she finally located the sheets.

She peeped into the kitchen and saw that Jonah was asleep, so left him to it.

After making up the beds, the sisters hung up their clothes and put them in the drawers, which didn't take long, then Leah went to find her sister.

Rosa was at her bedroom window again staring out at the moors.

Leah put an arm round her and they stood quietly together for a minute or two. 'I think we're going to be happy here, don't you? The house has a nice feel to it.'

'It's a splendid house.'

When they went down, Jonah was still asleep and didn't even wake when they forgot about him and walked into the kitchen chatting.

'Shh!' Leah put one finger to her lips. 'Let's go out the back way and have a look at the garden, give him more time to rest.' What an effort he must have made today if it tired him out so much. She must look after him, see he didn't overdo things from now on.

They found a part of the garden with square beds marked out by lines of stones. All they'd seemed to have grown this year was a fine crop of weeds.

'I intend to grow plenty of vegetables next year,' Leah said.

'Do you know how? We've never had a garden.'

'I can learn, can't I?'

Beyond the vegetable patch they saw a sheltered area containing a few smallish trees, so went across to explore it. There were quite high stone walls on three sides.

'What are those things on the ground?' Rosa moved forward. 'Oh Leah, look! They're apples! Just fancy having our own apple trees. What a pity some have fallen off.'

'Windfalls, they're called.' Leah picked one up and studied it. 'Most of this one is all right.'

Rosa pounced on another apple. 'So is this one. And this.'

'We can cut the bad bits out and stew the rest. How wonderful! Our own apples.'

'Hold out your apron!' Rosa darted to and fro picking up the windfalls, laughing with glee at how many she found, looking like the carefree child she'd been before her father died.

When the apron was full, Leah took her load into the house and piled them on the kitchen table.

Jonah mumbled something but didn't open his eyes.

She smiled fondly at the sight of him sleeping like a baby in her father's chair. That well-known chair standing in her new kitchen seemed to pull the two families more closely together.

Then she realised she was daydreaming and there was still a lot to do. 'Could you nip down to the village shop, Rosa, and see if they have any milk to spare? Tell Mrs Buckley I'll be down tomorrow to put in a regular order for milk and bread.'

As she gave her sister the last of her money, Jonah woke up and blinked as if he didn't quite know where he was at first.

'Oh. We're here. Sorry to abandon you on our wedding day, Leah. I was so tired I couldn't stay upright.'

'You're in your own home now, so you can sleep whenever and wherever you want.'

'Our home.' He stood up and stretched, then caught sight of the hamper on the floor next to the table. 'You haven't opened this yet.'

'I'd forgotten it. Rosa and I were making up our beds.' She opened the hamper and gasped. 'Oh, my goodness! Look at all this food!' She pulled out tins and packets, so many of them. 'What a thoughtful present.'

He picked up a tin of biscuits. 'Look. Mum's put in some of my favourites.'

'Do you think of her as your mother, not stepmother?'

'Yes. She's a lovely woman. You'll like her.'

'See what I found outside.' She pointed to the sink, where she'd dumped the windfalls.

'I used to love Granddad's apples. None of the ones from the shops ever taste as delicious as an apple fresh from the tree.' He reached out to pick one up.

She took it from him. 'Let me give it a good wash and cut off that bruised bit, then you can eat it. Do you like apple pie? I could make one tomorrow.'

'I love apple pies.'

She opened a door in the rear kitchen wall and beamed at the huge pantry that was revealed, with its L-shaped stone shelf running round at waist height.

'This will keep things beautifully cool in summer!'

As she turned, she bumped into Jonah, who pulled her into his arms and kissed her. It was the first real kiss they'd shared, because you couldn't count the public peck he'd given her in church. His lips were warm and soft, and the way he framed her face with his hands made her feel . . . cherished . . . wanted.

He ran one fingertip down her cheek. 'Your skin feels as soft as it looks. You have beautiful skin.'

'That's a good job because I can't afford face powder.'

'You can now, but I hope you don't buy any. I don't want to kiss face powder. I want to kiss *you*.' He chuckled. 'You look wide-eyed and surprised, as if you've never been properly kissed by a man before.'

She blurted out the truth. 'I haven't.'

'Why ever not?'

'I had Rosa to look after and the house to manage from when I was fourteen. There never seemed to be time to mess about with lads. And none of them wanted to walk out with a lass who already had a child to look after. Well, they wouldn't, would they?'

'No, I suppose not. I like having Rosa around, but I like having you here even more. I hope you didn't dislike the kiss, because I shall want to do it quite often.'

'I liked it very much.' She raised her hand to her cheek where his lips seemed to have left a lingering warmth.

They put away the contents of the hamper in the pantry together, but though it'd been a big hamper, most of the shelves were still empty.

'We'll have to fill them up,' he said.

She nerved herself to confess, 'I, um, don't have any money left and I need to do some shopping.'

'I'm sorry, love. I should have thought of that. I'll leave some in a jar, if you have an empty one. You won't want to carry it round with you all the time.'

She had plenty of empty jars. It was full ones she was lacking, she thought, watching in astonishment as he put several pound- and ten-shilling notes and a few coins in the jar she'd found.

'Just take what money you need and I'll put more in when necessary.'

'Don't you want to tell me how much to take each week for the housekeeping?'

'How would I know? You mustn't skimp on yourself. Buy the food we need and let me know if there's anything else you want as well.'

'You're making it all seem so easy.'

'That side of things is easy. Leah love, may I—'

She was sorry that Rosa came running in just then, because he'd seemed about to kiss her again. And she'd wanted him to.

After a simple tea, Leah would have liked to go out for a stroll, but she could see that Jonah wasn't up to it, so after she and Rosa had cleared up, she sat down across the fire from him. She must start some knitting, didn't like to have idle hands.

Rosa yawned. 'I think I'll go up now. Can I read in bed?'

'Yes. But be careful with that lamp. Make sure it's turned off properly.' Leah looked apologetically at Jonah. 'We're not used to oil lamps. We had gas lights before.' Some lucky homes in Birch End had electric lighting, but Mrs Harris hadn't modernised any of her houses.

Leah was tired now as well. Butterflies were fluttering in

her stomach and she was trying not to show how nervous she was feeling about what was to come.

'You're looking apprehensive, my dear.'

'I suppose any woman would on her wedding night.'

'No need. I know what I'm doing and I'll do my best to make tonight pleasant for you. Why don't you get ready for bed and I'll join you shortly?'

She ran up to the bedroom to get her nightdress, then came down to use the bathroom. It was so convenient to have the lavatory indoors and most of the time she'd make do with cold water to wash her hands.

She got into bed and lay there, waiting, sucking in a deep breath when she heard Jonah climb the stairs.

He was naked apart from a towel wrapped around his waist.

'I didn't know where my pyjamas were,' he said cheerfully.

'Under your pillow.' She should have taken them down when she took her own.

'But I'd only be taking them off again, so that doesn't matter.'

When he dropped the towel and stood there naked, she could feel herself flushing and didn't know where to look.

'We soon lost our fear of being naked in the Army, then in the hospital. I forget sometimes that other people usually keep their bodies covered. Charlie and I never bothered. Marion's in for a few shocks if she's prudish.'

He lifted the covers and joined her in bed. 'Let me kiss you again.'

He touched her body gently as he kissed her and she didn't quite know what to do with her own hands. But he seemed very confident so she let him guide her.

After some kissing and stroking, she felt a pleasant tingling in parts of her body. The books hadn't said anything about that. What did it mean?

She had thought making love might be difficult, but it wasn't, not with Jonah, his lovely kisses and gentle hands. She soon forgot her fears, and let him do what he wanted.

When he groaned, she thought for a moment something was wrong, but he said in a harsh whisper, 'I can't wait any longer.'

The final part didn't hurt at all but she couldn't understand what men saw in it. What she really enjoyed was the way he held her close afterwards.

'Did I hurt you?' he asked when his breath had steadied again.

'Not at all.'

'Good. But I didn't give you any real pleasure, either, did I? I'll make sure you enjoy it properly next time, I promise.'

Could that happen? She'd never heard the other women in the street talk about *enjoying* it.

But she'd lost her fear of bed play, at least. And it pleased her to think that she was now a proper wife, Mrs Jonah Willcox.

6

The day after the wedding Leah finished the unpacking, then got out her scrubbing things. 'You'll have to sit in the front room while I do the floor in here,' she said cheerfully to Jonah.

'You mean you're going to scrub it?'

She nodded.

He took the scrubbing brush away from her. 'That isn't necessary. I'm sorry I forgot to mention it before, but I've spoken to Ginny Dutton from the village and she's going to come in twice a week, more if necessary, to scrub the floors and do some of the dirtier jobs for us.'

'There's no need. I'm perfectly capable of looking after my own house.'

'I don't want you to do the rough work. It wouldn't be right.' He hesitated, then added, 'You'll be living differently now, Leah. The wives of men like me always have help in the house.'

'Well, I don't need it so you can save your money.'

'I wouldn't be comfortable seeing my wife down on her knees scrubbing the floors. And don't tell me you enjoy doing it.'

'Of course not. No one does. But it needs doing.'

His voice remained calm but something about his expression was different, more determined than she'd ever seen before.

'No, Leah. We'll have Mrs Dutton in to do that. And while

I'm at it, there's a washerwoman in the village and Mrs Buckley at the shop says she's really good, so please arrange to send all our washing to her.'

'Jonah, there's no *need*!'

'I think there is. I didn't marry you to get an unpaid housemaid.'

'But I don't *mind*.'

'I do.'

No one she knew had ever had a servant. But when she tried to persuade him that she'd prefer to clean her house herself, she might have been talking to the gatepost.

Jonah never raised his voice, not once, but he didn't yield an inch of ground either and in the end, she said huffily, 'I feel as if I'm banging my head against a wall of pillows with you.'

'Well, at least you won't hurt your head doing that.' He took her hand and raised it to his lips. 'Please bear with me on this, my dear. I may not be much of a husband, but I can make sure you don't have to do the heavy work.'

'But—'

He pulled her into his arms and kissed her, not letting her speak.

Mrs Dutton came in twice a week to do any heavy work needed.

She knocked on the door the first time and said at once, 'Thank you for giving me this job, Mrs Willcox. I can't tell you how grateful I am for the extra work. It'll make all the difference to us, that money will, especially if you don't tell the Means Test man about it. If he finds out, they'll take it off my husband's dole money, you see.'

Leah stopped protesting. Times were hard for most people in the valley, and especially in little Ellindale. Who was she to prevent someone from having things a little easier?

But what was she going to do with herself while Mrs Dutton scrubbed her floors?

Three weeks after their own wedding, Jonah and his new family went to Charlie's wedding, which was a lavish affair compared to theirs.

It was the first time Leah had mingled with what Charlie called 'the better class of people'. Charlie smiled wryly as he warned her about the snobbishness and insistence on certain ways of behaving that she might meet from some of them.

She wasn't surprised when even he behaved in a quieter and more serious way at the wedding but her brother-in-law still seemed able to hold his own in any company. She heard one of the male guests say in an approving tone that he was a 'rising fellow' in the valley.

She knew her own table manners were correct now, because she'd watched Jonah and learned from him how to hold knives and forks 'properly'. Not that she'd eaten in a sloppy way before.

She'd prompted Rosa to take the same care, making a game of it. Well, it was a game really. Holding your knife and fork correctly didn't feed a hungry child, did it?

Not many people talked to her, though they nodded politely. They were probably waiting to see how she behaved in her new role. She didn't mind that. She enjoyed watching what was going on and she didn't want to make any mistakes, for Jonah's sake.

These women might be from better homes but they were gossiping in little clusters, just as the women in her old street did. Some seemed to be avoiding others. Some seemed to be the bossy, talkative ones. Not so different then, for all their fine clothes and fancy jewellery.

She kept an eye on her sister and was glad to see that she

was behaving perfectly. She watched in approval as Rosa went across and introduced herself to the only other child of her own age at the wedding, a rather shy girl who'd been standing in a corner on her own looking uncomfortable.

That was typical of Rosa. She was innately kind, like their father had been, and more confident than any of them. She'd often wondered where that came from, his side of the family or their mother's.

Marion's mother was moving round the room, chatting to people. She paused for a moment beside Leah.

'Who's that Rosa's talking to?' Leah asked. 'She seems a nice girl.'

'That's Thomas Carpenter's daughter. Evelyn is a very nice little girl, but rather shy. She'd make a good friend for your sister. His wife's an invalid, poor woman. Heart trouble. She had rheumatic fever as a child and can hardly walk across the room now.'

'That must be hard for them all.'

'Yes. We weren't sure whether they'd come today, but I'm glad he made the effort to bring the child. Evelyn needs to get out and learn to behave in company. I must say, your sister is doing very well today, very well indeed.'

She sounded surprised that Rosa had good manners, which rather annoyed Leah, but she kept that to herself.

Mr Carpenter chatted to one or two of the men and then Marion's mother stopped to have a word with him. They both stared at his daughter, then at Rosa, so it was obvious what they were talking about.

After a sumptuous meal and various speeches, the newly-weds changed their clothes and left for a honeymoon. They wouldn't say where they were going, but Jonah had let slip to his wife that it was London.

She envied them the travel.

As soon as they'd gone Mr Carpenter took his watch out

of his waistcoat pocket and studied it, then beckoned to his daughter. She took Rosa to meet him, then they left.

He must be getting back to his wife. If she was an invalid he'd not want to leave her for too long.

On that thought, Leah studied Jonah. He was starting to look tired, so she went across to join him and suggested they go home.

He didn't protest so the hotel manager called the taxi.

While Charlie and his new wife were in London on their week's honeymoon, Jonah went into the shop every day to keep an eye on things, staying longer than usual. To Leah's dismay, after the first two days, he was exhausted.

He refused to leave the shop to run itself, even under Vi's capable management, so Leah insisted on him travelling by taxi instead of waiting for the bus and walking up from the village at the end of the day.

'I don't know why I didn't think of that,' he said. 'Yes, I'll send a lad into Birch End with a note to Robert to collect me every morning in the taxi for the rest of the week.'

'Rosa can take a note for you.'

'No, let the lad earn his shilling.'

'He'd do it for sixpence.'

'But his mother will appreciate the shilling and I can afford it.'

Jonah was so kind and never seemed to count the pennies. She'd never lived like this before. She wished she knew more about his finances, but she didn't dare ask. She knew that few men told their wives all the details.

When Charlie came home from the honeymoon, he managed to catch Leah for a quick, private word. 'Jonah looks tired. Was I asking too much of him?'

'Unfortunately yes. He can't work full-time, I'm afraid.

But he does enjoy coming into the shop, so please don't try to stop him working there.'

'I won't. He's actually very good with the accounts, much more careful than I would be. Every single halfpenny is accounted for.'

'He enjoys figures.'

'Yes. And I hope you don't mind me saying, but he looks happier since he married you as well.'

'I'm looking after him the best I can. But the air out at Ellindale will help too. He loves it there, even now, when it gets quite chilly in the evenings, and says he's sleeping better these days.'

He looked at her smugly. 'I was right about you. You are exactly the right person for Jonah.'

'Oh, well. I'm glad you think so.' She could feel her cheeks getting hot; she never knew what to say to compliments and was relieved when he changed the subject.

'The air in London was shocking, all smoky, and everywhere you went was crowded. You couldn't turn round without tripping over someone, and I never saw so many cars in one place in my whole life. All in all, it made me glad I'm a northerner and can live near the moors.'

'I thought you enjoyed bigger towns and cities.'

'Not as much as I like our valley, though I prefer living lower down. Ellindale is too small.' He stared up at the moors for a moment or two. 'Mind you, life is much better for most people down in the south than it is here in the north. There are still men on the streets there selling shoelaces, or other odds and ends, but not half as many as here. Most fellows seem to have a job of some sort.'

After a thoughtful pause, he added, 'One day it'll be the same here, but I doubt it'll be cotton mills that give people employment, well not as many people as they used to. Who knows what else will take their place in the future? Perhaps building motor cars like they do in the Midlands. But whatever it is, you can be sure I'll jump on the nearest bandwagon. I mean to make a big fortune before I'm through. Just so you know.'

Jonah rejoined them in time to hear Charlie add, 'Oh, and Marion wanted me to tell you she's at home on Thursday afternoons from two till three.'

Leah stared at him, baffled. 'What does that mean? Where else would she be?'

'It means it's her afternoon for receiving friends and visitors, you know for a chat and a cup of tea. It'll be a good way for you to meet people.'

'I don't think I'll bother with that sort of fussing around.'

'You should, if you want to fit in. Tell her, Jonah.'

He took her hand. 'You should do it, dear, call on her.'

But she didn't want to. It sounded so silly and artificial to her. She'd not know what to say.

When Charlie had left, grumbling that the taxi was late today, Jonah said thoughtfully, 'I really must buy a car. I've been thinking of it for a while. I know how to drive, even though I haven't done so since the war, and it'll be much easier than waiting around for Robert's taxi, not to mention the difficulty of letting him know I need him, since they haven't installed telephone lines up here in Ellindale yet.'

'Oh, that'd be wonderful!' It didn't take her more than a few seconds to realise that here was a chance for her to do something new and interesting as well. 'Will you teach me to drive the car too?'

He looked at her in surprise. 'There's no need. I can take you wherever you need to go.'

'I think I'd enjoy it, actually. Women drove during the war, I read about it, and not just cars but motorbikes and lorries.

They even flew planes. No one told them there was no need then, did they? What if I had to get you to the doctor quickly? Or there was another war?'

'We just had the war to end all wars.'

'The history books tell of war after war, even before the Norman Conquest, so I don't believe that.'

'Hmm. I've never thought about it that way. But that's beside the point. I haven't needed a doctor for ages.'

'How long is "ages"?'

He shrugged. 'Oh, a couple of years. I came down with pneumonia and they had to put me in hospital for a couple of weeks.'

'Then I definitely need to know how to drive.' She held her breath, because it was the first time she'd refused to give in to him on something important and she wondered if he'd be intractable about this.

He looked at her thoughtfully, not, thank goodness, with his placidly stubborn look, then spread out his hands in a gesture of surrender. 'Very well. I'll teach you to drive.'

Delight filled her and she forgot to be careful with him. Flinging her arms round him, she danced him round the room, making him laugh.

His next words surprised her. 'You're growing more confident, my lass. That's good. One day I won't be here to help you.'

Her delight evaporated instantly. 'I wasn't thinking of that, Jonah. If it's up to me, you'll live for ever.'

'On this point we should face facts from the start, my dear. I won't make old bones, though I think I'll last longer up here in the clean air. Shh.' He put a finger on her lips. 'Just keep it at the back of your mind.'

She could only hug him close. She had grown fond of him, even in this short time, and didn't want to think about losing him, even at the back of her mind.

The probability of an early death was so firmly fixed in the forefront of his mind that she felt it couldn't be doing him good. Well, if at all possible, she was going to turn his thoughts to happier things.

'Always believe you can succeed,' her mother used to say. 'Whatever you're doing.'

But how could she convince Jonah that he wasn't going to die young? That they had a bright future together? She would find a way, somehow.

The following week Jonah came back from the Birch End shop beaming and it was his turn to dance her round the kitchen. 'I've heard of a man in Rivenshaw who's selling an Austin Seven Swallow. The car is only a year old but he's not well and needs the money. Swallows are building up a good reputation and the company is having difficulty keeping up with orders, so I thought it'd be easier to buy from him than order a brand new one and then wait months for it.'

He paused. 'Want to come and see it with me?'

'Of course I do. Is Charlie coming too?'

He looked mischievous. 'No. I'm doing this on my own. He hasn't learned to drive and he'd just tell me to use taxis. He'd no doubt prove – to his satisfaction if not to mine – that it's a better way to get about. Only I know it isn't, not for me. So I'm going to take him by surprise, for once.'

He patted her lightly on the backside. 'Go and get your coat and hat. Quick! Robert's waiting outside.'

'But our tea. It's stewed beef and I haven't got it started yet. It needs a lot of cooking.'

'We'll bring a pork pie back with us from Rivenshaw.'

She hadn't had a shop-bought pork pie for ages. Her mouth watered at the mere thought of it. 'Just let me write a note for Rosa, then.'

She sat in the back of the taxi listening to the two men

discussing the merits of Swallow motor cars. She didn't understand half of what they said, but one day she would, she vowed. If she was going to drive a car, she was going to understand how it worked.

The vehicle they were shown was immaculate, with a yellow body and a black top. It looked bright and cheerful on a chilly day, Leah thought.

The seller was pale as a ghost, however, and after a while he went back into the house and his wife stayed with them to answer questions.

Robert knew a bit about car motors, so checked out various things, starting the car and listening intently to the sound it made. 'Runs smoothly enough, Jonah, as far as I can tell.'

'What do you think, Leah? The Swallow is a re-bodied Austin Seven, but so much more stylish, don't you think?'

She was flummoxed. Re-bodied? 'I don't know much about cars. It looks very neat, though.'

He turned to the woman. 'How much does your husband want for it?'

She hesitated. 'You're really interested?'

'Yes.'

Tears came into her eyes. 'You'd better come inside and discuss that with him, then.'

The man was sitting in an armchair, looking as if he'd have difficulty getting up again, and his wife went to stand behind him.

'How much is it?' Jonah asked.

'It cost me a hundred and seventy-eight pounds when it was new, Mr Willcox. It was one of their first saloon versions.'

Leah could see the desperation in his eyes and hoped Jonah wasn't going to bargain too hard.

'Since it's immaculate, I'll give you what it cost,' Jonah told him quietly.

The man burst into strangled sobs and covered his face.

Oh, it hurt to see him and she could sense his shame at his own weakness, so Leah said hastily, 'You and your wife will want to discuss it. We'll wait outside.' She tugged Jonah's arm.

Shortly afterwards the woman joined them. 'Thank you for your generosity, Mr Willcox. We're both grateful. He'll never go back to work, you see.' She hesitated and added, 'Are you sure you can afford it? You don't look all that well yourself. You sound as if you were gassed in the war.'

'I was. But not too badly. And I can definitely afford it. I'll give you a cheque.' He got out his cheque book.

'Thank you. You may as well take the car with you now. I can't drive the dratted thing. It's just sitting there, making him feel a failure.'

Jonah finished writing the cheque. 'Are you sure? Wouldn't you rather wait till this cheque is cleared?'

'I trust you, Mr Willcox. You've got an honest face, as well as a kind one.'

The man came out as Robert and Jonah were trying to check that everything was there.

'I'll show you . . . what goes with the car,' he said between gasps of breath.

Under his guidance they put everything into the vehicle. Then he stepped back. 'I presume you know how to drive it?'

'I'm a bit rusty, but I dare say it'll come back to me. I can't do much harm if I drive slowly.'

The man held out his hand and they shook, with Jonah clasping the other man's hand in both of his.

'Thank you.' The man gulped and shuffled into the house again.

Jonah looked at Leah, who was mopping her eyes. 'I do hope those are happy tears.'

'Happy at what you've done. I'm proud of you.'

'I hope you still feel that way by the time we get home.'

He wasn't as bad a driver as she'd expected, and though he was rather tense to start off with and clashed the gears a few times, he relaxed visibly as he grew used to driving again.

When they got home, he closed his eyes and let out a long, shuddering breath in relief, then grinned at her. 'I did it.'

'I knew you would.'

Seeing the other man's condition and the wife's helplessness had only reinforced Leah's conviction that she needed to learn to drive as well.

'I'm not nearly as bad as he is, am I?'

'No, Jonah love. That poor man's in a bad way.'

As autumn turned into winter Leah settled into a very pleasant pattern of living, with a home she loved and plenty to eat, and generous fires to keep the house warm. No skimping on coal here, because they had a good stock of it in the coal shed.

She and her sister had warm clothes and good shoes, thanks to Jonah's generosity.

She was looking forward to her driving lessons. To her surprise no one would be checking up officially on whether she knew how to drive safely. 'You mean, anyone can get into a car and drive it round, whether they know how to do it properly or not?'

Jonah laughed at her. 'What? Do you think there's an examination in driving?'

'Well, yes.'

'Some people think there should be, but no one in the government seems to care.'

Three mornings a week, Jonah drove off into Birch End and worked in the pawnshop.

He gave her a driving lesson nearly every day and said she'd taken to it like a duck to water.

But as the weeks passed, Leah still found herself with too much free time on her hands, since she had help with two of the major jobs of a housewife's week, the washing and the scrubbing.

She didn't like fiddling around with hobbies; she preferred to be doing something *useful*. Sewing her own clothes was one thing, she saw the value of that, but embroidery, which Marion did intermittently, was just a way of filling time as far as Leah was concerned. And she couldn't sit and read books all day, either, much as she enjoyed a good story at the quiet end of the day. It didn't feel *right*.

Jonah teased her that she was a 'doer', a person who had to be doing something, not sitting thinking or even chatting. And he was right.

She was used to struggling, always having too much to do, used to having other women to chat to in short bursts, as well. But since they lived outside the village, they had no near neighbours.

Auntie Hilda visited her a couple of times, but she had her lodgers to see to and couldn't spend more than an hour or two away from her own home.

Other married women seemed happy to stay at home, but they had children to look after, while Leah had shown no signs of conceiving a child over the first month or two of her marriage. Which was a pity.

She didn't like to complain about being bored, so tried to content herself with her library books and Jonah's companionship. He knew so much more than she did about the world that every conversation taught her something.

But even that wasn't enough to make her feel her life was completely satisfying. She needed something *useful* to do.

Having time on her hands was the last thing she'd expected of married life.

Oh, she should be thankful for her good fortune and not cry for the moon!

7

One morning there was a knock on the door and when Leah opened it she found Charlie outside, grinning and holding a hessian bag of something that looked lumpy.

'I've brought you a present.'

'Oh, right.' She looked at it in puzzlement, calling into the house, 'Your brother's here, Jonah.'

'I'll carry it in. This way, Robert.' Charlie led the way into the kitchen, followed by the taxi driver. He dumped his bag on the table. 'Put the box there, Robert, and come back for me in an hour.'

'No need,' Jonah said. 'I can drive you back. It's my day doing the accounts at the shop, anyway.'

Charlie hesitated. 'You said you were nervous of driving at first. Are you sure you're all right now?'

'O, ye of little faith! I'm quite safe to be let loose on the roads. Stop doubting me.'

Leah could have clapped. She'd been aching for Jonah to stand up for himself. His brother meant well, but was too bossy.

When the taxi driver had driven off, Jonah asked, 'Is this what I think it is?'

Charlie nodded and both men turned their attention to Leah.

'Why are you looking at me like that?' she asked, puzzled.

'What you've done is tempted us,' Jonah said. 'We both love ginger beer, so I asked Charlie to get the necessary ingredients and we're hoping you'll make a batch or two for the family. You're always saying your mother's recipe is better than the stuff they sell in the shops. Well, now's your chance to prove it.'

She looked in the bag eagerly and found several lemons (and how expensive must they have been, especially at this time of the year?), a big packet of ginger powder and two blue paper bags of sugar. The box contained a dozen brand new bottles with flip-top stoppers.

This, she thought happily, was going to be fun. 'Thank you. The first batch will be ready in two or three weeks, depending on how long it takes to ferment and you two get the first taste. I have a couple of other ingredients to buy before I can start, though.'

'Oh, what?' Charlie asked at once.

'Never you mind. My mother swore me to secrecy about the recipe and only Rosa is going to get the full details.'

'I'll take the ingredients back if you don't tell me,' he threatened. 'I'm family after all.'

'You're not a Forrest, like my mother was before she married. It's their family secret.'

She was surprised at the sudden sharpness in his voice and not at all sure he was joking. But she wasn't going to be bullied by anyone, so she pushed the ingredients towards him. 'Take them back, if you must.'

Jonah looked surprised at her vehemence.

Charlie pushed them towards her again, giving her a quick smile that didn't reach his eyes. 'Don't be silly. I was only teasing.'

She'd known he liked to be in charge, but this was ridiculous. '*I* wasn't teasing, Charlie. It's *my* family recipe and it's staying in my family. Anyway, you have to develop a nose and a sense of taste to make really good ginger beer. Even if I told you all the details, you'd still not be sure what you were doing unless I taught you a few tricks as well.'

He scowled, but didn't press the point.

When the men went off to the shop, she was left alone with the things Charlie had brought. She put them away in the pantry then went down the road to Mrs Buckley's shop. After a quiet word, Mrs Buckley agreed to keep quiet about what Leah was ordering, now and in the future.

You're not going to control every detail of our lives, Charlie Willcox, Leah thought as she strolled back up the slope to Spring Cottage. Not even Jonah tries to do that to me. She smiled. He wouldn't. He wasn't that sort of a man.

When she got back, Leah put her shopping away, stared round her immaculate house and decided to go for a walk on the moors to use up some of her abundant energy.

She walked for about half an hour, enjoying the views and following a path she had noticed from the back bedroom window. She'd wondered where it went and planned one day to follow it as far as she could see to find out. But she wouldn't go that far today, just enjoy the nearby scenery.

Just as she was about to turn back, she saw a man coming over a small rise downhill. Jonah had told her there was an old track to Ellindale beyond the farm fields, one of a network of small tracks that led across the moors. He'd asked her not to use it as it led past a farm whose owners were known for their rough behaviour and thieving ways.

The stranger was staggering slightly as if he was drunk. That seemed strange at this hour of the morning. She was sure she could easily outrun him so waited a little longer in case he was hurt and needed help.

He was moving awkwardly and there looked to be blood on his face, so her second guess was right: he was hurt.

When he caught sight of her, he straightened up and tried

to speak, but his eyes rolled up and he crumpled to the ground. As he lay there, she saw that his thin jacket was badly torn at one side. Had someone attacked him? She looked round to make sure they weren't still nearby, before going to help him.

Strands of dark hair were blowing across his forehead, his face was chalk white and there were new bruises on his left temple and cheek, the sort made by another person's fist.

She'd seen other men out on the tramp looking for work. They'd been willing to do any odd job in return for a square meal and didn't usually have the energy to go looking for trouble.

This man didn't look capable of physical work at the moment, which was the only sort usually offered. He was so painfully thin he looked as if he was made of sticks, not soft flesh and blood. His eyes were a vivid blue with long dark lashes and his hair was nearly black.

She knelt beside him and lifted his poor battered head off the damp ground, manoeuvring it on to her lap with some difficulty before stroking back his hair to examine the injuries to his face.

He opened his eyes and blinked, his gaze gradually coming into focus. 'Are you an angel? Have I died and gone to heaven?'

'What? No. You fainted and I came to see if I could help you.'

He tried to sit up and she shushed him, as she would a child. 'Lie still for a minute or two, give yourself time to recover. What's your name?'

'Ben.'

'I'm Leah. Did you have a fall?'

He let out a bitter laugh. 'Aye. When two men held me and another punched me, I soon fell to the ground right enough.'

She was shocked and looked round again, but they were alone on the windswept moor. 'Why did they do that?'

'Because I was on the tramp and they didn't want me at their farm. I'd have gone away if they'd just said there was no work, but they invited me in, told me they'd give me a piece of bread. Only as soon as I went in their yard, they started punching me – to teach me a lesson, they said.'

'What for?'

'I don't know. I didn't go on to their land till they invited me. I'm not from round here so I've no idea who they were. Madmen, it seemed to me. There was a sign saying Crag Hey Farm. I'd done nothing to them, nothing, but they *enjoyed* hurting me, missus. Enjoyed it, they did.'

She watched him gather his strength and this time he managed to push himself into a sitting position, so she edged back a little. But he still didn't attempt to stand up.

'It's all spinning.' He pressed one hand to his forehead and used the other to hold himself upright.

'Let me help you. I'll take you to my house. It's about a fifteen minute walk back, but we can go slowly. And I promise that I really will give you some bread and butter once we get there.'

He studied her face. 'You have a kind look to you, missus. Thank you. Most poor folk are kind when they can afford it, but not as many of those who're better off like you bother to help someone up off the ground.'

That comment surprised her and she looked down at her clothes, which he must be judging her by. They were a long cry from the shabby old things she'd been wearing before she got married.

'Can you just give me a minute or two more to pull myself together?' he asked.

'Of course.'

He took a few deep breaths and finally managed to stand

up. She had to help him and was surprised to find that he was much taller than she was.

'Have you no family to help you, Ben?'

'Yes, but I won't go on taking their bread. My brother gave me shelter when I lost my job, but he has two children who need the food more than I do. So I left while they were asleep one night and went on the tramp. Better that way. They're lovely little kids.'

He sighed. 'I'm going to miss them and I'll miss Rochdale, too. But there's no other work for me there, not now.'

She encouraged him to continue the conversation because talking seemed to take his mind off the painful task of walking. 'What job were you doing?'

'I was apprenticed to a stonemason, a good man, George Dryden. I was right at the end of my apprenticeship when he died suddenly and after a couple of weeks his son told me to leave. Well, there was only just enough work for him because folk are putting off building things.'

He stopped to gather his breath then went on, 'I didn't know George had been using his savings to pay me, so that I could finish my apprenticeship. His son was angry about that when he found out. But what use are all those years of hard work to me now if George isn't alive to sign the papers to say I've completed my apprenticeship?'

'Can't the son do that?'

'Leonard says it'll cost him money and he's none to spare. When will all these hard times end, that's what I want to know? I lost my eldest brother in the war. The other came back to a land supposedly fit for heroes. Ha! Fit for dogs, more like. The war's been over for more than ten years now and his family is living in two rooms in a slum and he's grateful to have a job digging roads and ditches. Fine thanks *he* got for the years he fought for our country.'

He stumbled and clutched her for a moment, panting slightly.

'I was lucky. I was too young to be called up. Dad got me the apprenticeship. It took all his savings, but he knew I'd pay him back as soon as I was earning. And I would have, but he and Mum are dead now, so there's only me and Ned left.'

They walked up the last slope and she said, 'That's my home. Spring Cottage, it's called.'

'It's old . . . pretty, too. Been there since before Queen Victoria became queen, those cottages have.'

'There were two cottages once but they've been made into one house now.'

To her relief, Jonah arrived home just then. As soon as he saw them he got out of the car, but when he tried to hurry towards them, he had to stop to catch his breath. He was looking bone weary, as he sometimes did.

'Are you all right, Leah?' he called.

'I'm fine, but this poor chap has been attacked at Crag Hey Farm. Stay there, Jonah. We can manage.' She added in a low voice, 'My husband was gassed in the war and he can't do much physically.'

There was wry humour in Ben's voice. 'Nor can I at the moment. Can you look after two of us?'

'I'm happy to help anyone in trouble.' People had helped her. Even Mr Harris had tried. It came to her suddenly, there on the cold moors, that this was something she could do: help others. There were all sort of schemes to help those out of work, or to feed hungry children. She could even start up her own scheme to help people in her own village. At present those going hungry in Ellindale had to get themselves and their families down to Birch End where there was a soup kitchen run by the church.

She stopped moving for a moment, as if she'd been struck by lightning. *That* was what she would do. Not embroidery or gossiping at tea parties, but helping people. Until she had children, anyway.

She sighed at that thought. Another month had just passed without her falling pregnant, to her deep regret.

She had to half carry Ben into the house because as he reached the little gate in the rear wall, he seemed suddenly to have run out of the last shreds of energy and fell to his knees.

'He's dirty,' Jonah whispered as he helped her support the stranger.

'What does that matter? He needs food before we see to his other needs. We can help him, Jonah, and afterwards I'm going to help others like him. I can't spend my life being useless when people are struggling to fill their bellies.'

He gave her a wry smile. 'I told Charlie you needed some occupation, but he thought Marion could teach you how to get on with the other ladies.'

'What? Spend my life like she does? No, thank you.' Leah blew out a scornful breath at the mere thought of tittle-tattling over teacups, then turned to help the man sit on one of the wooden kitchen chairs.

She got the milk jug from the cold shelf in the pantry and poured some into a glass, only half-filling it. 'Sip it slowly. If you've been without food, you have to eat little and often. I'll give you some bread in a few minutes after you've kept that down.'

'Thank you, missus.'

She could see what an effort it was for him not to gulp the milk.

Jonah was frowning at the sight of the bruising on Ben's face. 'What did you say happened to him?'

Leah repeated what Ben had told her. 'Do I have that right?' she asked him.

'Yes, missus . . .'

'What's your surname?' Jonah asked.

'Lonsdale.'

'Our name is Willcox.'

Ben repeated the name, then set down the empty glass, leaned his elbows on the table and rested his head on them with a low groan.

Jonah stood frowning in thought. 'Crag Hey Farm! I thought the Huttons had left the district looking for work. Thad Hutton is a brute and he's been in trouble since he was a lad. His brothers might not be as bad, but they do as he tells them, probably daren't do otherwise.'

Ben lifted his head. 'They didn't introduce themselves, but they did call the biggest fellow Thad.'

'He's the eldest, so I suppose it's his farm now his father's dead. I don't know what they live on. No one in Ellindale would employ a Hutton, that's for sure.'

Their guest seemed to have drifted off to sleep, his head on his hands.

'We ought to make him up a bed,' Leah whispered.

'In our home? We know nothing about him but what he's told us. No, love, I'd rather not have him sleeping inside the house till we're more sure of him.'

Their glances locked for a moment or two and she could see that determined look settle on Jonah's face. She supposed what he said was sensible, but she felt quite sure Ben wasn't a danger to them.

'How about the old barn? You said the nearest end was weatherproof. Could we make him up a bed in a corner?'

'Yes. If you can get what's needed, I'll keep an eye on him while you do that, Leah. We don't want him falling off his chair.'

She cut a slice of bread first and smeared it thinly with butter. 'If he wakes up while I'm gone, give him this.'

She had the house sorted out now and quickly found some frayed sheets and blankets she'd set aside for rags, and a lumpy flock pillow as well.

'I'll come and unlock the barn door for you,' Jonah said. When he'd done that, she sent him back to look after Ben.

The barn door creaked loudly as she pushed it open with her shoulder. The interior felt cold after the warmth of the kitchen. But to her relief, the floor and walls of this section showed no signs that the roof had been leaking. At least he'd be sheltered from the worst of the wind here.

She'd been meaning to spend some time in here and sort through things, but she needed help to move the heavier pieces of machinery and old furniture, and Jonah wasn't strong enough to do that, so she'd left it for the time being. It wasn't urgent, because they didn't need the barn for anything.

She managed to drag various smaller tools and objects back to leave a bed-sized space on the ground. As she looked round again, she saw a piece of stained canvas slung carelessly across one old farm machine. 'Aha!' She dragged it across to the space and laid her bedding on it. Not very comfortable, but it'd keep him off the damp ground. There was even a rusty old bucket he could use for his personal needs.

As she was walking back to the house, she met Rosa coming home from school and explained about their guest.

'It's like the Good Samaritan,' her sister said. 'How wonderful of you!'

'Oh, pooh. There's nothing wonderful about helping a poor man who's half starved.'

'It's nice to be able to help people, though, isn't it?' Rosa stopped and put her hand on her sister's arm, looking excited. 'I saw Evelyn as I was coming out of school and she wants me to go round to spend next Saturday with her. Is it all right if I do that? I'll do my chores before I leave.'

'Yes, of course. It'll be a lot of walking for you, though. They live in Birch End. Shall I ask Jonah to drive you down and pick you up later?'

'No need. I'll enjoy a good walk after sitting at a desk all week. I like Evelyn but I've never talked to her much at school. The poor thing's so shy she went bright pink when she asked me to visit her.'

'You'll never be shy.'

Rosa chuckled. 'Why should I? It doesn't do any good, does it, just leaves you standing in a corner on your own? I feel sorry for Evelyn, but she can be interesting to talk to when she forgets her shyness.'

Where her sister got her cheerful confidence from, Leah didn't know, but she hoped life wouldn't beat it out of her. In the meantime she was growing fast into her woman's body and was big for her age.

Ben looked up as the door opened and smiled at his rescuer, then stared at the rosy-cheeked girl who followed her in. 'This lass must be your sister, Mrs Willcox. There's a close resemblance.'

'Yes. This is Rosa,' Leah said. 'How are you feeling now, Ben?'

'A bit better, thanks to you and your husband. It's good to be out of that wind and have something in my belly. Haven't had butter on my bread for a long time.'

'You're welcome. Just sit quietly and rest now.'

'Is the tea still hot?' At Jonah's nod, Rosa plonked her school satchel down near the door and went to pour herself a cup, whispering to her sister, 'Shall I give Ben one?'

Leah studied him. 'Yes. Just a half.'

He nodded his thanks and sipped the tea, his hands clasped round the warm cup. He was watching them warily now as if expecting to be turned out at any moment.

'I've made up a bed in the barn for you, Ben,' Leah told him. 'You'll only be lying on a piece of canvas on the ground, I'm afraid, so it won't be very comfortable, but there are some blankets and you'll be sheltered from the weather, which is the main thing. It was starting to spit with rain again when we came in.'

'Thank you, Mrs Willcox. I'm very grateful. I'll leave first thing in the morning and—'

'No need to leave,' Jonah said. 'Unless you have somewhere to go?'

Ben looked surprised. 'No. There's nowhere. I just follow the road. But people don't usually want vagrants to stay for more than one night.'

'I think you'll need more than one night to recover,' Leah said frankly. 'You look at the end of your tether.'

He looked from one to the other and blinked hard, probably trying to prevent the humiliation of shedding tears of relief. 'I am tired,' he said in a husky voice. 'It was too cold to sleep much last night. I could only find a wall to lie near.'

'Stay here in the kitchen till you've eaten something more substantial then I'll walk across with you and help you get settled,' Jonah said. 'We'll talk in the morning and see if there's some way we can help you. I think you ought to report the attack on you to the police, for a start.'

Ben's attempt at a laugh was a mere croak. 'They're three to my one. No one will take my word against theirs.'

When Jonah followed her into the scullery, Leah gave him a quick kiss on the cheek.

'What's that for?'

'Being kind.'

So he kissed her in turn. 'You're kind as well.'

Two hours later, during a lull in the showery weather, Ben followed his host across to the barn. He stopped in the doorway to examine the stonework by the light of the candle lantern. 'I think this is even older than the cottage.'

'Is it? We don't know anything about the original owners. My grandfather bought the place before I was born. Anyway, this is where you'll be sleeping. I'll leave you with this candle lantern and some matches. If you need anything, or there are any problems, don't hesitate to come and ask for help, even if you have to knock us up. Oh, and if you could empty the bucket into the privy behind the house in the morning, I'd be grateful.'

'I'll do that. And I won't need to waken you. I'll do fine here.'

As his host left him to his draughty bedroom, Ben sighed with relief to have a roof over his head, and vowed that one day he'd repay the Willcoxes for their kindness. He used the bucket and put it near the door, then a yawn took him by surprise. Rolling himself in one blanket, he covered himself with the other doubled over, and managed to tug a flap of the stiff canvas over the top of that as well.

They'd even given him a pillow! It was wonderful to be out of the weather, to have privacy, to know he'd not need to move on in the morning. He blew out the candle and snuggled down.

The next thing he knew it was morning and something had woken him up. Oh, yes, the sound of a car being started.

Light was slanting down from windows on the upper level. There were shutters over the ground-floor windows. He hadn't noticed them last night. He hadn't noticed much at all.

He got up and walked stiffly to the bucket, then opened the door, trying to work out from the sun what time it was. Later than he'd expected. They must have left him to sleep.

After he'd emptied the bucket he wandered over to the main house and studied its stonework. Definitely not as old as the barn, but well built.

He took a deep breath before knocking on the door. He

wasn't used to such generosity and kindness, and didn't know what to expect today.

Leah was alone in the house, since Rosa had long gone to school and Jonah had just left for a meeting with Charlie at the shop. He'd worried about leaving her alone with the stranger.

'What? You're joking. Ben's so weak even I could fight him with one hand tied behind my back.'

'I hope you won't need to try.'

'Don't you trust him, Jonah?'

'As much as one can trust a complete stranger, yes. But you're so precious to me that I don't want to put you at even the slightest risk.'

She kissed his cheek and would have moved away again, but his arms went round her and he gave her a proper kiss. Then he caught sight of the clock and pulled back reluctantly.

'I have to go now. I do wish there was someone with a telephone in the village. Just in case you need me.'

'Oh, get on with you. I'll be fine.'

A few minutes later she heard the door of the old barn creak open and went to peep out of the front window. Yes, Ben was awake. He looked scruffy but much more alert than yesterday. He'd be ravenous, poor man. He was carrying his bucket.

When there was a tap on the front door, she simply called, 'Come in!'

He was hesitant, standing near the door. 'I wondered if there was anything I could do to earn my bread.'

'Yes. But first let's feed you.' She poured a cup of tea and handed it to him, then gestured to the egg she'd put ready. 'I thought a soft boiled egg might make a nice light meal for you.'

He licked his lips involuntarily. 'Are you sure?'

'Very sure. We get lovely fresh eggs from a woman in the village. And after that I have an idea about a job or two you could help me with.'

'Made-up work?' he asked drily.

'No, actual work. And even if it was made-up work, you should accept people's good will when it's offered.'

He flushed. 'Sorry. I'm just . . . it's been hard to get used to charity.'

She had pushed a small pan of water over the hot part of the range top to boil the egg in. While it was cooking, she cut two slices of bread and buttered it more generously than she had the day before, when she'd been worried about making him sick.

When she looked round, he was still standing up. 'Sit down, do.'

He slipped into the chair she indicated and within minutes she had the food in front of him.

'Now, eat it slowly, remember.'

He nodded and chewed his food thoroughly, his expression blissful.

She let him finish his meal in peace, then cleared away his plate and sat down again opposite him. 'The barn you slept in is full of old machinery and who knows what. It's also falling down at one end. Jonah told me you thought that building was even older than this house.'

'Yes. You can tell by how it's built.'

'You really are a stonemason?'

'I've had the training, yes, Mrs Willcox. Only I'm not entitled to call myself that since the final apprentice papers haven't been signed and put in.'

'I'll get Charlie on to it. He's better at sorting out problems like that than my Jonah.'

'Charlie?'

'I keep forgetting that you're not from round here. Charlie

Willcox is my husband's younger brother. He lives down the
hill at Birch End. He's a very good businessman and seems
able to persuade people to do just about anything he wants.
If Jonah drives you back to Rochdale and Charlie comes
with you, then you can see your old master's son and find
a way to get his help.'

'I doubt he'll give it. Leonard was furious at his father
spending his savings on my wages, though I had no idea
George was doing that.'

'Well, Charlie will find a way of persuading him to help
you, if anyone can. It'll make a nice drive out. I might come
with you.' She studied him. 'But not till we've got you looking
fitter and found you some decent clothes.'

'I have no money for clothes, Mrs Willcox. I had to pawn
my best things in Rochdale so that I could leave money with
my brother. I left my tools with him, too, in case he's desperate
and needs to sell them. Well, I could hardly carry a heavy
box on the road with me, could I?'

'We'll leave it to Charlie to sort out some clothes as well.
He owns two pawnshops, so he'll be able to find you something
to wear and I bet he's got a few tools he can lend you as well.'

She turned away and pretended to busy herself clearing
up the kitchen, because Ben seemed overwhelmed by the
help she was offering. He must have had some very hard
times in the past few weeks.

When she turned round, he was finishing his egg, polite
enough not to lick the plate, as she'd seen hungry children
do, but looking as if he wanted to. 'How did you sleep? Were
you warm enough?'

'I must have been because I didn't stir.'

'Good. Then you won't mind sleeping in the barn for a
few nights.'

'I'd be grateful for the shelter, and for the work. And Mrs
Willcox . . .'

'Yes?' She turned round.

'One day I'll repay you properly for your help.'

'It's I who owe you a great deal.'

He gaped at her. 'How can that possibly be?'

'You showed me what I can do to fill my days. I married above me recently, so Jonah insists I have help in the house, but I'm not used to idleness. For years I've watched people round here struggle to survive, find jobs, feed their children. I was struggling too after my father died. Now I have time on my hands, so if I can do something to help people in trouble, that will give me great satisfaction.'

'Oh. I see.'

'I lay awake for a while last night, thinking how to set about it. So I'd be grateful for any advice you can give me about the best way not to hurt people's feelings.'

"That's easy. Don't offer them charity, offer them work if you can. Any kind of work. Charity makes you feel less of a human being, even when it's freely offered and you need it through no fault of your own.'

'I'll remember that, Ben. Thank you.'

He picked up his plate and brought it across to the sink.

'I've sorted out some old clothes of Jonah's and we have a bathroom, though there's only cold water available so I'll bring you a kettle of hot water through. I'm sure you'd like a bath, and then I can wash those clothes for you.'

She hadn't felt so full of energy for a good while. She glanced out of the window. The weather was much brighter today. And so were her spirits.

8

Saturday was the day Rosa was going to Evelyn's. Leah hoped the two of them would become real friends. Her sister put on one of her new outfits, a matching blue cardigan and skirt, with a pale flowery blouse. She looked lovely, a sister to be proud of.

'Put your best coat on, and take your umbrella in case it rains,' she warned. 'You don't want to catch a chill.'

'Stop fussing! I'll be fine. And it's not as if it's snowing or anything like that. I'm only going to play with Evelyn and have dinner there, though they'll probably call it "luncheon".' She chuckled. 'You've taught me how to eat politely, so I won't shame you. And no, I won't forget to say thank you for having me before I leave.'

'Well, make sure you don't. We'll take you there and look for you on the way back, but I think we'll be home earlier than you.'

'I hope Charlie can help Ben get his papers finalised. I like Ben, don't you?'

Jonah came to join them. 'Will Evelyn's father be at home? Her mother isn't well enough to keep you two in order.'

'I don't know. And we're nearly grown up, so we don't need looking after.'

'Almost eleven isn't grown up,' Leah pointed out.

'I *feel* grown up.'

The two sisters stared at one another for a moment or

two, then Leah said, 'Don't finish growing up quite yet, love. Enjoy some carefree time first.'

Jonah judged it wise to change the subject. His wife's voice had wobbled. She'd had her childhood taken away from her by her mother's sudden death and wanted Rosa to have time to grow up. 'I knew Thomas Carpenter when we were lads, but he's not getting out much these days, because of his wife. I was surprised he even came to Charlie's wedding.'

'It must be hard, Mrs Carpenter being in such poor health.'

'Evelyn says her father has to travel into Manchester every day to work,' Rosa said. 'He has to set off really early and drive to Rivenshaw in the dark, then take the train from there. He doesn't get home till after teatime, so in the winter she doesn't see him in daylight at all during the week.

'Sometimes Evelyn's mother doesn't feel well, so she stays in bed all day and if it's not one of Mrs Salter's days to do housework and get the tea ready, Evelyn has to get the tea. She says she likes cooking. I don't.'

'No, but you like eating!'

'And you're a good cook. What's for tea?'

'I don't know yet. Come on, we don't want to keep Jonah waiting.'

They found Ben outside, looking nervous. 'Are you sure your brother doesn't mind me seeking his help?' he asked Jonah yet again. 'I don't want to impose.'

'He's agreed to do it, hasn't he? He likes to be in on everything that's happening and we neither of us mind helping hard workers. Look how you've made a start on clearing out the old barn, even though you've not got your full strength back yet.'

'I like to pay my way.'

They dropped Rosa at her new friend's house in Birch End, then drove to the pawnshop to collect Charlie.

Jonah left the other two in the car and went in to collect his brother.

'Still pleased with him?' Charlie asked.

'Yes. We both like him and he's a hard worker. What's more, his skills will come in very useful for a little plan of mine.'

'Tell me more.'

Jonah shook his head. 'Not yet. I've only just started thinking about it.'

'You and your plans. Are you sure Rochdale isn't too far for you to drive?'

'I enjoy driving. I may need a rest before we start back, though. Or I could ask Leah to drive for a while. She's coming on quite well, but she doesn't like driving in towns, gets a bit flustered.'

The car windows were open and Ben must have overheard them. 'I know how to drive, Mr Willcox, so I can help too. If you trust me, that is. I used to drive George to and from jobs in his van sometimes.'

Charlie looked at him thoughtfully. 'You're a man of many parts, Ben Lonsdale. Now, I've got some clothes put aside for you at the shop. Come in and try them on. You'll want to look smarter than that.'

'I'll stay in the car and wait,' Leah said. She always enjoyed watching people.

Another car slowed as it drove past the Swallow and jerked to a sudden halt as the driver braked hard. 'It *is* her,' the passenger said, acting as if Leah was deaf. 'It's not right, a slut like her lording it in a car.'

Mrs Harris's voice was recognisable anywhere, but Leah tried not to give any indication that she'd heard her. She continued to stare ahead and after a moment the car set off again, driven by Sam Griggs. What horrible creatures those two were, always being nasty about people, or attacking them!

Ben came out of the shop looking much smarter, with his old clothes in a parcel under his arm.

'Is something wrong, Mrs Willcox?'

'Does it show?'

'I can see something's upset you.'

'It doesn't matter.'

He looked as if he was going to disagree, but she turned to wave to a woman walking past and Jonah and Charlie came out of the shop, laughing about something.

Jonah's smile faded and he also asked, 'What's wrong, Leah?'

She hesitated, but knowing how stubborn he could be, she explained about Mrs Harris and the horrible way Sam Griggs always looked at her.

Charlie let out a snort. 'Just ignore him. Looks can't kill and he won't dare touch you now you're related to me.'

But she wasn't as confident as Charlie about anyone's ability to control a brute like Griggs. It was well known in the part of town where she used to live that he'd attacked other women who hadn't dared complain afterwards.

Griggs seemed more like a wild animal than a man, but a very cunning animal, who knew when to keep his claws hidden and which people were worth buttering up. He and Mrs Harris were clearly on very good terms.

Ugh! They were welcome to one another.

When they left Birch End they headed south, arriving at what was now Leonard Dryden's workshop mid-morning. The big side door was open but there was no noise coming from inside.

'They must be having a break,' Ben said. 'I'd, um, better go and see him.'

'I'll come in with you, lad,' Charlie said. 'Jonah, you stay here.'

Ben knocked on the open door. 'Anyone at home?'

A large man who was standing by a window scowled at them and walked across, speaking before Ben could even open his mouth again. 'I told you when Dad died that there'd be no more work for you here, so go away and don't come back again.'

'I'm not here to look for work.'

Charlie stepped forward. 'Better if you let me deal with this, Mr Lonsdale. May we come in, Mr Dryden, or do you want the whole street to know your business?'

Leonard studied him, then shrugged and went back inside, leaving them to follow or not as they pleased.

'That fellow's got *my* back up now,' Charlie said to Ben in a low whisper. 'Watch this.' He took out a little notebook and made a play of writing in it.

'What are you writing?' Leonard asked at once.

'I'm taking notes in case this comes to a court case.'

'Court case? What the hell do you mean?'

'My client wishes you to sign this letter stating that your father is dead, but you can swear that he's finished all the work necessary to complete his apprenticeship.'

'I'm signing nothing.'

Charlie at once began scribbling in his notebook.

'Stop that!'

'I have to take notes so that the judge can see that we've made every effort to do this the easy way.'

'Ben doesn't *deserve* me to sign anything. He used up my father's savings and left us with nearly nothing, damn him.'

'If he hadn't done that, would you sign the papers?'

Leonard shrugged. 'I might have done, but he did take the money, so now I won't.'

'My client is currently unemployed due to not having his papers as a stonemason. He is prepared to offer you a small sum as compensation for your loss, but he can't be held legally responsible for your father's decision, about which he knew nothing. So this is just for the goodwill.'

There was dead silence, then Leonard said, 'It'll cost him twenty pounds, then.'

'Ah. Well, sadly he doesn't have twenty pounds. I've loaned him ten pounds, but that's all I'm prepared to give. And we won't let you have the money till the papers have been signed and lodged, mind.'

Ben watched this little display of tactics without interrupting, but he didn't think the money would make any difference to Leonard.

'I want twenty pounds or I'm not signing anything.'

'We shall see you in court, then, Mr Dryden.' Charlie handed Leonard his business card which had a telephone number written on it. 'If you change your mind before Monday, get in touch with me, but if not, I'll lodge a complaint with the courts.'

As they walked out to the car, Charlie whispered, 'Say nothing! There was someone listening behind a door. I saw the edge of her skirt.' He stopped and pretended to tie his shoelace.

There was the sound of voices in the workshop, a woman's shrill tones and Leonard's lower rumble. She sounded furiously angry.

'Let's stand by the car and pretend we're going over the notes,' Charlie said.

Ben shrugged and did as suggested, not feeling hopeful.

Suddenly another woman joined in, screeching, 'Do something before they leave, you fool, or we'll not get anything!'

'Do you know who the women are?' Charlie whispered.

'George's widow, Leonard's mother that is. And his wife. The two of them gang up against him sometimes because he's a bit of a fool.'

The workshop door banged open. The women must have

shoved Leonard through it, because he staggered out at a run. A very small, scrawny woman with grey hair came to stand behind him in the doorway, arms folded. And behind her stood a younger woman with a baby in her arms, a baby which suddenly began to wail.

Leonard glowered at the people by the car and turned to glare at the two women as well. But the older woman made a shooing gesture with one hand, so he muttered something under his breath and said to Charlie, 'My mother thinks I'm being too hard on Ben.' There was a silence and he seemed to be fumbling for words.

'Go on! Ask him,' the older woman said.

'How much can he pay me if I finish those papers?'

'Ten pounds,' Charlie said. 'As I already told you.'

'Can't you make it a bit more?'

'No, not a penny more, because Ben's had to borrow it from me and that's all I'm prepared to risk.'

'Then how come he can afford to hire you as his lawyer?' Leonard snapped.

'He can't but I've got a cousin who's a lawyer and he's agreed to help us out. He's doing it pro bono.'

'What the hell does that mean?'

'It means for free. He helps men who're out of work sometimes. He can't bear to see people badly treated.'

While this exchange was going on, Ben stared down at the ground, the very picture of embarrassment.

The older woman sighed and came forward, shoving her son out of the way. 'We'll take the ten pounds, Mr Willcox. I'm sorry to have to take anything, Ben lad, but we're not doing so well since my George died. My son isn't as good with people, but I'm going to organise the jobs from now on, so things should improve.'

Charlie pulled out his wallet and extracted a one pound note. 'This is to show our good faith. As soon as Ben's papers are in and everything's sorted out, you can have the other nine pounds.'

She took it and nodded as she put it carefully in her skirt pocket.

Her son didn't move for a moment. 'I want it understood that I'm doing this for my family, not for *him*.'

'That's understood. Do you have the papers here or do we have to get them from somewhere?'

Mrs Dryden stepped forward again. 'I've got them. I used to do most of the paperwork for my husband. He'd filled the papers in already but he dropped dead before he could sign them. He thought well of Ben, said he was good with stone. So now all we need is a letter to go with the papers, explaining about my George dying.' Her voice faltered on the last few words.

'Could you write the letter now? My client is very anxious to get things sorted out and we don't want to have to keep driving to and from Rochdale. I'll pay you an extra pound.'

Her voice softened. 'Yes. Do you want to come in, Ben?'

'Thank you, Mrs Dryden, but I'd better not.'

'How about we come back in an hour and collect the letter?' Charlie suggested. 'I think your son should sign it and you'll need two witnesses. Perhaps some of the neighbours?'

'It'll be ready,' she said grimly. 'And properly signed.'

'You'll remember that it's the Amalgamated Union of Building Trade Workers that it goes to now,' Ben said anxiously.

'I'll remember. Eh, ten years ago they amalgamated and George was still grumbling about it the day before he died.'

As Jonah drove the car into the town centre, Charlie laughed aloud. 'I enjoyed doing that. I reckon I'd have made a good lawyer.'

'Why don't we go round to Ben's brother's and pick up the tools while we're here?' Leah suggested.

'Can't we do that later?' Charlie asked. 'I'm parched.'

Jonah laughed. 'You drink more cups of tea in a day than anyone I've ever met. Let's get the tools now, and make sure they're safe, then Ben can stop worrying. Tell us where to go, lad.'

Ben's brother was indeed living in a slum, but there was bread on the table and after the two brothers had hugged and thumped each other on the back, Ned brought out the heavy bag of tools.

'Here you are. I'd only have pawned these as a last resort, lad,' he said. 'You know that. But I've had a few bits of luck, odd jobs here and there, so we're all right for the time being. The Means Test man is letting me have the dole the weeks I'm not working, even. He's a lot kinder than the old one. It's you we've been worried about. Eh, why did you leave like that without telling anyone? Where have you been? You don't look at all well.'

'I was a burden you didn't need. Anyway, I've had a bit of luck myself, meeting Mr and Mrs Willcox.' Ben explained quickly what he was doing and his brother thanked Leah and the two men several times.

'We have to get back to the workshop for the paperwork, then find somewhere to have a cup of tea and a sandwich,' Charlie said.

Jonah added, 'We'll have to do that quickly. I don't like driving in the dark.'

With the tools letting out an occasional clank from the boot of the car, they drove back to see George's widow. 'Here you are. They're all filled in properly, Ben, except for your new address. You can fill that in yourself. And could you give it to me as well, just in case I need to contact you?'

Charlie scribbled Jonah's address down and tore a page

out of his notebook, then took out ten pounds and gave them to Mrs Dryden.

She didn't offer any of the money to her son, but folded the notes and put them away. 'Thank you. It'll take a few weeks for everything to go through, I expect, but those papers will get you fully accepted as a stonemason, Ben. I've done them a few times before for George so I knew exactly what to do. He enjoyed training lads. Eh, he was a lovely man.'

She gave Ben a big hug. 'I miss you, lad. Our Leonard's moved in, as was only right, but he's a grumpy devil to live with. I don't know how his wife puts up with him. If I had any other children, I'd go and live with them, by crikey I would.'

'Let's get going,' Jonah urged. 'It's a long drive.'

9

Rosa enjoyed her day at Evelyn's house, but gave herself plenty of time to walk home before it got dark. She went to thank Mrs Carpenter before she left, though she hadn't seen much of her friend's mother, who was lying on a chaise longue in the sitting room.

'Is it that time already? I must have fallen asleep. Is your father home yet, Evelyn?'

'No, Mother.'

'Oh dear. He said he'd come home early and drive Rosa up to Ellindale. It *is* a Saturday, after all, so he's only supposed to work in the morning.'

As Rosa repeated her thanks and made a move towards the door, Mrs Carpenter lifted one hand to stop her. 'It's a long way and all uphill, dear. Why don't you wait? Mr Carpenter ought to be home soon.'

'I'll be all right, Mrs Carpenter. I'm a good walker and it won't get dark for a while yet.'

She set off briskly, leaving Evelyn waving from the doorstep. She was glad of the fresh air after spending most of the day inside the overheated house so that her friend could fetch and carry for her mother.

She met an old playmate in Birch End and stopped for a chat, then the church clock struck the hour and she realised how long they'd been talking. 'Oh dear! Is it that late already? I'd better go. It's getting dark.'

To her dismay there was a sudden shower and she realised

she'd left her umbrella at Evelyn's house. Drat! She was getting soaked. Oh, well. There wasn't much further to go and she could change her clothes as soon as she got home.

It was as she was walking up the gentle slope that led through the fields between Birch End and Ellindale that a car stopped beside her, an old rattletrap of a thing with three men inside it.

She didn't like the look of them and when one of them jumped out, she backed away, afraid of the expression on his face.

'How about coming for a little ride in our car, girlie?'

Terrified, she set off running back towards Birch End. Footsteps thumped along the ground behind her, but she managed to keep ahead of the man cursing behind her.

The car started moving and must have turned round, because its engine noise got louder and louder. She sobbed aloud. She couldn't outrun a car and there was no one in sight to help her, though she'd passed a young man working in a field a few minutes ago.

Then she slipped in a muddy patch and fell headlong. Before she could get up, the man pounced on her, pulling her to her feet and keeping tight hold of her arm.

She began to scream for help, but he slapped her so hard her head spun and she couldn't think straight for a few moments, by which time someone had opened the rear car door and she'd been dragged inside.

William Carpenter arrived home well into the afternoon feeling annoyed at being kept back at work for no good reason. He knew his employer spent more time there than he needed to because he didn't want to go home to his wife, but that didn't mean his employees should have to work longer hours. It wasn't as if they were paid any extra money for it.

Sadly, in times like these William didn't dare complain; he was desperate to keep his job.

By the time he got home, it had started raining again, a chilly downpour, so he left his car in the drive and didn't bother to open the doors of the garage to put it away. He was hungry and was longing for a cup of hot, sweet tea. He'd see to the car later after it had stopped raining.

His daughter was sitting at the kitchen table reading a book so he waved to her and went along to the sitting room to greet his wife. It was uncomfortably hot in there, as usual. He kissed her cheek. 'How did the day go, darling? Are you feeling any better?'

'A little.'

Alice always said that but when he looked at her, she seemed white and frail, as always.

'Evelyn enjoyed her friend's visit, but I'm a bit worried that Rosa had so far to walk, and all on her own, too. Evelyn said Rosa forgot her umbrella. If she took shelter somewhere she might not have got home yet. You couldn't . . . ?' she hesitated.

'Surely you don't expect me to go after her in this?'

'Please, William. I didn't like her going home alone in such weather and I feel guilty for not insisting she wait for you to come home. It'll only take you a few minutes to check that she got there safely.'

He stared at her and sighed, knowing anxiety wasn't good for her.

'Please. If only to set my mind at rest.'

'Oh, very well. But next time she comes to visit, her family must send someone to pick her up.'

'Take Evelyn with you. She'll enjoy the ride.'

Grateful that the rain was easing off, he helped his daughter into the car. It didn't take long to drive through the village and up the hill.

He had to brake hard as a lad ran into the road suddenly and waved frantically to stop him.

He wound the window down. 'What the hell's the matter? I nearly hit you. Oh, it's you, Timmy.'

'I just saw them Huttons snatch a little lass off the road and drive off with her in their motor car, Mr Carpenter. Grabbed hold of her, they did, and forced her into the car. They went up the track to that farm of theirs. I didn't dare follow them on my own.'

William's heart sank. 'A lass with dark hair?'

'Yes. I think she was from that new family at Spring Cottage.'

'Oh, hell! Run back to the village as quickly as you can and get some more help. Tell them to hurry. I'll go after those Huttons.' Even they wouldn't dare attack him for no reason.

William knew the turn-off to Crag Hey Farm and slowed down to check for recent tyre marks before leaving the main road. Yes, there were some, showing clearly in the mud.

He hesitated, but didn't want to leave his daughter alone out here. 'Climb into the back of the car before I set off again, Evelyn. Quickly! Hide under that blanket and whatever happens when we get there, you are *not* to show yourself to these men. If it wasn't raining, I'd make you get out and wait for me here.'

He found the gate to the farmyard open and a rusty old car with a dented side parked outside the tumbledown house. Lights showed in the windows and as he got out, he heard screams from inside.

He ran into the house without thinking, yelling, 'Stop that!' at the top of his voice.

To his utter horror, they'd got all Rosa's outer clothes off, but they were so startled by his appearance that the one holding her let go.

She hurled herself into his arms and he pushed her quickly behind him, glaring at the men. 'What the hell do you think you're doing?'

'Having a bit of fun. She's a big girl. She was enjoying it. They always do in the end, don't they, Griff?'

The smallest of the three grinned and nodded.

'You filthy devils. She's only ten!'

'What? Well, she's well grown for her age. Nicely grown.' Thad, whom he recognised by sight, winked at him, then turned to his brothers. 'Looks like we've caught ourselves a trespasser, Griff, as well as a little girlie.'

William was uneasily aware that this Hutton was known for his violent behaviour, and started to feel afraid for his own safety. But he knew it'd be fatal to back down. They'd be on him like a pack of vultures. 'I've sent for help.'

Thad laughed. 'Who could you find to send at this time of day. There was no one on the road when we drove up it and there aren't any houses nearby, neither. You'll not fool us and maybe after we've taught you a lesson, you'll not interfere in our affairs again. That lass came with us willingly.'

'I did not!' Rosa shouted.

The poor child was shivering and clinging to the back of his jacket. William whispered, 'Try to get away if a fight starts.'

Sure enough the three brothers began to move towards him, going slowly as if to taunt him. He looked for something to defend himself with and all he could find within reach was a rickety wooden chair. He grabbed it and held it in front of him, praying the lad would bring help quickly.

The three men laughed at his efforts and it only took one of them to drag the chair out of his hands.

As he did so Thad yelled, 'Dammit, she's got out! Go and fetch her back inside the house, Jeb.'

Two of them grabbed William and the third one ran outside.

Timmy was running towards Birch End to get help. To his relief a car came into sight before he got to the village and for the second time that evening he ran out in front of a vehicle waving his hands and yelling, 'Stop! Stop!'

'The Huttons have kidnapped a little lass!' he cried. 'Mr Carpenter's gone after them and— Oh, it's you, Mr Jonah. It's your lass they've taken.'

'*Rosa?*'

'Yes, sir.'

'Who's taken her, did you say?'

'Them Huttons. My dad said they've been up to their old tricks again, pinching stuff, but they've never kidnapped a lass before.'

'I know where they live.'

As Jonah set off, Charlie stuck his head out of the car window and yelled, 'Fetch more help, Timmy, quickly!' He turned to Ben. 'Are you with us on this?'

'Of course I am. I'm not very strong, but I owe them sods for beating me up. They can thump me again too, if it'd keep that lass safe.'

Charlie glanced at Leah, who had anguish on her face. 'Have we got anything we can use as weapons?' she asked in a tight voice. 'Because if they've hurt Rosa . . .'

'There are some hammers and spanners among my tools in the boot,' Ben said. 'We could use them.'

'Good. As soon as we stop at the farm, you find something big and heavy for Charlie and me. Leah, you stay in the car and—'

'No. She's my sister and I'll kill them myself if they've hurt her.'

*   *   *

They jolted along the uneven track to Crag Hey Farm as fast as Jonah dared drive in such muddy conditions. It was no longer raining, but there were deep ruts with puddles in them all along the track.

When they stopped, Ben flung open the car door, ran to the boot and grabbed some tools, handing suitable ones to the other men and a big spanner to Leah.

'That's Carpenter's car!' Charlie exclaimed. 'He must be inside. You go round the back, Ben, and yell out if they try to escape that way.'

Just then the house door opened and a half-dressed girl came running out. She didn't see them at first because she was looking back over her shoulder.

'Rosa!' Leah ran to her sister before the men could stop her, pulling her into her arms but keeping a wary eye on the door.

For a moment Rosa shrieked in panic, then she realised who was holding her and clung to her sister, sobbing her name over and over.

The man who'd been chasing Rosa stopped dead when he saw them, but before he could turn and go back inside, Charlie ran forward and lashed out with a large hammer, hitting him hard on the upper arm and sending him crashing to the ground. He didn't attempt to get up again, but moaned and cradled his injured arm.

Another man peeped out then ducked back inside again. Someone in there cried in pain.

Charlie edged forward. 'Can you deal with this one on the ground, Jonah? If he tries to get up, hit him as hard as you can on the other arm. Ben and I will go and help Carpenter.'

Shoving her sister towards the car, Leah yelled, 'Get in! Now!'

Rosa hesitated, seeming disoriented, then did as she was told.

Leah rushed to the man on the ground, shoved her husband aside and brandished the spanner. 'You're filth, you are! Scum of the earth. Give me half an excuse to hit you and I'll do it happily.'

But he just lay back and moaned.

Inside the house, Thad tried to bolt the door and cursed as he saw that the keep was missing. He backed away from the entrance.

His brother asked. 'Where's Jeb? Didn't he catch the lass?'

'No. They've come to rescue her, so this sod must have sent for help after all.' He kicked Carpenter, then went across to a narrow door at one side of the room. 'Time to get out of here.'

'What about our Jeb?'

'He'll have to look after himself.'

'Nay, I'm fetching him.' Griff headed towards the door.

'You're a fool,' Thad muttered. He slipped out of the door and guessing they'd expect him to run for the moors, he crept up to the attics. He knew a good hiding place he'd used as a lad to escape his father's beatings.

As the men went into the house Leah concentrated on keeping the injured man from following his brother back into the house.

It was a moment or two before she realised how badly it hurt him to move. There was no mistaking the agony in his face if he even tried. Good. Serve him right. She'd like to break his other arm for what he'd done to her sister.

She risked a quick glance back at the car, relieved to see the pale circle of Rosa's face pressed against the window.

The rescuers went into the kitchen and they nearly bumped into Griff Hutton, who immediately moved back and ran towards a door.

Charlie got to him first and yanked him back by the coat, but he started lashing out with fists and feet.

'Think I'm frightened of softies like you,' Griff taunted. 'That one can't even breathe properly.'

'Stand back, Jonah. Leave him to me,' Charlie ordered. As the man lashed out again, he brought his hammer out from behind his back and got in a good swipe at the fist coming towards him. He only half connected with it, but hurt his attacker enough to make him roar in pain.

Griff grabbed a chair to protect himself from further blows, thrusting it at Charlie as if it too were a weapon.

But from where he lay on the ground, William seized his opportunity and grabbed Griff's ankle, holding on tightly, not letting the fellow kick him off. He managed to make him fall to the ground.

It took all three men to subdue Griff, though, because by now, Jonah was having difficulty breathing and Ben was still too weak to follow through on their attack properly.

'We'd better tie this one up,' Charlie panted. 'Jonah, see if you can find something.'

Griff tried to heave him and Ben off, but failed and after a struggle, they got him tied up with what looked like a frayed clothes line.

'Leah hasn't called for help, but you'd better go and see if she's all right, Jonah,' Charlie said. 'Keep your hammer ready and don't hesitate to use it. This one can't give us any more trouble, but I'm keeping an eye on things in case the other comes to his aid.'

Jonah came back to report, 'Rosa's in the car and Leah's all right. The other Hutton must have a broken arm. He's in agony and making no attempt to escape.'

'Good. Serves him right.'

'What are we going to do with the two we have got?'

'Haul them into Rivenshaw and give them to Sergeant Deemer, then let him go after Thad.'

'Is the sergeant good at his job?' Ben asked.

'Oh, yes. Deemer grew up here and transferred back to Rivenshaw to spend his last few years working as sergeant in charge before he retires. He was trained in the old ways of dealing with villains and I guarantee *he* won't treat any of these devils gently. Let's get this one outside.'

Evelyn, who'd been watching the melee from under the blanket inside her father's car, saw Rosa sobbing as she got into the other car. After waiting to make sure no more men were coming out of the house, Evelyn got out and ran across to join her friend, letting Rosa sob against her and wrapping her in an old blanket that had been protecting the leather seat.

When Leah joined the girls in the car then, she looked at Rosa's half-clad body in horror. She had to ask, 'They didn't, um, get your knickers off, did they, love?'

'No. They were tossing coins for who'd do that. Why did they want to undress me? It was horrible.'

'Because they're wicked,' Leah said, adding, 'Thank goodness for that!' under her breath as she held her shivering sister close. 'Are you all right, Evelyn?'

'Yes, Mrs Willcox. I hid in Dad's car.'

'Good. We'll stay here together till the men come back, shall we? We'll keep each other warm and won't get in their way.'

From the back seat, she and the girls watched as the men came out of the house, dragging one of the Huttons.

'The other one got away,' Charlie yelled, kicking Griff's feet from under him and standing over him with the hammer. 'If you try to get up again, I'll break your damned leg.'

Griff turned to look at his brother.

'They've broke my arm,' Jeb whispered. 'Don't give them an excuse to break yours.'

Griff cursed, but remained where he'd fallen.

Mr Carpenter came across to the car. 'Is the little lass all right? He didn't—'

The men all looked towards Leah as she opened the car window.

'Rosa's all right. They didn't . . . um, hurt her too badly. But we need to get her home.'

Her sister might have escaped the worst, but she was only half clothed and shivering violently, even wrapped in the blanket. Leah closed the window to keep out the wind and held her close.

She couldn't believe that those brutes had been intending to rape a child. What sort of creatures were they even to think of that? *She* didn't know a word bad enough to describe them, that was sure.

Just then another car came bumping down the lane that led to the farm.

Four men tumbled out of it and ran across to them. Charlie let out a groan of relief. He knew all of them by sight.

'How is she?' one of them asked immediately.

'She's upset but we got here just in time,' Charlie said grimly.

'Were they trying to—' He looked towards the car and saw the children.

'Yes. They got some of her clothes off, but they didn't finish the job, thank goodness. We'll discuss that later.'

Evelyn got out of the car and ran round to her father, who was limping. 'Daddy, are you hurt?'

'Just a bit bruised.'

'Daddy, why did they take Rosa's clothes off?'

Her words echoed out clearly and the men who'd just arrived muttered to one another and glared down at the captives.

Mr Carpenter took a deep shaky breath. 'We'll talk about it another time, Evelyn, and your mother will explain it to you better than I can.'

One of the men standing near the two captured brothers said in a furious voice, 'We'll hand you over to the police, but if I ever see any of you Huttons in Birch End or Ellindale again, I'll kick you where it hurts first and ask what you're doing in the valley second. I've got a little lass the same age as Rosa Turner and I'd do far worse to anyone as touched her than break his arm. I'd use a very sharp knife on him, that I would.'

They both winced.

'Filthy devils like them should be hanged or at the very least, castrated,' another said. 'I could do it now. I've practised on bulls. I'd not miss the important bit.'

Rosa didn't seem to be taking in what was happening around them, and both girls were too innocent to understand exactly what was being discussed. She didn't speak again and just continued to sit pressed against her sister, shivering from time to time.

Charlie, Jonah and Ben came across to the car. Jonah was wheezing badly, which gave Leah an additional layer of worry.

'I think the best thing we can do now is get Rosa home,' Charlie said. 'Are you all right to drive, Jonah?'

'Yes.'

'Shall we go home now as well, Evelyn?' William asked. He was bruised and muddy, still furiously angry, and all he wanted was his home and a warm fire.

'Yes, please, Daddy.'

'I'm sorry,' he said to Leah. 'I was going to bring her home by car, but I got delayed at work. If there's anything else I can do—'

'Nothing at the moment.'

Charlie went across to have a word with the men guarding

the Hutton brothers. 'Can someone send Robert out to Spring
Cottage with the taxi in about an hour to pick me up. I think
Jonah needs to rest now.'

'Is he all right to drive home?'

'He says so.'

By the time he got back to the car, Jonah had got in and
started it up. He was still wheezing but he ignored that and
drove off slowly down the muddy lane.

No one spoke on the way back to Spring Cottage.

When they got there, Leah took charge, telling Jonah to
sit down and rest before ordering Charlie and Ben to stoke
up the stove to heat some water for a bath.

Then she sat on the sofa holding her sister close.

From time to time tears trickled down her cheeks and she
brushed them away impatiently.

Her sister, lively little Rosa, was like a frozen shadow of
herself, barely moving, clinging to her big sister whenever
she could.

Leah felt she'd let her sister down badly.

There was no sign of Thad Hutton, though Sergeant Deemer
in Rivenshaw organised a thorough search of the farm and
surrounding moors the next day. But the ongoing rain made
it more difficult to find any tracks and after a long, cold day,
the volunteers had to give up.

'Does that sod know the moors well?' the sergeant asked
one of his searchers as they drove back to Birch End.

'Like the back of his hand. All them Huttons do.'

'That family has always been trouble. You should see the
notes on them at the police station.' He shook his head. 'I
don't think anyone knows much about this present generation though.'

'Since their parents died, the brothers have been coming
and going, not attempting to farm the place. No one knows

where they go or what they get up to. I doubt it's honest work, though.'

'Well, those two who were caught won't be getting up to anything for a good few years,' the sergeant said grimly. 'They'll not be able to hurt any more little girls. How is the poor lass going?'

'I haven't seen her myself but I hear she's been very quiet, not at all like her usual lively self. Which isn't surprising. But at least she escaped the worst.'

And there they had to leave it, though there was more than one man in the district ready to turn out at a moment's notice if there was any chance of catching Thad Hutton.

10

As the weeks passed, Leah worked hard, buying presents, planning food, determined to make their first Christmas together a happy time. But how?

She was desperate to cheer up her sister, who had refused to go to school in the weeks since the incident. Rosa didn't willingly leave the house at all, even scurrying across the yard to the old barn as if afraid of the whole world.

'Come and help me, Rosa. We don't need to set the table yet, so let's have a look at the ginger beer,' she urged. 'It takes longer in winter for it to start fermenting, but it should get going soon. If the bubbles are rising, we'll need to feed it every day for a week. I remember how careful Mum was about that. Perhaps you could take charge of doing it?'

Rosa shrugged. 'You'd better do it. I might forget. I've a lot on my mind just now.'

Leah bit back some sharp words and went to check on what her mother had always called the ginger beer *plant*. 'Oh, it is fermenting. Look!'

But her sister was staring blankly into space.

'Fetch me the sugar, will you? *Rosa!* Wake up.'

'What?'

'Fetch me the sugar jar, please.' She opened the tin of ginger powder and carefully measured two teaspoonfuls into the 'plant', followed by four teaspoons of sugar. 'There. We'll need to feed it every day for a week, at least.' She waited. 'Well? Don't just stand there. Put the sugar away.'

With a sigh, as if she was being put upon, Rosa took the jar back in the pantry. She hadn't even glanced at the ginger beer plant.

Jonah, who had come home not long before, came across to stare at the mixture and seized the opportunity to give his wife a quick cuddle. 'I'm looking forward to drinking this.'

'It's going well, should be ready in time for Christmas. We haven't made any ginger beer for ages, have we, Rosa? This is just about the perfect stage for starting to feed the plant. Look at the small bubbles, coming up in short bursts. That's how you tell, Rosa. You should be able to—'

'Can we do this another time, please, Leah? I'm not in the mood for fiddling about with ginger beer.'

Jonah had been about to take his usual armchair near the window, but he turned and said sharply, 'That's not a very polite thing to say to your sister.'

Rosa flung herself down at the table and opened a book without replying.

This was so unlike the normally cheerful child that Leah and Jonah exchanged astonished glances.

When he walked across and twitched the book out of her hands, Rosa scowled at him and tried to snatch it back.

'Listen to me.'

She tried to get up but he pushed her down into the chair, knowing they couldn't let her wallow in her unhappiness. Life was hard. He knew that only too well. She'd just had her first hard lesson. His heart ached for her, but she had to toughen up as she faced the vagaries of life.

'Listen, I said. Since the Huttons kidnapped you, you've been impossible to live with. You're rude to your sister, who is worried sick about you. *She* didn't do anything to hurt you, so she doesn't deserve treating like that.'

He waited but Rosa continued to scowl down at the table,

lips pressed tightly together. 'You've been lazy about doing your chores and you've refused point-blank to go to school. Well, you're not the only person in the world who's been hurt and you've had enough time to start getting over that incident now. You're going to school tomorrow if I have to drag you there myself, and you'll do your share of the household jobs when you're at home. Leah isn't your servant and neither am I.'

'You don't understand!'

'Don't I? Do you think I haven't been hurt? How do you think I felt at being turned into a wheezing wreck of a man at twenty-one? There is no cure for what I've got!' He paused, looking her in the eyes, his wheezing way of breathing the only sound in the room.

She flushed and began to bite her lip, as if uncertain what to say or do.

'Even so, I'm grateful to be alive. How many men do you think I've seen killed? I've seen them with their limbs blown off, screaming as they died. What happened to you was frightening and horrible, yes, but you were rescued before those brutes could really hurt you and you're not missing any parts of your body.'

Leah opened her mouth to ask him to go more gently on her sister, then caught a quick head shake from him and closed her mouth again. She'd tried being gentle and it hadn't worked. Maybe his way would work.

'Bad things happen to everyone, Rosa,' Jonah went on. 'No one escapes them. No one! It's part of life. You're growing up now and must learn to cope, as we all do.'

'But it's not *fair*!'

'Well, there you are. Unfair things happen and some people get more than their share of them.'

'You're not my father so you've no *right* to talk to me like this! Dad wouldn't have been unkind to me. *He* wouldn't have scolded me.' She pushed past him and ran out of the house, heedless of the icy wind blowing.

Jonah looked at Leah and spread his hands helplessly. 'Do you think I was too severe with her?'

'No. We've tried being kind. That didn't work. So we'll try being strict.' She wiped away a tear. 'It'll be difficult, though.'

'Does she understand what they were trying to do to her?'

'She does now, sort of. She asked me why and I did my best to explain. I mustn't have done it very well, because all she could say was she was never going to get married if you had to let men do horrid things like that to you.'

Jonah put his arms round her and she leaned against him for a few moments.

'I wish they could catch the other brother, Jonah. People say he's the ringleader. I know she's worried that he'll come after her.'

'They will catch him sooner or later, and I'm sure they'll send the other two to prison for a long time.'

He kissed the top of her head. 'Rosa will miss something important if she doesn't marry. I'm really glad Charlie found you for me. I'm such a stupid fellow I might not have found anyone half as good myself, even if I'd plucked up my courage to go out and look. I'd turned into a semi-recluse, living in my books and newspapers. I'm very happy with you, Leah. I hope you feel the same.'

'I am happy, but . . . there's one thing missing.'

'Tell me.'

'I wish—' She broke off, then finished her sentence. 'I wish I could fall for a baby.'

Seconds ticked slowly past and his voice sounded sad as he answered. 'That might not be your fault. Being gassed might have . . . made that more difficult for me.'

She could only hug him close and pray he was wrong.

It'd break her heart if she couldn't have any children. It had been one thing to resign herself to being a childless spinster. It'd be much harder to accept being a barren wife.

After a while, she pulled away from him and said more briskly, 'How about we bring Ben in and discuss our building plans with him? He's looking a lot better now he's eating and I think he's worrying about paying us back.'

'Yes. It's time to give him something to do with his life.'

Ben looked up as Rosa ran into the tumbledown end of the old barn, where he was working on a small job he'd found for himself, making good some damage to a wall to pay the Willcoxes back for their kindness. She didn't see him at first and ran to the far corner, sobbing loudly, like the hurt child she was. His heart went out to her.

When she saw him, she exclaimed, 'Oh, no! Isn't there anywhere a person can be private round here?'

She turned to leave but he was worried about her, so moved quickly to bar the way. 'Don't go. Tell me what's wrong.'

'What do *you* think is wrong?'

There was a silence, before he asked gently, 'I know. But what upset you just now?'

'Jonah. And Leah. They've been nagging me, telling me to buck up and go back to school. I can't. Whatever they say or do, I'm *not* going to school.'

'Why not?'

She looked at him in puzzlement. 'That's obvious.'

'Not to me. Tell me.'

'Because everyone there will know what those men tried to do to me and they'll say horrible things about it.'

'Ah. And that's what you're afraid of, a few words?'

'I'm absolutely *humiliated* about the whole thing, if you must know.'

His tone was bitter. 'If feeling humiliated is the worst thing that ever happens to you, Rosa Turner, you'll not be doing badly.'

'You grown-ups all stick together! That's what Jonah said to me. Well, let me tell you, I don't *care* if worse things happen to other people. I care about what happened to me.'

'So you don't care about how your sister feels?'

'What?' Rosa frowned at him then stared down at the floor, moving some flakes of stone around with her foot. 'Of course I care about Leah, but she's not the one who was kidnapped and . . . and had her clothes taken off. It's me who'll have to face everyone at school about that. They'll laugh at me, I know they will. I'll never live it down.'

'Actually, she's very upset indeed about what happened to you. And you'll have to face the people at school sometime because the law says you have to go to school till you're fourteen, so you're not old enough to leave.'

'They can't make you go if you're *ill*!'

'You're not ill; you're being cowardly. I'd thought better of you, Rosa.' He turned away and went on sorting through the stones, ignoring her.

She began to cry again.

It hurt him to hear it, but he resisted the temptation to hug her. Once she'd quietened down a little, he said, 'Crying doesn't help, love. I've tried it, and believe me, it solves nothing.'

That caught her attention. 'Men don't cry.'

'Don't they? I did when I was on the road with no home, no work and no food. I cried more than once, I can tell you. But each time I had to carry on walking the next day, because there was nothing else I could do. Sometimes you just have to carry on.'

He picked up a smaller stone, studied it and put it on the end pile.

After a few moments of watching him in silence, she asked in a hesitant voice, 'What are you doing?'

'Going through the stones that fell when part of the end wall collapsed. I'm seeing how many are usable and sorting them into roughly similar sizes. I'd like to do something to pay your sister and her husband back for their kindness to me when I was at my lowest point ever, so I thought I'd rebuild this wall.' He stopped as he heard footsteps coming towards them.

Jonah appeared in the doorway. 'Oh, there you are, Rosa. Leah's worrying. Go and reassure her that you're all right, please. I need to speak to Ben about something.'

Her shoulders sagged but she turned and trailed back to the house without protesting.

'It *is* a humiliating thing to have to face,' Ben said quietly.

'I know. But she can't hide in the house for the rest of her life, so the sooner she gets that over with the better.'

'I suppose so. Anyway, did you want something?'

'Yes, to speak to you.'

'If you think it's time for me to leave, I—'

'Not at all. We want to hire you to do a job for us.'

'A job?' Ben frowned. 'A *real* one? Or a made-up one?'

'A real job. We want to ask your opinion first, and see if you can do it for us. If you come to the house we can— ' He stopped and looked round, as if noticing for the first time, the neat piles of stones. 'What are you doing here?'

'Sorting out the stones. It'd be quite easy to repair that end wall. Well, it would if you'd buy me the sand and cement. I wanted to repay your kindness.'

Jonah clapped him on the shoulder. 'Great minds think alike. Come and talk about it. Brrr! It's cold out here.'

When Rosa came back into the house, she looked so uncertain Leah didn't scold her any more. 'Can you go up and make the beds, please? Jonah and I need to talk to Ben about doing a job for us.'

Rosa didn't move for a moment or two, then burst out, 'Ben says the same as you. That I have to face people. How can I, Leah?'

She went across to hold her little sister close for a moment, only Rosa wasn't so little any more. She seemed to have grown in the few months they'd been here, probably because she was now eating well.

She wasn't a woman yet but not quite a child, either. 'You'll face it bravely, love, and one good thing will come out of it.'

'A *good* thing?'

'Yes. You'll find out who your real friends are because they'll stand by you. I bet Evelyn will be the first to do that. The ones who aren't kind to you, well, you'll know not to trust them in future. Will you go back tomorrow? I'll give you a note for your teacher.'

Rosa sighed, hesitated, then said, 'All right. And . . . I'll do my best.'

Leah watched her go slowly up the stairs, her shoulders drooping, moving like an old and weary woman. She wondered if she'd ever stop feeling guilty about not keeping Rosa safe. But too much sympathy would do no good now. Life went on. You could only go on with it. A hard lesson but there you were. Few people went through life without meeting troubles of various sorts.

She turned as the men came in. 'Do sit down, Ben.' When he was seated opposite her at the table, she gestured to Jonah to continue, but he shook his head.

'You tell him, Leah. It's more your project than mine, after all.'

Another of her husband's gentle reminders about his state of health, she thought bitterly. 'Ben, I've told you before that

I need something to occupy my time, something worthwhile, since my dear husband doesn't like the idea of me scrubbing floors or doing the washing. And anyway, the women who do those jobs for me need the money desperately and we don't. So . . . Jonah's been reading about a new organisation that's just starting up called the Youth Hostels Association. It'll help young people from poorer backgrounds to go on holiday and get to know the countryside by providing them with cheap accommodation.'

'There's one hostel opening in Wales this very month,' Jonah put in. 'I think that's the first one but others are being planned.'

'What a good idea!' Ben said at once. 'I didn't know much about the Pennines till I went on the tramp, but even I couldn't help noticing how beautiful some places were, worried as I was about finding something to eat and somewhere to sleep. Do you think enough people will still come hiking in times like these to make it worthwhile, though?'

'Yes. We already get quite a few walkers coming up the valley in the warmer months and although Nancy tells me numbers went down in the twenties, some hikers still came. Despite the bad times some people have managed to keep their jobs, and since prices of many things have fallen over the past few years, that gives the ones in work more money to spend on enjoying themselves.'

Jonah took over. 'People in the south are much less affected by the Depression, so let's encourage them to spend their holiday money here in the north. Every penny they spend is a penny earned by someone who lives here, and that passes on to other people in turn. It's called the multiplier effect, I think. I learned about it in a book.'

Leah carried on as he fell silent. She'd already learned to recognise Jonah's distant, I-am-thinking look and knew he'd stop talking for a few moments unless prompted. 'The hostels aren't for families, Ben, they're for younger people, hikers usually. I should think some of them would definitely like to stay overnight here, because it's very pretty countryside once you're away from the towns.'

She laughed and added, 'When it's not raining that is. They could use a hostel as a base and head off in a different direction each day instead of having to move on to a town which has rooms to let. And even those rooms are too expensive for some, who can afford to pay a few pennies, but not a few shillings, so they just do day trips and see only places close to their homes.'

Ben nodded. 'Go on.'

'A hostel should not only offer young people cheap accommodation in dormitories but give them somewhere to prepare simple meals. We have the old barn already and it's quite big, so if it could be made habitable, given a water supply and sanitation, it could provide holiday accommodation for quite a few people.'

Jonah nodded vigorously to endorse this. And although he'd told her to do the explaining, he couldn't help joining in. 'Leah and I thought if we opened a hostel it would provide a couple of part-time jobs at least, and that would help our own people.'

'And the hikers would buy things at the village store.' Leah hesitated and added, 'I thought we might also use the end part of the barn to provide free shelter for men on the tramp.'

'They're not all well behaved,' Ben warned.

'No. But the part you've been looking at today could be kept separate from the hostel. We don't want young women put in danger from rough men on the tramp.' She broke off for a moment, remembering what those brutes had done to her little sister. 'Are there any women on the tramp?'

Ben thought about this and said, 'I didn't see women on their own, though you couldn't always tell whether some of them were men or women. Some people didn't want to talk to anyone, but I did see a few families and they often stopped for a chat. Some of them were walking to relatives in another part of the country, others were just . . . walking.'

'If any women tramps come here, we'll manage somehow. Do you think my basic idea will work? Is our old barn still sturdy enough to be made habitable?'

'Oh, yes. It was very well built. It'll outlast us with just a little help occasionally.'

'And could *you* manage to make it habitable for us?'

He stared at her, mouth falling open. 'You want me to be *in charge of doing it*?'

'Yes. We trust you.'

Ben swallowed hard, couldn't get the words out. He felt like a drowning man who'd been pulled out of the water at the last minute and then handed a pile of treasure as well.

'I'd love to do it, but I don't have the necessary papers to say I'm allowed.'

'They're on their way. Charlie sorted that out.'

'I still can't do it, I'm afraid. I've got my tools, but you need barrows and ladders, all sorts of equipment. And I'd need a labourer to fetch and carry for me. Some jobs take two pairs of hands, you see.'

'We thought the labouring job could go to a man or lad from round here, rather than bringing in an outsider, and if he's good, he could even get apprenticed to you and learn a trade.' Jonah waved one hand dismissively. 'Though that's a decision for much later, of course.'

Leah smiled at Ben's amazement. 'We can supply the money you need to start up so that you can buy equipment, and you can pay us back later once you're on your feet again.'

It took him a few shaky breaths before he could form any words that made sense, then he said in a choked voice, 'I'd love to do the job for you, not only because it's a job, but because it's a very old building and such places are often pulled down when there's no need. I love old stone houses.'

He went to the window and looked out, blinking hard. 'That old barn has been defying the wind and weather for two or three hundred years. It gave me hope just to see it when I first arrived. Our forebears knew how to make buildings that last.'

'And how to breed men who can last, too,' Jonah added softly. 'We got through the war and defeated the Germans. We'll get through this depression as well, see if we don't.'

Ben turned and gave them a wobbly smile. 'Will you excuse me? I need to . . . pull myself together, get used to the idea. It'd be a dream come true, a feast for a hungry man to have my own business and jobs.'

He was out of the house before they could answer.

Upstairs Rosa stood on the landing near her bedroom door with tears in her eyes. She couldn't help sometimes overhearing what her sister and Jonah were saying. Today she'd listened deliberately in case they were discussing her with Ben.

But they weren't. Of course they weren't. Jonah was right. She wasn't the only person in trouble in the world. He'd had his health ruined and Ben had nearly died out on the moors.

After listening to their plans, she felt something change inside her. Her sister was going to do wonderful things, help people, build for the future. With Jonah's support, of course. He must have quite a lot of money tucked away to do all this. Strange, that. She'd thought all rich people were like Charlie and his wife, talking loudly and showing off their wealth.

Ben had been in despair when he came here, his face

almost skull-like. He was still thin, but he looked a lot better and was putting on flesh again. Now, he was overwhelmed by the opposite situation: hope for the future. How wonderful that was for him!

She too had felt in the depths of despair since *it* had happened. But she suddenly felt that if Ben could climb out of his terrible situation, much worse than hers, and start a new life, so could she.

Could she be brave enough to face up to the people in the village? She looked down at herself. She had all her arms and legs. And most people in the village were kind, like Auntie Hilda and Mrs Buckley.

She mustn't be a coward; she had to try.

She was dreading it, though.

Her dad had helped her out of a scrape just before he died, and he'd told her afterwards to plan what she was going to do instead of rushing headlong into things. She could hear his voice saying, '*Plan* what you do with your life, love. Don't let things just happen to you. You've got the chance of a good education. Seize it with both hands. Make me proud of you.'

If ever there was a time to follow his advice, it was now. She would start by planning what she was going to say tomorrow, how she would deal with people's curiosity.

Would that be enough to get her through the humiliation she was sure she'd be facing? She was dreading going to school, absolutely dreading it. But if she didn't go, she'd not get an education and that'd be letting her dad and Leah down.

The following morning, Rosa got ready for school. She was quiet and didn't eat much breakfast, but no one nagged her to clear her plate.

When her sister said, 'You'll be all right,' Rosa nodded, praying Leah was right.

She set off to walk into the village to catch the early morning bus. To her relief, Evelyn was already waiting at the bus stop. Her friend's smile made her feel better at once.

'Oh, I'm so glad you're coming back to school. I've missed you so much.' She began to go through what had been happening, but Rosa cut her short.

'What are they saying about me?'

Evelyn flushed and looked uncomfortable. 'Some people are being unkind, saying . . . well, that those men had their way with you. I don't know exactly what that means, my mother went all red when she tried to explain it to me and said she'd tell me next year. But from the way they talk about it, it sounds bad.'

'Well, that doesn't matter because Leah told me what it means and those men definitely didn't have their way with me.' She took a deep breath and said it as she'd planned. 'They were tormenting me, taking my clothes off to embarrass me. Only your father came and saved me before they got all my clothes off. It was just like . . . um, like being seen in a swimming costume. If I'd been on a beach, it wouldn't have mattered at all.'

'Oh, I see. How absolutely horrid of them!'

'Some people are horrid. Your father was wonderful. He was a hero.'

Evelyn beamed at that compliment.

The bus came shortly afterwards and they got on.

At school, Rosa avoided the people she didn't like and when anyone asked her, she went over what had happened briefly and then asked them about school and what she'd missed.

Luckily for her, one of the boys had broken his leg the previous day trying to climb up to the top crosspiece of the swings in the boys' side of the playground. And since half the school had seen that happen, it had taken some of the attention away from her.

Of course a few people still made snide remarks, girls she didn't get on with. She'd expected that and told them straight out not to be so rude.

Her teacher stopped her on the way out of the classroom at lunchtime and asked if she was all right.

'I'm fine, thank you, Miss Grey.'

'Good, good. If anyone annoys you or – or says silly things – just let me know and I'll give them a good telling off.'

Rosa vowed she'd die before she did that. She was going to cope with this on her own if it killed her, and she was going to study even harder than before, to make Leah and Jonah proud of her. 'I'm more interested in catching up with anything I've missed, Miss Grey. I want to try my best to get an Esherwood Bequest, so if you can give me any extra work or suggest anything that would help, I'd be very grateful.'

'Good girl. I'll plan some extra work for you.' The teacher patted her on the shoulder and went off to the little room where the five teachers ate their lunches.

Rosa took a deep breath and went outside. She'd got through the morning. It hadn't been easy but she'd done it.

She could get through the afternoon, too.

By the time she and Evelyn got on the bus to go back up the valley to Ellindale, she felt so exhausted she could have lain down and gone to sleep.

But she'd coped! Her dad would have been proud of her, she was sure.

11

And then it was Christmas, the first of Leah's married life. She was determined to make it memorable. But when she asked Jonah about inviting Charlie and his wife for a meal, he looked a bit embarrassed.

'Marion's arranged for them to spend Christmas Day with her parents and other relatives. They're going to her parents for the midday meal, then spending the evening at an aunt's house. She didn't ask Charlie, just arranged it. He looked unhappy when he told me. And so he should. Talk about off with the old, on with the new.'

She could see that Jonah was hurt by this abandonment and said cheerfully, 'Well, that's good because we're invited to go and have a meal and a drink of port and lemonade with Auntie Hilda. Port is her annual extravagance. I'd like to go if you don't mind.'

'Am I included? I hardly know her.'

Leah was annoyed at how insecure his brother's treatment had made him feel. 'Of course you're included. You're my husband! As if she'd ever invite me without you at Christmas! As if I'd even think of going anywhere and leaving you on your own! Auntie Hilda says to bring Ben along as well because she doesn't like to think of him being alone at such a time.'

'That's extremely kind of her.'

'She *is* kind. I'll take a few food treats with us because she can't afford anything lavish. I'd have invited her here but she has her lodgers to look after.'

'She works hard, doesn't she?'

'Very. But she's always preferred to keep busy. I never remember her sitting around doing nothing. She was a wonderful help to me when my mother died, as if she was really my auntie.'

As she put away the shopping, Leah cocked her head. 'Listen. Ben's whistling again.'

They smiled at one another as the tuneful melody was punctuated by the thuds of rocks being moved. After Christmas, Jonah and Ben would go out to buy the necessary equipment and then Daniel Pollard from the village would be starting work as a builder's labourer.

'Daniel's so happy at the prospect of bringing home a pay packet again,' she said. 'I wish we could provide jobs for more people.'

'We're doing our share. I'd never have thought of creating a hostel if it weren't for you.'

'I didn't realise we could afford it. Jonah, you never talk about money, but we *can* afford it, can't we?'

'Yes. Look, I think I'd better explain our finances because everything will come to you one day.'

'Don't talk like that.'

'You have to face facts, but we won't dwell on them. Anyway, this is a good opportunity to go through the details because we're on our own. This isn't for Rosa's ears. Wait there and I'll get out my account books and papers.'

She sat down, glad of a few moments' rest, because she'd been on her feet all morning.

He came back and spread out some papers, then they sat together going through them.

After he'd finished she stared at him, feeling as if she'd never really seen him before. 'I didn't realise you had so much money! Does Charlie know?'

'No. And he's not to know. Even in times like these, it's

possible to invest your money to make more.' He glanced sideways and smiled at her shocked expression. 'I don't want anyone to know except you. When Charlie started talking about finding me a wife, I especially didn't want one who'd marry me for the money, so I kept quiet about my finances. And you didn't even think of the money side, did you?'

'I did think of having enough to live on but I don't think I'd have married you at all if I'd known how rich you were.'

'Darling Leah, I'm not rich, just modestly comfortable.'

'It seems rich to me.'

'Well, we live so economically that I've hardly touched my money since we came to Ellindale. Charlie wanted to give me an allowance but I told him I had enough to manage on. He must be thinking of investing in something because he didn't argue. He's bought a lot of property during the last year or two. Pawnbroking is a flourishing business in times like these and property prices are low.'

He gathered the papers together. 'So now you know my dreadful secret.'

She planted a quick kiss on his cheek. 'I still shan't waste any money, however much you have.'

'*We* have. I think frugality was bred into you, my dear.'

'I might buy us some new sheets, though, if you don't mind. Ours are very worn.'

'Far too extravagant,' he said with a straight face.

'Oh, you!' She gave him a mock slap on the arm.

'One more thing: if Rosa doesn't get a scholarship to the grammar school, we can afford to pay the fees.'

She hugged him from behind as he sat in his armchair, then kissed the top of his head. 'That's a lovely thought. Thank you.'

When he came back after locking his papers away, she greeted him with, 'Let's try the ginger beer on Christmas Eve, and if you don't mind, I'd like to give Mrs Buckley at the shop a bottle for herself. She has no one to give her presents now, you see. I've already started a new batch, though it isn't fermenting yet.'

She didn't talk about the money again, but she thought about it a lot.

Fate had been very kind to her since her father's death, as if making up for her losing both parents. She wanted to be kind to other people in return. She *would* be. A few pennies could make a huge difference when your purse was empty, as she'd found out.

On Christmas morning, Jonah produced the presents he'd got for the ladies during an excursion into Manchester with Charlie. He gave each of them a book, *The Murder at the Vicarage* for Leah, which the bookseller said was Miss Agatha Christie's first novel about an elderly lady detective called Miss Marple.

'It seems strange to think of an old lady being a detective, but then, old people often see more than younger folk realise.' She said pointedly to Rosa, 'Life doesn't end at forty, even though you'd think it did to hear younger people talk.'

Jonah chuckled. 'Well, the bookseller said it was a really good story and he predicts another huge success for the author.'

For Rosa, Jonah had bought *Swallows and Amazons*, a novel for older children, also highly recommended by his bookseller.

Rosa stroked the cover reverently. 'You couldn't have bought me anything better than this, Jonah. Thank you so much. One day I'm going to have a whole bookcase full of my very own books.'

After seeing the way her eyes lit up as she shared that dream, he promised himself to buy her a bookcase for her birthday and then set about helping her fill it. Without books he didn't know how he'd have coped with the problems his wartime service had given him. And since his marriage he'd been very happy. With a smile at his wife, he turned to his own presents.

Leah had made him some handkerchiefs with his initials in one corner, and Rosa had embroidered him a bookmark in cross stitch with his name on it.

Charlie's present was a parcel of expensive food treats and a bottle of wine.

But Jonah valued the gifts made by Leah and Rosa much more highly. It was the first time he'd ever received such special, personal items.

When they drove into Birch End, Auntie Hilda greeted them with a beaming smile and kissed everyone, Jonah and Ben included.

She greeted their presents and contributions with little cries and exclamations, though Leah had warned Jonah that the silk scarf he'd insisted on buying for her would probably never be worn, but kept in tissue paper 'for best'. Her dear friend would cherish it, though, and take it out of the drawer occasionally to gloat over.

The food Leah had brought made Hilda blow her nose vigorously. 'You shouldn't have.'

'Of course I should. We would have needed to eat if we'd stayed at home, so I brought a few things with us.'

'But you brought so much.'

'So that you can keep some for yourself, for a treat.'

She took hold of her adopted niece's hands. 'Oh, Leah, I'm that happy you're settled with Jonah. Your mother and father would be happy too, I know. He's such a nice chap, not at all like his brother.'

'Don't you like Charlie?'

She looked round to make sure Jonah couldn't overhear.

'I don't dislike him exactly, but he's sharp and I'd not like to go into business with him, because he'd always want to take the lion's share of whatever profits you made. I've met men like him before. And look at that wife of his. He married her to show off, not to love. He treats her like an expensive toy and she looks like one, not like a real woman.'

'You're a very wise woman, Auntie Hilda.'

The older woman flushed slightly, not used to compliments. 'Go on with you!'

They ate their meal crowded together with a card table set up at one end to extend Hilda's draw-leaf table. There was much laughter, especially when it was Hilda herself who got the silver threepenny bit in her helping of Christmas pudding and tried to give it to someone else.

Afterwards, they had a sing-song, because one of the lodgers could play the piano by ear.

Leah was waiting to see Jonah's reaction to the singing and he was indeed amazed.

'What a beautiful voice you have, Mrs Gordon!'

Hilda blushed. 'I do enjoy a sing-song. And Willy here plays the piano so well. Anything he's heard he can play, doesn't need music at all. How could anyone not sing along with a piano player always available?'

As he was driving them home Jonah said, 'That's the best Christmas I've ever spent.'

Leah was amazed that a simple party could have given her husband this much pleasure. 'Well, I'm glad about that.' She gave his hand a quick squeeze and saw him smile.

When they got home, however, their joy was quenched abruptly. Someone had broken into the house and wreaked havoc.

'Whoever it was deliberately damaged things,' Leah said in a low voice, as if afraid of being overheard. 'They've smashed my crockery for no reason, all my mother's best dishes.' She couldn't hold back a sob.

Rosa looked down. 'They've trodden food into the rug. That's not an accident either.'

'You don't suppose they're . . . still in the house?' Leah whispered.

'I doubt it,' Jonah said. 'I'll go upstairs and have a look. Stand at the door and be ready to run down towards the village for help.'

'Let me go upstairs,' Ben said. 'I'm quicker than you.' He didn't wait for Jonah to agree, but grabbed the poker and crept up.

The others waited by the outer door, motionless.

'If we have to run . . . don't wait for me,' Jonah wheezed.

Leah looked at him anxiously. When anything upset him, his breathing seemed to worsen very quickly.

'No one in the bedrooms!' Ben yelled down. 'Don't come up yet though. Just to be absolutely safe, I'm going to check all the wardrobes.'

'I'll take a peep at the best room.' Leah ran off to do that before Jonah could stop her but was back almost immediately. 'They haven't done as much damage in there, but it looks like they poured milk all over the sofa and they've sliced the curtains into shreds.'

She brushed away tears, huddling her arms round herself and beginning to pace up and down from the foot of the stairs to the door and back again.

The opening and shutting of wardrobe doors stopped and Ben called down, 'There's definitely no one up here.'

'Lock the front door, Jonah.' Leah left him to do that and went up the stairs at a run.

Whoever it was had slashed the bed sheets and blankets too, and punctured the pillows, scattering feathers everywhere.

Leah opened the wardrobe door and gasped as the stench showed the person had urinated all over their clothes.

She shivered. 'Who could have hated us so much?'

Jonah, who had followed her slowly up, looked round with a grim expression on his face. 'Only one person that I can think of: Thad Hutton.'

On the other side of the landing, Ben paused at the door of Rosa's room before going in to comfort the sobbing child.

'They spoiled my s-school uniform and they t-tore up my b-books. It's a good thing I took my Christmas book to show Auntie Hilda.'

Leah came to join them. 'Let's go downstairs and see if we have enough left to make a pot of tea.'

But the tea leaves had been scattered all over the floor and some of the stock she'd made for soup had been poured into the sugar tin.

'Ben, will you go and see if Mrs Buckley is still up and will sell us some tea, sugar and condensed milk. Wake her if necessary. She won't mind when you tell her why.' Leah could hear how tight and unnatural her voice sounded, but at least she was managing not to cry, well, but for a few tears. 'I'd better start clearing up, I suppose.'

Jonah looked round. 'Not till the police have seen it. I'm going to drive into Birch End and fetch Constable Burns right away. I'll call in to see Mrs Buckley and ask her to send up a few groceries, but Ben must stay with you ladies in the house. All right, Ben?'

'Yes, of course.'

'Lock up after me.'

Mrs Buckley sent her neighbour's two hefty sons up to Spring Cottage with a box of essentials and her very best wishes. They gawked at the damage from the doorway, then went back to spread the news.

Jonah returned half an hour later with the policeman from Birch End in the car.

Constable Burns walked round the house looking shocked rigid. 'I've never seen the like,' he muttered a few times.

After he'd looked at all the rooms from the doorways, he said, 'This is too serious for me to deal with. I'll have to fetch Sergeant Deemer.' He turned to Jonah. 'Can you drive me into Rivenshaw, Mr Willcox? I know you're tired but he'll want to deal with this straight away.'

Jonah was indeed looking exhausted and Leah was about to say he was too tired. She didn't feel confident enough to drive there herself, though she would have done in an emergency, so she was relieved when Ben said, 'I could drive the constable, if you like.'

She looked at her husband, ready to argue, but he nodded at Ben and said in a whisper of a voice, 'Thank you.'

'I think we should stop in the village on our way through and find someone to come up here and keep guard,' the constable said. 'Wasn't Daniel Pollard going to work for you? He'd come for a few shillings and he's a strong chap. He'd be good in a fight.'

'I don't want to spoil his Christmas.'

'Not much of a Christmas when you're on the dole, sir. If you pay him a few shillings, he'll come running. Shall I send him up to help you, Mr Willcox?'

'Yes. Please do. I'll pay whatever he thinks fair.'

When the others had gone, Leah cleared a chair, dropping the mess on it to the floor with a shudder and wiping it with a dampened cloth. She made Jonah sit down and rest.

'Sorry . . . to be . . . such a crock.'

'You did more today than I'd have expected, so actually, I think you're improving in health.'

He froze, hand halfway towards hers. 'Do you really? Well, I hope you're right. I'm sorry you've had to face this, Leah.

It *must* be Thad Hutton. I can't think of anyone else who'd have any reason, though why he'd blame us for what he did wrong is more than I understand.' He took her hand and held it in both of his for a moment.

'It's all my fault,' Rosa said. 'I should have waited for Mr Carpenter to drive me home.'

'Of course it isn't your fault. Criminals sometimes try to blame other people for what they do, but it's they who decide to commit a crime, not the people they hurt. I hope the police catch Hutton and shut him away till he's too old and feeble to do more than hobble along the street.' He reached out again for Leah's hand and sat holding it.

Rosa watched them, smiling now. 'I like the way you two are kind to one another, even when things have gone wrong. As soon as the police have seen this, I'll help you clear up, Leah.'

'Thank you, darling.'

Daniel from the village arrived ten minutes later, a bit breathless from having got out of bed and hurried to dress and rush up the hill, but clearly delighted to earn a few extra shillings. He was indeed a strong fellow, which was why Ben had chosen him. He wasn't tall, but was sturdily built, though like many of the young men who had no work, indeed, like Ben himself, he was too thin and had a hungry look to him.

Leah showed him the damage and he grew angry, not only because someone had broken in but because they'd wasted so much good food when others were going short.

'Ought to be thrown down a pit and left to starve, whoever did this ought,' he said a few times as Leah showed him round. 'Just let me get my hands on him. I'll give him what for.'

When they got back to the kitchen, he said, 'I think I'll patrol outside, Mrs Willcox. We used to play at hiding in the shadows when I was a lad. I haven't forgot how to do it.'

The three of them sat inside and waited for the police. Sergeant Deemer was so highly respected in the area that Leah was praying *he* would come out in person not send another constable.

To her relief, he did. Not only Sergeant Deemer, but also Charlie, who had seen Ben driving his brother's car and run to find out why, worried that Jonah might be ill.

He'd arranged for the taxi to come for him later but the fact that he'd come at once went a long way towards making Leah forgive him for abandoning his brother at Christmas.

When the sergeant had examined everything and taken careful notes, he said, 'Can't do anything now till daylight. Don't touch anything outside till I've checked it, but you can clear up inside. If you're anything like my missus, you'll be fretting to clean up.'

'Do it in the morning,' Jonah said.

'I couldn't sleep, knowing it was in such a mess. I know you're exhausted, so you must go to bed. No, love, I insist. Rosa, will you check that there's enough clean bedding and help Jonah with it? I'll just see Charlie out. His taxi should be here any minute.'

He hesitated.

'In the morning you just tell me and Daniel what to do and we'll do it,' Ben said.

Jonah went upstairs and lay in bed with tears trickling down his cheeks, ashamed of his own weakness but helpless to do anything else after such an exhausting day.

Charlie spoke in a low voice. 'I'm sorry you're faced with this mess.'

She shrugged.

'And I want to apologise for not putting my foot down about Christmas. Next year we'll definitely get together.'

He stood by the door, looking round, eyes narrowed in

thought. 'We must take advantage of this new council scheme to encourage electricity. Life would be so much easier if you had it up here. People are being encouraged to put in electricity all over England now. And you need a phone as well. I think I'll talk to one or two people at the council and push them to get the phones out to Ellindale.'

'I've never had electricity in a house but I've envied those who did. Electric lights are so clear and bright. I don't have anyone to make telephone calls to, though, even if we do have a phone put in.'

'There's the doctor, for one. Lives are being saved every day because people can phone for a doctor in emergencies.' She knew he was thinking of his brother.

The taxi arrived just then, but he didn't get into it straight away. 'We both know that Jonah will never be a well man. He's managed to avoid pneumonia all except that one time, but it's even more of a killer for men who've been gassed than it is for other people. So if he ever gets it you'll need to call in the doctor straight away and get Jonah into hospital.'

'I'll always look after him, you know I will. But that's definitely the best reason of all for getting the telephone.'

She didn't want to lose Jonah. He was more a friend than a lover. It was no wonder they hadn't managed to start a family because he didn't play around in bed very often, but oh, he was such a dear kind friend.

Charlie nodded to her. 'I know you look after him. I've never seen him as happy.'

She wondered sometimes if Charlie was happy in his marriage. Or even if he wanted to be. His first love seemed to be making money. Perhaps that was enough for him. It'd never be enough for her.

12

Leah woke with a start, hearing voices below, which was strange because the house was usually quiet when she awoke. She couldn't think why she felt so muzzy-headed, then she remembered what had happened and jerked upright in bed.

The room was still in chaos but they'd cleared the stinking clothes out of the wardrobe at least. She only had a few bits and pieces of clothing left now, and Jonah was in the same state.

He must have got up very quietly. He should have woken her because there was so much to do. She hadn't gone to bed after Charlie left but had cleared up until utter exhaustion overcame her.

Daniel and Ben had helped her, then Daniel had volunteered to keep watch in the kitchen during the rest of the night.

'I might doze, Mrs Willcox, but I'm a very light sleeper and if I pull a chair behind the door, no one will get in without waking me.'

'I'll doze a bit, too,' Ben said. 'But I'll wake if I hear any unusual sounds near the old barn.'

'Thank you. You've both been very helpful.'

Their presence had enabled her to sleep soundly, but now she got up, had a quick wash and flung on the clothes she'd been wearing on Christmas Day. She wasn't quite sure what other clothes were left, but these were at least untainted.

Rosa came to her bedroom door. 'I'm just finishing going through my clothes, then I'll come downstairs to help there. I'm going to wear yesterday's clothes. Thank goodness he didn't treat mine like he treated yours.'

'Throw anything that he might have dirtied out, including things you're not sure about.'

Her sister shuddered. 'Don't worry. I will.'

Downstairs she found Mrs Dutton scrubbing the floor with her usual vigour.

Leah stared in surprise. 'It isn't your day to come here.'

'Sergeant Deemer stopped at the pub on his way back to Rivenshaw and told those who were still up what had happened, and they knocked on doors and spread the word. The sergeant asked them to yell for help if they heard anyone creeping around.'

'But that still doesn't explain what you're doing here today.'

'I'm helping you get cleaned up again and I won't take any payment for it, either. We stick together here in Ellindale and you're one of us now. I know I'd want to scrub my place from top to bottom if anyone broke in and did this.' She gestured with one wet hand.

There was a sound from the best room and she looked at Mrs Dutton for an explanation.

'Mrs Hayden from next door to me is working on your best room. It wasn't as badly messed up as this one, but he still did some damage. And Nancy Buckley's sent you some extra cleaning materials, no charge.'

Tears came into Leah's eyes. 'Oh, how kind of you all.' She went across to hug Mrs Dutton, something she'd never dared do before, and got a quick, shy hug in return.

Jonah had been watching from the kitchen range. 'I've poured you a cup of tea, Leah, then everyone can have breakfast with us. We've enough clean food to go round, thanks to Mrs Buckley. No, I insist you join us too, Mrs

Dutton, and your neighbour. No one can work as hard as you have on an empty stomach. We can buy more food later today.'

He turned back to his wife. 'Daniel's wife is going through all the things we're throwing out to see if she can use any of them. And Ben says he'll need some rags when he starts the building work. Mary says even if bedding is ripped, she may be able to sew bits and pieces together to make blankets and she'll be happy to take the clothes the burglar messed up and give them a good wash if you don't want them, because her family can certainly use them.'

'I definitely don't want them. I couldn't bear to wear those clothes again.' Leah shuddered at the memory of how bad the inside of the wardrobe and its contents had smelled. 'I know it's extravagant, and they could be washed, but I just can't put them on my body. I'd keep imagining I could smell them.'

'Then don't. Daniel and his family have been through some hard times and they've got growing children to clothe.'

Leah leaned against her husband for a moment's comfort.

'It's an ill wind . . . ' he said quietly.

There was the sound of a car drawing up outside and Jonah turned his head to look out of the window. 'Charlie's here. There's a woman with him.'

'It can't be Marion!'

He chuckled. 'No. I can't imagine her ladyship getting her hands dirty. Ah, it's Vi. They're pulling bags of stuff out of the boot.' He went to throw the front door open and greet the new arrivals. 'Welcome! Be careful where you tread. We have a team of people working here.'

Charlie came and clapped him on the shoulder then peered into the house. 'Someone's been working hard.'

'Our neighbours. And they won't take money for helping us,' Jonah said in a low voice. 'Isn't that kind of them?'

As the two men moved to the door, Mrs Dutton pointed a finger at them. '*Don't move!* You can't walk on some parts of the room till they're dry. And they won't get dry if you let my nice warm air out, either. Just a minute.' She bent to peer across the flagstone floor. 'If you go straight to the fireplace from the door, it's dry all the way. Don't move from in front of it till I give you the word.'

'Yes, ma'am.' Grinning, Charlie gave her a mock salute and tiptoed across to stand warming his hands.

Mrs Dutton smiled at Vi, who was shutting the door again. 'We don't often see you up at this end of Ellindale, love.'

'We don't often get emergencies like this, do we?'

Mrs Dutton's smile faded. 'I hope they catch the rascal who did it. Did you see the pile of things we've had to throw away as you walked to the door? Daniel's wife is going through them. She's desperate for clothes.'

Vi gave Leah a sympathetic look. 'Someone certainly went to town on your house, Mrs Willcox. Anyway, we've brought you some new bedding and some clothing. Luckily I know your sizes from last time.'

She plonked two loaves wrapped in white butcher's paper on the table. 'The baker had some bread left. It's not fresh, because today's first baking has all gone, but it'll make good toast.' She added a bowl of eggs. 'From my own hens.'

Leah nodded, not daring to speak or she'd have sobbed. Such kindness eased something in her heart after the destruction that an unkind person had wrought to both her home and her feelings.

Jonah put his arm round her shoulders. She could see that he too was beyond words.

'Marion sends her commiserations,' Charlie said.

But Leah couldn't help noticing, and she was sure the others did too, that he didn't bring anything from his wife. She saw Vi and Mrs Dutton exchange knowing glances.

Charlie scowled at that but said nothing.

Leah had thought she was strong, could deal with bad situations, but tears came into her eyes whenever she tried to talk about what had happened. There was something particularly horrible about a person coming right into your home and damaging your most intimate possessions, even your underwear.

And there was something particularly moving about neighbours helping out, which brought more tears.

Once the rest of the kitchen floor was dry, Mrs Dutton and Vi got together to organise food, giving Rosa the job of spearing the bread on a toasting fork and holding it in front of the open fire.

She watched the girl for a moment, then said, 'Make the handle a bit longer, love. It pulls out.'

'I forgot. I'm tired and dopey this morning.'

'I'm not surprised.'

When the food was ready, Charlie asked, 'Shall I take something out to Ben and Daniel?'

'No, they're joining us in here,' Leah said. 'They've been real troupers about helping us.'

Soon everyone was crammed around the table while the two women served breakfast.

'Daniel will be staying here for a while to make sure no more intruders get in,' Jonah told his brother.

'Good.' Charlie took another piece of toast, buttering it lavishly while Rosa stood by the fire with the last slice of the loaf on her long wire fork.

'You're going to need some more bread later,' Vi said abruptly.

'There'll be bread at the village shop,' Leah said. 'Or I can make some pancakes, thanks to your eggs.'

'What about your tea tonight? You'll need more than bread for that, with menfolk to feed. Nancy Buckley said to tell you to come down to her shop and get some tins or what-ever else you need.' Mrs Dutton chuckled and added, 'She says hang Sunday closing laws! This is an emergency.'

That made everyone smile briefly.

'Marion and I will be providing tea,' Charlie said. 'If you two and Rosa come to the Green Man Hotel, we'll all eat there. Robert will collect you in his taxi and take you back afterwards. You're looking a bit too tired to do the driving, Jonah lad, and no wonder.'

His brother sighed, but didn't protest.

'I can drive you there and back,' Ben offered. 'No need to pay a taxi. Daniel will keep an eye on things here while I'm gone.'

'I'll call my brother in, just in case,' Daniel volunteered.

'Ben can come and eat with me while he's waiting,' Vi said at once. 'It won't be fancy but I'll make something that will stick to your ribs, Ben. Mr Willcox will tell you what time to pick them up again from the hotel.'

'Thank you, Miss—'

'Mrs Cobham. I'm a widow. Number Eleven Porter Road. And I prefer people to call me Vi.'

He nodded and repeated, 'Thank you, then, Vi. I'm grateful.'

Before he left, Charlie said, 'This break-in is a bad busi-ness. Does Sergeant Deemer think it's Hutton? And, more to the point, can he catch the fellow?'

'He thinks if it's Hutton he'll have left the district again, but I'm not so sure,' Jonah said. 'The sergeant is going to get the constable to check the Huttons' farm regularly to see if anyone is using it.'

'Until the fellow who broke in is caught, you're going to need protection for yourselves and the house.' Charlie looked round. 'It's a pity there's no one living closer. I'd better hire someone to stay here if you can find him sleeping space in the barn.'

'I've already got someone sleeping there: Ben. He's going to repair the old barn for me and he'll hear if anyone starts prowling around. Daniel's happy to stay with us at night as well till we're sure the burglar's been caught.'

There was the sound of a car horn outside; the taxi had arrived to collect Charlie.

'I'll see you at teatime. I'll book a table at the hotel for five o'clock. Marion says only common people eat that early, but I get hungry and you won't want to stay out late, so she'll have to put up with it for once.'

When Charlie had left, Ben went out to the old barn and Daniel went home for a rest, taking his first five shillings' pay to gladden his wife's heart.

Leah went to examine the bundles Charlie and Vi had brought. 'Wasn't that thoughtful? I need to sort through these and put them away. I like this blouse, oh, and this skirt, too.' She tried to prevent herself from yawning, but failed.

Jonah caught hold of her hand and pulled her down on the sofa next to him. 'Finish that later. Let's just rest quietly for half an hour. I'm tired too. I'm not used to all this to-ing and fro-ing.'

'Can I go and read in my room?' Rosa asked. 'At least I still have my Christmas book. I don't know what the library is going to say about the damage to their books. I hope they don't stop me borrowing other books.' She stretched and wiggled her shoulders. 'Actually, I might have a little nap. I'm still tired.'

When she'd gone, Jonah said, 'Mrs Dutton is desperately short of money but she wouldn't take a penny for her help today.'

'I know. We have to do something for them. What the people in the village really need is a way of earning a living. I'd start up a proper business if I could. But what? The Youth Hostel will only provide occasional work.'

He yawned and that made her do it too.

'I'm too tired to think straight at the moment, Leah. I think I'll follow Rosa's example and go upstairs for a nap. You should have a rest, too, or you'll never last the evening. What time did you come to bed last night?'

'About two o'clock in the morning.'

'You didn't wake me.'

'No. You were sleeping peacefully.'

'I don't often get nightmares since we married.'

'That's good. I'll just tell Ben we're having a nap, then I'll join you upstairs. Now that things have quietened down, the lack of sleep has hit me. Set the alarm clock for four, will you? It wouldn't do to be late for anything where Marion's involved.'

'I think that meal is Charlie's way of making up for his wife ignoring us at Christmas.'

'And not offering any help today.'

'She's a spoiled brat. I don't know how he could marry a woman like that. I couldn't live with her for one day, let alone pander to her selfishness time after time.'

'Well, I'll put up with her happily this evening because I'm glad not to have to cook.' Leah pushed him towards the stairs. 'Go on. I'll be up in a minute.'

That afternoon a shabby old Austin 7 drew up at the rear of Nancy Buckley's shop, as it sometimes did. No one in the village ever mentioned it to outsiders because she'd asked them to keep it quiet.

She looked out of the window to see who it was and immediately put the kettle on because Adam Harris liked his cups of tea. Usually she put a red card in the window so that Mrs Greenhalgh next door would pop in and mind the shop while she entertained her guest, so she did that quickly.

Eh, the poor chap looked even more tired and upset than usual today. What had that wife of his been doing now? She'd drive him to an early grave, she would, and dance at the funeral too.

You had to wonder why he kept that old rattletrap of a car. Was it because *she* didn't want him to spend money on a new vehicle or was he fond of it, as he claimed, and liked to drive it himself? If he did buy a new, bigger car, he'd have to pay a higher yearly engine tax, but surely he wasn't short of money now? He'd done a good job of reorganising the laundry to make up for his father's poor management.

Mind you, the new system of taxing cars had caused a lot of anger among the wealthier motorists who had bigger cars and had to pay a higher engine tax. Robert in the village was annoyed about it too, since he used his car as a taxi to make his living, not for riding around in luxury. He'd had to put up his fares to cover the new tax.

She just wished she had a car, any sort of car. It'd be so useful. But she didn't know how to drive, and even if she did, she'd never be able to afford even the cheapest one, so that was a silly dream.

As she opened the back door, Adam dredged up a tired smile. 'Happy Christmas, Nancy, even if I am a bit late wishing you well.'

'You don't look as if you've had a good one.' She never minced her words or pretended with him.

'No. This is for you and have you got a cup of tea for a tired old chap?' He handed her a box of chocolates, the sort she didn't sell in her shop because who in the village would buy such an expensive item?

'Thank you. They're my favourites. I shall eat one a day to make them last. I've always got tea for you, Adam, after what you did for my Stanley when they sent him back from the war to die.'

'I grew up with both of you. It was the least I could do to help.'

'And as for old, you're the same age as me and I don't reckon thirty-six is old!'

'I'm a bit older, turned thirty-seven in November, and I feel ancient today.' He caught sight of the bottle of ginger beer standing on her sideboard. 'Is that what I think it is?'

'Ginger beer. I was given it for a Christmas present but there's too much for one person to drink so I've been waiting to share it with a friend.'

'It looks home-made.'

She saw him lick his lips without realising it and hid a smile. 'How about we share it now? It'll remind us of when my mother used to make it for a Christmas treat, won't it? Sit down while I find two of her best glasses. We may as well drink it in style.'

She got out two prettily engraved glasses, polished them carefully, then opened the bottle with a satisfactory pop and poured them each a drink.

They clinked glasses.

'To old times and old friends,' he said.

'To old friends and new ones too. It was a new one who gave the ginger beer to me, Leah Willcox.'

'Did she make it herself?'

'Yes, she did.'

'I remember now, her mother used to make it.'

They sipped, savoured the fizzy liquid, and sipped again with happy little murmurs.

'This is excellent, Nancy. Some of the best I've ever tasted. As good as your mother's, I do believe.'

Both were taken back to their childhoods by this simple act and sat lost in their memories for a few moments.

Then he set down his empty glass and said thoughtfully, 'If Leah could make this regularly, you could sell it in your shop and then you could both make a profit.'

'Who's got the money to buy fancy drinks in times like these? And she doesn't need the money. I think Jonah Willcox is very comfortably off. They never stint on what they buy from me.'

'Still, she might enjoy making it. Some of the hikers would buy it and I'd buy a dozen bottles at a time. I don't drink alcoholic beverages, as you know – I leave that to my wife – but I'd drink this happily. Perhaps Ethel would drink less gin if we had some ginger beer in the house. And maybe that would improve her temper.'

And maybe not, Nancy thought. Ethel Harris would still be a nasty bitch even if she stopped drinking so heavily in the evenings. Well, look at the scar on the poor man's forehead from her last violent attack.

Just out of curiosity, she asked, 'How much do you think people would pay for a really good ginger beer?'

'Double what the cheap stuff costs, though it'd need a pretty label on the bottle so that it looks as special as it tastes.'

'Really?' She stared down at the bottle, undid the flip top and poured them another glass each. 'Then we'd better not let it go flat if it's so valuable. It never tastes as nice the second day.'

'It wouldn't hurt to ask Leah if she'd be prepared to make some for me, a dozen bottles every month, say, to start off with. I'll pay whatever she thinks right.'

'Jonah Willcox might not like the idea of his wife making ginger beer for sale. But I will see if she's interested because it sounded as if she'd enjoyed making it and I'm always looking for ways to earn a bit more in the shop.'

He leaned back in the armchair, closing his eyes, and soon drifted off to sleep. Nancy nipped the empty glass out of his hand and sat watching him. Did that wife of his know where he went when he left the house after their arguments? *She* only ever went out with someone else driving her, like that horrible rent man of hers. She spent a lot of time with him. People called her Lady Muck behind her back, and she was.

Handsome is as handsome does, Nancy's mother had always said, and she agreed. Look at Leah Turner. She hadn't turned into a snob in spite of coming up in the world.

Nancy sighed. At times like this she missed her Stanley something cruel. Adam and the two of them had been good friends as children, as close as brothers and sisters in spite of the Harrises owning the laundry. And now Stanley was dead and Adam was living a desperately unhappy life.

It was no use expecting a gentle person like him to stand up to a shrew like Ethel, either. He never would.

But sometimes, when things got particularly bad, he had to get away for a few hours and he usually came here. He often fell asleep once he'd calmed down and Nancy liked to sit and look at him and think of the old days.

He was still quite an attractive man – when he wasn't looking frazzled. What a waste, a man like him being married to a woman like her!

When Adam woke he felt refreshed, just as he always did after a visit to Nancy. On his drive home he decided to pull himself together and stand up to Ethel once and for all. His wife had gone too far recently. She was getting worse and he was going to make some changes to his life with her. Or he'd sell up, give her half the money and leave her.

Some might call that running away. He'd call it saving his own sanity. But it'd mean leaving Ellindale too. Could he bring himself to do that?

His wife was waiting for him in the sitting room, dressed in her best, her face plastered with make-up. She looked more like a painted doll than a flesh and blood woman tonight.

'Had a nice time with your mistress?' she sneered by way of a greeting.

'I don't have a mistress. I was visiting an old friend, the widow of a man I played with as a lad.' He always said this. She always ignored it.

'You seem to have forgotten that we have people coming round for a drink tonight.'

'Who?'

'Those new people who moved into the old Culshaw house. The Borton-Smythes. They seem very nice, our class of people. And they must be comfortably off, from the changes they've made to the house.'

'That's because he's a spiv. He made his money in war profiteering and horse racing. He still wins a surprising amount through betting. I wonder how he manages that?'

'Well, *I* like them and I want you to be polite to them.'

'Oh, I can do that quite easily. Unlike you I always try to be polite.' He ignored her gasp of shock at his sharp answer. 'What time are they coming?'

'Seven-thirty, after an early dinner. They're coming for cocktails.'

'Very well. I'll be ready. But I'll stick to lemonade.' He turned to leave.

'Where are you going?'

'To change my clothes.'

When he came down, she was about to pour herself another gin.

'You won't make a good impression on them if you're tiddly when they arrive.'

She glared at him. 'I *never* get tiddly.'

He hadn't dared to say it before but he did now. 'You get tiddly most evenings, unless we go out. Your speech becomes slurred and your eyes go unfocused so that you look as if you're squinting.'

She gaped at him.

'It doesn't matter when we're staying at home, because I no longer care what you look like, but it's well known in the village that you're a secret drinker.'

She opened her mouth and took a deep breath to yell at him when the doorbell rang. As she snapped her mouth shut again, footsteps pattered across the hall, their long-suffering maid going to answer the door and show in the visitors.

Adam took little part in the conversation, but played his part as host, keeping their glasses filled.

'Aren't you joining us in a proper drink, old man?' Borton-Smythe raised his glass and took a gulp.

'I don't drink alcohol. It doesn't agree with me.'

'Really? Poor you! It agrees with me very nicely indeed.' And he proceeded to prove that by drinking several G&Ts, which seemed to be everyone's favourite drink tonight.

When they'd gone, Adam looked across at his wife. She'd held back a little on her drinking but her speech was slurred now and her eyes weren't focusing properly.

No wonder she was so nasty to everyone. She must always be hung over.

'I'm going to bed now,' he said abruptly.

'Just pour me a nightcap before you go up.'

'No. You've had enough. If you insist on drinking more, you can get it yourself.'

The glass came sailing across the room but missed him by a mile.

He left her to it, his mind already on work. He was going to check all the machinery and if anything needed replacing, he was going to get it done. He still felt guilty about Stan Turner's death. If Ethel hadn't persuaded him to wait to spend all that money, poor Stan would still be alive.

Thank goodness Leah had married Jonah Willcox and got herself and her sister away from Birch End. He'd offered her a job in the laundry because it was all he could do to help her, but he knew her father wouldn't have wanted his clever daughter to work there.

Ben drove the family into Birch End and deposited them outside the Green Man Hotel.

Leah listened to his cheerful whistling fade into the distance as he drove off to Vi's house for a meal. What a difference there was in him already! He was still thin, but he looked stronger and had colour back in his cheeks – and hope in his eyes. What a help he'd been after the break-in!

No, she mustn't think of that. They might as well enjoy themselves tonight. Daniel and a friend were keeping watch over Spring Cottage, so there would be no unpleasant surprises when she got back.

Marion was sitting in the hotel lounge, drumming her fingers on the arm of her chair and looking bored. Charlie was standing in front of the fireplace, enjoying the warmth as he often did. It seemed to be his favourite place to stand.

'Ah, there you are!' He came across to greet them. 'Why don't you sit down and have a drink? I'll let them know that we'll want to eat in quarter of an hour or so.'

His wife sighed heavily and he winked at his brother.

'Glass of wine, Leah?'

'No, thank you, Charlie. A glass of lemonade would be nice, though. I love fizzy drinks.' Actually she wanted to taste it carefully, to see what other people produced, in case she decided to make lemonade as well as ginger beer one day.

'Beer, Jonah?'

'I'd rather have a white wine, if that's possible.'

'Anything is possible,' Charlie joked.

They sat and sipped their drinks, then Marion asked a few questions about how they were managing. She sipped her usual dry sherry so delicately Leah wondered if she'd even finish the drink tonight.

As the conversation flagged, Marion told them that she'd bought the sheet music for her favourite songs, 'Honeysuckle Rose' and 'Ain't Misbehavin'', and was learning to play them on the piano.

Leah had heard of them, but had never had the time to care about such things. It must be nice to be able to play the piano, she thought wistfully.

She nodded and agreed to most of the things people talked about, but it was a relief to go into the dining room and talk about something more relevant to her life.

They were placed at the families' side of the room. Rosa was very quiet, but Leah could see that her sister was staring round, taking it all in.

The food was excellent and Leah suddenly realised she'd eaten hardly anything since yesterday. No wonder she was hungry. Rosa was making a hearty meal of it too, but Jonah, who never ate a lot, was merely picking at the food in front of him. She nudged him and whispered, 'Don't waste good food. You need to feed yourself to keep well.'

He smiled at her and whispered back, 'Yes, mama!'

Charlie was watching them approvingly. He might have brought them together, Leah thought, but he couldn't take credit for making the marriage a pleasant one. That had to go to Jonah, who was the most considerate person to live with that you could ever wish for.

The meal progressed through brown Windsor soup, roast chicken and potatoes, and apple pie and custard. She did it all justice and ignored the scornful way Marion watched her clear her plate.

She was relieved when it was time for Ben to pick them up, though, because she found it difficult to converse with her sister-in-law, who seemed always to be looking down her nose at her and Rosa.

★   ★   ★

Charlie came out to the car to see them off. 'Next year we'll definitely get together, perhaps on Christmas Eve. Make it a family custom, eh?'

He looked back at the brightly lit hotel, eyes narrowed in thought. 'I've spoken to one or two people at the council, and they're going to work on getting electricity and phones out in Ellindale. I said I would, didn't I?'

'You did. Thank you, Charlie.'

'I do care about my family, you know.' He grinned. 'In my own way.'

She smiled back. He was irrepressible, always bubbling with ideas. Had her husband been like that as a lad?

'Tomorrow we'll draw up a shopping list for your building supplies,' Jonah said as Ben drove them home. 'And the day after we're going into Manchester to buy what we need for the house after the break-in. It's about time we had new furniture anyway, something more comfortable on the back.'

He looked at Rosa. 'And all of us need to buy new clothes. Can you stand doing that, young lady?'

She beamed at him. 'I shall enjoy that very much, thank you, Jonah.'

When they all went up to bed, Leah lay awake for a while, tired though she was. It was strange how things turned out. The burglar, whoever he was, had shown her what lovely people lived in Ellindale.

And that in turn had left her determined to do something to help her neighbours build better lives for themselves. She didn't know what she could do yet, or whether she could succeed, but she was definitely going to try.

Well, she'd turn her attention to that once she'd got the house set to rights again, and them all supplied with new clothes.

13

Before Leah went into the village on the Monday morning, she made a list and found she'd need to buy a lot more groceries than she'd expected. It seemed the burglar hadn't just destroyed things, he'd also stolen some of their food, plus two of her bottles of ginger beer.

The latter theft infuriated her most of all, which was irrational, but there you were. She hadn't brewed the ginger beer for the likes of him and hated to waste her efforts! She hoped it would choke him.

She'd have to report that to Sergeant Deemer. Could it be . . . Was the intruder stocking up a hideaway somewhere in the area? This made it even more likely that it was Thad Hutton. He'd know this part of the moors well. She shuddered. She didn't want him hovering nearby, then returning and creating more havoc.

She left Rosa chatting to Ben as he worked, sure her sister would be safe with him, especially as Jonah was nearby in the kitchen.

When the shopping was done, Mrs Buckley suggested finding a lad to take it all back up to Spring Cottage in a handcart.

'That'd be good. I'll give him a shilling for his trouble.'

'They'll be fighting to do it for that. Sixpence would be enough.'

'Find me a lad who'll give it to his mother and it'll be a shilling.'

Mrs Buckley didn't comment but she gave a nod, as if approving of this.

When a scrawny lad called Bertie was ready to leave with the groceries, Mrs Buckley slipped him a biscuit 'to feed your muscles', which made him beam at her and take a huge bite. Then she asked if Leah could spare her a few minutes.

'Of course.' She turned to Bertie, who was just finishing the biscuit. 'Tell my husband or whoever's there that I'll be back in a few minutes. Take everything into the kitchen at Spring Cottage and unload the bags on to the table. And wipe your feet before you go in.'

She gave him the shilling and watched him put it safely in his inside pocket, then leave with another beaming smile.

'Let's go into the parlour, Mrs Willcox. I'll just get my neighbour in to look after the shop, then we won't be disturbed. You sit on that chair. It's the most comfortable.'

She explained about Mr Harris's offer to buy ginger beer regularly. 'Of course I know you don't need the money, but come the summer, I'll be able to sell some in the shop and even before then, you could sell it to The Shepherd's Rest and perhaps even the pubs in Birch End. It's that good, Mrs Willcox, it really is. Best ginger beer I ever tasted.'

Leah stared at her, mouth open, as the idea sank in and sparked off another idea. There it was! Something that would create a job or two for the village, even if only part-time. 'What a good idea! But I'm going to need some help to do it properly in bigger quantities. Do you think I could find someone from our village to work for me part-time?' Her mind was racing ahead. She could find out how to make other fizzy drinks as well as ginger beer, maybe starting with dandelion and burdock which she loved herself.

'They'd be queuing up for any sniff of a job.'

'I'm going to turn the old barn into a Youth Hostel, so that should give you more customers too. But maybe we

could use one end of the barn for making ginger beer. I'll
have to discuss it with Jonah first, of course, but still, I think
it'd work, don't you?'

'You're a clever woman, Mrs Willcox, if you don't mind
me saying so.'

'Am I? Well, so are you. Look at how you started this
business. And couldn't you call me Leah?'

'If you'll call me Nancy.'

It felt good to have made a friend. Nancy was more than
ten years older than her but it didn't seem to matter, they
got on so well.

On the way home Leah passed the lad who'd delivered her
groceries sauntering down the hill, whistling cheerfully.

She found the sacking shopping bags of food waiting for
her on the table, as she'd requested.

Jonah was sitting in a chair, reading as usual, but he put
his book down when she came in.

She began to unpack the groceries, but was so excited
about the prospect of starting up another little business that
she abandoned them to sit down and tell him all about her
new ideas.

He looked at her as if he'd never seen her before. 'I didn't
realise I'd married an entrepreneur.'

'I don't even know what that is.'

'It's a French word for someone who starts a business and
takes the risks of doing so.'

She felt her excitement and certainty falter. 'Would it be
very risky? I don't want to lose you money.'

He reached out for her hand. 'Every part of life has its
risks. Never hesitate to try something, or at least to see if
it's possible, my darling. After all, we'd not be investing ten
thousand pounds in your business, just a few pounds to get
you started.'

'Oh, you are so kind!' She raised his hand to her cheek for a moment, then became brisk again. 'I can't do it on my own, though. I need your help.'

And then she had another brilliant idea. She could involve him in the work, give him something useful to do. But she didn't tell Jonah about that part of her idea. Instead she just said casually, 'There are so many details I'm going to need to find out about. I wonder how you go about looking into this sort of thing?'

There was a minute or so of silence, during which Leah was almost holding her breath, willing him to volunteer so that he'd think it was his own idea. Finally he said, equally casually, 'I could help you with that, if you like. You know how I love reading and finding things out.'

'Oh, would you? It won't be too much trouble, will it? Only you're so much better with that sort of thing than I am.'

She saw him swallow hard and blink a few times, and knew she'd found an even better reason for starting her fizzy drink business.

'I'd find it interesting, Leah. But we'd need more help with the recipes and ingredients than I could offer, however many books I read. A chemist might be the person to ask. In the past they were the ones who made flavoured drinks for people, you know, cordials and fizzy water and other concoctions.'

'Including ginger beer?'

'Of course. What do you think of dandelion and burdock?'

'Oh, I love that drink! But even though I'd recognise dandelion and burdock plants – who wouldn't? – I have no idea how to make it from them.'

'Precisely. When I was a lad my grandmother used to buy the ingredients from the chemist to make it with, not the grocer's. I used to have a glass when we visited her. You and I could try a chemist.'

'The one in Birch End, you mean?'

'Why not? Keep it all close to home and give our neighbours the chance to earn money. I can go and see whether the library in Rivenshaw has any books on herbal drinks. The librarian is always very helpful when I'm hunting for information.' His grin made him look more boyish than usual. 'I'll pretend it's for me, say it makes me feel better to drink it. I've only got to wheeze once or twice and the librarian will believe me.'

The thought of his poor health clouded her happiness and her expression must have given her worries away.

'Leah, I don't want us ever to pretend about my health.'

She stopped him before he could elaborate. '*Don't talk like that!*'

'I have to. I can't let you be dependent on me. You must learn to depend on yourself and to manage money, too, because I've made a will leaving everything to you. But I promise you, I'll live as long as I possibly can because you make my life so happy.'

He paused, then changed the subject. 'I think starting a fizzy drink business is a very good idea. I shall enjoy helping you, and I needed another interest. There are barely three half days a week of book work in Charlie's office most of the time. My body can't cope with physically active tasks for long, but my mind is just fine.'

'Are you going to tell your brother about our idea?'

He screwed up his mouth, something he did when thinking hard, so she waited again. 'No, I don't think so. He'd try to take over. No, we'll do this ourselves and surprise him.'

'But won't he notice?'

Jonah grinned. 'I'll tell him you've got a new hobby and I'm helping you. He knows you're not going to be like Marion, living to dress prettily and gossip to *the right people*.' He changed his voice to imitate Marion's affected tone and did it so well, they both burst out laughing.

'I'm beginning to think Charlie isn't the only sneaky person in the family.' She tried to look at him severely, but he just chuckled and ruffled her hair.

She put up one hand. 'Don't! I spent ages getting it neat.'

'Ah, but I like your hair better when it isn't neat. Now, there's something else we need to decide. Do you want to go to the New Year dinner at the hotel in Birch End? They put on a fancy show every year and Charlie drags me along for an hour or two.'

'Good heavens, no. Well, not unless *you* want to go.'

'Heaven forbid. It usually bores me to tears, and the men smoke cigars, which makes it hard for me to breathe. But I would like to celebrate our first New Year together in some special way. How about . . .'

'How about what?'

'Throwing a village party at The Shepherd's Rest in Ellindale. We could pay for everyone to have, say, two drinks each, with lemonade for the children, and Matt Baker can play the piano for a sing-song. Much more fun than a starchy party with snooty people.'

It sounded lovely; then she sighed. 'I daren't leave the house. It might be broken into again.'

'I'll organise a roster of men from the village to keep an eye on it. They can do that in pairs and I'll pay them for their trouble. Believe me, they'll be happy to miss a couple of hours of celebrating in return for a few shillings.'

'You're so kind to people.'

'I saw too much death and unhappiness during the war. And now hard times like these have brought unhappiness to many again. You've brought me out of my hermit's cave! Now, I feel more a part of the world and it'll make *me* happy to brighten people's lives in any way I can.'

'That's a lovely thought.'

'You're kind as well, Leah. It's one of the things I like most about you.'

She felt shy of what she wanted to tell him, because she hadn't been brought up to give or receive compliments easily, but he often complimented her, so she took a deep breath and said her piece, 'I . . . um, like a lot of things about you, Jonah. I'm glad I married you.' His smile warmed her heart.

'Let's hope that 1931 will be a better year for everyone. I've come to the conclusion that the government should consider bringing the pound off the gold standard. Some experts think that might make a difference to the country's finances and I agree with them. It's a long time since we've used gold sovereigns for money. We've settled into using banknotes in this modern world, for heaven's sake.'

'It'd be heavy to carry sovereigns around, if you had them, that is.'

'I read recently that there are two million unemployed. They don't have anything much and that's a lot of unhappiness and hardship, Leah. The government should do more for them. They could afford to pay a slightly higher amount of dole to those in the greatest need.'

He was a thinking man, who'd had a good schooling before he went into the Army, and who'd made his life through books when he came home an invalid. Sometimes she had trouble keeping up with him, but she was never embarrassed to admit that she didn't understand something, because he clearly liked to teach her things. He'd made her feel good about seeking knowledge, too.

They were quiet for a while, then he said, 'Let's drive down into Ellindale now and talk to the landlord at The Shepherd's Rest about a village party. He'll be delighted to earn some extra money, I'm sure. It's been hard times for landlords as well as for their customers.'

As he started the car, he chuckled suddenly. 'My brother will throw a fit at me spending money on this sort of party.'

'Let him. Um, are we providing food for them or just drinks?'

'Oh, food as well, definitely. Good hearty fare, not fancy stuff. There will be quite a few hungry people there.'

Don Dewey stared at them in shock. 'You want to throw a party . . . here at The Shepherd's Rest . . . for the whole village?'

'Yes. A real, old-fashioned village party. Would it be all right to hold it here? And can your wife cater for it? I'll pay her well, because it's a lot of extra work.'

'She'd love it. Izzy! Come through here a minute. I've got some good news for you.'

Mrs Dewey came to the door at the back of the small bar. Leah had only seen her in the distance before. She was a scrawny woman with grey hair tied back under a headscarf and a big apron wrapped round her. Her hand went up to her mouth at the sight of them. 'Oh, dear! I must look a right old mess. I was just scrubbing out my kitchen.'

'Doesn't matter what you look like, Izzy. Listen to what Mr Willcox wants to do.'

As she listened, tears came into her eyes. 'What a lovely idea! It'll cheer people up no end, that will. Me and Don are just scraping along these days, but the party will help us get a bit ahead, and that'll cheer *me* up, I can tell you.'

Jonah put his arm round Leah's shoulders and asked Don and Izzy, 'Will you do it, then?'

'Like a shot!'

'And will you please buy as much as you can from the village shop or local farmers,' Leah put in.

'You could get some things cheaper at the markets in Rivenshaw, Mrs Willcox.'

'I know, but Nancy needs the money too.'

'How much do you want to spend?'

'Enough to give everyone in the village a full belly and a couple of drinks,' Jonah said promptly. 'You'll know how much that will take.'

Leah saw her shock and said coaxingly, 'Just plain, hearty food. Can we leave it to you to organise that? I'm sure you won't waste money but we do want people to eat well.'

'I have catered for parties before but not recently. I used to love doing it.' Izzy still seemed to be shocked by it all.

'Once you've worked out what to serve, come and discuss it with me. There isn't much time. We can pay for someone to help you with the catering if you need it.'

'If it's the whole village, I shall definitely need help. Look, I'll start working it out straight away and come up to see you this very afternoon, because Nancy will need to order extra supplies in and there isn't much time before the new year. Oh dear, it'd all be so much easier if someone in the village had a phone.'

'My brother's looking into that,' Jonah told her. 'Charlie doesn't like me being out of touch and he doesn't drive. We're hoping to get a telephone line into the village some time after the new year.'

When they were outside, he said, 'Let's drive down to Birch End and see the chemist while we're out and about. We'll ask him about ingredients and helping us with the fizzy drinks.'

'You don't wait around when you decide to do something, do you, Jonah Willcox?'

'No, I don't.'

The chemist's shop wasn't big. Leah hadn't needed to buy anything from it since her marriage, but she'd come here from time to time on errands for her mother. It hadn't changed over the years. The shop space was about the size of the front room in her family home but seemed smaller because the walls were covered in shelves, right up to the ceiling. Most of them were crammed with neatly arranged small items but there were spaces on the shelves that hadn't been there before, as if Mr Nolan was carrying less stock.

And of course in the shop window were two big bottles containing red and green liquid. They had never changed, not since she first noticed them as a child and admired the pretty colours.

Andrew Nolan had an Irish name and the slightest hint of an Irish accent, presumably picked up from his parents, but he'd been born and bred in Lancashire. Like many others, his parents had immigrated to England for a better life. His father had been the chemist before him and Leah had a vague memory of a balding man with spectacles.

As they went in, Mr Nolan came out from the workroom where he made pills and bottles of medicine with a warm smile on his face. He had looked the same for as long as Leah could remember, not old exactly, but not young either, with sparse grey hair neatly parted in the middle.

'How can I help you, Mr and Mrs Willcox?'

Jonah explained what they were thinking of doing, ending, 'But we need someone with more knowledge of plants and chemicals to work with us. Would you be interested in doing that?'

'I would indeed. But I'm afraid I couldn't invest any money because my wife and I are living partly on our savings.'

'On the contrary, we'd pay you for your expertise.'

'Pay me! Now that's got a fine sound to it.'

'But we'd expect you to keep the details of our methods and recipes secret, especially now, when we're just planning things.'

'Where will you be making these beverages?'

'We have an old barn which we're having renovated.'

'I've seen it when out walking. It could be a handsome place but it's been neglected. I shall be glad to see it restored. I always feel sad when I see old buildings crumbling. What are you doing about equipment?'

'We haven't even thought of that yet because it's early days.'

'I can help you there, if you like. I have a friend who manufactures and sells equipment for chemists.' He flushed. 'He would pay me a small commission for sending you to him, but I'd still get you better prices than you could find anywhere else, I promise you, and his equipment is excellent. Also, you'd not have to run around hunting for the equipment.' He looked at them anxiously.

'That would be very helpful,' Jonah told him. 'It's my wife's business, so you'd have to deal with her about practicalities.'

Mr Nolan smiled at her. 'Well, that's good, because my wife is the one who does my books and puts in the orders for me. I couldn't run the shop without her.' He pushed the curtain aside from the doorway to the back room. 'Hazel, my dear! Can you come and join us?'

The woman who joined them was younger than her husband and wearing a wrap-around pinafore as many women did during the day to protect their clothes. When he explained what was proposed, her face brightened.

'You're like manna from heaven, Mr and Mrs Willcox. A miracle, even. I'll be frank: I've been wondering how long we could keep the shop going with so little money coming in.' She cast a fond glance at her husband. 'My dear husband is rather a soft touch, you see. He can't bear to send people away empty-handed when they're in urgent need of medicine, and who can blame him, especially when it's children who're ill?'

Mr Nolan flushed and Leah saw his hand grasp his wife's for a moment. She looked from one to the other as she added, 'We'll have to make our ginger beer in much bigger batches, so we'll need bigger containers to ferment it in, bottles, all sorts of things. Perhaps you could obtain a catalogue from the manufacturer and come up to Spring Cottage to discuss what needs ordering once the barn is finished?'

'God bless you both,' Mrs Nolan said quietly. She held out her hand and the two women shook solemnly to seal their bargain.

As they walked away, Leah whispered, 'That felt strange. Women don't usually shake hands with people in that way.'

Jonah whispered back. 'They don't usually set up and run businesses, either. You're very special, my dear, although you're a quiet woman too. You don't shout at the world, you get on with doing your best. I admire that.'

She linked her arm in his and they walked back to the car in happy silence.

14

On New Year's Eve the village party began at five o'clock with a fine hearty meal set out on the bar in the main drinking room. Plates of sandwiches jostled with two huge oblong baking tins of potato pie, fresh from the oven. Bowls of pickled red cabbage were set beside each of them to add a tangy relish to the dish. Cold pork pies were cut into pieces and laid out in patterns, while smaller pasties were piled on plates.

The 'afters' were set out on the back shelf of the bar, a whole crumbly wheel of tasty Lancashire cheese from a local farmer and several big apple pies.

People sighed as they studied this feast, but they'd been told in advance that Izzy would be serving the food *after* the arrival of the Willcoxes, so no one pushed forward or even tried to form a queue, for all that some of their stomachs were growling audibly. Instead, they accepted a glass of hot punch or port and lemon, or a half pint of beer from Don and found themselves places to sit or stand.

When Jonah and Leah came in, followed by Rosa and Ben, they found that one table near the bar had been left free for them. They were met with a rousing round of cheers and applause, and Don brought across a beer for Jonah and smiled at Leah. 'What's your pleasure, Mrs Willcox?'

'Do you have any cider?'

'Only the bottled sort. We don't get enough custom to keep barrels.'

'Then I'd like a glass of cider, please, and my sister would love a glass of lemonade – without the port.'

When Izzy began serving the food, she insisted the benefactors went up to the bar first. Don stayed out of his wife's way to one side of the room, making himself useful by indicating which group was next to get their food. A young woman was helping Izzy. She looked flushed and happy.

More than one person had tears in their eyes as food was heaped on their plate. A woman wept openly as she took her serving back to the table. Don bent to whisper in her ear and she looked at him open-mouthed, then gave him a watery smile.

Leah had suggested making extra to give to the poorer families and guessed this was what he'd told her.

No one minded eating from plates balanced on their knees or sitting on windowsills, or even standing in the corner and managing with one hand.

Two younger men were served first after the Willcox group, so that they could relieve those keeping watch at Spring Cottage. Ben went across to whisper instructions to them and also took an early plate of food.

As usual, the three old spinsters who lived in Moor Cottage had taken over the tiny snug at the side of the building, which was the only other drinking space in the pub. It was more a large alcove than a room and was usually kept for women, but tonight the three sisters didn't glare at the men who came to join them. Indeed, the older one who was sitting at the outer end elbowed the sister beside her. ''Utch up a bit, our Annie. We can squeeze a few more in here.'

The next old lady obligingly 'utched up', sliding along the circular bench to make room for some more older men and women.

All the children were behaving impeccably, because no one wanted to be sent home and miss the feast.

When the plates were scraped clean, they were taken away to be washed then brought out again for the afters. Big slices of apple pie were served with wedges of 'sharp', crumbly Lancashire cheese and more bread and butter if wanted.

'It's a right old feast, this,' one man said. 'I haven't seen the like of it in years.'

'That'll line my kids' bellies for once,' a woman commented, her voice thickened by emotion. 'I just hope they don't make themselves sick.' She leaned across to clout one lad on the ear. 'What did I tell you, our Brian? Eat slowly or I'll take it away from you.'

When the plates were once again cleared away, a big teapot was brought out and those who wanted more beer or port or cider had to say whether they'd had two drinks already or not.

One man opened his mouth to claim he still had a drink owing, but his wife looked at him warningly and instead he said meekly, 'I'll buy a half of beer now, if that's all right, Don.'

When everyone had something to drink, the oldest man present was helped to his feet and Don banged for everyone's attention. Simeon then thanked Mr and Mrs Willcox on behalf of the whole village. 'We's getten our bellies filled tonight, sir and missus, and right good food it was, too. We thank you with all our hearts.'

More cheering greeted this, then people settled down to chat happily.

It wasn't till Jonah and his family were getting ready to leave that Ben took him aside.

'Hutton tried to break into your house tonight.'

'*What?*'

Ben gave a grim smile. 'He didn't succeed. Peter Toddy has a bit of a bruise, but he reckons he got in a good punch or two. They chased Hutton off and yelled at him to stay away. He stopped and yelled that he'd be back, so Peter shouted that if he did return, the whole village would go out on the hunt for him and they'd search the moors till they found him. He told me Hutton would probably be camping out in Blacklea Dell, so maybe we can suggest Sergeant Deemer has it checked. There's a sort of a cave there.'

'I'll definitely speak to the sergeant. What I can't understand is why Hutton is going on with this . . . this vendetta.'

'Because he's got a warped mind, that's why. If he tries to hurt any more little lasses from the village, he'll find himself missing a useful part of his body. The men are furious with him. But there's no doubt now that he has it in for you, so you'd better be careful till he's caught. It might be best to get hold of a gun.'

'I don't like guns.'

'No sane person does, unless they're hunting for food or being attacked by an enemy. But you need to be able to protect your family. I can ask around, see if someone's got a gun left over from the war that they could lend you. There are quite a few "souvenirs" still around.'

'No. No, don't do that. You're right that we need to protect ourselves and I have no problem with using a gun to *defend* my family. I'll get my brother to find me one and I'll teach Leah and Rosa how to use it, as well.'

'Good. I thought I'd have to work harder to persuade you. I know how to use a gun, too, Mr Willcox. If you can lend me one, I'll keep it safe and can watch your back. Sorry to spoil your evening with this news.'

'It didn't spoil the party.'

'No. Everyone looked very happy, didn't they?'

'They did indeed.' Jonah thought for a moment then added, 'I'll hire extra men to stay on guard tonight.'

'You don't need to. They've already volunteered. And they won't want paying, either.'

'I can't ask them to work for free. Not when they're so short of money.'

'Tonight you should accept their gift, if you don't mind me saying so. It'll be better for their self-respect if they can pay you back for the party. Tomorrow you can start giving them jobs again.'

'You're very wise for a man so young.'

'I've had some sharp lessons in life this past year. Very sharp. And it was you who got me back on track again. So you can always count on me. Always.'

Once the Willcoxes had gone home, the piano was opened and a sing-song began. People were less inhibited now that Jonah and his family had left.

The pianist knew all the old songs from the Great War and didn't need music to play from, so they all had a hearty sing. One or two people who had particularly good voices were persuaded to perform solos from time to time, and there was much tapping of feet and patting of knees to the rhythm.

When midnight came, the landlord counted down the last few seconds from his big parlour clock and led a loud greeting to 1931.

Everyone wished each other a better year and then began taking their glasses back to the bar and collecting their smaller children from wherever they'd found a place to lie down and sleep.

Don and Izzy came out with bowls and gave them to some of the poorest families.

'We don't need any more charity tonight,' one father of seven growled.

'It's not charity. Mrs Willcox ordered so much food, there's a good bit left. We're keeping some, but there's too much for my family and the rest will go bad if we can't find people to eat it. But I'd be grateful if you'd wash my bowl before you bring it back. Save me the trouble.'

The man's wife tugged at his arm and looked at him pleadingly. With an angry mutter, he took the bowl and carried it home, while she concealed under her shawl the loaf that had been thrust into her hand as well.

Don looked at the small group of his personal friends who were left. 'One more for the road?' he asked. 'This one's on me.' It had been a long time since he'd been able to offer that to his friends.

They nodded and sat down again.

'It's good that Mester Willcox moved to Ellindale, isn't it?' one man said. 'Good for the village, I mean.'

'Aye, it is that.' Don lifted his glass. 'But it's even better that he got married to such a sensible woman. Here's to the Mester and his wife. She might be quiet but she's a canny lass, that one.'

'Here's health and happiness to them both!'

As Jonah and Leah lay in bed, because they were both too tired to stay up until midnight, she said abruptly, 'I heard what Ben said to you.'

'Ah. I was going to tell you in the morning.'

'There's always a fly in the ointment, isn't there?'

'We'll catch this particular fly before we're through. And forewarned is forearmed.'

'Let's not talk about that horrible man, Jonah. Let's think about our future instead. What do you want from 1931?'

'More happy times with you, my love. And success to our little venture.' He pulled her close with a happy murmur and for once he loved her as a husband should. From what she'd heard, most men liked their bed play more often than Jonah did.

Afterwards, he fell asleep quickly, but Leah stayed awake

for a while, praying with all her might that this time they'd conceived a child.

It was the only thing lacking now. Why she was worrying when they'd only been married for a few months, she didn't know. But she felt impatient for a baby in her arms, his baby, to make them into a proper family.

She needed to do that while she still had him, she thought, then got angry at herself. She was starting to think like him.

She wouldn't let herself do that, look on the dark side. Her father had always said you should look on the bright side and then it was more likely to come true.

PART TWO

1931

15

As soon as he heard that Hutton might be hiding nearby, Sergeant Deemer led a search party to Blacklea Dell. He didn't take any risks with such a dangerous criminal and was accompanied by a constable and two sturdy farm labourers.

They found signs that someone had been living in the narrow slit of a cave, with old planks laid to sleep on, candle wax drippings on a protruding spur of rock and a small hearth full of ashes and one half-burned twig. But whoever it was must have moved on.

Deemer was puzzled by a pile of smashed glass near the entrance – bottles, it looked like. He put the top part of one bottle in a brown paper bag and carried it back in to show to Jonah. 'See. They were flip-top bottles, like the ones your wife uses for her ginger beer. Not very common, those. I can't understand why he smashed them, just sheer bloody mindedness, I suppose. But he's gone and good riddance to him. I see no reason for him to come back now that we know his hiding place and have destroyed everything in it.'

Ben, who'd been listening, shook his head slowly. 'I don't agree, Sarge. This part of the Pennines is his home territory. From what the men who live round here have told me, his family has lived at that little farm for several generations, making up for the poor living it gave them with a bit of thieving here and there.'

He let that sink in and added, 'Hutton stayed nearby till now, didn't he, even in the depths of winter? He must have foraged in his home for blankets and provisions, something to cook in as well. And he stole more provisions from Spring Cottage. I reckon he'll be back once the weather improves, if only because he doesn't know anywhere else.'

'I agree,' Jonah said. 'Does he have any relatives other than his brothers, someone he might be staying with occasionally?'

The sergeant looked thoughtful. 'I'll look into that when I have a moment. But if you see any signs of trespassers in this area in the meantime, let me know. With only me and two young constables to police the whole valley, we're stretched a bit thin.'

'I'll spread the word,' Ben promised.

Leah banged her pots around the kitchen for a while after she heard about this. It was silly to let such a minor act of destruction upset her, but smashing the bottles seemed to send a message to her particularly: that he'd smash anything she and her family tried to do. At least, that's how she read the gesture. She tried not to let her feelings show to her husband, but the anger wouldn't go away and continued to simmer inside her.

Ruin her things, would he? And that after attacking her little sister. It was the sort of thing that made decent people feel sick to the core. Well, if she got the chance, she'd ruin Hutton. He was a dangerous, violent man who needed locking away before he attacked other children.

When Jonah mentioned the gun she told him she wanted one of her own and the sooner he got hold of guns for all three of them, the better.

'You'll have to teach me how to use it. You're sure you remember how?'

'Oh, yes.' Jonah nodded. 'No one who fought in the Great War will ever forget what they had to do.'

'Mr Dryden taught me to shoot,' Ben said. 'He was in the Great War, too, and he believed every Englishman should learn, in case our country went to war again. He had quite a bee in his bonnet about that. It must have been bad.'

'You can't imagine. And I pray your generation will never find out. The trench warfare was bad enough but when the gas came rolling towards you, you were helpless.' Jonah shuddered and closed his eyes, taking deep breaths till he'd calmed down.

Later Jonah got the car out and drove into Birch End to work in the pawnshop.

Charlie was waiting for his brother. He clapped Jonah on the back. 'Good news. They're extending the telephone lines up the valley to Ellindale, *and* the gas and electricity too. Unfortunately, they consider you to be living outside the village, so if you want them to put them in at Spring Cottage, you'll have to pay extra. You don't need to worry about that, though. I'll see to it.'

'How much extra is it?'

'Twenty pounds.'

'I can afford that.'

'You don't need to. And I won't let you. I'm doing well, Jonah. Consider it a present for all your help here.'

For a moment the two brothers stared at one another, then Jonah gave in, spreading his hands helplessly. Since he managed the account books, he knew how very clever Charlie was at making money, even now, and how much he liked to spend it on his family. If times had been better, he truly believed his brother would have been a millionaire by now. 'Very well, and thank you. I must say, I didn't think they'd bother to bring the services out to the top of the valley yet.'

'The local councils have been given money by the government to employ men who've been out of work for more than six months on jobs that help the community.'

'Ha! That'll mean employing men who won't have been eating well enough to keep up their strength, even if they were manual labourers before. It'll nearly kill the poor sods.'

'Well, we'll feed them up a bit in the early days if we have to. It won't cost much to send up some bread and cheese mid-morning to the ones working on it. I'm not letting anything stop us from getting the telephone out to Ellindale, especially with Hutton still on the loose. I want to be able to pick up a phone and call you if I need something, and I want you to be able to phone for help if . . . well, if bad things happen.'

That was as close as Charlie got, Jonah knew, to expressing the deep love between the two of them and he too had difficulty putting his feelings into words. He just wished Charlie had married a more pleasant woman, then the four of them could have got together socially more often. It wasn't that Marion was unfriendly, exactly, but she seemed to look down her nose at them and he wasn't letting her treat Leah like that.

Charlie nudged him. 'Stop day-dreaming. I said, I've got hold of some guns for you. They're locked in my safe. Let's have a look at them now and you can take your pick. I think you're right. Leah should have her own. You never know.'

'And one for Ben. He's proving very useful around the place, a real hard worker, and he gets on well with people in the village. But I can't help wondering what the hell we fought for when people like Hutton can still threaten violence in England.'

'Violence is always happening somewhere and will continue to pop up as long as there are thieves and criminals trying to take advantage of law-abiding citizens. But we'll keep you and yours safe, whatever it takes.' Then his tone of voice changed. 'And what's this I hear about you two spending time with Andrew Nolan? Is Leah setting up as a chemist now?'

Trust Charlie to have his ear to the ground. 'No. She's going to make ginger beer in bigger quantities for a few people who'll pay her for it.'

'You don't need her to earn such tiny amounts of money!' Charlie protested. 'If you're a bit short, you just have to say and I'll—'

'I'm not short, but Leah needs something to occupy herself with, and other people can make money from what she's doing. We're paying Nolan a small amount, and he's said he'll sell our ginger beer in his shop. Don at The Shepherd's Rest is going to try it out on his customers. Oh, and Adam Harris has offered to take a dozen bottles a month from Nancy Buckley. He doesn't drink alcohol.'

Charlie chuckled. 'He doesn't need to. Everyone knows his wife drinks his share.'

'The poor man doesn't lead a happy life, does he? Anyway, he tried some of Leah's at Christmas and loved it. She has her mother's recipe and the ginger beer is the best I've tasted, I must say.'

'You'll have to give me a few bottles.'

Jonah grinned at him 'You taught me too well for that, Charlie. We'll give you *one* to try, then *sell* you a few bottles if you like it.'

'At ten per cent off the usual price.'

'Five per cent.'

Charlie let out a cackle of laughter. 'All right. Never mind the free bottle, I'll take six when the next batch is ready and see how we go.' His voice softened. 'I found you a good wife, didn't I, my lad? You seem very happy with her and you're more like the old Jonah these days.'

'You did well for me and I'll always be grateful. Leah's good company as well as an excellent housewife. She makes me feel better about everything. I wish I weren't so . . . you know.'

Charlie's smile faded and he nodded. 'I know, lad. Anyway, let's look at these guns. Mind, you're not to say who got them for you.' He opened the safe and took out some cloth bundles, unwrapping them one by one and laying out the guns in a row on his desk.

'If anyone asks, I'll say I bought them from some passing tramps,' Jonah promised.

'Good story. No one can check that, with all the men on the road.'

They spent some time studying the handguns, checking them out as well as they could without firing them.

After a few moments Jonah hefted one of the revolvers, an expression of distaste on his face. 'I used a Webley Mk IV like this one in the war. They were given mostly to the officers, even junior ones like me. I hated using the damned thing, but at least it was reliable. Most of the chaps would rather have had a Luger, though, because the Webley jumps when it's fired.'

'I can't get the ammunition for the Luger as easily,' Charlie admitted.

'I'll take three of the Webleys, then. I'll need plenty of ammunition, because I have to teach Leah to look after a gun as well as how to fire it, and to check that Ben's telling the truth and he does know how to shoot. I might not be around all the time and if Hutton turns up, they should be able to protect themselves.'

His brother sighed. 'You wouldn't need the guns if you didn't live out in the middle of nowhere. Can't I persuade you to move into Birch End?'

'No. We like living in Ellindale. It's home. I can breathe

better out there, and the water's good so Leah can have her business and sell fizzy drinks.'

'You're a stubborn sod.'

'Pot calling the kettle black.'

They punched one another on the shoulder, grinning, then Jonah said, 'Let's go and try out the guns, eh? Somewhere away from the village.'

'I'll call the taxi.'

'No need. I can drive us up on to the moors and the fewer people who know about the guns the better. You really ought to learn to drive, you know.'

'I'd need spectacles to see well enough and I don't want to wear the damned things. They make you look old.'

'Who'd have thought you were so vain?'

'It's not vanity; it's good business to look smart.'

'You can still be smart in glasses.' But he might as well talk to the wall. His brother had his mind firmly set against wearing them.

Jonah drove them to a former quarry on the edge of the moors and tried the pistols out. He was still adept enough to hit the targets. When he'd finished, he put three of the six handguns to one side. 'I'll take these three Webleys. How much do I owe you?'

Charlie looked pained. 'As if I'd charge you. Anyway, I didn't pay for them. I did a bit of swapping.'

'Very well. Thank you. But I will pay for the ammunition.'

'Oh, all right. You'll be careful?'

'Extremely careful. I have a lot to live for these days. And yes, I'll teach Leah and Ben to be careful too.'

As he got into the car, however, Jonah shook his head sadly. 'I never thought I'd be using a gun again.'

Charlie scowled into the distance. 'I never thought I'd have to find some for you. In a small village like Ellindale, of all

places! Well, what are you waiting for? Let's get back. I'm
freezing. I reckon it's going to snow.'

Jonah looked up at the sky. 'You could be right. I'll ask
old Simeon. He's the best at predicting weather of anyone
I know.'

But there was no need to ask, because it began to snow
as Jonah was driving back into Birch End; tiny dry flakes
whipped across the moors by an icy wind, just a few at first,
so that you wondered if it really was snow at all.

During the next two hours, however, there was no doubting
it. The snow got heavier, with bigger flakes that settled and
built up, till everything was coated thinly in white.

'If this goes on, I doubt you'll be going to school tomorrow,'
Jonah told Rosa later as the snow continued.

'I don't mind. It's nice to have a day off now and then.'

'You've only just gone back after the Christmas holidays.'

'That was weeks ago. And if you don't sit near the radi-
ators in our classroom, your fingers get so cold it's hard to
write neatly.'

The next morning they woke to a white world. Everything
outside was still, the usual faint, omnipresent sounds of life,
both animal and human, muffled by the snow.

Ben came across from the barn for breakfast, leaving tracks
in the white next to the faint marks left by birds. He stamped
his feet at the door and banged his jacket with his hands,
but was still shedding snow from his garments as he came
inside.

'We had about six inches overnight, I'd guess,' he told
Leah.

'Were you warm enough?'

'Yes, thanks to your new blankets. But someone turned
up last night. I was just checking that everything was all
right when I saw this old tramp staggering down the path

from the moors. I put him up in the end place, as we'd planned, our first guest there, and lit him a fire. I hope you don't mind me using the extra wood but he smelled too bad to have him in with me.'

'It's what the end part is for, isn't it? It's a good thing you saw him.'

'Yes. Can we feed him and let him stay till the snow clears?'

'Of course.'

'He's far too old to be tramping the roads.' Ben gestured towards the window at the snow which had started again and was piling up at the bottom of each pane of glass. 'Just look at it!'

'Bring him across for breakfast.'

'Um, better not. He can't have washed for a good while.' He pinched his nose and mimed a bad smell.

'Oh. Well I don't have any old clothes but maybe he can wrap himself up in a blanket while I wash his things? They'll soon dry in front of the fire.'

'I doubt he'd thank you. From what I can tell, he's been sewn into that shirt for a while. I asked him why and he said it stops people dragging it off his back and stealing it.'

Leah quickly put a platter of food together, bread topped with a fried egg, more bread, buttered and spread with jam and a big mug of tea.

Ben took it across the yard and went into the end room, finding the tramp awake and toasting himself in front of a good fire. 'Mrs Willcox sent you some food. You can stay till the snow thaws, if you want. I'll bring you some more wood later.'

The old man looked at the food suspiciously. 'Why would she do that?'

'Because she's a kind lady. She took me in too when I was near dead from tramping the roads. Get that food down you while it's still warm.'

The old man sat down at the rough plank table, licking his lips. 'Say thank you for me. She won't want me to go near her.'

'No. But since you're staying for a while, how about telling me your name, at least?'

'Mitch.'

'Is that a first or a second name?'

'First.'

'Got a surname?'

'Yep. But I don't use it if I can help it. I don't get on with most of my family.' He filled his mouth with egg and chewed it quickly, as if afraid of it being taken from him.

'I'd still like to know who I'm talking to.'

This was greeted by a loud sigh. 'Well, I won't lie to someone as has been kind to me, but promise you won't throw me out if I tell you. I'm not like the rest of my family, curse 'em.'

'I won't throw you out.' Ben waited.

'The name's Hutton.'

Ben could feel himself stiffening.

The old man looked at him warily. 'See. Soon as you heard the name, you scowled. Not all the Huttons are bad 'uns, you know. That's why I left Ellindale. The good 'uns usually do leave. I've been on the road for years now, ever since the war ended. I like travelling round. If I were rich I'd get on one of them big liners and travel all the way to America. Always fancied seeing New York.'

'Do you come back here often?'

'No. This is the first time. I didn't mean to come here but I must of took me a wrong turn. It were that cold up on t'moors, I couldn't think straight.'

He waited a moment, then added, 'From the look on your face, my brother's lads are still upsetting folk. How many of them are there now? There were four in all, I do know that. But I think one were killed in t'war, or were it two? No, just the one. Three of 'em left, then, and that's three too many for my liking. I'd as soon they don't find out I'm here.'

'They won't. Two of them are in prison, the other's on the run. Thad, that is.'

'Ah, he's the worst. He was vicious as a child even.' He glanced sideways. 'I suppose you want me to leave now you know?'

'No. We'll give you a chance to show you're not like them.'

His shoulders sagged in relief. 'Thanks. I'm grateful. I'll be off soon as it thaws, though. Don't want to stay round here in case Thad hears and comes after me. We came to blows last time we met. The others had to hold him back to let me get away.'

'Where are you going?'

'Got a sister over Todmorden way. She gives me a bed sometimes in the winter. I try not to outstay my welcome.' He lifted his fork to his mouth again and shovelled in some more food, gulping and snorting.

'Right. Well, enjoy the rest of your meal.'

Ben whistled softly as he made his way back to the house. This time he took off his coat and settled down at the table with the other three to eat breakfast.

'Did he tell you his name this time?' Leah asked.

'Yes. Bit of a surprise. He's a Hutton.'

'*What?*' Jonah put down his knife and fork. 'And you left him there?'

'He says he doesn't get on with them, only came here because he took a wrong turn. He's heading for Todmorden.'

'Do you believe him?'

Ben considered this for a moment, then nodded. 'Yes, I do. I couldn't say why but he just seemed . . . well, genuinely afraid of running into his nephew.'

'I'll come across and meet him myself later,' Jonah said.

Ben shrugged and addressed his food. Life threw some strange things at you. He didn't blame Jonah for being careful.

They began discussing the barn as they finished their meal, a continuing subject of interest. With Ben's advice, Jonah and Leah had decided how best to adapt it, and there were only the details to sort out now.

They'd agreed to divide it into two parts, and now that the outer walls were finished and weatherproof, Ben was working on the interiors.

About two-thirds of the old barn would become the youth hostel, with a bedroom for men on the smaller top level, where hay had once been stored, and a bedroom for women on the ground floor, as well as a living area and kitchen. Each would be supplied with bunk beds.

The idea of these cheap lodging places for young hikers had caught the fancy of both Jonah and Leah, and they were sure it would bring a little extra money to the village shop and perhaps the pub, as well as providing part-time cleaning work for one or two of the village women.

The smaller section of the barn was near to where the spring came out of the hill, and it was here they would make and bottle ginger beer, dandelion and burdock, or any other drink that seemed suitable. They intended to install an underground pipe taking the water to a small storage tank in the barn.

At the rear, near the perimeter wall and linked to the barn by a small passage, were one-storey outhouses which had now been divided into two small dwellings: the two-room cottage where Ben was living and what they were calling the 'doss house', a room where men on the tramp would be allowed to sleep on wooden bunk beds, with a lean-to area for ablutions. The men would be given one night's shelter free of charge, with simple food provided in the evening and morning.

'Do you mind sleeping cheek by jowl with vagrants?' Leah asked.

Ben gave her one of his gentle smiles. 'I don't mind at all. I know what it's like to be on the tramp and I'm happy to help them, Mrs Willcox, truly I am.'

So she went back to planning her manufacturing area with Hazel Nolan, ordering the equipment they'd need, discussing the drinks they'd make – though the ginger beer came first – and where they'd put the big coppers she would be using to brew it. They'd also need to make an area for washing the bottles, and another for filling them and putting them into boxes.

She listed ingredients, consulting Andrew Nolan rather than his wife about what ingredients would be needed and how best to store them.

In his enthusiasm for their project, Jonah insisted they should make several types of fizzy drink. For instance, he'd tasted an unusual one called Coca-Cola at a soda fountain in London a couple of times, and had enjoyed it greatly.

But Leah managed to persuade him that exotic drinks like that wouldn't go down well with her Lancashire customers, and anyway, they should start small.

After some spirited discussions, she got her way about limiting what they made to just the two drinks to begin with: ginger beer, and dandelion and burdock.

She'd been shopping in Rivenshaw enough times to see how popular Schweppes' mineral waters were with those who could afford them, and realised that her little business couldn't compete with big companies like them. So she was going to offer something a bit different, something special, and she only expected to sell it locally.

While they were still in the planning stage, Jonah read his

morning paper one day and cried out in shock. 'No! Not again!'

'What's wrong?'

'There's been another underground explosion at a colliery in Cumberland, with twenty-seven killed. Twenty-seven! There was an explosion in Staffordshire only last October. I think there were fourteen killed then, or was it fifteen?'

'That's terrible. Why can't they make the mines safer? This is the twentieth century, after all.'

'Even when they know ways to make things safer, they don't do it, because it'd cost more money and reduce profits.'

'Better lower profits than costing lives.'

'Some men can only think of money.' He went back to the newspaper, muttering to himself.

She smiled fondly. He always liked to start the day with that newspaper of his, had paid extra to have it delivered early, though the few other people in Ellindale who could afford newspapers picked them up from the shop.

Mitch stayed for three days, mostly sitting quietly by the fire. He couldn't seem to get enough of the warmth.

When Ben found out their guest was able to read, he brought him one of Jonah's old newspapers. But then he had to find a magnifying glass before the old man could read it.

'I had some specs once, but someone stole them. Steal anything, some people will, curse 'em.'

Before he left, Mitch went to the house door to thank Leah and Jonah personally, then turned and tramped off down the hill, walking with a slight limp, as if one hip pained him.

'Funny old world, isn't it?' Leah said. 'I never thought we'd be sheltering a Hutton.'

'Ben doesn't reckon he's a bad chap. Too old to cause

trouble anyway. It's all he can do to survive. I doubt we'll see him again.'

By mid-February, Ben had the main structural work completed, because most of the old barn was still in reasonable order and the outside didn't need much work – though it could do with repointing in a few places once the weather was finer.

When he told Jonah that the place was weatherproof, he got ready to lay the wooden floor in what they were calling the 'fizzy room'. The big flagstones there were not in a good condition, but could be re-used outside.

Planks had already been ordered and delivered, and had cost a lot of money. Ben was happy to do the floor as well, though he warned them he could only do plain woodwork, not the fancy stuff.

Leah worried about the cost but Jonah just smiled and said he could afford it, and that they couldn't employ people and expect them to work on the bare earth or broken paving stones in these modern times, now could they?

The area for the Youth Hostel had a flagged floor that was in much better condition, and the big square stone slabs just needed a little attention before they were level again and ready for use during the summers.

Jonah had shown her his accounts, beautifully neat columns of figures, and spent hours teaching her to keep her own accounts in the same way. She'd enjoyed that, because she'd always loved doing sums.

She hadn't had the faintest idea of it at the time, but she'd married a man who was comfortably off and Jonah could indeed afford to pay for her small business. She was practising making dandelion and burdock, and kept trying out her drink on her family and neighbours!

People in the village now asked her how things were going with the fizzy drinks when they met her at the shop, and seemed excited about the new business. She hadn't decided who to offer jobs to and would take Nancy's advice on that later on.

Then everyone grew even more excited as work started to bring in electricity to the village. Given the harsher moorland weather, it had been decided to put it underground, to save maintenance and repair costs. It'd be wonderful to have light at the flick of a switch in the dark evenings, and to have access to the BBC radio service would be a joy, she was sure. Not just music but plays and news would be available to while away the evenings.

Like everyone else in the village she'd listened to radio programmes at friends' houses further down the valley and come back feeling envious. Charlie, of course, had a particularly elaborate radio set, with a gramophone turntable included in the elegant apparatus.

The women talked excitedly in the shop about having a wireless. Even if you did have to pay for a radio licence, ten shillings a year was still a cheap form of entertainment for the whole family, and it came to you right there in your own home. Some of the women had already started saving their pennies and asking their husbands to cut down on their drinks or tobacco to add their share to the cost. Others wouldn't be able to afford it but felt sure they'd be asked in to listen to someone else's radio.

No one was particularly excited about the prospect of the telephone line being brought into the village, because most could see no need for it. Telephones were for better-off people such as doctors or shopkeepers like Nancy, not for ordinary folk.

The Willcoxes were definitely having a telephone installed and Leah wondered if this would put her and Jonah more at Charlie's mercy. He seemed to think he was still in charge of their lives, but he wasn't going to take charge of *her* life, she vowed. Only her husband could try to tell her what to do, and thank goodness, Jonah wasn't the sort to order you around.

In the mcantime she continued to get ready to start her business, not boasting about it, that wasn't her way, just getting on with the work that needed doing.

16

Adam Harris brought in an engineer to check all the machinery in the laundry and when he got home Ethel berated him for wasting money. Which meant someone had told her what he was doing. He could guess who, but knew they'd have been threatened into revealing what was going on, so didn't say anything.

It was hard to keep anything secret, even in a large village like Birch End, which some people preferred to call a 'small town'.

For once he stood his ground against his wife. 'It's necessary, Ethel. A man was killed last year because I listened to you about saving money. That will be on my conscience for the rest of my life, so I'm not risking it happening again.'

'*Conscience!* Cowardice, I call it. You're too soft for your own good, you are. Workers are ten a penny. There's no benefit to an employer in spoiling them. They'll only take advantage and work more slackly.'

'What gives you that idea?'

'Everyone knows it. Look at the women in the laundry. They're like animals, coarse, rough-housing with one another at the drop of a hat instead of getting on with their work. I've seen them. All they're good for is hard physical work.'

'Well, I believe they deserve better of their employers than to be put in danger. And if they want to have a bit of fun occasionally, who can blame them? I'll thank you to keep out of my laundry in future. *Stay—right—away.*'

'Why should I? You're in business to make money, not pamper the lower classes, and you weren't making money when we got married. You *need* my advice and I'll continue to give it.'

'No, I don't need it. It was my father who lost money, not me.' He'd heard the saying 'If looks could kill' many times, but he was shocked because he'd never seen a death wish written so clearly on someone's face. 'I'm not arguing, Ethel. I'm doing it my way from now on. And if you turn up at the laundry I'll have you thrown out.'

He turned away from her, but winced when he heard something thud against the door behind him.

He felt sick with disgust and yes, with fear, when he went into the small room where he spent most of his evenings. Anything to be away from *her*.

But she seemed to be growing more violent . . . more dangerous. He didn't know what to do about it. Was he imagining it or was he really in danger?

He wished he could get a divorce, whatever it cost, but you had to have evidence of adultery and she had spared him that, at least. She didn't even seem interested in bed play these days, and thank goodness, because he could no longer bear to touch her.

A few days later Adam was working late in the office at the laundry when he heard a sound outside on the shop floor. Had someone broken in? Or was he just imagining things?

When he heard the sound again, he knew someone must have got in, so went to investigate. He found some of the machinery's drive belts running, the quieter ones at the end. Surely these had been switched off when the laundry closed for the day?

He couldn't see anyone and nothing seemed to have been disturbed except for the two machines. He decided to go into the engineer's workshop and switch them off, then check the place from top to bottom.

When he turned, someone shoved him hard towards the dangerous machinery and as he jerked backwards, he saw that the guard grille had been unlatched. Letting out an involuntary yell, he grabbed one of the upright supports.

It was only by sheer good luck that he managed to catch hold of it, but the person tried to push him again and he knew he was fighting for his life. If he fell among the whirring belts, he'd be killed.

He tried to see who his attacker was but there wasn't enough light to see more than a silhouette, and the fellow had a cap pulled down low and what looked like a scarf tied across his lower face.

Terrified that whoever it was would try to push him again, he slid quickly down on to the floor, out of the way of the gap into the danger zone, wedging one foot against the nearest strut. The solid lower part of the machine was very stable but he was only too aware that he was still in a highly vulnerable position. He had never been any good at fighting.

As his attacker's shadow fell across him and the man raised one hand, Adam saw that he was wielding a hammer. There was nothing Adam could do to protect himself against a blow from that. Even if he protected his head, it'd break his arm and then he'd be helpless.

Then a woman screamed shrilly from the walkway above. 'Mr Harris! Mr Harris! What's happening?'

The hand lowered and his attacker stepped quickly back, disappearing into the dimness. Adam heard his heavy footsteps running away but didn't dare risk standing upright yet in case this was a trick.

Someone came clattering down the metal stairs from the upper walkway and then across the floor towards him. But these footsteps were much lighter, the pattering sound made by a woman's shoes. Surely a woman wasn't one of the attackers?

He groaned in relief as Bessie, one of his hardest workers and charge hand of her section, came into sight.

She knelt down beside him. 'Are you all right, Mr Harris?'

'I think so.'

'I saw you from the walkway, lying on the floor. I thought at first you were hurt and someone was trying to help you up. Then I saw him raise a hammer to hit you so I screamed.'

'Thank goodness you did. You probably saved my life. He ran off when you cried out. Whoever it was had just tried to push me into the machinery and was trying to finish the job.' He shuddered and it was a moment before he could move and let her help him to his feet.

She stood still with her arm around his waist, saying in shocked tones, 'You mean . . . Oh, surely not? Why would anyone try to kill you?'

'I don't know but I'm certain he was trying to do that. Did you see who it was?'

She hesitated, and the silence went on for too long, but eventually she shook her head, avoiding his eyes.

He didn't press her, but he was sure she knew who'd attacked him and was afraid of being attacked herself if she named him.

To his mind, that could mean only one person: Sam Griggs, his wife's rent collector. It was Ethel who'd said Sam didn't have enough to do for her and arranged for him to do small jobs at the laundry. Sometimes he drove the delivery van or helped carry heavy loads of wet washing around.

Ethel said she sent Sam because she didn't like to see him wasting time, but Adam guessed that was merely an excuse for him to keep an eye on the laundry for her.

All the women who worked here were afraid of the fellow

and went round in twos when he was there, but he had never touched any of them as far as Adam knew or he'd have sacked him.

Sam had threatened or even thumped tenants of his wife's houses, though, if they fell behind with their rent, and there were whispers that he sometimes did worse.

'It was Sam Griggs, wasn't it?' he said in a low voice.

'I daren't say. He'll kill me if I do. Please don't tell anyone I recognised him.'

'I won't.' But if Sam had tried to kill him, there was only one person who could have set him on to do it and what would Ethel try next?

'What are you going to do about it, Mr Harris?' she asked. 'You can't just let it go.'

'I haven't decided. But I daren't go home yet.'

She gave a tiny nod as if she understood exactly why. 'You should see Sergeant Deemer. Lay a complaint at least.'

'I have no proof. I couldn't see my attacker's face.'

'Then get yourself a bodyguard. There are enough men out of work who'd jump at the chance.'

He thought about it for a moment or two, then nodded. 'Good idea.'

It suddenly occurred to him to wonder why Bessie was in the laundry at this hour, so he asked.

'I left my handbag here with my purse in it. Silly of me, but Jane had hurt herself, a really bad cut, and it wouldn't stop bleeding, so I had to take her to the doctor. You said I should do that if there was an accident and you'd pay. I hurried her out and forgot my own bag and it took ages for the doctor to see her and stitch up the cut.'

'No one told me there had been an accident.'

'You weren't here when it happened and Mrs Harris said not to bother you with details.'

'My wife was here?'

Bessie nodded. 'In your office.' She hesitated then added, 'I heard her opening and shutting the drawers.'

'Hell fire! I told her not to come here any more. That settles it. I'm going to get the locks changed straight away, and if you know a strong man I can trust with my safety, I *will* hire one. I'd be grateful for your help there.'

'I know half a dozen. How about Bert Falton? He's a big, strong chap and he's such a strong Methodist, you can be sure no one will be able to bribe him to look the other way.'

'Good idea. Do you know where he lives? Will you show me the way?'

'You'll be careful . . . at home?'

'I'll be keeping Bert with me until I see my way clear. Now, if you've got your handbag we'll lock up and see Bert, then we'll visit the locksmith and ask him to change the locks on all the doors in the laundry.'

'What about hiring a nightwatchman as well? Just for the time being. And getting an alarm bell fitted, an electric one that you just have to touch a switch to set off and call for help?'

'Good idea.' She was an intelligent woman. If her parents hadn't been so poor, she'd have gone to the grammar school, but they'd needed her wages, however small.

What sort of woman had he married, though? What was he going to do about her?

Adam didn't return to the laundry till he'd hired Bert to guard him and visited the locksmith. The latter was delighted to have such a big job and agreed to change every lock in the place, even if he had to work all night to do it.

As the evening passed, Adam sent the locksmith's lad out for fish and chips for them all, after which he waited impatiently in his office for the work to be finished. He found his papers only slightly disturbed. He'd not even have noticed if Bessie hadn't told him Ethel had been in there.

He didn't go home till two o'clock in the morning, accompanied by Bert still. He put one finger to his lips before he opened the front door. There were no lights showing in the house but with a street lamp outside, he didn't need to switch on the hall light. He was quite sure Ethel would be listening for his return and wanted to take her by surprise.

With Bert tiptoeing behind him on the strip of carpet that ran up the middle of the stairs, Adam crept up and tried to open his wife's bedroom door. It was locked. He banged on it with his clenched fist. 'Ethel! Get up! I want to speak to you this minute.'

It was rare for him to go to her bedroom. He hated its cloying perfumed smell. No one had ever invented a perfume that covered up a nasty nature like hers.

'There was no need to wake me up,' she yelled. 'Whatever it is can wait till morning.'

'No it can't. I need to speak to you now.'

He was surprised at how long it took her to open the door and she sounded to be opening and shutting drawers. When she finally opened the door she tried to hold it nearly closed, but he was angry enough to shove it backwards and her with it.

He stared round, trying to work out what she'd been trying to hide, then he saw the wardrobe door move slightly. Suddenly he knew why she didn't want to share his bed now and what she was hiding. She had someone in there, betraying him in his own house!

'Get out of my room,' she snapped and tried to push him on to the landing.

He sidestepped her and yanked open the wardrobe door before she could stop him.

Sam tumbled out. He put up one fist as if to punch

Adam, but Bert was there, moving between them, smiling slightly.

'Just give me the chance,' he told Sam.

'Get out of the house, Griggs!' Adam said. 'And don't come back again. You're fired.'

'You can't fire *my* rent man,' Ethel said at once.

'I can if he's in my wife's bedroom with his flies unbuttoned.' He pointed to Sam's trousers and when he turned to his wife, he saw that her nightgown was unfastened at the front, and her face and neck bore the marks of whisker burn.

Silence. Then she tossed her head, not looking upset at all. 'You'd better leave, Sam. I'll see you in the morning as usual. I'll have something sorted out by then.'

As he moved towards the door, she took a step after him, looking at him fondly, her lips puckered for a kiss. At this blatant provocation, Adam grabbed her arm and swung her round to face him instead. Sam stopped with a growl of anger but looked at Bert and left.

'You'll be too busy moving out of my house and seeing your lawyer in the morning to meet your damned lover, Ethel. This is grounds for divorce. I even have a reliable witness to your adultery.'

Joy filled him in a huge surge. This meant he could get rid of her and he wouldn't have to leave Lancashire to do it. He could divorce her for adultery.

He looked across at Bert. 'I didn't expect to be facing this, but we both know what we saw here.'

Bert nodded. 'Yes, Mr Harris. I'll be happy to testify in court if you need me. Everyone knows I'd not lie after an oath sworn on a Bible.'

As Bert was a well-respected lay preacher, Adam nodded. He couldn't have found himself a better witness.

'Send that man of yours away and we'll talk about this.'

Ethel's speech was slightly slurred and he could smell the gin on her breath.

'Perhaps you could also smell my wife's breath, Bert. She's clearly been drinking again.'

'Yes, she's been on the gin, definitely. I can smell it from here.' Bert gave his employer a sympathetic glance.

Adam took the key out of her bedroom door and pushed her further inside. 'I'll have to lock you in for the night, I'm afraid. When you leave in the morning, you'll be going for good, so you'll need to pack your things.'

'Don't you dare lock that door!'

'It's that or throw you out of this house now in what you're wearing.'

She glared at him, but stepped back, dragging her dressing gown closed for the first time since he'd come into the room. 'Can I just say that—'

He didn't wait to hear what she wanted to say and enjoyed slamming the door and turning the key in the lock.

She began yelling and kicking it but he ignored that and walked along the landing to his own bedroom. 'I sleep here, Bert. For tonight, I'd be grateful if you'd keep watch on both bedroom doors and the hall below. Don't let my wife leave the house or anyone else come in. Tomorrow I'll hire another man to help you guard me and my home. I think I'm going to be in danger for a while. Would you like a blanket to wrap round yourself?'

'Yes, please. And is there a chair I can sit on?'

'There's a comfy one in my bedroom. You stay there. I'll fetch it, then we'll go round the house and make sure all the outer doors are bolted. You'll need to learn your way round.'

'I'll soon do that. Do you have a fireplace in your bedroom?'

Adam was surprised by this question. 'Yes.'

'Better put the poker near the bed from now on, then. You can't be too careful.'

Adam was halfway down the stairs when another thought occurred to him. He stopped and turned round. 'What about your own family? Sam knows who you are. Will they be safe?'

Bert grinned. 'My brother and his family are living with us to share expenses, because we're both out of work. He's a strong lad and he hates Sam too, because that sod used to bully us at school. You never forget people who treat you badly, do you? So if you want someone else to stand guard for half the day, or night, Tim will be happy to do the job.'

'Good. He's hired.'

Adam got to bed half an hour later, not expecting to sleep, but feeling better than he had done for a long time.

He knew nothing more until he was woken by yelling and screaming just outside his bedroom door. He jerked awake, realising with a shock that it was daylight and the shrill noises were being made by his wife.

Scrambling into his dressing gown he went on to the landing, to find Bert with two new scratches on his cheek barring the top of the stairs.

'She said she had to go to the bathroom, then she tried to hit me over the head with a candlestick,' Bert said.

'Tell your tame brute to let me past, Adam Harris. You're a poor sort of a man to need someone to protect you from a woman half your size.'

'I'm happy for you to leave, Ethel, but I would prefer to see you off the premises myself and I won't do that until *after* I've checked what you've got in your bags.' He pointed towards two suitcases just inside her bedroom door.

'It's just my clothes. You're surely not going to take those off me.'

'Of course not. But I let you wear some of my mother's jewellery and you're not taking that. I told you at the time it was to stay in the family.'

'You'll never get a family. You don't know how to pleasure a woman in bed.'

He could see his guard blush at that. 'Keep hold of her, Bert.' He tried to open a suitcase but found it locked. 'Give me the keys, Ethel, or I'll break the locks open.'

'No. What's in the case is mine. I've more than earned it marrying a long streak of nothing like you!'

He got the poker from the hearth and raised it over the suitcase lock.

She darted between him and the case. 'No, don't!' After trying and failing to stare him down, she said, 'I'll give you the keys.'

She began to sob pitifully as she fumbled for them in her handbag, but he ignored that and opened the suitcase, upending it on the bed and tossing her clothes back in one by one.

Some small leather boxes were left. 'My mother's jewellery,' he said. 'Bert, make sure she doesn't leave the room but please witness what I've removed from her case.' He opened each little box and showed the other man its contents. 'This is hers, a brooch she said belonged to her mother, so I'm putting it back in the case. But this was my mother's and she has no right to keep it.'

When he'd finished, he refastened the suitcase and put it on the landing, ignoring her complaints about crumpled clothes, then opened the second one and upended it. When her clothes were put back in the case, some small silver ornaments were left on the bed.

'These belonged to my grandmother,' he told Bert and snapped the locks shut.

'If you'll carry the cases down and put them outside the front door, Bert, I'll just have a private word with my wife, then escort her out.'

Ethel waited till they were alone to say pleadingly, 'Don't

do this Adam. It'll cause a terrible scandal in the town. I'll stop seeing Sam and we can—'

'I don't care about you and Sam, and I definitely don't want you back. I've been wanting to be rid of you for years. I have ample proof now of adultery and I'm sure it was you who tried to have me killed last night. I shall be suing you for divorce.'

'Well I have proof too!' she yelled. 'You go and see that Nancy Buckley regularly, and everyone in the village knows it.'

'I've never laid a finger on Nancy. She's the widow of a good friend of mine.'

'Tell that to the court. I won't go down without a fight. You've been seen with her and I'll swear you were having an affair, say I saw you kissing.'

He managed a smile. 'Ah, but I can *prove* that I didn't touch her.'

'I don't believe you!'

'She always called in a neighbour to mind the shop, so we were never really alone. And she left the sitting-room lights on and the curtains open, so anyone who passed could see what we were doing. You can't keep secrets in a small village.'

At the front door Ethel stopped and said challengingly, 'The car is mine. I bought it with the rent money.'

'You're welcome to it. Pity you don't like to drive it yourself.'

'Sam will go on driving it for me, as usual. He's a good rent collector, as well as a better man than you.'

'Where will you live?'

'I shall throw someone out of one of my houses. Pity that little pet of yours married that cripple. I'd have enjoyed throwing *her* out.'

He saw Sam Griggs standing waiting at the corner.

'Fetch my car please, Sam,' she called.

'It's waiting round the corner, madam.'

'Then bring it here. I'm leaving in style.'

When the car drew up, she said in a low voice, 'You'll regret this, Adam Harris.'

'Not as much as I've regretted marrying you.'

He walked back into the house, shut the door and sagged against it.

As the sound of the car engine faded, he said, 'She's a terrible woman, Bert, terrible.'

'Everyone knows that from the way she treats her tenants. You're well shut of her.'

'I know, but I fear things will get worse before they get better, because she'll tell all sorts of lies and blacken honest people's names.'

'She might not realise how much people have seen,' Bert muttered.

Adam didn't quite catch what his bodyguard had said, but was too weary to ask. He'd been shocked to the core by what he'd found out. He shouldn't be shocked at anything Ethel did, but he was. To commit adultery in their own house, with her husband only two bedrooms away was . . . a filthy trick.

She'd have laughed while she did it, that nasty, cruel little sound he hated so much, he knew she would.

And oh, dear God, she was going to try to blacken poor Nancy's name now. Thank goodness Nancy had never been able to afford to leave the shop untended.

After some thought, Adam decided he'd have to report the incident at the laundry to Sergeant Deemer. But first he had to wait for their maid to arrive for work and tell her what had happened, to make sure she knew not to let his ex-wife in.

Ex-wife! He loved using that word.

When he heard the sound of a key in the back door, he went to the kitchen, which made the maid jump in shock. 'Sorry, Minnie. I didn't mean to startle you.'

'That's all right, sir. Is Mrs Harris not up yet? Will she want me to get her some breakfast? I left everything ready for her, as usual, but nothing seems to have been touched.'

'Sit down and let me explain . . . '

When he'd finished she surprised him by smiling. 'I'm glad to hear that, sir. I was going to give my notice at the end of the quarter, because Mrs Harris isn't easy to work for.'

'Do you still want to leave?'

'No, sir.'

'I hope you'll stay, then, because I've always been satisfied with your work.'

'Thank you, sir. Um . . . what about Sam Griggs?'

'Did you know what was going on between him and my ex-wife?'

She flushed bright red. 'I did suspect something, sir, but it wasn't my place to tell you. It was one of the reasons I was leaving.'

'I'm going to have the locks changed on all the doors, and no keys are to be given to anyone else without my say-so. You'll need to keep the outer doors locked at all times until . . . well, until certain matters are sorted out.'

She looked at him thoughtfully. 'I think you'd better not give me a key. It'd be easy enough for that Sam to stop me and take it from me by force.'

'What do you suggest we do, then?'

'You're usually up when I get here. Mostly, you can let me in. It'll be awkward to do the shopping, though.'

'Can you manage by phoning through the orders for the next few days? You'll be in charge of everything from now on, so I'd better raise your wages, I think.'

'Oh, sir! Mam will be that glad.'

'You'll have to let Mrs Carrick in when she comes to do the laundry and scrub the floors.'

Minnie frowned.

'What's wrong?'

'She's that Sam's auntie.'

'Oh, dear.'

'And she's been taking advantage of it, slacking off, telling me he won't let her be dismissed when I say she's not done something.'

'Well, we'll have to let her go, then. Do you know anyone else who'd come in and help?'

'Yes, sir. My Mam will come like a shot. Dad's still out of work and she'll be glad of the money, I can tell you. I've been having to live in lodgings or they'd have had their dole cut because of my wages. Those Means Test men who decide on what men will get paid if they're out of work are cruel. They take the children's wages as part of the dole.'

'Would it be easier if you lived here?'

'Not on my own, sir.'

'Ah, yes. Of course. If we hired another maid would it be all right?'

'Yes, sir, as long as she and I could share a bedroom.'

'Yes. I see. It's all going to be very complicated for a while.' He wasn't going to pretend. 'But I think you and I will both be happier with new arrangements in place, Minnie, don't you? So go ahead and find me another maid.'

'Me find one, sir?'

'Well, you're going to have to share a bedroom with her and you'll be the head maid, with higher wages.'

'Ooh, sir. Thank you ever so much.'

It was nice to see someone happy. Hiring another maid was a small expense compared to what a divorce would cost and he couldn't have anyone thinking he was sleeping with Minnie.

He didn't have nearly as much money as Ethel, but he was well acquainted with Wesley Brand, who now ran his family's small law firm in Birch End. He doubted Wesley would even consider representing Ethel, because none of his friends had ever liked her. But he'd represent Adam, and make sure Ethel didn't get any maintenance payments, surely?

What a pity she could look so attractive and be so charming when she wanted. Adam had been dazzled by her, thrilled that she'd chosen him, when he wasn't very good with women, believing that she loved him.

Oh, he'd been such a fool!

But he would try very hard to do better with his life and relationships in future.

17

Of course word got round in the valley about Mr and Mrs Harris splitting up, and Leah soon heard about it. You heard many things in the village shop. No one was surprised that the couple had separated, just that he'd waited so long to get rid of her.

Mrs Harris had apparently moved out of the house or been thrown out by her husband, according to who you listened to. She was now living in a much smaller house, having turned her tenants out at a moment's notice. No one expected a snob like her to go on living in such a small place, though.

By the following day, word was also going round that Mr Harris was divorcing her because he'd caught her out in adultery. How that information had got out was a mystery. *She* was saying she was glad to get rid of him. *He* wouldn't comment on the separation or divorce, no matter who asked him.

However, he wasn't looking unhappy, no, he was looking more relaxed than he had for a long time. People could see that with their own eyes. *She* was brazening it out, living in the small house with only Sam Griggs' aunt to do the house-work.

No one except posh people dared to be anything but polite to her, though, because when she went out, that Sam Griggs was usually hovering nearby.

It didn't take long for people to notice that she wasn't

going to her former friends' houses in the afternoons to take tea with the other ladies, and not in the evenings either, when people usually went out in couples. They'd dropped her, people said gleefully. She wouldn't like that. What would she do with all her fine evening clothes now?

Leah listened but didn't comment. She'd never forgotten the day Mrs Harris had scolded her so harshly about mopping the pavement, the day she'd been at her lowest ebb. Or the way Sam Griggs had tried to rape her. It was a word people tried to avoid saying out loud, but it still lingered in her mind because that was what he'd been trying to do. And who knew how many other women he'd attacked and got away with it?

He and Ethel deserved one another as far as Leah was concerned. But they'd probably go on making money and living luxuriously. It didn't seem fair that such horrible people could go on treating poorer people so badly and get away with it.

One day in early March, Jonah drove his wife down to the village shop to take a few bottles of ginger beer to Nancy. They'd decided not to trouble Mr Harris about buying it. Well, the poor man's life was very unsettled, to put it mildly, and she was selling one or two bottles a week to farmers and people with a bit of money to spare.

'Adam Harris hasn't called in lately. He's probably got his mind on other things and has forgotten about the ginger beer,' Nancy told Leah while Jonah was outside chatting to a man he knew. 'But it'll be worth all the trouble if he gets rid of *her*. My Stanley thought a lot of Adam, said he was one of the kindest men in Lancashire.'

Leah nodded. She didn't usually indulge in gossip, but there was no one else in the shop so it couldn't do any harm.

'My father thought well of Adam too. He was upset when

he decided to marry Ethel Garton and prophesied it'd not go well. He did think Adam would manage the laundry better than his father, and he has. His father had let the laundry run down; Adam built the business up again but *she* kept nagging him to tighten up still further and look where that led.'

Nancy looked at the crate of ginger beer bottles. 'I can probably sell some by the glass to hikers on finer weekends. They don't seem to mind the cold, but they don't come out hiking much in the rain. Would you let me have six bottles on consignment, this time? I'm a bit short of ready cash this week as I've had to pay a few bills.'

'Yes, of course.' Who wouldn't trust Nancy Buckley?

As it turned out, a large group of day hikers stopped at the shop for refreshments the following weekend and polished off all but one bottle of her stock, to Nancy's delight.

She handed over payment for the bottles the next time Leah went shopping. 'I told you it'd sell to the hikers, didn't I? I doubled what I'm paying you on that, doubled it!'

'Yes, you did tell me.' It would only mean a few extra shillings coming in but that would make a big difference to a woman who was always balancing on a knife edge where money was concerned.

'Could you let me have more bottles, do you think? After all, they won't go bad, will they, so they'll sell sooner or later?'

'I can let you have eight bottles, so I'll leave it to you to divide them between yourself and Mr Harris, if he asks for any. I have to give the other two I've got left to Don. He heard about you selling so much of the last batch and he's keen to see if it sells by the glass to his customers at The Shepherd's Rest. I doubt it will, because it's mostly locals who go there.'

'Some might like it. Them farmers' wives always have a

penny or two tucked away from their egg money. And I shall pray for fine weather on Sundays from now on. They won't come out hiking if it's like today.'

Both women looked out of the window at the clingy rain that hadn't stopped since early morning. *Unremitting* was the word that came into Leah's mind every time she glanced out at it.

'It takes time to build up stocks of ginger beer, but I've got my equipment in place now, Nancy, and my first big batch is bubbling away. I've had to buy some more bottles. And you get me my secret ingredient.'

They exchanged conspiratorial smiles.

When Leah went out to the car, she saw that Jonah had moved to sit in the passenger seat. Her heart gave a little lurch and she drew in a deep breath to calm her nerves before getting into the driver's side.

He greeted her with, 'You need all the practice you can get, love. You can drive me into Birch End.' He stopped to stare at her. 'Goodness, I didn't expect you to be so nervous. You seemed to take to driving up and down the lane very well.'

So she told him what was worrying her. 'I'm not bothered about changing gears and double de-clutching, I think I've got the hang of that, and I'm all right driving into our village. But, well, I've been wondering whether I might need glasses for driving. I'm all right with things that are close to me, I can see them fine. But things that are further away are rather blurry. You did say I had to keep my eyes on what's going on ahead of me, but it's difficult when the roads are busier, especially with moving objects some distance away.'

'Ah. That could account for your poor aim when we've been practising shooting.'

'I suppose so.'

'Charlie's the same, near-sighted, only he says he's too vain to wear spectacles. If you need them, Leah, you must get some. We'll have your eyes checked straight away.'

She sighed. 'I'm just as vain as Charlie, Jonah. Spectacles don't exactly flatter people. So . . . well, I'm not sure I want to bother with the driving.'

'Nonsense. You'd be pretty with or without glasses, because your kind nature and your . . . your decency show in your face. And you have really lovely hair.'

'What a nice compliment!'

'I mean it. Come on, Leah, you can't let a little thing like needing glasses prevent you from driving. Pluck up your courage.' He waited for her to respond.

'I suppose you're right, Jonah. I'd better arrange for an eye test.'

'We'll go into Rivenshaw right now and make an appointment to get it done as soon as possible. But I think I'll take over the driving once we get to the outskirts of Birch End.'

She wished he'd take over immediately, but wasn't going to show how very anxious she was feeling. Well, she hoped she didn't betray it.

To her dismay the optician could fit her in straight away. She felt like a lamb being led away to the slaughter as she followed him into the inner room. No young woman that she'd ever met would want to wear glasses, and she was no different. She'd always felt sorry for the kids at school who had to because other children yelled 'Speccy four-eyes!' at them. At least people didn't yell that after adults. Well, not usually; maybe the odd naughty lad would if there were no adults standing nearby to clip him round the ears for his rudeness.

The test took nearly half an hour because Mr Purdon prided himself on his thorough testing methods. After that he insisted on speaking to her husband.

'Your wife needs spectacles for driving and long-distance viewing, I'm afraid.'

She stared at him in shock. He'd spoken to Jonah as if she wasn't there! Some men were like that, but these were *her* eyes and she wasn't going to be left out of any discussions.

'Excuse me, Mr Purdon, but I'm not deaf and I do understand English.'

He looked at her in puzzlement, but Jonah winked at her and nodded as if to encourage her to continue.

'I'm afraid I don't understand what you mean, Mrs Willcox.'

'You tested *my* eyes then you didn't tell me the results, but spoke to my husband.'

'But . . . it's the husbands who pay for the glasses.'

'And it's me who'll have to wear them . . . *if* I decide to take your advice and wear spectacles. I may go and discuss it with an optician who will notice my existence.'

The optician cast a desperate glance towards Jonah, who kept his eyes focused on Leah. She could see the right-hand corner of his lip twitching as it did when he was holding back laughter.

'Um, I didn't mean to upset you, Mrs Willcox, really I didn't.'

'Wouldn't it upset *you* to be ignored?'

'Um . . .'

Jonah took pity on Mr Purdon, who didn't seem to know what to say next. 'What do you think about it then, darling?'

She knew she'd be cutting off her nose to spite her face if she did what she wanted and marched out of the shop never to go back there again. Stupid patronising man! 'I really want to learn to drive so I suppose I will need glasses, unfortunately.'

Mr Purdon looked from one to the other, turning his head from side to side like someone watching a tennis match. She could see Jonah still trying to hold back a smile. She might have found it funny too if she weren't the one needing glasses.

'Would you, um, like to see some frames, Mr and Mrs Willcox?'

'Yes, please.'

'Do you want my help, dear?' Jonah asked pointedly.

'Yes, please.'

He watched her try on several pairs of frames without any lenses in them, then look at him each time.

'I rather like the gold ones,' he offered. 'The darker ones seem too heavy for your face.'

She studied the gold spectacles again, then caught sight of the little price label and gasped. 'Look how much they cost!'

He waved one hand dismissively. 'If you're going to wear them regularly, you'll want to look nice. Some of the film stars are wearing glasses now, you know. I was reading about it only the other day in the newspaper.'

'They are?'

'Yes. Not only glasses but darkened sunglasses. Not that you'd need those very often here.' He turned back to Mr Purdon. 'So, we'll take the gold frames. What do we need to do now?'

'If you'll kindly leave a deposit, I'll order the lenses to be made. That'll take a week or two, and I can either drop you a postcard or telephone once they're ready.'

'It'll have to be a postcard because the phone hasn't been put through to Ellindale yet.'

When they walked out of the shop, Jonah let his laughter out. 'Well done, darling, for standing up for yourself! That poor man didn't know how to deal with you.'

'That poor man treated me like an idiot.'

'He won't make that mistake again, believe me. And I

know you're worried, but you didn't look at all bad in the gold glasses. I wonder what Charlie will say when you learn to drive and he's still restricted to taking taxis. His eyes are much worse than yours, you know. He'll have to change his mind eventually and get some glasses for everyday use, whether he drives or not. I wonder what Marion will say about you wearing glasses.'

She shrugged. 'It doesn't matter what she says. I need the horrid things to drive safely, so that's that.'

The thought of Marion made her feel sad. Her sister-in-law was expecting. Charlie had shared the good news with them last week, after inviting them out again for a meal at the Green Man in Birch End. He'd been cock-a-hoop about the coming baby.

Leah had felt almost sick with envy at the sight of Marion with that glowing look on her face that pregnant women often got. She just hoped she hadn't shown it.

In Todmorden, Cissy Greenby opened the door to find an old man leaning against the wall, wheezing.

'No beggars,' she said firmly.

'Cissy, it's me . . . Mitch. Don't you recognise your own brother?'

'Good heavens, come in. You look dreadful.'

'I feel dreadful. Can't seem to shake this cold. I get rid of it for a week or two then it comes right back again. Can you give me a bed for a night or two, love? I hate to trouble you, but I'll die if I have to spend another night out in the cold.'

'Yes, of course we can find you somewhere to sleep, though it may not be a proper bed. I've always got room for family, even ones I disapprove of. Thad was here for a few days just after Christmas. He'd been hurt, so I couldn't say no but he wasn't an easy guest, not at all grateful for what we did for him.'

'Thad came here?'

'Yes.'

'Did he tell you what he'd done?'

'Not exactly, just that he'd got into a fight. Well, I could tell that by looking at his face.'

'He kidnapped a little lass last year and started undressing her. He's always in trouble, that one.'

Cissy's face turned white. 'He didn't!'

'He did. Luckily they rescued her in time.'

'Oh, dear heavens! The monster. And I had him staying here. Well, he's not staying again.'

'He's a real bad 'un, he is. I'm not bad, Cissy. I stay on the road because I can't stand being shut up in a house.'

'I know, Mitch love. Let's get you sorted out, eh? You'll have to sleep in the attic because Pam's come back to live at home, she and her husband *and* their two kids, all in our second bedroom.'

'Out of work, is he?'

'Yes.'

'There's a lot of fellows without work still. You're a kind sister even to think of taking me in on top of them. And your attic will be a lot warmer than sleeping under a hedgerow or behind a wall, so I am really grateful.'

'You'll have to take a bath first, though.'

'*What?* Aw, Cissy, not a bath.'

'I mean it. You stink worse than I've ever known you to before and I'm not having my whole house smelling nasty. We'll do it straight away before the children come home from school.' She held the door open and turned to call, 'Pam? It's your uncle Mitch.'

A younger woman peered out of the kitchen and grimaced as the smell wafted towards her.

'He's going to take a bath straight away.'

'He certainly needs it.'

'Can you put some pans of hot water on the gas stove, then you can help me get the tin bath in from the outhouse. We'll have the bathing over and done with while there's just us, then we'll wash his clothes in the same water.'

The two women had to drag the clothes off Mitch, unpicking the rough stitches on some of them, and he complained the whole time, horrified when they even ignored his pleas to leave a fellow some privacy.

'Get away with you!' Cissy said. 'You've got nothing I haven't seen before. And our Pam's a married woman with a son, so you won't surprise her.'

Still protesting loudly, he was bundled into the bath and only then did he quieten down, lying with his head against the tin rim, eyes closed. 'You forget,' he murmured.

'Forget what?'

'How nice it is to lie in a warm bath.'

'There you are. It's nice to feel clean, too. Here. Let me wash your hair and back properly for you.' Ruthlessly she used soap and flannel on every part of his anatomy, ignoring his occasional outraged yelps, then she got him out and wrapped him in an old sheet while she washed his clothes in the bath water.

She stopped suddenly, hands deep in suds. 'I've been wondering what clothes we can lend you and I've just remembered Dick's father's old clothes. We put them up in the attic after he died. Plenty of wear in them yet. It must be ten years ago now, but they'll still be there.'

'I'll go and get them,' Pam said.

'They're in the old trunk at the far end. They'll need airing but they were put away clean. Dick's father was about the same size as Mitch. A bit taller, maybe.'

After they'd helped Mitch put on the clothes and rolled up the trouser legs a bit, Cissy looked at him in dismay. 'Eh, you've lost a lot of weight. You aren't looking after yourself, my lad.'

'I manage. These are hard times. Folk don't have as much to share as they did once.'

'You used to be able to manage better than that, though, finding yourself odd jobs here and there.' Her voice softened. 'Stay with us for a while, Mitch love. We'll feed you up again.'

'Well, just for a few days. It's nice on the roads in summer, you see, well, it is as long as it doesn't rain. And I enjoy a good tramp over the tops. Can't beat the views from up there.'

'You're too old to live on the road, my lad. You're staying here from now on and I'm not taking no for an answer.'

She knew how weak he must be feeling when he didn't protest at that edict, and exchanged worried glances with her daughter. Mitch was ten years older than her, but he'd never been this feeble before.

Ten days after the eye test a postcard was delivered to Spring Cottage by the second post, saying the spectacles were ready.

Jonah chuckled at the expression of dismay on his wife's face. 'You'll look fine in them. And you won't have to wear them all the time, will you?'

'No. I suppose there's that to be thankful for, at least. When shall we go and pick them up?'

'Straight away. Let's get it over with. I have to work tomorrow, remember.'

They drove off down the hill, with Jonah trying not to smile. Leah wasn't often grumpy, but she was today.

Oh, he was so lucky to have met her, so very lucky. And lucky to have such a caring brother, too.

And he didn't mind the glasses at all. They made her eyes look bigger.

★   ★   ★

Leah hesitated at the door of the optician's shop, then took a deep breath and followed Jonah outside to the car.

Of course Charlie would have to be walking along the street just then, a meeting she'd hoped to avoid till she was used to the feeling of spectacles on her nose.

He stopped to study her. 'Hey, you've got them. They don't look as bad as I'd expected, I must admit.'

'Tactful thing to say, Charlie,' Jonah snapped.

'What? Oh, sorry.'

Leah squared her shoulders. She wasn't having Charlie pitying her, or anyone else, for that matter. 'I can see what's down the street clearly for the first time in my life, and that's the point, surely? When are *you* going to be brave enough to get yourself some and learn to drive, Charlie Willcox?'

'I don't need to drive. And what's more, I don't believe in women driving. They can't cope with mechanical things.'

'My goodness, I didn't think you were that old-fashioned, Charlie,' she said sweetly.

'Old-fashioned? What do you mean?'

'Saying such silly things about women really makes you look bad and *old-fashioned*.' She turned to Jonah. 'We'll change places on the outskirts of Rivenshaw and I'll see how my spectacles work for driving, eh?'

Jonah lingered to poke his brother in the chest. 'She's right, you know.'

'What do you mean?'

'That was an old-fashioned thing to say, Charlie. Don't let Vi hear you talking like that. Does she realise you think any man could do her job better than she does?'

'I don't think it.'

'You sound as if you do when you talk like that.' Whistling cheerfully, he got into the car.

Charlie watched them drive away, then looked at the

optician's thoughtfully and took a hesitant step towards it. Wouldn't hurt to find out— No! He shook his head and walked away very briskly.

18

There had been one or two small burglaries in Ellindale and Birch End, but after Sergeant Deemer visited the houses and warned people to keep their doors locked at night, the thefts stopped and no one thought any more about it. It must have been a passing tramp.

He wished he had more men and could do more to pursue criminals and sort out problems, but at times like these the authorities were reluctant to spend any more money on policing this relatively peaceful area.

But he wouldn't give up. He'd keep putting the pieces together until he could see the whole picture more clearly.

Recently there had been a few violent incidents in Rivenshaw, with people getting bashed in the street. No one had actually reported these attacks to him, so he had decided it was no business of his if people wanted to let others black their eyes.

It was only when someone casually mentioned *who* had got hurt, that he was puzzled. Not one of the victims was the sort of person usually associated with fighting. In fact, they were all shopkeepers.

His heart sank as he had begun to suspect what was going on, only he needed proof to get his superiors to act.

Now another shopkeeper in Birch End had been beaten up. This time he felt certain that the attack would be reported, because Mr Champlin was very much in favour of law and order and not the sort to give in to bullying. But again, no complaint was made. Surely the man had seen the person who had attacked him?

Deemer decided it was time to do something about this, proof or no proof. No one was going to turn his peaceful valley into a place where crimes were committed with impunity.

He had only two constables to help him, which was normally adequate: a new inexperienced young constable, Archer, who had recently been appointed to Rivenshaw police station to replace a man who'd been promoted; and Parker, with four years' experience, was stationed out at Birch End and normally did a very thorough job.

After some thought about how to tackle this problem, Deemer called them together for a meeting about the situation. 'A pattern of attacks like this usually means someone is forcing the shopkeepers to pay protection money. I saw it happen more than once during my years in Manchester. If that's what's going on here, it needs nipping in the bud very firmly.'

Archer gasped. 'I've heard it on the news on the radio, and seen it in the pictures, but I never thought we'd get that sort of crime here. What can we do about it, Sarge?'

'Nothing much until someone lodges a complaint. Parker, you and I will go and see Mr Champlin in Birch End. He hasn't complained but he was beaten up badly enough to put him in bed. Archer you can keep an eye on the station while we're out.'

The young constable looked disappointed but knew better than to protest.

'We'll go straight away,' Deemer said. 'I'll get the police car out.' He didn't always use the vehicle, because you heard and saw more about what was going on if you patrolled on foot.

The Champlins lived over the grocery store they owned.

When Sergeant Deemer and his constable went into the shop, Mrs Champlin let out a gasp and looked at them apprehensively.

'Is your husband at home, Mrs C?' the sergeant asked, noting the reddened eyes that showed she'd been crying.

'He's ill, I'm afraid, had a bad fall. Can't see anyone for a few days.'

A customer came in and Deemer waited till she'd finished serving the woman and the door had shut behind her, then rested his hands on the counter and leaned forward so that he was closer to her. 'We both know your husband was beaten up. And if you don't take me upstairs to see him, I'll go up on my own and make a big, loud fuss about it, one that can be heard right down the street.'

'Please, Sergeant, let this drop. You'll only make things worse.'

'I can't actually do anything official unless Mr C lays a complaint, but I can at least gather information for possible future use.' He waited a few seconds and added, 'I'm definitely going to do that, Mrs C, one way or another.'

Someone else came into the shop just then and she said in a different tone of voice, 'No. I won't let you disturb my poor sick husband, Sergeant.'

Deemer looked at her in surprise then studied the customer more closely. Sam Griggs. Was it him, then? The expression on Mrs Champlin's face could only be described as 'terrified'.

When he moved closer to her to speak quietly, Griggs moved closer too, standing right beside the sergeant now.

'My husband fell down the stairs and that's all there is to it. Now, I have customers to serve.'

Deemer scowled at her and left the shop. As he drove off, he looked in his rear-view mirror and saw Griggs standing on the pavement outside the shop watching them go. He then began to walk down the street after them, which showed he hadn't gone into the shop to buy anything at all.

As the two policemen discussed what had happened, Deemer took a decision. 'I'm coming back here tonight to get the full story from them.'

'She looked scared to death. I don't think she'll tell you anything, Sarge.'

'No, but her husband might. If he really is injured, I'd guess he was brave enough to stand up to their threats, so he may well be brave enough to tell us what really happened, even if he daren't press charges.'

'Can I come too, Sarge? After all, I'm based here in Birch End.'

'Not this time, lad. Champlin will talk more freely if there's just me. I'll walk up from Rivenshaw after dark, then cut across the fields and get to their backyard along the side streets. We don't want anyone seeing the police car or me, and telling those cowardly devils about it.'

He told Archer what had happened, then let the young fellow put the car away in its garage as a reward for his sensible attitude and behaviour. The lad was a good driver, better than Deemer himself. Well, youngsters were more used to cars, weren't they?

When the constable brought the keys back, Deemer made sure he understood the importance of what they were doing. 'Remember, extortion is worse than simple thieving. If we don't stop it, more people will get robbed and beaten into submission.'

Archer echoed the other young constable's words, 'I wish I could come with you tonight. It's not often something exciting happens in the valley.'

'Once you've had a year or two in the job, you'll be glad for the days when nothing exciting happens, believe me.'

As he started to go through the post, he muttered, 'I'm

going to catch Griggs if it's the last thing I do, and whoever is working with him.'

'Do you know who that is?'

He looked up from the pile of letters and laughed gently. 'I can make a good guess. It's someone who's a lot cleverer than he is, that's for sure. I've dealt with Griggs before. Brute force, not stupid, but not clever enough to organise something like this, either. They'll both get their come-uppance, however long it takes me, I promise you that.'

Deemer walked slowly along the public path that crossed the field next to Birch End. There was enough moonlight to pick his way and it was a well-defined path. He stopped for a moment to check there was no one ahead.

It was a big village these days and he studied it for a few moments before moving on into the side streets, remembering what it had been like when he was a lad. None of these streets of new semi-detached and detached houses had existed then, just huddles of cottages and the occasional larger house.

He moved cautiously and hid a couple of times to let people pass by. When he got to the rear of the grocery shop, he was pleased to see a light in the upstairs sitting-room window. He picked up two handfuls of gravel from the back lane and tossed one against the window.

Nothing happened, so he repeated his action with the other handful.

Someone put out the light and the window opened. 'Who's there?'

He moved forward to show himself. 'Howie? It's me, Gilbert.'

They had been in the Great War together, same regiment. That left a bond, even though Deemer was older than Howie.

'Oh hell, can't you leave well alone?'

'No. And I'm going to raise my voice and yell at you if

you don't let me in. Do you really want to wake the neighbours and let them see you talking to a policeman?'

Silence then, 'All right. Wait there.'

When the back door was unlocked, Deemer slipped inside.

'Better come up to the sitting room,' Howie said. 'But I'm *not* laying charges, whatever you say or do.'

'Threatened your wife, did he? Griggs is very brave about hurting women.'

Howie stopped dead, mouth falling open in shock. 'Who told you it was him?'

'I didn't need telling! I know my valley. Who else could it be? Him and Hutton are the two worst villains round here, but Hutton's run off, and even if he's hiding nearby, he wouldn't dare come into town in daylight, which leaves only Griggs.' He waited for that to sink in, then asked more gently, 'He did threaten your wife, didn't he, lad?'

'Yes. I had no choice, Gilbert, no choice at all. I refused at first but he bashed me and said he'd bash her worse next time. I'm only one man. I couldn't be with her every minute of the day and even if I could, I'd not be able to fight a brute like him.'

'I know, Howie. Your wife's safety is the only thing that'd make a man like you give in to extortion.'

Mrs Champlin came into the room from the bedroom, standing in the doorway, glaring at Deemer.

'Ah, good evening, Mrs C. I hope you had a good day's business.'

'We had a good day till you turned up.'

'Stay out of this, love,' Howie pleaded.

She shook her head. 'No. I want to know what you say to him.'

He looked sadly at his friend. 'I'm *not* laying charges. I'm not risking my May's safety.'

'Tell me a few things, then. That'll help a bit. How much is he making you pay?'

Howie named a sum. 'It's not that much. Won't break the bank.'

'That's only a starter sum. He'll raise it in a few weeks, then raise it again, till he's taking more money out of that shop than you are, till you're having trouble paying your suppliers.'

Both of them looked at him in shock.

'Nay, he won't do that,' Howie said. 'I told him I'd not pay more.'

'He's only to bash your wife and you'll cave in. And if he feels he can get away with it, he'll buy the shop off you eventually, and for much less than it's worth.'

'No one could be that wicked!'

'It's how thieves like him operate, Howie lad. I saw it in Manchester, aye, and more than once.'

Mrs Champlin began sobbing and her husband put his arm round her.

'What can I do? We've worked so hard for this shop. I *can't* just give it away.'

'What you can do is tell me every single detail, yes, and who else he's extorting money from. And from now on, you can tell me if he does anything else or tries to put up the amount you pay. Every detail counts, do you see? Helps me build up a picture, see their weaknesses. There's someone working with him. Did you get any idea who?'

Howie hesitated, then said, 'Tell him, May.'

'I saw Mrs Harris sitting in the car waiting for him each time he called. I was peeping out from the upstairs.'

Deemer whistled softly. He'd wondered. How could a woman who'd had a comfortable life turn to something like this? Eh, people said there was nowt as queer as folk, and they were right. He reckoned these two had told him all they knew so stood up to leave.

'I'm on the telephone at the police station and so are you here. You don't have to be seen coming to see me.'

'It's still not safe. The operator listens in and she's a gossip.'

Gilbert thought for a minute. 'You've only to say my order is ready and I'll come round. Or you can send a letter. If you post it before nine, I'll get it the same day by second post. One way or another, I'm going to get the proof I need to stop Griggs and his accomplice. Then, once I've gathered enough information, we'll get in men from other areas and pounce on the sod, catch him in the act.'

'I think my wife's right and it is Harris's wife who's managing it all,' Howie blurted out suddenly. 'Ex-wife, I should say. Harris is well shut of her.'

'Go on, Howie. Did you see her with him any other times?'

'Yes. When I gave him the money the third time he came here, I peeped out of the shop window and she was in the car again. He made a victory sign when he went back out and she laughed . . . clapped her hands together and laughed, she did, damn her to high heaven!'

Deemer thought hard, then sat down again. He noted it all down and Howie signed it, much to his wife's dismay.

He walked slowly back across the fields, heartsick for Adam Harris and Howie both, hoping desperately that he could stop this before anyone else got hurt.

Sam Griggs went into the pawnshop and asked to see Mr Willcox in private. Vi stared at him coolly. 'What about? We deal with pawning things. And since there's no one else in the shop, it's as private here as anyone could wish.'

He moved along to the gap in the counter and raised the flap, easily preventing her from pushing it down again. 'I'll tell *him* what it's about, not the fiddler's monkey. Now, go and tell him I need to see him, or else I'll do it myself.'

Vi stared at him in shock, then found that he was letting

her lower the counter flap, so took a quick step backwards. 'Wait here!'

She went into Charlie's office, which was just round the corner at the back.

He was going through some accounts with Jonah and they both looked up in surprise when she burst in without knocking, shut the door and leaned against it.

'Sam Griggs is here, Charlie, and I don't like the look on his face. He's demanding to see you. He tried to push his way through to the back.'

'Oh, is he? You stay here. I'll deal with him.'

She sat down suddenly as if her legs felt wobbly and Charlie studied her. 'It's not like you to show fear.'

She shivered. 'He frightens me. I felt . . . well, that he would kill me for twopence.'

'In that case I'll take this with me.' He took a small cosh from his desk drawer, putting it in his belt, just under his jacket. He'd used it once or twice on troublesome customers.

'Be careful,' Jonah said quietly. 'Sam Griggs is a big chap and nasty with it.'

'I'll be very careful. But I don't like the thought of him *demanding* to see me and it takes a lot to put the wind up Vi here. I've heard some nasty rumours about him recently.'

Charlie walked out into the shop, staying back from the counter. 'How can I help you, Mr Griggs?'

'You can take me through to that office of yours so that we can talk privately, and then send that woman back out here to serve your customers.'

'What do you want to talk about?'

'You'll find out when we're in there.' He started to lift the flap again.

Charlie whipped out the cosh and slammed it down on

the counter flap, surprising Griggs and making the flap drop with a loud bang. 'I don't take people through to the back without a good reason.'

The noise Griggs made in response sounded more like a snarl than a word. He reached for the counter flap again and as Charlie threatened him with the cosh, he laughed and snatched it from his hand.

He lifted the counter flap and took a step forward. 'You're all mouth and trousers, you are. You couldn't fight your way out of a paper bag.'

'No, but he has backup,' another voice said.

Sam looked sideways and laughed. 'What, you? A cripple who can't even breathe properly. I'm really frightened now.' He pretended to tremble.

Jonah pulled out his revolver, which he now carried at all times since you never knew when trouble would hit. He'd expected any attacks to come from Thad Hutton, so had waited to see what Griggs was after and whether he'd be forced to use the gun.

'You'd not know how to fire that!' Griggs mocked.

Jonah smiled. 'Oh? I wonder what they taught me in officer training in the Army, then? You were too young to serve, but my brother and I weren't, and we both know how to use guns. Charlie, I'm afraid I was right and you were wrong. You will need to carry a gun at all times till we get this little problem settled.'

Griggs scowled at them and stepped back. 'What problem? There's nothing to settle. I wanted to see you privately because I'd prefer folk not to know my business. I, um, apologise if I was too pushy. But since you're so unwelcoming, I'm going to take my custom to another pawnshop.'

'You do that,' Charlie said. 'And don't even come through the door of either of my shops again, because you won't be served.'

The look Griggs gave him was a threat in itself, but he said nothing more as he walked out.

The brothers stood shoulder by shoulder watching him leave, then moved from behind the counter to peep out of the window. Griggs got into a waiting car which drove off straight away.

'Isn't that Mrs Harris driving?' Jonah asked.

'I can't see clearly enough from this distance.'

'You really do need to be able to see who's coming and going, my lad. You don't want to be taken by surprise.'

Charlie let out a heavy sigh. 'All right, all right. My eyes have been getting worse, so I was going to make an appointment to see Purdon about some glasses anyway.'

'Go now, while I'm here. I doubt Purdon will be busy. And make sure there's always someone here to stand guard over Vi and the shop.'

'The rumours must be true, then.'

'What rumours?'

'That Griggs has been threatening shopkeepers into paying him money to protect them. Protect from who! It's Griggs himself who's attacking people.'

'Why the hell didn't you tell me?'

Charlie shrugged. 'Because they were just rumours and anyway, I only heard yesterday.'

'Well, they're more than rumours now. That must be what he wanted to speak to you about. We've seen how Griggs operates, even though he backed down today. You'd better go and see Deemer as well while you're out and tell him what happened.'

'Griggs did nothing illegal and he even apologised. There's nothing the police can charge him with.'

'Nonetheless, go and tell Deemer. Information is always useful and he's a wily old bird. I'm sure he'll already be aware of what's going on, so he'll believe you.'

* * *

Charlie walked along the street to the optician's and wasn't best pleased to find Mr Purdon free to give him an eye test immediately. Custom was down in nearly every shop, which just showed he'd done the right thing going into the pawn trade, whatever his parents had said. At times like this, it was one of the few thriving businesses.

He put up with the fiddling around of the eye test, chose a pair of spectacle frames at random – how the hell did he know which one would look best? – and went along the street to the police station.

Sergeant Deemer wasn't there, only a young constable, who thought the sergeant might be back in half an hour or so. Charlie wasn't going to hang around wasting his valuable time, so decided to return later.

Back at the shop, he told Jonah the sergeant was out, but that he'd ordered some glasses.

'You sound delightfully grumpy.'

'You don't think I'm *pleased* at the prospect of wearing the ghastly things?'

Jonah's smile broadened. 'You'll like it when you can see what's going on around you properly. You can only have passed your army medical by cheating. I bet you never hit anything on weapons practice, either.'

Charlie gave him a wry smile. 'I hit the target board several times . . . but never close to the bull's-eye. Why do you think they had me working in the office?'

'You could have got out of serving with your eyesight.'

'I didn't want to get out of it. I was determined to do my bit. No one was going to give *me* a white feather.'

'Well, from now on, I think you'd better carry a gun like I do, whether you can hit anything with it or not. I didn't have to fire mine but it saved you some trouble today. Don't let Deemer see it. He's against casual gun carrying, though how he expects to stop it when so many men brought "souvenirs" back from the war, I don't know. You have to tell him what happened, though.'

'I'll call in on the way home tonight.'

'You should go back after that half an hour has passed. I'll stay on here.'

'You're a nag, that's what you are.'

Jonah was suddenly very serious. 'I know you're angry about needing glasses, but we can't let this thing with Griggs go, Charlie.'

'No. You're right really.' A moment later, he muttered, 'I don't know what Marion will say about the glasses. She cares a lot about appearances.'

His sister-in-law cared too much about that sort of thing, Jonah thought, but didn't say it aloud. The important thing was that Charlie had ordered glasses and was giving Deemer the information.

Sergeant Deemer was standing behind the counter of the police station, lost in thought, and it took him a few seconds to acknowledge Charlie's presence. 'Oh, sorry, Mr Willcox. Did you want to see me?'

'Yes. We had an incident at the pawnshop in Birch End today. I thought you should know about it.'

The sergeant was suddenly very alert indeed. 'What sort of an incident?'

'Sam Griggs came in, acting the bully.'

'What did he want?'

'He didn't say exactly, but if my brother hadn't been there, he might have thumped me. In fact, I'm pretty sure he would have.'

Deemer questioned him, but agreed that there was nothing you could charge the man with.

'Sorry to waste your time coming here,' Charlie said apologetically. 'Only, my brother insisted I let you know.'

'It's not a waste of time when it gives me more information.'

'That's what Jonah said.'

'He's right. You'd better watch out for yourself from now on and tell him to do the same. I can't prove it yet but I'm certain Griggs is extorting money from several shopkeepers in Birch End by threatening them with violence. Someone beat up Mr Champlin quite badly when he resisted.'

'Oh, hell. I'm not a fighter.'

'Then I'd suggest you hire someone who is to keep an eye on you and your shop. I mean it, sir. We have a tricky situation on our hands and it could turn nasty in the blink of an eye. Well, it *has* turned nasty: Howie Champlin got badly bashed. There are enough men out of work for you to get help.'

'What is the world coming to? After the war they talked about a land fit for heroes. Ha! It's gone from bad to worse.'

'Things will get better, I'm sure. Now, your shop does a lot of business, so Griggs and whoever he's working with will be very keen to dip their fingers in your pie. And they won't want others who're paying them protection money to see you getting away without paying, either. So that's two reasons for them to pursue this further and you to take great care.'

Charlie walked slowly back to the shop, sent his brother home and asked Vi to hire him a bodyguard. 'No, find me two of them, one to work as a night watchman.'

'What about the Rivenshaw shop?'

'Oh, hell, there's that, too. This is going to be expensive.'

'It'd be more expensive to give in to that horrible man. Anyway, it's an ill wind,' she said. 'The men will be glad of the money.'

'Aye, well, I wish fate would find a better way of providing jobs than forcing people to spend their hard-earned money on hiring bodyguards. My brother's had to do the same, even out at Ellindale.'

He could hear how bad-tempered he sounded, but he didn't care. It had been a rotten day so far.

And he still had to tell Marion about the spectacles.

Deemer returned to the police station where young Archer said nothing much had happened except a man had come to see the sergeant and hadn't wanted to wait in the public space near the counter.

'So I put him in the backyard, Sergeant. I hope that was all right.'

'Very sensible. Did he look respectable?'

'Yes, well, sort of.'

Deemer went out to the back, thinking *What next?* But he smiled when he saw who it was. 'Finn lad, where did you spring from?'

'Oh, here and there. I've been helping out over Todmorden way and the inspector said you might have a little job for me.'

'He was right. I do. You couldn't have turned up at a better time. And I'm glad you kept out of sight. I don't want folk to know you're working for me.'

'Good.'

'You look a lot better, lad.' He had been sorry when Finn left the force after the sudden death of his young wife and unborn child. He'd vanished for a year or two, then come back to the district and made it known that he was available to do occasional jobs when they were short of men. Pity he hadn't wanted to rejoin the police force, but he'd been adamant about that.

'I'll get young Archer to make us a cup of tea, and while he's doing that I'll tell you about what's going on round here and where I think you can help . . .'

★ ★ ★

When Charlie went home, Marion went on and on about her day's doings. He tried to be patient but she did the same thing nearly every day and he was getting fed up of hearing her complaints.

She'd tried to make him change his clothes in the evenings and join her in a cocktail whenever they weren't going out, but he didn't see the need to change and anyway, he wasn't a boozer. If he drank anything, it'd be a beer, but she thought beer was common and wouldn't keep it in the house.

In the end, he broke into her monologue to say abruptly, 'I'm getting a pair of spectacles.'

'What?'

'I'm short-sighted. *Very* short-sighted, Mr Purdon says.'

'I did wonder. What sort of frames did you choose?'

He shrugged. 'They all looked alike to me, round wire eyepieces with bits of glass stuck in them and annoying little side hooks that make your ears itch.'

'Tomorrow I'll go back to the shop with you and check that you've chosen the most flattering frame. If you have to wear glasses, we need to be sure they make you look like a successful businessman, not a schoolboy swotting for exams.'

He opened his mouth to protest but she got *that look* in her eyes, so he closed it again. She was right, really. Might as well make the best of a bad job.

And she had a gift for making things look good. It was one of the minor reasons he'd married her.

19

When Jonah came home from the shop, he asked Ben to join them in the house and told everyone about Sam Griggs' attempt to bully Charlie. 'So you'll all need to be particularly vigilant in future. It's not exactly isolated here, but it's out of sight from the village, so keep your guns handy, Leah and Ben. I'll tell people to come running if they hear any shots. In fact, we'll use two quick shots as a signal that we need help.'

Leah stared at him in dismay. 'What next? Things seem to be going from bad to worse lately. I know I said I'd carry a gun but I hate the thought of having to use it.'

'I'm sorry if this upsets you, love, but you needed to know.'

'Of course we did. I'm sorry if I sounded to be blaming you. Anyway, if you've no more *bad* news, let me tell you my piece of good news. The rest of the equipment will be delivered tomorrow. They sent a postcard to let us know.'

'That's excellent. I have some good news as well. They'll be putting in the last stretch of telephone and electricity cables tomorrow, then connecting up those who want to be on the phone, which are only us, the shop and The Shepherd's Rest in Ellindale for the moment. But I think anyone who can afford it will want to have electricity connected.' He smiled as he added, 'If only to listen to the radio.'

Her face lit up. 'How exciting! That'll make us feel very modern and in touch with the wider world, won't it? We can get your radio set out, so that we can listen to concerts and plays; hear the news. You must have missed it and I've never had the chance to listen. What a difference electricity will make to everyone's lives.'

'Yes. And once the phone is in, you'll be able to call for help if you need it, which is the most important thing at the moment as far as I'm concerned.'

Ben stood up again. 'If that's all, Jonah, I'm in the middle of a job and I don't want the mortar to harden, so I'll get back to work. You can be sure I'll keep my eyes and ears open for strangers and I'll tell the lad helping me to do the same.'

When he'd gone, Rosa looked at the other two anxiously. 'I wish I had a gun as well.'

Leah knew her sister still had nightmares about the incident with Thad Hutton and didn't want anything else to upset her. 'You can learn to shoot mine, can't she, Jonah? Then if I can't get to it, you'll be able to.'

'Really?'

'I don't see why not,' Jonah said.

As Rosa smiled and went upstairs to do her homework, he turned to his wife. 'She's a bit young to be handling guns. Are we doing the right thing?'

'Whatever makes her feel more secure is right, as far as I'm concerned. It's not as if she's likely to be shooting anyone, after all.'

'You'll carry the gun with you at all times?'

'How can I? Women's clothes aren't made for guns and certainly not when I'm doing the housework. I'll keep it handy and that's the best I can do without letting people see it.'

'I suppose so.' He frowned for a while, then changed the subject. 'Are you ready to start making the dandelion and burdock for selling now? You've been experimenting for long enough, surely? The last lot tasted delicious to me.'

'Yes. But I just have one small adjustment to make to the recipe. We've got to produce drinks people think are special, because we can't sell them as cheaply as the big companies do, no matter how careful Mr Nolan and I are about buying the ingredients. He's found us more supplies of dried burdock roots now, thank goodness. He says he'll lay in a big stock this spring, pay folk to go out herbing for burdocks and dandelions, then dry the parts we need himself. He knows a shed he can hire for the drying and storing, and he's quite excited about it all.'

'That's good. People keep asking me how it's all going and when we're going to start selling the drinks. Most people in the village won't be able to afford them, sadly, but a few have a little money to spare for the occasional treat and those who've tried your ginger beer at the pub have been very complimentary.'

She took a deep breath and confessed in a rush, 'Jonah, I'm still worried about one thing – the selling side of things.'

'I've been concerned about that too, I must admit. I think we're going to have to involve Charlie, after all.'

'Oh, dear. Can't we just pay someone else to go out and sell for us? It's not that I don't like your brother, but he's so bossy. I know he'll want to take the business over and I don't want that. I'm enjoying the planning and experimenting.'

'Charlie would be upset if we didn't involve him, or at least ask him if he wants to be involved, especially if we brought in strangers. Besides, he's really good at buying and selling things, always has been. Even if I had more energy, *I* wouldn't know where to start.'

There was a brief silence then she sighed. 'Unfortunately you're right. If we're going to provide jobs for local people, which is the most important thing, we'll need to have decent, steady sales. I don't expect to sell our fizzy drinks anywhere except in the district, but even that should be enough to provide work for two or three people. I know how it feels to have no money at all, and to have hunger nagging away at you day after day.'

'Did you often go hungry?'

'After Dad died, I never got quite enough to eat. Towards the end, there were days when I had nothing beyond a slice of dry bread.'

'So you had no choice but to marry me.'

She saw the sadness on his face and grabbed his hand. 'I'd not have married you if I hadn't liked you, whatever state I was in.'

He gave her a searching look, then relaxed a little. 'I believe you mean that. So you've no regrets, then?'

'You know I haven't. I like living with you, being your wife.'

He bent to kiss her. 'I'll speak to my brother about the selling side of the business, then.'

'I want to be there when you do.'

'Of course. It's your business, not mine. But I'm going to insist on a legal agreement being drawn up before we start working with Charlie. You and I will have the majority share in the business. We'll have to settle on a name for it, too. We've whittled it down to three, but—'

'I still like Spring Cottage Mineral Waters best,' she said promptly.

He gave her a quick hug. 'I was going to say, we might as well go for the one you like most. We'll have to design labels and since it's a new company, they'll have to be really attractive ones.'

'Oh, dear. There's so much more to be done than I'd realised. I'm not very artistic, Jonah. The teacher used to laugh at my drawings. I drew a horse once and she thought it was a dog, and a badly drawn one at that.'

'Well, it's not surprising there are some tasks that are new to you and me both. We've neither of us done anything like this before. You didn't think of it as capable of providing full-time jobs for several people when you first got the idea, either. You were just thinking of part-time jobs for a couple of women. But wouldn't it be marvellous if it did provide several jobs, for both men and women?'

'Yes.' She hesitated, then shared her main fear. 'Am I reaching for the moon, Jonah? Trying to do too much?'

'In a way, yes. But then again, why not?'

'Because it's your money that's going into it, that's why not. What if our business fails and you lose it all?'

'I won't put in more money than I can afford to lose, I promise you. Leave me to worry about the financial side of things. That at least I'm capable of.'

He sat tapping his fingers on the table, then shrugged. 'Right then. We'll speak to Charlie tomorrow about the sales side of things.'

Thad Hutton made his way slowly across the moors, avoiding the signposted hikers' paths and keeping out of sight of people. He moved slowly with the occasional rest because he was carrying a heavy bundle and a canvas holdall. He breathed deeply, enjoying being back. There was nothing like the moors, not in any other part of England that he'd visited. You could earn reasonable money in the south, and he had done, but you had to live cheek by jowl with other folk, and that irritated him.

He stood in the entrance to the long narrow cave. It was more like a crack in the rock, he always thought, but it was enough to provide shelter from any kind of weather.

The place hadn't been touched since the police had been here last time, he could tell. And they wouldn't expect him to come back, so why would they bother to tramp across the muddy moors to check it out again? He was counting on that.

He'd go back to the house tomorrow and see what else he could scrounge. Unless someone else had moved in and if so, he'd have to get rid of them without arousing suspicion that he was back. It was still his house, even if he didn't dare live there. As long as he paid the rates, no one could take it from him, at least he didn't think they could. Just let them try!

The cave felt damp, but his wood supply was still there, kicked around. He picked it up and piled it neatly again, then sat on a small stone outcrop just inside the entrance and looked out across the moors. He could see right down the Vale of Ellindale, though Rivenshaw, at the bottom end, wasn't very clear, and only the southern part of the village of Ellindale was visible at the top end.

He'd have liked to keep an eye on Spring Cottage but it was hidden by the curve of a higher part of the moor. Pity. He wondered how that bonny little lass was going on? He'd dreamed about her a few times.

He'd often wished he had a telescope to see into the distance and now he'd got one. Bit of luck that. He'd only intended to break into the house in Cheshire for some food and there it had been, sitting staring at him from the windowsill, a neat little extendable telescope. It had been begging him to carry it away.

He got it out of his pack and used it, delighted to be able to see everything much more clearly. He'd find out what was going on in the valley, but they wouldn't even know he was here.

He set his things out carefully. He had a place for everything here. It was surprising how comfortable you could make yourself in a cave.

He had two stones the same size for standing his pan on

when he was cooking. He'd chipped out the stone so the pan was held safely in place. He had a paraffin burner now, to heat up water for a cup of tea or warm up a tin of something to eat. But he'd still boil his kettle on the fire whenever it was safe to do so because he couldn't nip to the shops in Rivenshaw for more paraffin and it was a hell of a long walk back to the next town.

It was surprising what food they were putting into tins these days. He'd taken a few tins from each of the houses he'd broken into. You could only carry so many, though, when you were on the road. It'd save him spending his own money on food.

He had to keep a money reserve in case he had to go on the run again. He scowled at the mere thought of leaving. Not if he could help it. This was his *home*. If he lived here quietly, surely he could stay for most of the spring and summer then he would go south again during the worst of the winter and earn more money.

Charlie left Jonah in charge of the shop while he went with Marion to look at spectacle frames.

It turned out she'd rung up the shop that morning and had instructed Mr Purdon not to send off the spectacle frames he'd chosen until she'd approved them.

She took one look at them and gave her husband a punch in the upper arm. 'Charlie Willcox, don't you *ever* choose something so important without consulting me again. Those are old men's spectacles.'

'They're very expensive frames,' Mr Purdon protested.

'Yes. But for older men than *my* husband. Show me some others.'

Charlie tried on frame after frame at her bidding, not daring to protest because she had *that look* on her face again.

Mr Purdon got everything at all possible out of his shop

cupboards. She was so picky and uncomplimentary that he thought she'd never find anything, which would mean a lost sale.

In the end she narrowed it down to three frames and waved one hand imperiously. 'Put the others away, Mr Purdon. They're not nearly nice enough for my Charlie.'

In the end she chose the square spectacles.

'They'll be more expensive to make,' the optician warned her. 'It's not a popular style.'

'What has that to do with anything? My husband has a position to maintain in our community and we'll pay what we have to, since he'll have to wear the spectacles a lot of the time. I don't want to look at a fuddy-duddy across the dinner table. Now, how quickly can you get the lenses made?'

'A couple of weeks?'

'Phone up the lens makers and tell them these are needed in a hurry.'

He did this, sounding so uncertain and apologetic she took the telephone from his hand. 'This is Mrs Willcox here. We need those spectacles within the week. I shall send to London for lenses otherwise.'

She listened for a moment, her foot tapping impatiently, then cut the voice short. 'We'll pay the extra.'

There was silence then the person at the other end said something.

'That's more like it.' She handed the telephone back to Mr Purdon and smiled triumphantly at her husband. 'You'll look rather good in those, Charlie.'

As they left the shop, she said again, 'Don't ever make decisions like that without consulting me. You have no sense of style whatsoever. Nor does your brother. *My* family is noted for their taste and elegance, and I won't have you Willcoxes letting us down.'

She looked at the little fob watch pinned to her jacket. 'Is it that time already? I have to meet a friend in Rivenshaw. Call the taxi for me and tell him to hurry up.'

He did this from his shop, watched Marion change a display while she waited and talk to Vi about it. He breathed a sigh of relief when she left.

'Mrs Willcox has an excellent eye for detail,' Vi said as she came back behind the counter. 'I don't know why I didn't think of setting things out that way myself.'

He didn't comment, just asked her to make him a cup of tea and went back into his lovely, peaceful office.

Later in the day, Jonah asked, 'Could you come home with me for an hour tonight, Charlie? There's something we want to discuss with you. I'll drive you there and bring you back home to Birch End afterwards, so it won't take too long.'

'Why do we need to go to your house? If you've something you want to talk about we can do it here. Vi will stop anyone disturbing us if we ask her.'

'Leah and I both need to talk to you, and also we need to show you some things up at Spring Cottage.'

'What things?'

'I'll tell you when we get there.'

'Oh. All right. But why you need to make a mystery of it, I don't know.'

Jonah made sure they got away early, leaving Vi and the night watchman to lock up. As they drove out of Ellindale, they passed some men who'd been digging the trench by the side of the road. They were climbing into a lorry, chatting and laughing now the working day was over.

'Soon have the telephone at your place,' Charlie gloated. 'Not many people in the village have bothered to order it.'

'They will once the business world finds its feet again.

These bad times are coming to an end. I can feel it in the air. It's just starting, so don't expect things to happen overnight, but I keep seeing little signs.'

'Well, that's more than I can feel or see.' But his brother did seem to have a keenly honed instinct where business and money were concerned. He'd often surprised them with his predictions.

Charlie got out of the car as soon as it stopped and strode into the house without waiting for Jonah. 'Nice to see you, Leah. How about a cup of tea for your favourite brother-in-law? It never tastes as good when we make it at the shop.'

'I'll brew a pot in a minute or two but I have another drink I want you to try first.'

He looked at the row of glasses on the table and brightened. 'I hope it's some of your ginger beer.'

Jonah went to kiss his wife's cheek, then they all sat down. 'Over to you, darling.'

She took a deep breath, suddenly nervous. 'It's about my new business, Charlie.'

'Business? Making fizzy drinks, you mean? I thought it was more of a hobby.'

'It started off that way, but . . . well, hikers have been buying the ginger beer at Nancy's shop and they love it . . . and Mr Harris has ordered some . . . and they've even started selling it at the pub. So I think we can sell it all over the area. We'll make money from it, but best of all, we can create jobs for a few people from the village.'

Charlie leaned his chair backwards, balancing on the two rear legs, whistling softly. 'Well, well! You are a dark horse.' He glanced at his brother. '*Leah's* business? Not yours?'

'I'm involved and I shall own a share of it, but it was Leah's idea and it was her recipe that started it off.'

'So why did you bring me here? I don't know anything

about making fizzy drinks, though I'm always willing to taste them for you.'

It was Leah who answered. 'We need your help. Neither Jonah nor I know how to sell things to other businesses and you do. We thought . . . well, you might like to take a share in the business and help get it going. I've heard you say a few times that you like to spread out your investments. It'll only be a modest profit but every bit counts, don't you think?'

She took a bottle of light brown liquid from the dresser. 'Do you like dandelion and burdock? Oh, good. I want you to try this before we go any further. It's made with my new recipe. See what you think.'

He took the glass from her, watching the tiny bubbles rising and bursting for a moment, then sniffing it. 'It certainly smells right. Dandelion and burdock was one of my favourite drinks as a lad.'

He took a sip, rolled it round his mouth and sat staring up at the ceiling before swallowing it. Nodding, he took another sip.

The others didn't say anything till he'd finished the whole glass and put it down.

He looked at them. 'It's good. Really good.'

'I knew you'd like it,' Jonah said. 'Is there a glass for me, Leah?'

'You'd drink all my stock if I let you.' But she poured him some and when Charlie held out his empty glass, refilled that.

She watched them savour the drinks. Jonah winked at her. Charlie took his time, studying the liquid a couple more times in between mouthfuls.

'We've bought the main equipment to do things properly. It's out in the old barn. Would you like to see it, Charlie?'

'Definitely.' He drained the second glass, got up and followed her out.

Jonah stayed where he was, his mouth twisting a little and his expression sad. Then he poured himself another half-glass. 'Clever Leah. You'll be all right . . . whatever happens.' He raised the glass as if drinking a toast to her.

Everything in him strained to go and join them, but he didn't allow himself to do that. He wanted it to be clear that *she* was in charge.

He never lied to himself and he knew that over the years his breathing had gradually become more strained. It had helped to come out to live in Ellindale, but he wasn't going to make old bones, or even middle-aged ones, probably.

He was determined to train Leah to be self-sufficient, enterprising and businesslike before . . . well, before his lungs gave up on him.

That wouldn't be for a few years yet, he hoped. It was happening very slowly, after all. Surely he would be granted more time with her? A child, even. They were both longing for one. He swiped a tear from his eye and breathed in and out deeply to settle himself.

Out in the old barn, Charlie nodded a greeting to Ben, who was working at a corner bench. 'You do woodwork as well?'

'Not the fancy stuff, but my dad liked making things and I used to help him.'

Charlie looked slowly round, taking his time.

'It's looking good in here now,' he admitted. 'What about the other side, the youth hostel?'

'We're finishing the fizzy drinks section first.' Leah smiled. 'We can't decide what to call it, so the nickname "fizzy" stayed. I know you want the business to sound very posh, but this is just between us.'

He walked over to a bench. 'Tell me about the equipment.'

'We've bought enough to start up, though if the business does well, we'll have to buy some more – but it's easy to get hold of. We bought bigger vats to ferment the ginger beer in, or mix the dandelion and burdock. That narrow table with raised edges is to do the bottling on. The pipes will be attached to whatever container of drink is ready and it'll have to be hand pumped to start with.'

'You'll need a lot of bottles and somewhere to store them.'

'I know. Ben has made the roof of one of the outhouses waterproof and we're putting them in there. We'll use the end of this room as a washing place. Mr Nolan says we have to use only perfectly clean bottles. I'm thinking of buying overalls and caps for the workers so that they're immaculately clean too.'

'What about the ingredients? You'll need good stocks in case you have a rush on something. You don't want to run out of supplies.'

'Mr Nolan will help us get the ingredients to make a steady supply and he'll check the recipes, too, to make sure there's nothing harmful in them. He's been teaching me about sterilisation for the bottles. It's what Mum did anyway, but we'll be doing it on a bigger scale. We're also thinking of making fizzy water. He says he's seen it on sale in London.'

'Fizzy water! Why bother? Water's tasteless, whether it's fizzy or not.'

'Fizziness feels nice on the tongue. I've been reading about it. Some spas have naturally fizzy water. Scientists have worked out how to add fizz to ordinary liquids. We can try it out, see if it sells. The water from our spring is very good, you know. Mr Nolan has had it analysed for us. It has some excellent minerals in it. Rich people pay a lot of money for such water.'

He looked at her as if he'd never seen her before. 'You've been a busy lady, Leah! What about labels for the bottles? If I'm to sell them I need something people will like the look of.'

'That's another thing I can't do on my own, Charlie, however many books I read. I'm not at all artistic. I wouldn't know how to design labels or check that a design is good enough for our purpose. I do want them to look expensive, though.'

'Very special mineral waters,' he murmured.

She beamed at him. 'Oh! That sounds just right. We could put it on the labels. I've been racking my brain for days, trying to work out what to say about our drinks, and you came up with a good slogan without even thinking about it.'

'I like playing with words.'

'I enjoy words, too, but I'm not witty. Charlie, we really need you for the selling. You know instinctively how to do it. I don't understand that side of business yet. I can make the drinks, yes, and very good ones. I'm thinking of making some brand new drinks later on too, not just the well-known types, by the way.'

'Not ambitious, are you?' he teased.

'I'm ambitious most of all to provide jobs for people in Ellindale.'

He smiled at her. 'In your own quiet way, you're going to make a big difference if you succeed in doing that.'

'With your help, we shall succeed. I have a very good sense of taste, and my mother's and grandmother's recipes are stored here.' She tapped her forehead. 'Recipes with little differences that no one else knows about, but which make the drinks much nicer.'

'That knowledge is the capital you're bringing to the business. Jonah seems able to supply the money. I didn't know he had so much. I'll put some money in, too, of course, and I'll take charge of the selling.'

She waited, watching him look round the barn again, studying it more carefully now, then he turned back to her.

'Let's go back and talk to Jonah, shall we? I don't want

to have to repeat everything to him. He says it's your business, but it's still his money.'

'I know. I wish he wouldn't keep saying the business is mine so firmly.'

They looked at one another and such a stricken look came over her face that he gripped her shoulder and said, 'We'll keep him alive. They didn't think he'd live this long when they invalided him out of the Army towards the end of the war, but Mum looked after him and later on, I did.'

'I'll look after him too. That's more important than anything else. I'm very fond of him.'

'It shows. I think this business will help him. He used to get very down in the dumps sometimes, bored by sitting around so much. But he doesn't seem to have been downhearted since he married you.' He gave her a nudge with his elbow and said yet again, 'I chose well, didn't I?'

'Yes. Very well.'

They walked back to the house together, both with a lot to think about. She felt closer to her brother-in-law than she ever had before.

Jonah looked up as they came into the kitchen.

Charlie sat down opposite him at the table, Leah sat beside Jonah and threaded her hand in his, giving it a quick squeeze.

'You keep saying this is Leah's business,' Charlie began, 'but I'm not getting involved unless we're all three of us in it together. That includes you, and not just your money.'

Jonah shrugged. 'Of course I'll be playing my part, but it *is* Leah's business because it was her idea. We'll do everything legally, with a proper contract drawn up.'

Charlie stiffened. 'Don't you trust me?'

'I don't trust fate. I want to know Leah will be safe if anything happens to me. Or you, come to that.'

Charlie had opened his mouth, but at this he shut it with a snap. The look he gave his brother made Leah realise how very fond of one another they were beneath all the joking and banter. Their love shone from them.

She changed the subject hastily, because they'd gone far enough down a sad path. 'So . . . what do we do about designing labels? It's very important to make a good first impression.'

That shut them up and she let the two men think about it in peace.

'I'll ask Marion,' Charlie said at last. 'She likes arty things. She'll know someone who can do it or one of her friends will.' He rolled his eyes. 'You should have heard her this morning, going on at poor Mr Purdon about the spectacles I'd chosen. You'd think we'd committed a crime. But the ones she chose for me do look better.'

'She has superb taste, always dresses beautifully,' Leah said wistfully. 'I've never seen anyone look as elegant, except for movie stars.'

He nodded. 'She does, doesn't she? There's no one as stylish as my Marion. She'll probably set a few new fashions in maternity clothes too, once she starts showing.'

Leah hoped her jealousy wasn't obvious.

When they were in bed that night, Jonah put his arm round her. 'I'm sorry I haven't given you a baby yet.'

'It might be my fault, for all we know. It's silly to blame someone. I think it's just . . . fate.'

'Well, let's give fate a hand, eh? You're not the only one who's jealous of my brother and his wife. I'd love us to have a child.'

She turned eagerly in his arms, praying that this time the miracle she longed for would occur.

And once again, the lovemaking, although quite pleasant, left her wondering why people got so enthusiastic about it all. At least it wasn't painful. Some of the women where she used to live had complained about their husbands' attentions not being comfortable.

Anyway, what did such details matter? She might not be madly in love with Jonah but she had grown very fond of him and was glad she'd married him. She too wanted a child, no, not a single child, several children.

What if she never had any? Tears came into her eyes at the mere thought of that.

Surely life couldn't be so unfair, so unkind?

20

Sam stood by the window, scowling out as he buttoned his shirt. 'I don't like Willcox getting away with it. When folk hear about that, some of them will try to stop paying as well, I know they will.'

Ethel yawned and stretched, feeling good after an energetic session in bed. Sam might not be the most intelligent man in the valley, but he was an indefatigable lover. 'We'll work out how to deal with that when it happens. I think we'll drive into Rivenshaw tonight and have a meal at one of the hotels.'

'I'd rather have fish and chips at home. I never enjoy my food as much when I have to fiddle with knives and forks. And fancy stuff that costs the earth isn't as filling, either.' He flexed his upper arm. 'I need good, hearty food to keep my body strong.'

'Well, I want to go out. I'm missing that sort of meal.'

'Let's go to the Green Man, then. At least they served a nice steak last time.'

She grimaced. 'And people stared at us. I'd prefer to go further afield.'

'Looks don't kill. We'll go to the Green Man if we go anywhere.'

'I said—'

He picked her up by the front of her dressing gown and shook her so hard she cried out to him to stop hurting her.

'I'm fed up of you always telling me what we do, Ethel. I say we go to the Green Man.'

She opened her mouth to protest, then something in the way he was looking at her made her back off and say, 'Oh, let's just get some fish and chips.'

He smiled, not a nice smile. She hadn't noticed how cruel he could look before, because he'd never stared at her in quite that way. But then, she'd never been in his power before.

No, he wouldn't dare! She pulled herself together and stared right back at him. If she showed she was afraid of him, he'd take over.

He shrugged and looked away. 'All right. I'll get us some fish and chips on my way home from the pub.'

'From the pub? What am I going to do while you're out?'

'What women usually do when their men aren't around. How should I know?' With that he turned and strode out of the house.

She watched him go, feeling indignant – well, more than indignant. She was beginning to worry about him. She'd believed she could control him but he was starting to call the shots in a way Adam never had, a brutal way. The other day he'd punched her in the stomach. Not enough to injure her, but not playfully, either. It had been meant as a warning

She didn't like feeling physically afraid, never had been before, but she couldn't manage without Sam at the moment, so she'd have to tread carefully.

Not for the first time she wished she hadn't let herself get carried away just because he was a good lover. When she had enough money saved, she'd leave him and go to live somewhere like Bournemouth, posing as a widow. She wished she had as much money as she'd pretended to Adam, but however much you threatened tenants, if they had no money coming in and had pawned most of their possessions, they couldn't pay you.

Bournemouth would have to wait, but her time would come. Widows with money could lead a very pleasant life.

Well, at least she couldn't get pregnant nowadays. Going to see that dreadful woman to get rid of the baby had taken one worry off her mind. Unfortunately, Adam had had to rush her to hospital afterwards when she started bleeding, so he'd found out what she'd done. The doctor had said she'd not be able to have any more children and Adam had never been the same with her since, never been as easy to manage, either.

Sam wouldn't be able to come after her when the time came, because she'd plan it carefully and leave a false trail that suggested she was going to emigrate. She was good at making plans, good at fooling people too. She should have gone on the stage.

She'd fooled Adam for years until the baby incident. He was such a soft touch. But stupid about money. She'd made extra money for him in the laundry and he'd not been at all grateful, even though it'd saved it from bankruptcy.

His father had messed everything up and without her guidance, Adam would mess things up too and that laundry would go bust within a few years. But her houses would still be standing, bringing in rents. She'd sack Sam, making him think she'd sold them.

She smiled at the thought. She had a woman picked out to manage them and pose as the new owner. Women had fewer opportunities than men, so needed good jobs more. This one would never betray her.

There was a lot to plan. If Sam started leaving her alone, he had only himself to blame if she found a way to take his share of the money as well. She smiled. Well, why not? It'd be the icing on the cake.

*   *   *

Adam found it wonderful to have got rid of Ethel and have the house to himself. Minnie and her sister were quiet young women who liked to sit in front of the kitchen fire in the evenings and read his wife's old magazines. He let Minnie have her young man in, on condition he never went further than the kitchen. It was an added protection for the two young women.

He lived in fear of Ethel returning. However, his lawyer said she'd have no right to come back unless he let her, and Adam knew that however weak he'd been in the past, he wasn't going to do anything that would allow Ethel back into his life. Since she'd murdered his baby, he'd hated even the sight of her.

Ethel turned up at the laundry one day, incandescent with rage because she hadn't been able to get into the house, insisting she needed to collect some other bits and pieces.

'Give me a list and I'll have Minnie pack them.'

'I want them now and if you don't let me in, I'll rip up everything I can lay my hands on here.'

As she lunged for a pile of papers, he grabbed hold of her and called for help. She might not be very big but she made up for that by sheer violence.

Together, he and his manager got her to the door and pushed her into the street.

'If you come back, I'll call the police and have you arrested for trespass.'

He thought she'd still defy him, but a woman started laughing inside the laundry, and when he turned he saw faces pressed to the nearby windows. The laughter grew louder.

Ethel went bright red and strode off down the street.

'Never let my ex-wife in here,' he said to Jim. 'Spread the word. She's not to set foot across the threshold, even if you have to use force to keep her out.'

He went home to pack anything of hers he could find. It was a good thing he did this with his usual care, because he found various items hidden among her old clothing in the spare bedroom – ornaments and pieces of silver, things that were light and would fit into a pocket.

It made him feel dirty even to touch her things. What had he ever seen in her?

The following day he set about making the laundry a safer, happier place to work. Some of the workers were still a bit stiff with him, but they'd come round.

The following week he went to Rivenshaw to get the wage money out of the bank. As he was walking back to his car, he saw Ethel turn into the street at the far end, coming in his direction. He ducked into the nearest shop to avoid meeting her.

'Can I help you, Mr Harris?'

He spun round and only then realised he was in a haberdasher's and a woman was looking at him enquiringly from behind the counter. He could feel his cheeks growing hot with embarrassment, because it was usually ladies who shopped in these places and he couldn't think what to ask for.

He didn't know the woman but she had such kind eyes he confessed, 'I just nipped in to avoid meeting the female I consider my ex-wife now since we're separated and getting a divorce. Do you mind if I shelter here for a moment or two?'

'Not at all, Mr Harris.'

He went to the door, started to peer out, then ducked back. 'Oh dear, she's stopping to look in the window of the next shop. I hope she doesn't come in here.'

'Why don't you go through to the back room till we're sure she's gone away?'

'Would you mind? You must think I'm foolish.'

'No. I think you're wise to avoid her. She's a very loud woman when she's angry, isn't she? I haven't been in Rivenshaw for long but I've seen her berating people. I'm Christina Galton, by the way. This used to be my aunt's shop. I inherited it after she died. It's hard times to make a living but I scrape by, because people have to do a lot of mending to keep their clothes wearable. This way.'

She held up the counter flap and he went through it into a neat room which seemed to be both office and sitting room.

He was just in time. The bell on the shop door rang and he heard his wife's voice calling for service.

Miss Galton rolled her eyes at him, then went back into the shop. 'Good afternoon. How can I help you?'

'The correct thing to say is, "How *may* I help you?" Did no one ever teach you grammar?'

There was utter silence, which continued for a surprisingly long time, then his wife asked for some pink thread to mend her petticoat. He didn't remember her ever sewing before. Why would she need to do it now? Surely she couldn't be short of money?

Miss Galton was perfectly polite, but somehow her voice had lost the friendly tone. She didn't chat to Ethel, but responded mainly in monosyllables and it wasn't long before her customer left.

He peeked out through the partly open door and saw Miss Galton walk to the door and stare through the glass panels. When she turned and saw him, she said, 'You'd better stay in the back a little longer, Mr Harris. She's looking in the next shop now and doesn't seem in a hurry.'

'I'm sorry she was so rude to you.'

She shrugged. 'Rudeness reflects badly on her, not me.'

'You're sure you don't mind me staying?'

'Not at all. Would you like a cup of tea? I was just about to brew one when you came in.'

'Yes. That would be very welcome.'

'It's one of the advantages of living behind the shop. I can do other things while I wait for customers.'

She continued to chat as she pushed a small kettle on to a gas burner, breaking off twice to go back into the shop and serve customers with thread and pins.

The sales were for pennies only each time. 'It must be very hard for shopkeepers to manage in these troubled times,' he said when she came back.

'Yes. But I do manage. I don't have rent to pay on the shop, or I might not be able to. My aunt owned it, so as long as I can pay my council rates, I can wait for better times to come.'

'Do you think they will?' He'd come back from the war into more than a decade of deepening economic depression and hadn't owned the laundry through any good times.

She set a cup down in front of him and pushed a sugar bowl towards him. 'We have to believe they will, don't we? I listen to the radio and try to understand what they're saying about how the country is going. I'm sorry I can't offer you any biscuits. That's one of my little economies.'

He liked the way she didn't pretend. He couldn't help noticing how weak the tea was and how little milk she'd put in. A lot of people had to re-use the tea leaves these days.

When they'd finished, she stood up. 'I'll just go and check that your ex-wife has left the street.'

'If you wouldn't mind.'

She came back a minute later. 'Mrs Harris just came out of the grocer's and she's walking back this way.'

'Whatever is she doing, hanging around like this?'

'Filling in time. A lot of people walk up and down aimlessly without buying anything.'

'Ethel's still living in Birch End, though, in one of her own houses in Crowther Street, not in Rivenshaw.'

Miss Galton went to look out again and he stood in the doorway to her little sitting room, ready to move back.

'How strange! She's studying each shop very carefully. It's almost as if she's waiting to see who goes in and out. Why would she do that, Mr Harris? Come and look.'

He did. 'She's not window shopping, that's for sure.'

He'd overheard one of the workers at the laundry whispering to the woman folding sheets with her that Sam Griggs was threatening shopkeepers in Birch End, demanding and getting protection money from them.

Adam had thought it just a foolish rumour, but as Ethel stood for quite some time in front of a shop, it occurred to him abruptly that if this was true, she might be involved with Griggs. She was living with the fellow, after all, and was far too sharp not to notice what he was doing.

Ethel had a strange attitude towards the world. She seemed to crave excitement and if there was none, then she'd provoke a row, throw things, her eyes glittering with the thrill of it. But surely she wouldn't break the law?

Only she'd done that already, and more than once, now he came to think of it. She'd not only threatened tenants who got behind with the rent with violence, but had boasted to him about getting Sam to thump them or turn them out of a house roughly, so that their furniture got broken. She'd laughed at Adam when he protested and dared him to go to the police about it.

In fact, she wasn't a good landlord in any way. Oh, she kept her houses waterproof, but she did nothing to the insides unless forced to, and she had no sympathy whatsoever with her tenants' problems.

He didn't say anything to Miss Galton, wasn't going to tell anyone about his conjecture until he'd thought it through properly. Two could play the game of keeping their eyes open.

'Mrs Harris has turned off the street now.'

'Good. And thank you so much for helping me today, Miss Galton. If I can ever help you in any way at all, don't hesitate to ask me.'

She looked at him thoughtfully. 'I think you actually mean that.'

'I do.'

'Then if I ever get desperate, I'll come to you.'

He drove back to Birch End, lost in thought. Surely his wild guess couldn't be right? Surely Ethel wouldn't be breaking the law to that extent? She had no *need* of the money. She was richer than he was, had taunted him with that many a time.

But she did seem to need excitement in her life, need it quite desperately!

To Jonah's surprise, Charlie turned up at the pawnshop scowling darkly at the world. What on earth had got into his normally cheerful brother?

Charlie jerked his head in the direction of the office, so Jonah followed him, surprised when his brother slid the bolt on the door.

'They've arrived.'

'What?'

'Those damned spectacles. Purdon sent word late yesterday. Marion made me wear them all evening. Thank heavens we weren't going out anywhere, that's all I can say.'

'Let me see how you look in them.'

Charlie hesitated, then pulled out a little leather case and took out the spectacles, hesitating again before putting them on. He didn't say anything and just stood scowling even more darkly as he waited for a comment.

'Actually, I like them.'

'You don't have to pretend, Jonah.'

'I'm not pretending. If you're going to continue in business, expand into other areas once times are better, as you've told me, you'll look more responsible and clever in them.'

'Marion told you to say that, didn't she?'

'No. I haven't spoken to her for days.' He went across and put his arm round his brother's shoulders. 'Why are you so upset about needing them, Charlie?'

'Because no one wants to wear glasses. And . . . because of the way I tormented other kids at school. Every time I've put these damned things on I can hear myself yelling, "Speccy four-eyes". Donny Harper gave me a pasting once for doing it to a friend of his. He was a kind lad, was Donny. And then he was killed in the war, poor sod.'

'Ah. You're suffering from guilt. It's a bit late to change what you did when you were a lad, but if you want to make amends, you can find Donny's wife and give her a helping hand. I've heard she's having a tough time. Maybe that'll assuage your guilt.'

'Is she still around? She's never been in here. She used to be quite pretty.'

'I saw her only the other day. She's not pretty now. She's scrawny and looks worn to the bone.'

Charlie sneaked a look at himself in the little mirror Vi used to check that her hair was tidy. 'And you really think they make me look more efficient and businesslike?'

'Yes. Really.'

'Have Leah's glasses arrived yet?'

'Not yet.' He chuckled suddenly as the humour of it caught him. 'Like you, she doesn't want to wear spectacles and is embarrassed by the change.'

Charlie's expression brightened a little. 'Well, when they do arrive, we could all go out for tea at the Green Man, then she and I can wear them and face the world together. It'll get it over with.'

'It wouldn't hurt. She's not happy about having to wear them, that's for sure.'

'We'll do it then.' Charlie turned, then stopped to add, 'I will help Donny's wife, if I can. Do you know where she lives?'

'With her parents in Bentinck Street, end house, next to the fish and chip shop.'

Charlie left the pawnshop earlier than usual that night, making his way to Bentinck Street and shuddering as he walked along it. The whole street reeked of poverty.

Women were dressed alike, wearing wrap-around pinafore dresses, all faded, some downright ragged. They were standing at their doors gossiping in spite of the evening chill. None of them spoke to him, but all of them stared at him, and he knew this wasn't because of his new glasses. It was because he was well-fed, out of place here.

He stopped at the house next to the fish and chip shop, wrinkling his nose at the smell. The house door was closed and he almost walked on past it, but he'd never been a coward, so he drew a deep breath and stopped, knocking.

A woman's voice called to a child to get away from the door and footsteps sounded on the other side of it, coming closer.

The woman who opened the door looked beaten. She was thin and hunger sat in her eyes and in the droop of her whole body. The children peering from the other side of the room were thin too, but not as thin as she was.

'Have you a minute, Mrs Harper?'

'What for? I don't need to pawn anything, thank you, Mr Willcox. I've nothing left that's worth pawning.'

'I'm here to give you something.'

'What's the catch? I told you: I don't have any money.'

He'd got a story ready made up. 'There isn't a catch. An old relative left me some money on condition I find three war widows and give them each something from her. She was widowed too, in the Boer War, you see.'

The woman waited, arms folded across her faded pinafore, looking sceptical.

'You were married to Donny Harper, right?'

Her whole face softened. 'Yes, I was. He was killed at Ypres. He was a wonderful man.'

'Then you'll qualify as one of the three recipients.'

'Why me?'

'Because I can choose who I give the first lot of money to. I knew Donny, which is why I thought of you. He and I were at school together. And when I was unkind to other kids, he tried to stop me. Now I'm the one they should call "Speccy Four-Eyes".' He indicated his own face.

'He always tried to look after people who were being bullied, my Donny did.'

'Anyway, can I come in and talk about my, um, aunt's bequest?'

'Well, all right.' She went back inside and he followed.

The children went to stand next to an old woman who was sitting in a creaking rocking chair by the fireplace, even though there was no fire lit. Her face was blank.

'That's my mum. She's a bit forgetful, these days. And those two are the neighbour's kids. She pays me what she can to mind them. She's got a job at the laundry. My lad is older and he's out scrounging for firewood.'

Charlie fumbled in his pocket pulling out the envelope he'd prepared. 'Here you are. It's ten pounds.'

She stiffened and made no attempt to take it from him. 'What do I have to do for it? I don't accept charity.'

'It's not charity, I told you. It's a bequest from my Auntie Janie.'

She hesitated then took hold of the envelope, peeped inside and sucked in her breath sharply.

'There's a condition.'

She thrust it back at him. 'No.'

'You haven't heard what it is.'

'I'm not giving my body to any man, whatever he pays.'

'Hell fire! I'm not asking you to, woman. I'm a happily married man and even if I wasn't, I'd never force a woman.'

'Sorry. What *are* you asking me to do, then?'

'You have to find me another widow for the second bequest. But it has to be someone who really, really deserves a helping hand.'

'How do I prove that?'

He shrugged. 'My aunt said there'd be no need for proof. She said if I chose the right first person, the others would follow. The second person has to find a third.' He heard his voice soften as he added, 'I'm sure you're the right sort.' He held out the envelope again.

Mrs Harper took it from him, stared at it for a moment, then clutched the envelope to her breast. Her hand was trembling now and her breath was shaky, as if this good fortune was just sinking in. 'I'm still not sure whether to believe you.'

'The money's the proof. If you bring the name of the next person to the pawnshop, I'll give the same amount to another woman. Give the name to me, not anyone else.'

'All right. I'll have to think about who needs it most. Thank you for choosing me, Mr Willcox. I'm sorry if I were suspicious. It's the last thing I'd expected from you. Or from anyone, these days.'

He paused at the door. 'I nearly forgot. You're not to tell anyone about it.'

'Don't worry. If anyone knew I had this money, they'd be begging for a share or trying to rob me. I shan't even tell my father about it. Oh!'

'What?'

'It's all in banknotes. How will I keep it secret if I have to change a whole pound? Everyone knows I don't have that much money.'

'You can come into the shop tomorrow and Vi will change it for you. You can keep coming for change. No one will be surprised if you come there.'

'Can I leave most of it with you after that? You'll have somewhere safe to keep your money. Just till I work out what to do with it? I don't have anywhere that's safe here. There are kids in and out of the houses round here, and they're into everything. My poor mum would be as likely to throw it on the fire as keep it safe.'

'Yes, of course you can. And here.' He fumbled in his pocket and pulled out a florin. 'You can use this to buy some fish and chips for tea.'

'Thank you. But you must take it out of the money when I bring it into the shop. I insist on that.'

'Are you always this stubborn?'

'I've had to be when protecting my own interests.'

As he walked home, Charlie let out a little huff of breath that was nearly a laugh. Being philanthropic was the last thing he'd expected of himself, too. And he'd let himself in for giving away money to two other women as well. Why had he done that?

He didn't know, but it wasn't till he got home that he realised he'd completely forgotten about having to wear glasses.

And actually, the world was much clearer with them on. He liked that.

Anyway, what did wearing glasses matter when some people were so near starvation? He'd not been into their houses before, just seen them in the shop. It really brought it home to you.

He looked up at the sky. If there was a god up there, he'd be laughing at the sight of a bespectacled Charlie Willcox turning into a philanthropist.

But maybe he'd approve of it.

Mr Purdon came running out of his shop just as Jonah was about to get into his car. 'Your wife's glasses have arrived, Mr Willcox. Can you ask her to come in and I'll make sure they fit properly before she takes them home?'

'Yes, of course.'

'They look very nice, I must say. I haven't seen that frame made up before. The quality shows.'

'I'll bring her in tomorrow morning.'

'Good.'

Jonah grimaced as he started the car. Now he had to persuade Leah that she looked all right in them. As far as he was concerned, she'd look good in anything but people were so silly about glasses. He wished *his* only problem was needing to wear spectacles.

As he drove out of Ellindale, the sun came out. Shame there were no neighbours nearby to chat to occasionally, but the old house near Spring Cottage had been closed up for many years. It'd need a lot of work doing if anyone was to live there again.

When he drew up at Spring Cottage, his spirits lifted, as they always did at the sight of his home.

Leah came to the door radiating happiness.

He got out of the car quickly. 'Something good's happened, I can see it in your face.'

'Rosa's been awarded the Esherwood Bequest. Isn't that wonderful? Isn't she a clever girl?'

'Oh, my goodness! That's marvellous.'

Rosa came to stand at the doorway, looking flushed and as happy as he'd ever seen her. 'The scholarship pays for my fees and books, Jonah, and even my uniform if that's needed, so I won't be a burden on you.'

'Well done, Rosa! I'd have happily paid for you to go to grammar school, mind, even if you hadn't won the scholarship.' He didn't say it but this award made her a very special girl indeed in the valley, since only one girl and one boy received an Esherwood Bequest each year.

'You can pay for me to go to university later on instead,' she said. 'I want to become an English teacher in a grammar school when I grow up.'

'That would be wonderful.' He gave her another hug for good luck.

When they went inside, he mentioned Leah's spectacles being ready, and she grimaced and shrugged. Within a couple of minutes she was smiling at her sister again, though.

21

'How shall we decide who to offer our jobs to?' Leah asked over breakfast the next day.

Jonah smiled at her, knowing how much she enjoyed picturing the future. He liked to see her busy and happy. 'You're getting a bit ahead of yourself, aren't you? We don't need to hire anyone yet.'

'I know. But when the time comes I want to be ready with all the details. I wish we could employ the whole village. I hate to see the men standing around with nothing to do, looking utterly miserable, and the children in such ragged clothes. I'm ready to start producing fizzy drinks but we can't really get going until Charlie helps us find some customers. And we can't do that till we have labels for the bottles and price lists and oh, everything.'

'Including a little van for deliveries.'

'Is a van harder to drive than a car?'

'Depends how big it is. Don't try to walk before you can run, love. You'll do well at driving the car once you have your glasses, I'm sure, but we'll employ someone else to drive our van.'

Our van. How exciting! She forced herself to calm down, but she was dying to do something.

'Perhaps you could leave the employment side of things to me, Leah? I know most of the people in Ellindale.'

'It should be people who're in desperate need, Jonah.'

'I know, love. But they also have to be capable and hard-working. Now, can I give you a ride into Birch End when I go to work today? You said you had a few things you needed to buy and you wanted Mr Purdon to adjust your spectacles.'

'Yes, please. I'll call on Auntie Hilda after I've done my shopping then come home with you later. I haven't been to see her for ages, and I want to tell her Rosa's news.'

When they went into the optician's shop, Mr Purdon was happy to adjust her spectacles. He tested them out again to make sure they sat properly on her nose, then stepped back.

'How does that feel?'

'Much better.'

'Are you getting used to them now?'

'Yes. I'm beginning to.'

She and Jonah went outside but when he offered to drive her to her aunt's, she refused. 'No need. It's only three streets away.'

She walked briskly along, greeting a couple of women cheerfully as she passed.

One called out, 'I like your specs, Leah.'

'Thanks. They make a big difference to how I see the world.'

She was already won over. Then she saw Sam Griggs coming towards her and faltered. Why did she have to run into him, now? He was looking at her so strangely. Surely he wouldn't try to annoy her here, in public?

But he did. When she tried to pass him, he stepped to the same side, and repeated the manoeuvre when she stepped the other way, making it plain he wasn't going to let her move along.

'Quite the fine lady now, aren't you? Though I liked you better without glasses. I'm remembering how soft your body is underneath those demure clothes. Mmm.' He licked his lips.

She gasped in shock at his crudeness, then rallied. 'From when you attacked me, do you mean? If I'd had any witnesses, I'd have reported you to the police.'

'I'll find you again, Mrs Bloody Willcox. I'll choose a time when you're on your own and then I'll finish what I started.'

She couldn't help flinching away from him.

'Are you having trouble, Mrs Willcox?' a voice said.

She turned in relief to Mr Harris. 'Yes, I am. This man won't let me past.'

'Causing trouble again, Griggs?'

Sam gave him a sneering grin. 'Ask your wife how much trouble I can cause. She doesn't seem to mind my . . . trouble.'

'As far as I'm concerned, she's my ex-wife now and you're more than welcome to her. I haven't been this happy in years.'

Adam offered his arm to Leah and she took it gratefully, allowing him to walk with her to her auntie's house.

'Next time I'll ask Jonah to drive me right to the door,' she said as she took her arm out of his.

'It'd be wiser, I think. That one's a born troublemaker and he seems to have something against you. He's been causing bother elsewhere as well, and we can only hope he'll get caught by the police before he really hurts someone.' They both stared down the street watching Griggs turn the corner.

'On a pleasanter topic, I've been meaning to ask about your ginger beer making, Mrs Willcox. Have you made a start?'

'It's gone beyond a start. We actually have a stock of bottles now. Do you still want to buy a few?'

'Yes. I'll drive up to collect them.'

'We could deliver them.'

'I'd rather buy them from Nancy, so that she can have a little profit. I was planning a stroll on the tops this weekend, so I'll collect them then if that's all right. I'm really enjoying the freedom of living alone. But I'll call in at Spring Cottage as well, if I may, because I'd like a word with you and Jonah about something else.'

The door opened just then and he raised his hat to Hilda. 'Mrs Gordon. I hope you're well.' He winked at Leah. 'By the way, I like the spectacles. The gold suits you.'

When he'd gone, she told her auntie what had just happened.

Hilda got very angry at the idea of Griggs accosting her openly like that. 'The cheek of it!' she exclaimed several times.

It was more than cheek, Leah thought. That man was evil.

Then her aunt said, 'Mr Harris is right. The glasses do look nice. The modern ones are so much nicer than they used to be in the old days.'

Leah nodded then changed the subject to Rosa's success and that brought a huge smile to her auntie's face.

When it came time to leave, Leah suddenly felt nervous at the thought of walking back along the street on her own, but didn't like to say so.

Her aunt guessed. 'I'll come with you, Leah love, because I need to go to the shops. While I'm out I'll spread the word that Sam Griggs has been making a nuisance of himself, annoying you. If he dares behave like that to you, he'll do it to other women as well.'

'Thank you. But please don't tell Jonah what happened. He has enough to worry about.'

'I'm sorry, love, but I shall tell him. He's your husband. He needs to know about that nasty creature pestering you, so that he can look after you better from now on.'

A minute later Hilda muttered, 'Just imagine it, harassing a decent woman and in broad daylight too! I don't know what the world's coming to, I really don't.'

* * *

Seeing Griggs annoying a nice lass like Leah Willcox settled it for Adam. He went straight from Mrs Gordon's house to the police station.

'Can I speak to you privately, Sergeant Deemer?' he asked in a low voice, looking meaningfully at a woman reporting a lost dog to the young constable.

'Certainly. Come into my office.' The sergeant gestured to a chair. 'What can I do for you, Mr Harris?'

'It's about those cases of extortion you mentioned to me. I'm beginning to think my ex-wife is involved.' He went through all he'd seen and heard lately, including the recent encounter with Leah Willcox. 'Do you think I'm seeing connections where there aren't any?'

'No. Griggs has never done anything on this scale before. Something has changed and they *are* living together, so she could well be involved. At the very least, she knows what he's doing.'

'The two of them deserve one other!' Adam exclaimed.

'Well, they'd better make the most of it while they can. I'm going to put a stop to his antics if it's the last thing I do, and if I have my way, he'll end up in jail.' The sergeant sighed and added, 'But he's playing it very cleverly, I have to say, more cleverly than he usually does. People are too afraid of him to complain.'

'No wonder. He's a big man. And perhaps he's being clever because my ex-wife's guiding him. She's good at organising things.'

'If we catch them out in criminal acts, she'll go to jail, you know. How would you feel about that?'

'I don't care what happens to her as long as she never comes back to me. She was the worst mistake I've ever made in my whole life.'

The sergeant nodded two or three times, then said quietly, 'I'm beginning to think we should set a trap for them.

Someone's going to get badly hurt if we don't stop this. I've seen it before. These violent men enjoy frightening people and start to think they can get away with anything. We don't want any serious injuries here in the valley, let alone a murder.'

'Murder!'

'Things escalate. Would you help me trap him, if necessary?'

'Definitely. What would you like me to do?'

'You could maybe let some false information drop to your wife.'

'Ah. I'd vowed not to speak to her again. And I prefer to call her my *ex-wife*.' Adam stared blindly into the distance. 'I don't want to live in a town where people go in fear of their lives, so I'll do whatever you need, as long as I don't have to let her into my house again. I have to be careful about one thing, though. At the moment I have witnesses to her infidelity. I can't be seen to condone it. I see her around town, though and could speak to her then.'

'I'll have a word with the area inspector. It's important to get his support. Then we'll work out exactly how to set about it. You'll probably only need to have a brief conversation with her, just to drop a few hints.'

When Adam got home, his maid was nearly bursting with news.

'Mrs Harris come to the door again today, sir, bold as brass. Tried to push her way in, said you'd forgotten to send some things she needed when you packed the other stuff for her.'

'I hope you didn't let her in, Minnie.'

'No, sir. You were very clear about that. But she's stronger than I'd expected. She tried to shove me out of the way. I thought she was going to knock me down. My sister was out shopping but luckily, my young man was having a cup of tea with me in the kitchen. He'd just delivered the meat and you said you didn't mind me giving him a cuppa now and then. So when I yelled for help, he come running and shoved madam outside again.'

'Tell him thank you from me. He's welcome to as many cups of tea as you wish to give him. In fact, ask him to come round whenever I go out at night, Minnie, until this is sorted out. I don't want you or your sister to get hurt if my ex-wife brings that Griggs into this mess.'

'Ooh, thank you, sir. That'd be lovely. Just so you know it's all above board and respectable, me and Jeff are walking out officially. We can't afford to get married for ages yet, because he's got the chance to buy the butcher's shop where he works. Old Mr Marston is thinking of retiring, you see, because he's not a well man. But it all takes some doing in times like these, and if Jeff's parents weren't helping him, there'd be no chance of us finding the money, even though the price of the business is cheaper than it would have been in better times.'

As she stopped to draw breath, Adam said quickly, before she could launch another torrent of words at him, 'Good luck to your young fellow. But mind you keep the chain on when you open the door in future, even in the daytime.'

'I will, sir.'

He heard her humming cheerfully as she set the table for his tea.

Minnie's happiness warmed his heart as he sat listening to the wireless after his solitary meal. His maid had really blossomed since his wife left and her sister was a nice girl, though shy. This was a much happier household now.

Jonah and Charlie took their wives out for a meal at the Green Man that same evening and of course the conversation turned to the fizzy drinks venture.

'I forgot to ask you,' Charlie told his wife, 'Jonah and Leah need someone to design the labels for the bottles. Who should they go to? You know more arty people than I do.'

She hesitated, then flushed slightly, which was unusual for her. 'I wonder if you'd let *me* have a try? You can always say you don't like what I produce, and it'll cost them nothing to let me give it a go, because it's family. And anyway, I love designing things. I've designed headed notepaper and made little Christmas cards for several of my friends to have printed.'

Charlie stared at her in surprise and she added hastily, 'Not if you'd rather bring in a professional artist, of course. I won't be offended.'

Leah had never seen Marion diffident about anything before and was intrigued. She glanced at Jonah but he gestured with one hand as if to tell her it was up to her. So she took a chance.

'I'd love you to try, Marion, but you'll have to let me pay you if you do the job well enough. I believe it's wrong for people to work for no pay.'

'Oh. Well.' She flushed. 'I've never actually earned any money before. It'd be an interesting job, too. If I'm good enough, that is. I was always top in art at school and the teacher wanted my parents to send me to art college, only they wouldn't. They said it'd be too bohemian and unsafe for a decent girl. And of course, money got tighter for everyone, so they didn't want that much extra expense when I would just end up getting married. But I used to get books out of the library about how to paint and draw, and practise.'

Charlie was staring at her. 'You never told me that.'

'What was the point? I didn't get the chance to study art and once I met you, I had other things on my mind.'

'Yes, persuading your papa that I would make a suitable husband. He still isn't sure.'

'Well, I am. I didn't want one of those boring men who work in banks or for insurance companies. I've friends married to that type and you're much more interesting. And you're not mean. You've let me spend money on my books and painting materials. I can't tell you how much I appreciate that. Some men only like their wives to spend money on running the house and check every penny that goes out.'

'I thought your painting and drawing was just a little hobby, something to pass the time.'

'It's more important to me than that. It makes me . . . happy.'

'Why haven't we got any of your paintings on the wall, then? I've seen you doing watercolour paintings, but you never show them off.'

She blushed bright red. 'It'd seem to be boasting.'

'You'll have to show me some and if I like them, we'll put some up and to hell with what anyone else says.'

Leah listened to the two of them and it suddenly struck her that they were gradually starting to feel like her relatives, too. 'How will you do it, Marion? I wouldn't know where to start.'

'I'll buy as many different bottles of pop as I can find and study the labels. I'm sure Charlie won't mind drinking the contents!'

He grinned at her and made a little mock bow.

'Then I'll try out a few ideas. Are you still going to call your business Spring Cottage Mineral Waters?'

'Yes.'

'We could have a picture of the spring itself, perhaps. Could I come and look at it, do you think? I could take a few photos. Is it pretty? I've never even seen it.'

'I'd like that to be on the label and of course you can come and look at it.'

★   ★   ★

Sam Griggs gave Ethel a slap across the face to shut her up and stormed out of the house. He was fed up of her uppity ways. It was one thing to work for her and to sneak into her bed, but quite another to live with her all the time.

She was a right old pain to live with, Mrs Bossy Breeches was. Well, she wasn't going to tell him what to do for much longer. It was driving him mad.

He went to the pub and drank three pints in quick succession, thinking hard about how to make Charlie Willcox give in to his demands and pay up regularly. The best way would be to get him worried about his brother's safety, really worried. Charlie must be made to understand that Jonah would only be safe if Sam was paid to 'protect' him.

He couldn't make Ethel see that people always protested and refused to pay him at first, till he gave them a sample of what might happen if they didn't pay up. Pain was a good persuader.

Sam would rather have got at Charlie and that fancy wife of his directly. He could have broken a few windows in their house, made a mess there, got the wife upset. Unfortunately, their house stood cheek by jowl with neighbours and made such tactics too risky. Someone might see him and his size made him too easy to recognise. What's more, some of the people out in that posh part of the village had telephones and might call in the police without him knowing.

But everyone knew how fond Charlie Willcox was of his crippled brother, and *he* lived out on the edge of the moors, with no neighbours and only a ruined house nearby. No one in Ellindale had a telephone yet so they couldn't call sneakily for help.

Workmen were putting the new lines in to connect them, though, so he'd better get the job done quickly before they finished.

He smiled as he thought how easy it'd be to get to Jonah

Willcox and his family without being seen. Pretty wife, he had. That might be a bonus. Sam was feeling the lack of variety in bed. That was the reason he'd never married. He always got fed up of a woman after a while. Always.

He might be well and truly fed up of Ethel now, but he wasn't fed up of the money she was helping him earn. And the rent money was mounting up nicely too now that he wasn't passing it on to her. When he had enough saved, he'd go and live somewhere else, leave her behind. She'd hate that.

He scowled at the thought of Ethel. When he'd told her what he intended to do tonight, she'd said it was a stupid plan and he'd be tempting providence by showing his hand so openly. She'd actually dared order him not to do it. He'd been forced to thump her to shut her up.

Sam tramped up the main road towards the top of the valley, hiding whenever he heard someone coming. Once he got beyond Birch End, he walked confidently up the middle of the narrow road. Who'd be driving up here at this time of night? There were no rich people with cars in Ellindale except for Jonah Willcox.

At Spring Cottage, he stopped in surprise. The car wasn't there. Then he saw the young sister come to the window and draw the curtains. He watched for a little longer, but there was no sign of the wife. They must have gone out and left the lass on her own. He smiled. He could make do with her for the first serious warning.

The front door was locked and when he went round to the rear, that door was locked as well. He'd have to break one of the doors down, which he could do easily enough, or go in by a window.

Maybe it'd be better to come back another time when the cripple was there. No, he was damned if he was walking all that way up the hill for nothing.

He found a small rock near the garden wall and lobbed it through the window. A scream from indoors told him he was on the right track and he smiled.

But after that things didn't go at all to plan.

Someone grabbed him from behind and while he was fighting off whoever it was, someone else inside the house fired a gun twice. They were either a terrible shot or else not firing at him, but he didn't want to stay around to find out.

Sam punched his assailant as hard as he could, grunting in relief as the man fell down and didn't get up again, just lay groaning.

He ran off down the hill as fast as he could. He was a bit slow to hear the car approaching, but turned hastily into a muddy field. He had to lie down in the sodding mud as the car drew level with him. He cursed in annoyance at the mess that was going to make of his clothes.

The car slowed down just where he was lying and he saw someone peering out of the driver's window. Had the driver seen him? No, he must just be slowing down for the hill, because the car didn't stop and it didn't speed up either, only chugged slowly onwards.

When it had gone into the gates of Spring Cottage, he set off again as fast he could, given the poor conditions. Clouds hid the moon and rain lashed down suddenly. That was all he needed after the mud!

He slowed down as he approached the cottages in Ellindale, then cursed as he had to lie flat on the ground again. Men rushed past him on the road and continued up the hill.

What the hell was going on here tonight? Had he caused this? Had the gun been a signal for help? And who had the fellow been who'd attacked him?

He got up and brushed in vain at the muck on his clothes. In case anyone else was out, he avoided the easy route down the main road and cut across the open countryside, falling a couple of times on the rough ground. He didn't hear anyone else on the road that ran roughly parallel to where he was walking, but he wasn't taking any chances.

It took a damned long time to get back home and Ethel hit the roof when she saw the state he was in and screamed at him in fury after she'd dragged out of him what had happened.

'*Now* will you listen to me, Sam Griggs? If you don't, you'll run your head into a noose. You're a fool. A stupid, idiotic fool. I don't know why I took up with you.'

He'd have liked to thump her, if only to take out his anger on someone, but unfortunately she was right. He had acted foolishly. He should only have had one pint, for a start. It clouded your brain, booze did, and you took risks you'd have avoided if you were sober. He'd do it properly next time, stone cold sober.

She continued to rant at him so he dragged her, kicking and screaming off to bed, where he roughed her up a bit more than she appreciated.

22

The previous afternoon Thad had decided to put the next part of his plan into operation: find out what Jonah Willcox and his family did in the evenings, so that he could work out what time of day was best to strike.

He'd spent a lot of time thinking about what he would do to *her* and to her little sister. The nasty things she'd called him had echoed in his mind while he was working down south. No woman was going to treat him like that! And anyway, that little lass had been a woman grown in her body, or he'd not have touched her. He'd only been going to give her a taste of what was to come.

Yes, and the girl deserved it, didn't she? She'd been flaunting herself at men, walking along the road in that short skirt with her long legs showing. And her skin had been soft when he'd touched her, so very soft.

He rubbed his forehead. He didn't remember all the details of that night very well, if truth be told. What stayed with him, galled him unbearably, was that his brothers were in jail and he'd had to run for it, leaving his home. Well, someone was going to pay dearly for doing that to him. By hell they were.

He set out from the little cave at dusk and headed towards Ellindale. The moon was nearly full so he could see where he was going.

It was good to have something to do. He was fed up of being alone, much as he loved being on the moors. He had to keep coming back to them but they weren't the only thing he cared about in life. He liked to go out for a drink of beer occasionally, for one thing. He missed that.

And he missed his brothers even more than he'd expected to. The three of them had had some good times together. He often wondered how poor Griff and Jeb were coping with being locked up in prison. He'd have gone to visit them if he'd been free to.

He'd kill himself rather than let them shut him away. He'd not be able to breathe in a prison cell. But he'd only kill himself as a last resort. He'd try very hard to kill anyone coming after him first.

Since he didn't want dogs being able to track him back to the cave, Thad took care to tramp along a convenient stream for some distance. His boots were well oiled and wouldn't let in water if he didn't stay in the stream for too long.

Later on, he couldn't resist making a small detour to his old home, which he'd visited secretly three times already. Someone had locked the house up carefully, but he knew where the spare key was hidden. There weren't any signs that people had been there since the police locked it up, but he hated to see the old place looking so dusty and bare of life.

His mum would have thrown a fit at the mess after the fight and about the broken chair, so he'd cleared that lot up for her, at least. He missed his mother, had done ever since she died. She'd been a tough one, but she'd managed to put food on the table after their father died and clothes on her sons' backs. They'd helped her as soon as they were old enough to go out scrounging.

He was at the point now where he wanted to find himself a wife and start a family, but what was the use if he couldn't live with them in the same home as his parents and grandparents – and their grandparents too, from the tales his granddad used to tell him?

He'd found a few bits and pieces in the house to make his life more comfortable in the cave, but he wasn't burdening himself with anything else tonight. He'd just take a breather at the farm and check that everything was all right.

To his annoyance, when he got closer Thad saw a faint light in one window. He crept round the edge of the farmyard, letting the soft earth mask the sound of his steps, and found that the scullery door had been forced open.

Someone had got inside, damn them!

Anger flooded through him. He wasn't letting anyone make free of his home. Opening the scullery door carefully, he crept inside. It felt warmer out of the wind and firelight was flickering invitingly from the kitchen.

He couldn't see into that room without moving forward and risking being seen himself, but there was no sound of anyone talking, so he decided there was probably only one person there. He could look after himself if it came to a fight.

Pulling the inner scullery door back slowly, he waited for someone to notice and call out, but no one did and he couldn't see the whole room from here. It took his eyes a minute or two to get used to the dimness then he took a cautious step inside the kitchen. The next thing he knew, someone grabbed him by the collar and yanked him forward, tripping him so that he stumbled to his knees.

'Don't move or I'll brain you!' a voice growled and a thick cudgel was brandished right under his nose.

He could see enough to tell it wasn't a policeman, at least. In fact, the fellow was wearing clothes as rough as his own and was unshaven.

'What the hell are you doing in my house?' he demanded.

'I'm just taking shelter for a day or two. There was no

one here so I thought the place was empty. I've done no harm. In fact, I mended a dripping tap.'

They stared at one another, two unshaven men who looked as if they were sleeping rough.

'Well, you can get out now. I'm back.'

'It's cold and wet outside.' The stranger paused and added, 'I could share my food with you if you'd let me stay till the morning. I've got a bottle of rum, and I'd share that too.' He grinned. 'It didn't cost me anything. Some people are very careless.'

Thad licked his lips at the thought of a drink. Hadn't he just been wishing he could call in at a pub? He gave in to temptation. 'All right. It's a bargain. But you'll leave tomorrow.'

'Or maybe we could make another bargain and you'd let me stay a few days if I could get you some more food? If you're coming back here to live, you'll need supplies, and if you're coming here secretly at night, you mustn't want to be seen in the village.'

'If you go stealing things round here, they'll come after you and that might lead the police to me.'

'I stay out of the way of them sods. Anyway, I earn a few shillings here and there so I don't need to steal. But it looks like the rain's set in and I'd soon as not set off across the hills till the weather brightens.'

Thad studied him again. 'Well, you certainly don't look as if you've gone without food. Most fellows on the tramp don't have any money.'

'You don't look hungry, either.'

'I've been working down south. There are always odd jobs to be found there.'

'Seems we have a lot in common. I came back to see my mother, give her a few shillings.'

Thad envied him that, wishing he could still sit and talk with his own mother by the kitchen fire.

It'd be good to sit in a comfortable chair in front of a good, warm fire for a few minutes, even better with a drink in his hands. And he wasn't in the mood for a fight tonight. 'All right. You can stay for the night if you share your food with me. We'll see about tomorrow. What's your name?'

'John. And you?'

'Thad.'

As the man got some bread and cheese out of his bundle, Thad wondered whether to jump him and take what he had by force. But give the fellow his due, he was careful how he stood and didn't give Thad even half a chance.

The food was good: fresh bread and ham and an apple. And when a bottle half full of rum was brought out of the knapsack, he got out two glasses and settled back with a pleased sigh.

Ah, this was just a man on the tramp. No danger from him. He was a stranger and probably didn't know anything about the Huttons. They had a nice chat about the world. The rum went down smoothly and Thad relaxed more than he had for ages.

Finn watched Thad Hutton carefully as he got out his food and shared it for the evening meal. He'd got the right man, fallen lucky straight away.

Sergeant Deemer was a cunning old devil; and there was more to the new inspector than they'd expected when a scrawny, bald fifty-year-old who talked posh took over the district.

As Finn shared his food, then his rum, he was surprised at how much Hutton let slip once he had a few drinks in him. He didn't say who he was planning to get back at, but he did talk about a woman and a girl he intended to kidnap, so it was easy to guess.

Eventually the rum ran out and so did the confidences.

So Finn pretended to doze off. But he didn't let himself sleep. This man wasn't to be trusted, not about anything.

When Hutton got up and tiptoed towards the knapsack, Finn said softly, 'I'm a very light sleeper and I don't like having my things messed with.'

'Can't blame me for trying.'

'Can't blame me for keeping an eye on you.' He pulled a chair round and balanced it carefully so that it'd tip over and wake him if Hutton tried to get near.

In the morning Finn got out the last of his food and shared it, then said, 'If you're going to let me stay, I'll need to get in more supplies.'

Hutton stared at him for so long he thought the trap wasn't going to work, then took a deep breath and shrugged. 'All right. See if you can get some more booze.'

'Fair enough. Thanks. It's good to have a comfortable place to rest every now and then, and the weather hasn't been good.'

Finn tramped down the valley right into Rivenshaw, walking off his sleepiness. He was grateful for a dry spell, but kept an eye on the clouds building up to the west.

Trying not to draw attention to himself, he slipped into the police station, relieved to find no one there except policemen.

One look at him and Deemer said jovially to the constable, 'You go and make us a cup of tea, lad. I know this chap from years back when he did me a favour, so I always give him a cuppa when he's passing through. You can get out the biscuits too before you do your first round of the town.'

The young policeman looked at Finn curiously but did as he was asked.

When he and Deemer were alone, Finn said abruptly, 'Hutton's taken the bait. And I've persuaded him to let me stay for a few days. He's there now. He talked a little when he was drinking, gave no names but the woman he mentioned must be the same one you told me about. I don't know yet what he's planning. Or when he wants to act.'

'Do you think it's safe for you to go back?'

'Oh, yes. I can look after myself.'

'You all right now?'

Finn shrugged. 'Of course I am.'

As rain was still pouring down outside, he took a nap in one of the cells, then conferred with Deemer about ways and means of setting a trap.

He went shopping before starting back up the valley. He bought a bottle of gin this time. Easier to pretend he was drinking this by filling his glass up with water.

He'd see if he could get some specifics out of Hutton tonight. They needed to find a way of catching him in the very act of committing a crime. No use just preventing it. He might get away.

You had to lock men like him up. They were a danger to society.

While John was out, Thad prowled round the house. He felt nervous to be so near the village in the daytime. He went up to the attic and watched people and vehicles passing on the road. They were a few hundred yards away, but that was still too close for comfort.

No one came anywhere near the farm, though, till much later, when a man trudged up the hill and turned into the lane.

Thad stiffened. He couldn't see who it was clearly but he had his things up here in the attic with him, ready to hide.

As the figure got closer, he realised it was John. He relaxed a little but kept watch till he turned into the farmyard, in case anyone else was following him. But John was definitely on his own.

He went downstairs to greet him, surprised at how good it felt to have someone to talk to. 'You took long enough. You've been gone all day.'

'I went down to Rivenshaw to do the shopping because there are more people there and a stranger wouldn't stand out as much. Then it began to rain, so I found a broken-down shed and took shelter.' He shrugged. 'I don't have a lot of clothes to change into and I wasn't in a hurry so I stayed there till it looked like being fine for a while.'

Thad watched as food was produced, and then a small bottle of gin. Not his favourite tipple, but better than nothing. 'I've got to go out before we have a drink. Something to check on. But I could do with some food.'

There was a meat pie. He'd eaten half of it before he realised it.

John grinned and took the other half. 'It's all right. Call it payment for my lodgings.'

It was still raining on and off, but Thad got ready to check out Spring Cottage.

'I want you out of here tomorrow,' he said before he left. 'No offence, but I've got somewhere to go and I want to lock the place up good and tight.'

John shrugged. 'All right. But you won't chuck me out tonight, will you? It's started raining again.'

'No. You can stay tonight, then leave in the morning.'

'Let's drink to that.'

'Later. I want a clear head for what I'm doing.'

'All right. Later.'

'Leave some booze for me.'

'I won't even start till you get back. My da always told me it's bad luck to drink alone. I just think it tastes better in company. I'll probably have another little nap while I wait for you to come back.'

*   *   *

Leah was in a happy haze as Jonah drove her home, thrilled that another step had been taken in her new business and also happy that she was getting on better with Marion.

He braked suddenly as they were going up the hill.

'What's wrong?'

'I thought I saw someone in the field. No, I must have been mistaken.'

That worried her. And her worries turned into fear when she saw lights on all over the house and two men standing in front of it as if on guard. 'Something's happened, Jonah.'

They listened to the tale of the would-be intruder and thanked the men from the village for coming to help.

'The little lass fired a gun, so we came running.'

Jonah swung round. '*You* fired the gun, Rosa?'

'Yes. Because that man knocked Ben out before Daniel could come running from the other side of the house. Leah let me practise with her gun so I knew what to do.'

He gave her a wry smile. 'You're a quick-thinking lass. Didn't it upset you to fire a gun?'

'No. I wish I could have fired a bullet right into him.'

'Did you recognise him?'

'No. But it must have been Thad Hutton, don't you think?'

'We don't know for certain who it was. But we can't do anything tonight.' He turned to the men. 'Anyone like to earn a bob or two keeping watch here till morning? Whether it was Hutton or someone like Sam Griggs, I doubt they'll come back tonight, but I prefer to make sure we're well guarded. We'll let Ben lie down and recover so that he'll be wide awake in the morning.'

They nodded, looked at one another and two men stepped forward.

'We can't let Sergeant Deemer know until then, but if anyone's going into Rivenshaw tomorrow, I'll pay them to take a message,' Jonah said.

Another man volunteered eagerly.

When Jonah and his wife were lying in bed, he said in a low voice, 'Who do you think it was? Hutton or Griggs?'

'I think it was Griggs, whatever Rosa says.'

'Why?'

'Because the other day he told me he'd catch me alone one day and finish what he began.'

'The hell he will! I may not be strong enough to defend you myself but I can hire people who are.' He held her close. 'You mean the world to me, Leah.'

She pretended to go to sleep, so that he would too, but she lay awake worrying for some time.

That same evening Thad cursed as he got outside and found it was raining again, and even harder than before. But he'd set his mind on checking what Jonah Willcox and his family did of an evening and what time they went to bed, so he didn't turn back.

He hadn't yet worked out how to get to the two women, but it'd come to him when he could see the whole picture. He never could make plans till he saw everything in his mind's eye.

As he left the farm and started across the fields, however, he heard a gunshot and stiffened. It was repeated a moment later. What stupid sod was firing a gun in peaceful Ellindale? People would be buzzing round in the village like angry wasps.

Well, that settled it. If there was some sort of disturbance going on, he might get spotted and blamed for something. No, dammit, he'd have to put off what he'd been going to do until another night. That bitch would still be there in Spring Cottage tomorrow. And the day after, if necessary. He'd get rid of John first. It'd been good to have a bit of company and someone to drink with but he didn't want to encourage the fellow to stay longer.

He went back into the farmhouse quietly, but even so John was awake and alert.

'Did you hear the shots?'

'Aye. What's going on? Did you see anything while you were out?'

'Who the hell knows? I saw nowt. But I'm not going anywhere near Ellindale if something's upset folk and made them fire guns. Where's that gin?'

Finn got out the bottle and they settled into drinking. He managed to fill his own glass with water while Hutton was outside relieving himself, so that he stayed more or less sober. He tried to lead the other man into confiding about when he planned to strike, but in vain.

In the end, he came to the conclusion that Hutton hadn't actually decided when to act or even made detailed plans. Pity.

Anyway, he couldn't do any more. It'd look suspicious if he came back to the farm again.

He might go into Rivenshaw, though, and discuss the matter with Deemer and then phone the inspector from the police station. They might need some help when the trap was finally set.

Thad set off early next morning, getting John out of the house first, then going up to the attic window to check that he really did leave. He wondered a couple of times what had made someone shoot a gun last night.

He watched John walk along to the road, then caught the occasional glimpse of what could only be him, trudging down the hill into the village. Good. He was gone. He was pleasant enough but he had better not come back again.

Before he set off, Thad waited till a heavy shower of rain cleared people off the road so that no one would see him on the open patch of ground beyond the farm. Not that there had been many people around.

After half an hour of plodding across the moors, he looked up at the sky and cursed the heavy black clouds which were gathering again. The rain wasn't going to stop today. He was so cold and wet by the time he got to the cave, in spite of his layers of clothes, that he made a sudden decision to spend a few days at his aunt's house. She was a soft touch and would take pity on him.

No use prowling around Spring Cottage or Ellindale until whatever had caused the gunfire had died down completely. He'd stay for two or three days with his aunt Cissy then come back and make his final plans.

The words seemed to chant in his brain of their own accord as he walked. They often did.

> *Lock away his brothers, would they?*
> *Chase him away from his home, would they?*
> *He'd make sure they regretted it.*

It was always the same words, like a song running through his head. They faded sometimes but never went away completely.

Oh, he'd definitely make sure they regretted messing him around.

Sergeant Deemer was roused early that morning by a man on his way to work.

'There's no telephone in Ellindale yet, Sergeant, so they couldn't call you for help last night but we went up from the village to help so the Willcoxes were all right. Mr Jonah asked me to let you know that they've had an intruder at Spring Cottage. Whoever it was smashed one of the windows, and they think it was Sam Griggs. Or Thad Hutton. Nobody's sure which.'

Furious at more trouble invading his territory as well as

eager to catch Griggs committing a crime, because it was surely more likely to be him, Deemer got ready to go and check the situation.

Just as he was about to leave Finn slipped in through the back door and a quick chat proved that it hadn't been Hutton. This time at least. Which was a help.

He left Finn to have a sleep in the same cell and drove straight up to the top of the valley to investigate. The ground was damp enough to show footprints but to his frustration, half the village seemed to have come up to Spring Cottage the previous night and trampled all over the evidence.

As he asked around, one or two people in Birch End and Ellindale claimed to have seen Griggs in the pub, then walking up the hill by the field path after he left it.

Deemer spoke at length to the watchman who'd rescued Ben from the intruder.

'I didn't really see his face, sergeant, because it had clouded over. But it could have been Griggs. The fellow I fought was big enough.' A pause then, 'In fact, it probably was him. There aren't many men that big round here, only him and the Huttons, and they're in prison, aren't they?'

'Thad isn't.'

'Ah. There you are, then. I couldn't swear it was Griggs on a Bible. He and Thad are much the same height and build.'

'I think it's more likely to be Griggs,' Jonah said. 'He tried to get my brother to pay protection money. This might be his way of forcing us. Though of course Hutton clashed with us, too, when he kidnapped Rosa.'

The sergeant didn't tell them about Finn, who could prove it hadn't been Thad this time. He'd save that information for the inspector.

When he got back, Finn had smartened himself up a bit. 'I've something to attend to in Manchester, but I'll call in on the inspector in a day or two to see if I'll be needed again.'

After he'd reported to the inspector, Deemer had a chat with his constable, bringing him up to date on what had happened. 'We're getting some pieces of the puzzle, but they're making up a damned strange picture.'

'What about Griggs? Was it him breaking in?'

'It must have been. But Hutton has a grudge against the Willcoxes too. I've never seen it happen before but I'm beginning to wonder whether we have two villains, each acting separately and neither aware of what the other is doing. And if I'm right, they're both going to return to Spring Cottage. That'd be a right old turn-up for the books, wouldn't it?'

'I never heard of such a thing.'

'I mentioned my idea to the inspector, but he doesn't think it's likely we're dealing with two villains here.' He tapped the side of his nose. 'I know it wasn't Hutton this time, but I have a feeling he'll be back. He's got a nasty streak to him. You get a feel for things when you've been in the force for as long as I have, and truth is sometimes stranger than the things you see at the movies, even.'

The constable listened carefully, looking thoughtful. He was a very willing and eager lad, so Deemer carried on.

'It'll be easy enough to set a trap to catch Griggs, though it may take a few days to set it all up, but I'm not so sure about Hutton. He's a cunning devil and though my friend Finn found out a few things, we've no way of knowing exactly when he's planning to strike or if he even is. I'll have to think about it all. If Hutton is going to cause more trouble in Ellindale, it'd be good to nab them both at the same time.'

He fell silent for a moment then added slowly, 'I wonder if I can manage it?'

Half an hour later, he said aloud, 'I have to try because

we don't want to be left with one troublemaker still running free and likely to come back when the furore has died down.'

Deemer thought it through again quickly and smiled at his own thoughts, still talking to himself. 'Ah, well. I never thought I'd say it, but thank goodness for the new area inspector. I wasn't sure about him when he took over, but he seems to be a right 'un. He's prepared to assign more men to us if we have good reason to set a trap. Well, he's been paying for Finn's time here already, hasn't he?'

They'd have to work it out carefully, not rush in. They didn't want to mess it up.

Thad arrived at his aunt's house on the outskirts of Manchester the following afternoon. He stood at the door, dripping water because it had been raining all the way and only two men had offered him a lift. Both had been driving open carts and he'd had to sit in the back in the rain. Neither of them had been going very far, either.

She stared at him with such disgust on her face that he wondered what she knew about him. Then just as he thought she was going to shut the door in his face, she let out a whoosh of air and gestured to him to come in.

'Stand on the doormat, Thad. I'm not having you dripping mud over my nice clean floors. I wasn't going to let you come here any more, not after what you did to that little lass, but you don't look well and—'

'I didn't touch that lass!' he said quickly, then had to stop speaking to cough.

'Don't lie to me.'

'Well, I didn't touch her in that way you mean. I just wanted to frighten her because I was angry at her family.'

She studied his face again. 'You promise me you didn't touch her . . . you know, like a woman!'

'I promise, Aunt Cissy.' He didn't let himself smile, but

she'd accepted his story. She was as stupid as most other people about that sort of thing.

'Oh, thank goodness! It's bad enough using a little lass to frighten someone else, but I wouldn't want to think a relative of mine was warped enough to touch a child in that way.'

She looked at him coldly. 'My daughter will say I'm too soft when she gets back, but you'll come down with pneumonia if you don't get out of those wet clothes and warm up a bit. I don't want your death on my conscience, so you can stay for one night, but that's it. You'll go on your way and I don't want you back here again. Come into the kitchen and get out of those wet clothes.'

She hardly said anything else, just barked out orders. If he hadn't felt a bit under the weather after getting soaked and chilled, he'd have left straight away in the face of such treatment.

He found he was sharing the attic with his uncle Mitch again, and the place was piled high with furniture.

'They've got enough stuff up here,' Thad said in surprise.

'Aye. My niece and her kids have had to move in because her husband lost his job in the coal mine and the Means Test man said they'd have to sell their furniture before they could get the dole.'

'Rotten sods, the government are, doing that to folk,' Thad agreed automatically.

'Anyway, Len's working down south and sending money now and then, and Cissy has a bit tucked away, so they're managing without the dole.'

'Good.' Thad shivered and when the old man tried to carry on chatting he told him to shut up. 'I'm too tired to chat.' He'd even turned down an offer of bread and scrape from his aunt, because he didn't feel hungry. What he wanted desperately was a good, long sleep. That'd set him up again.

★   ★   ★

In the morning, however, Thad felt worse and when he got out of bed, the room spun round him and he fell back on it again.

Mitch went for Cissy, who came up and stared at her nephew. 'There. What did I tell you about getting soaked through? You've caught a bad chill and serve you right. But I suppose you'll have to stay another night or two.'

During the next few days Thad was feverish and at night he had the strangest dreams. He fought off monsters, was hot one minute, cold the next, and couldn't help calling out when his enemies chased after him and nearly caught him.

'You shouldn't have made enemies then they wouldn't be preying on your mind,' his aunt told him unsympathetically.

It was a week before he was fit enough to move on and he'd rather have spent a few more days there. He hadn't eaten this well for a good long while.

But his aunt was adamant that he had to leave and packed his things herself.

His uncle Mitch was nowhere to be seen.

'Do not come back,' his aunt yelled then slammed the door shut behind him.

Thad stopped at the corner of the street to make a rude sign in her direction. Now, where should he go? He still didn't feel right.

Ah, there was only one place to go when you weren't well: home. He'd go back to the farm and hide out in the attic.

When his nephew had gone, Mitch left his hiding place in the front room and came to sit in the kitchen with his sister. 'I don't know what to do about Thad.'

'What do you mean? There's nothing to do – he's gone.'

'He's gone back to attack that family he's angry at. He was delirious and he kept going on about it, spelling out

what he was going to do. Talking out loud he was, so I heard
it all several times. Didn't you hear anything?'

'I did hear him talking in his sleep, but with the door to
the attic shut, I couldn't make out exactly what he was saying,
and anyway, I'm a heavy sleeper once I've got off.'

'I don't think he knew he was telling me what he intended
to do, so I didn't let on that I'd heard owt. But Cissy, I don't
like the thought of what he's planning to do. He's a rotten
sod, that one, nephew or not. He *is* planning to attack that
lass.'

'Nay!' She looked at him in shock and bit her lip. 'That
makes me feel sick. I wish now that I hadn't given him
shelter. Maybe if I'd left him out on the street, he'd have
died of the chill and saved us the shame.'

'You're a good, kind woman. You couldn't have done that,
even to him. And if I haven't said it before, I'm grateful for
how you've looked after me. Deeply grateful, my lass.'

'You're my brother. And you're a decent chap, even if you
do like going on the tramp.' After a pause she said in a tight,
unhappy voice, 'You have to tell someone about what he's
planning, Mitch, or decent people are going to get hurt.'

'I know. Who should I tell, though? Will the police here
be interested even?'

'Probably not, but I hear Gilbert Deemer is police sergeant
in Rivenshaw now. He's a shrewd fellow.' She smiled remin-
iscently. 'He and I walked out for a month or two when we
were young, but it didn't come to anything. I've always liked
to hear how he was doing, though.

'Rivenshaw? That's miles away. How will I get there, Cissy?
I'm not up to much walking at the moment and I've no
money for bus fares, even if I could stand the journey.'

'You're not even going to try, Mitch. I'll go to the local
police station and ask them how to get in touch with him.'

She let herself shed a few quiet tears as she walked into

the town centre, because they wouldn't show in the rain. Her brother was getting weaker, even though he didn't cough as much now. Poor Mitch wouldn't be going on the road again. He'd probably not see another autumn even. He got so breathless at times.

She'd seen that look on people's faces before, always thought of it as the 'death look'. They seemed almost transparent as if the flesh itself was preparing to fade away.

He was the last of her brothers and sisters. She'd been the youngest, what their parents had called an 'afterthought child'. There'd just be her left after he died. And how would she deal with those terrible nephews up in Ellindale if the police didn't keep them locked away?

They'd all come after her if they found out she'd reported one of them, she knew they would, aunt or not. A widow didn't have the same protection as a woman whose husband was still with her. Damned wars! They took all the good men from you. But she couldn't not report it.

Thank goodness her own children were good 'uns. They took after their father's side, not the Huttons, who were mostly bad 'uns. It was good to have Pam and the kids living with her. Families helped one another, well, the good ones did.

The policeman behind the counter looked down his nose at Cissy, which was a mistake, because she wasn't having that from anyone, let alone someone young enough to be her son.

'I need to get a message to Sergeant Deemer in Rivenshaw,' she said firmly. 'It's about a criminal he's looking for.' She wasn't sure whether Deemer was actually looking for Thad, but it was the only way she could think of to persuade them to put her in touch with him. 'I know where the fellow is and I've a fair idea of what he's planning to do next.'

'Tell me about it, Ma. If I think it's useful information, I'll pass it on to him.'

She saw an older policeman peer out from a back room so said loudly, 'I'm not your "Ma" and I'll have more respect from you, my lad, when I'm doing my duty as a law-abiding citizen and reporting something important.'

The older policeman came to join them at the counter. 'Is something wrong?' Then he looked at her more closely. 'It's Mrs Greenby, isn't it?'

'Yes. But I'm afraid I don't recognise you.'

'Tommy Piper. I used to play with your kids. I just got made up to sergeant.'

'Ah. I remember you now. Congratulations on your promotion.' She had to wait a minute to speak in order to get control of herself, because she was both angry at the young policeman and still upset about her brother.

In a voice which would wobble, however hard she tried to control it, she repeated what she needed them to do.

'You're sure Sergeant Deemer will want to know about this?'

'I'd stake my life on it, Sergeant. I can't afford the money for bus fares to Rivenshaw and anyway, it's my brother who overheard this villain talking, and he's so weak and ill I have to nurse him, so he can't go anywhere. Please help me to do this. My brother hasn't got long to live. He'd not lie about it. Not now. And he'll die more peacefully for getting something done about Thad.'

'I'd better come and see your brother myself, talk to him. Keep an eye on the counter, lad, and mind your manners with ladies in future.'

After Sergeant Piper had talked to Mitch, he turned to Cissy, 'You were right to come, Mrs Greenby. If you come back to the station with me we can ring Sergeant Deemer and tell him what your brother overheard.'

'Thank you.'

'For what?'

'For taking what I said seriously.'

'I realised when I grew older how hard you'd worked to stay respectable, especially with your family background. And your children are respectable too, unlike their cousins. I admire what you've done with your life, Mrs Greenby.'

The compliment made her day.

Sergeant Deemer put down the phone and rubbed his hands together, as he always did when he was particularly pleased. 'We've got it.'

'Sir?' Archer waited.

'We've got the information we need. I've just found out that Thad Hutton is on his way back here – may even be here already – and that he's planning to attack the woman and girl at Spring Cottage. He deserves hanging that one does. But if we can get him locked away for a long time, that'll be a help.'

'I never thought I'd hear about such happenings in our valley, Sarge.'

'Bad things happen everywhere, lad, everywhere on earth. Any road, I think we're ready to put our plans into operation so if you'll go and mind the front desk, I'll phone the inspector and we'll put our heads together.'

23

When he heard what had been reported to the police by a law-abiding member of the Hutton family, the area inspector came to Rivenshaw in person to confer with the sergeant. But he came in his own car, not wearing his uniform, because they didn't want to alert anyone to the fact that something was being arranged.

After they'd gone through everything twice, Deemer rang up the pawnshop to see if he could catch Charlie and Jonah Willcox. The inspector wanted to chat to them.

'Jonah's not working in the shop today,' Charlie told him.

'Damn! I'll have to send someone up the valley to let him know he's wanted.'

Charlie chuckled. 'No, you won't. They installed his telephone yesterday, so you can just pick up your phone. They're fitting electrical points into the whole house next week. Leah's over the moon about it. She's not fond of cleaning oil lamps.'

'Good timing with the phone.'

Deemer also sent a message to Finn, who'd just returned from Manchester and was staying in lodgings in Rivenshaw.

Charlie was with them ten minutes later and Finn soon after. Twenty minutes after the phone call, Jonah drove into Rivenshaw and parked in a side street away from the police station, which he approached via the back lane, as the others had.

The five men went over the details of how they'd set the

trap, and who else they could bring in, then the inspector leaned back.

'I'm still not convinced you'll be able to catch both these criminals in the same trap, Sergeant, but it's well worth a try because you stand a fair chance of catching one of them, at least. I'll leave you to organise everything as we've agreed. The sooner it's done, the better. If that aunt of his is right, Hutton will be taking action tomorrow.'

'I can go out after dark and check whether he's back at the farm,' Finn volunteered. 'I know my way around it and there's a real jumble of old sheds there. I've noticed one I can hide in. It won't be comfortable but it'll be worth it.'

Deemer saw the inspector to the door, then went back to join the others. He didn't intend to wait for trouble to hit, as the inspector had suggested, he was going to prod it along. The only gamble would be when exactly Hutton would act, but he was betting the fellow wouldn't wait around and Finn would be able to help them keep an eye on him.

He sat down to go over the details with the Willcoxes as well as Finn, and brought in his constable too. 'We need more men and I don't think we'll have trouble finding help. The valley folk, especially those up in Ellindale, are frustrated by the closing down of the mills and businesses round here. These past few years have been hard going, with intermittent part-time employment the best most of them could find.'

They all murmured sympathetically at the thought of that.

'The lucky ones have had just enough work to stay entitled to a partial dole. Some poor sods haven't even had that and have been on transitional payments or other charitable handouts. They'll be happy to take action against *something*, especially if we promise them a good feed afterwards.'

'I'll pay for that,' Charlie said quietly.

'And I'll help them in some other way,' Jonah said. 'I'm not having my wife and sister-in-law in danger.'

'Especially when your wife is trying to create employment,' Deemer said. 'If only two men from Ellindale can get full-time jobs in her fizzy drink business, and a few women can get part-time jobs, that'll be something well worth doing. So no one's going to harm her or delay what she's doing if I have anything to say in the matter. I admire your wife greatly, Mr Willcox. She's quiet but a hard worker and a caring woman. Well, she comes from good stock, doesn't she? The Turners have lived in the valley for generations.'

He waited for that to sink in, then picked up the phone. 'Now, I'll phone Mr Harris and we'll get things started. Ah, Adam lad. Can you come in for a meeting about you know what? It's time to act. That's good. Come in the back way.'

When Adam arrived, the constable was sent to keep an eye on the counter while the other five men put their heads together to sort out who was doing what and which other men they'd bring into it. It was a much livelier discussion than the one led by the inspector had been.

Once their plans had been laid, Deemer said, 'Remember, lads, if this goes as we hope, we didn't *plan* all this differently from what the inspector suggested. It just *happened* that way.'

The others nodded, looking grim and serious now.

Good chaps, these, Deemer thought. The sort who made Lancashire great and would do so again, when times improved. Eh, this was a bleak year, as bad as the previous one. No signs of better times yet, whatever Charlie Willcox said about feeling things were going to improve. The man was a born optimist. He cheered folk up but he couldn't change the world. Not even the King could do that.

He turned back to his companions. 'Thank goodness for the telephone. You got yours in the nick of time, Jonah lad. It means you can phone for help if you need it. And don't hesitate to do that. We don't want any dangerous heroics.'

'I've got a—'

Deemer held up one hand. 'Don't tell me about your gun. I don't want to know officially about such things.' He nearly laughed aloud at the surprise on their faces. Did they think he was stupid?

He stood at the back door to watch them go, before he went to brief his constable. How frail Jonah Willcox looked compared to his brother. Eh, the Great War had left a lot of damaged men in its wake. Britain had won, but at what cost?

When Adam left Rivenshaw police station, he went back to Birch End to do something he'd been dreading: speak to his ex-wife. Not that he was afraid of her, no, it wasn't that. But he loathed being near her since he'd found out about her affair with Griggs. It made him feel dirty.

Unfortunately some of the group's planned actions would depend on his success in dropping a hint to her, so he had to do it well and not make her suspicious about his motives.

Fate must have been on his side, because he saw her as he walked towards his home. She was sitting on a bench at the nearby bus stop, frowning. The relief on her face as she looked up made him wonder if she'd been waiting for him.

He didn't even need to think of something to say because one look at her and he gasped in shock at the bruises on her face. 'What happened to you?'

'Sam's been hitting me, Adam. I've never been beaten before.'

He watched her blink her eyes and that stopped him feeling sorry for her, because that was the way she blinked when she needed to force some tears.

She made a show of hunting in vain for a handkerchief, so he took his out and handed it to her. 'Why did he beat you?'

'Because he's stupid and you can't tell him anything.'

'You chose to go with him.'

'I didn't know how violent he could be. Adam, please can't you and I try again? I'll do my best to be more . . . pleasant, keep my temper in check . . . Adam, please?'

'No, Ethel. We can't try again. I just couldn't do it. You could always leave him, though. You have enough money.'

She scowled at him. 'Sam's taken my bank book and he's been keeping the rent money too. I've hardly any money left.'

'And you're letting him do that?'

'I have no choice. He gets violent. I'm afraid of him. *Please*, Adam, let me come back to you.'

'I'm sorry. I can't. Especially now.'

'Why not now?'

He pretended to hesitate, then said in what he hoped was a convincing tone, 'Oh, because I'm, um, making a new life. In fact, I've got some friends coming round tomorrow tonight. I've just been arranging it.'

'You don't have any real friends.'

'I was at school with the Willcoxes!'

'Them? You didn't have them round to the house before. Why now?'

'You didn't want my friends round before. You said they weren't good enough.' He stepped back. 'Keep the handkerchief.'

She jumped to her feet and tried to grab his sleeve to stop him going, but he moved away again. Then he put the clincher on the act. Well, he hoped it was the clincher. 'Look, I'd advise you to leave him and move somewhere else. I can't give you any details of why, but you should leave straight away, today if you can, tomorrow at the very latest.'

He hurried away, expecting her to call after him, but she didn't.

He did not, he found, want her to get involved to the extent of having to go to prison. He'd done his best to warn her, as well as plant the information, but he could do no more without spoiling their plan.

At the corner he stopped and hid behind some railings to look back at her. She was still standing where he'd left her. She had that thoughtful look on her face which meant she was weighing up what to do next.

He was still angry at being made a fool of by her and hoped what he and the others were doing would lead to Sam Griggs' downfall. And not just for his own sake. He hated to see decent people robbed and hurt as Deemer said some of the shopkeepers had been.

Adam was suddenly quite sure Ethel wouldn't take his advice. Well, on her head be it. He'd tried.

He telephoned Sergeant Deemer when he got back to the laundry. Mindful of the operator, he spoke cryptically, 'I think I did what you wanted. I think something is being planned even as we speak.'

'Well done. We stand a good chance of succeeding, I think. I've got a couple of lads keeping an eye on the local suspect. They're eager to earn a shilling or two and they'll let me know if he does anything unusual between now and tomorrow.'

Adam nodded. They'd tell the sergeant when Griggs left Birch End the next night and Adam had invited Deemer to station himself at his house because Rivenshaw was too far away for him to take quick action.'

He worked hard for the rest of the day, feeling more of a man because he was doing something about Griggs. But he slept badly that night. He always did after he'd had to deal with his ex-wife.

The following day seemed to pass even more slowly. Adam couldn't settle to work and went home from the laundry early, leaving his foreman to close up for the day.

He made himself a sandwich for tea, then left half of it because he had no appetite. He couldn't read the book that had greatly amused him the previous evening. *1066 and All That* was a wonderful parody of English history, so it just showed what a bad state he was in when he found he'd read the same page three times without taking any of it in, let alone laughing.

He switched on the radio, but couldn't be bothered to listen to that, even though there was a good concert on.

The only thing that calmed his nerves a little was pacing up and down.

Would Ethel be caught out, or would she steer clear? Did he want her to be caught?

He kept asking himself that, but got no answers. One minute he thought it served her right, the next he hoped she'd just go away.

'I wish it still got dark early,' Sam told Ethel. 'It'd make my job easier. I'll have to go up to Ellindale by a roundabout route tonight and wait nearby for Willcox to leave for his evening out with his brother. If he doesn't leave, if you've given me the wrong information, you'll be in trouble, my girl.'

'I told you exactly what Adam told me. I can't do more than pass that on, can I?'

'Mind your tongue and get me something to eat.'

Tears came into her eyes as she made him a sandwich. Perhaps she should have taken Adam's advice and left today while Sam was out collecting *her* rents? No, her husband had just been speaking as if something bad was going to happen to frighten her.

She'd thought she could manage Sam, but she couldn't. He was like a barely tamed beast once he had some power over you.

When he set off, she sighed in relief and lay down to rest. He was exhausting to live with. She'd have a good long nap while she waited for him to come back. She hoped he'd succeed in hurting Leah Willcox, because if he didn't, he'd take it out on her when he got back.

He'd probably take it out on her anyway.

She looked at the clock. There was still time to catch the last train into Manchester. She had some money tucked away, but he had her bank book. She could claim that it had been stolen, though, couldn't she? Or perhaps she could find out where he'd hidden it. He'd not been carrying it around with him.

What it came down to was, did she dare leave him or not? If he caught her heading towards the station, he'd half kill her. If she didn't leave him, he might still half kill her.

Out on the moors, Thad shivered and huddled in his blankets. But they felt damp and cold. He'd been here in the cave since yesterday and he'd been cold the whole bloody time.

Glancing out of the entrance, he was puzzled at how low the sun had sunk. He must have dozed a bit. It was later than he'd expected. Which was a good thing, really, because it meant it was time to act. He was fed up of waiting around.

He rubbed his forehead, which was aching again. It had been aching on and off since he had that bad cold. His aunt should have let him stay longer, recover properly. He might make a detour when he'd finished his business here and lob a few stones through her windows. That'd shake the old bitch up a bit.

He dragged himself out of the cave. Better set off now, before it got completely dark. Those clouds were low and promised more rain, so the moon might not be much help to him.

But he'd have a warm young body to warm him up later. He'd show those uppity women who was master. After he'd finished with them, he'd head south and find a job. He couldn't come here again, dammit.

The country was in a rotten mess and so was his life.

He rubbed his forehead again as he set off. This was a worse headache than usual.

He arrived at his farm and decided to have a last look round. Perhaps his brothers would be able to come and live here after they got out of jail. It'd be nice to keep it in the family.

A fit of shivering stopped him for a moment. What he needed was warmer weather. He'd seen pictures of Australia on the news at the cinema. It looked warm there.

He hadn't the money to pay for a passage, but he might be able to work his way there. He was big and strong. The captain would take one look at him and know he'd be useful.

Yes, that was what he'd do afterwards. Head out for Australia.

Finn got cramp in one leg just as Thad came out of the house. It nearly killed him not to move, not to groan.

Was it his imagination or was Hutton walking unsteadily? No, he wasn't imagining it. Thad was weaving about slightly as he walked.

Finn slipped out of the shed and stood in the shadows, taking a few moments to get his leg moving properly again. Then he set off across the fields, heading towards Adam Harris's house in Birch End. He went in the back way, nodding to the maid and her boyfriend, who were going to keep watch on the house after they left.

'They're waiting for you in the sitting room, sir,' she said. 'This way.'

Deemer and Charlie were there, so Finn made his report.

'Hutton came to the farm but he didn't stay there long. He'll be nearly at Spring Cottage now. I hope you've got some good men there to protect the ladies.'

'I picked them myself,' Deemer said.

A car drew up outside and Adam went to the window, moving the edge of the curtain slightly. 'It's Jonah. I'll let him in.'

The two men greeted one another a little more loudly than was necessary at the door. As he closed it, Adam said, 'The others are here. Come and warm yourself up.'

Sam watched the two men go back inside Harris's house then moved along the narrow alley he'd been watching the house from. Ethel had been right about the men gathering at her husband's house. Good. He'd be able to do the job tonight.

The sods would probably sit around like lords, drinking fancy booze and smoking cigars, like the rich people did in the movies. It wasn't right that some folk had such luxurious lives while others had to toil hard just to fill their bellies.

He'd been wondering whether it was worth it to pull Charlie Willcox into line about the protection payments, but the sight of those well-dressed men made him angry all over again, so he set off straight away. He had the use of Ethel's car when he wanted, but tonight he had to walk up the damned hill so as to keep out of sight, because the sound of a car engine would give his presence away. And the car itself would stand out like a sore thumb in poverty-stricken Ellindale. The first thing those women would know was when he burst in on them.

Ethel had insisted he wear a mask. Silly thing it was, but she might be right when she said he didn't want to give them the chance to swear that it was him attacking them. If he covered his face and wore ragged clothes that he threw away, it could have been any big man, and Thad Hutton was still on the run.

And of course, Ethel would swear that Sam had never left the house all evening. She was going to leave the front room curtains open and stuff one of his jackets with cushions, so that it looked as if he was sitting by the fire with her.

He grinned at the cleverness of this. She could be very useful at times, Ethel could. And not just in bed.

At one stage he wondered if he'd heard footsteps behind him, but when he looked round there was no one to be seen. Then a couple of sheep moved in the field next to the road and he smiled at himself. It was the animals moving about. He wasn't usually nervous, but tonight he was a little on edge.

He'd feel better once he'd made the point to Charlie Willcox: pay up or your family will suffer.

A lad knocked on the back door of Adam Harris's house. 'Message for the mester,' he said in an excited, breathless voice.

'Come in, love.' The maid took him through. 'Young Teddy's here, sir.'

The five men turned as one.

Deemer nodded to the lad to report.

'Sam Griggs waited outside till you'd all arrived, Sergeant, then he set off up the hill. I followed him to the first field after Birch End, like you said. Then our Luke took over and I come back t'tell you.'

'Was Griggs on his own?' Deemer asked.

'Yessir.'

'I have another job for you now. I want you to go and wait outside the house where Griggs is living. Just watch and do nothing. I want to know what Mrs Harris does.' He tossed a shilling to the lad, and added, 'There'll be another shilling for you afterwards.'

'Yessir.'

The lad ran off, beaming.

The group of men looked at the sergeant expectantly.

'We can't leave yet,' he said. 'Not till the next lad comes back. Don't worry. We'll soon catch up with him in the car.' He turned to Jonah, who was looking particularly strained. 'You've got men there. He won't get near your women.'

'No. But I'll be glad when this is all over.'

'It's always hard to wait,' Charlie said. 'We did a lot of waiting in the Army, didn't we? Nearly drove me mad.'

24

Sam slowed down as he got near Spring Cottage. The village was very quiet. There had been lights in a few of the houses, and there were clearly people in the pub but they weren't making much noise. Well, not many folk had the money to get drunk these days.

Walking quietly, keeping his eyes open in case anyone was out for a stroll, he continued past the old half-ruined house. Nearly there now.

There was a light in the kitchen but the curtains were drawn. He went round to the back and took out his lock-picking tools. Useful, they were, because tenants sometimes changed the locks on you.

He opened the door very carefully, relieved that it didn't squeak and give him away, and went into a sort of rear hall.

Just as he got to what he supposed to be the kitchen door, it opened and a young lass started to come out, saying, 'I'll just get it and—'

Her! The one he wanted.

She saw him and screamed loudly. Leah Willcox came rushing out and stopped as he grabbed Rosa and set his penknife to her throat.

'You don't want to make any more noise, missus,' he said. 'Get back into the kitchen.'

'What do you want, Griggs?'

'I'm not Griggs.'

'Of course you are. I can—'

She stopped speaking as he pressed the knife point a little deeper into her sister's throat and drew a bead of blood.

'I'm *not* Griggs. And anyone who says I am will be in a lot of trouble and their families will get hurt. Sit down.' He moved Rosa forward, keeping a firm hold on her. 'Now, take off your clothes!'

Mrs Willcox gaped at him.

'Do as I say. All of them. Take them off!' He pressed the knife still further into the lass's white throat.

She began to unbutton her cardigan.

Rosa moaned in fear.

'Shut up, you.' He moved the knife back a little so that he could give her a shake. As he did so, someone hit him from behind, but his cap took part of the shock of it and he had the wit to keep hold of the lass and whip her round between himself and his attacker.

'Try that again and the lass suffers. Now get out of our way. Me an' Rosa are going outside.'

The man stepped aside and Sam frogmarched Rosa to the door.

As he was dragging her over the wall, he had hold of her by one arm. He stood outlined against the sky while she was wriggling below him, trying to escape. A shot rang out and he fell to the ground.

Ben moved cautiously forward towards the prone figure. 'Don't move or I'll fire again.'

There was no answer.

'He's not moving,' Ben called to the others, 'but it might be a trick. Someone bring me a torch so that I can check.'

Ben stayed where he was until one of the men from the village came across with a torch and shone it on the body.

'Take off his mask. I think he's dead, but we need to be sure.'

He turned the man over and took off the mask, showing Sam Griggs' face, eyes blank and open, and a bloody hole in his throat.

'He's dead enough for me,' the man said. 'That were a good shot.'

Ben nodded, then a terrible thought occurred to him. 'Do you think they'll say I murdered him?'

'No. How could they? You saved that lass's life and they'll probably give you a medal.'

'Let me see him,' a voice said from behind them.

Ben turned to see Rosa standing back on their side of the wall. He moved to stand between her and the corpse. 'You don't want to see this, love.'

'Oh, but I do. I need to *know* he's dead, that he can't come after me again.'

Leah came to put one arm round her sister's shoulders. 'How could he possibly think we wouldn't tell people we'd recognised him? Oh dear, I feel sick.' After one look at the body she rushed to the edge of the garden to vomit, then leaned against the wall, shaking. 'Let's go inside. I could do with a cup of cocoa.'

'Can you phone Sergeant Deemer and tell him we've killed Griggs? Stay out of sight afterwards, in case Hutton is around. We'll stay here and keep an eye on the body. We can stay in the lee of the wall. It's deep in shadow.'

She turned to her sister. 'Are you coming inside with me, Rosa?'

'In a minute. I want to have another look at him.'

As Leah reached the back door, someone grabbed her, putting his hand across her mouth before she could scream for help. She recognised him, even in the darkness. She'd never forget what Thad Hutton looked like, not after what he'd done to her sister.

How could there be two wicked men coming after them

on the same night? Sam Griggs had been on his own, she was sure. And this one was a loner as well.

She struggled desperately, trying to get out one cry and bring them all running to help her, but he seemed inhumanly strong and all the response she got from him for her efforts was a soft laugh.

'You won't get away from me,' he whispered. 'An' I'll not let you cry out.'

A few minutes later, Rosa followed her sister into the kitchen and found it empty, with its one lamp turned low. 'Leah! Where are you?'

She rushed into the bathroom, checked the front room and looked in the kitchen again, this time noticing that the kettle hadn't been pushed on to the hot part of the hob.

She screamed at the top of her voice then because that was always the first thing Leah did when she came in, always.

Men came running.

'What's wrong?' Ben asked.

'Leah's not here.'

'*What?* She must be.'

'She's not even been here. See. The kettle hasn't been touched. I left it there. It's the first thing she does, push it further on the hob and get it boiling.'

'Go and check upstairs. Take this.'

Rosa took the torch from him and ran upstairs. It didn't take her more than a couple of minutes to confirm that Leah wasn't there and shout the news as she ran down.

Ben took the torch again and went to the back door, telling everyone to stand still. He looked down at the ground and though there was a mess of footprints just outside the door, there was a single trail of big boot marks showing clearly in the soft ground beyond it.

There were no smaller footprints near that or anywhere around to show where Leah might have moved away from the house, none at all.

'I think someone big has taken her. He must have been carrying her. Oh, damnation! We've failed.'

'Thad Hutton,' Rosa said at once, brushing a tear away impatiently.

'I'm going after them,' Ben said. He looked at the two men who were standing waiting for orders. 'One of you come with me, the other wait and tell anyone who answers this signal to follow us.' He took out his gun and fired twice into the air.

'I'm coming with you,' Rosa said.

'No, you're not.'

But when he'd gone, she ran upstairs, found her sister's gun, which was kept ready loaded, and followed him.

The man waiting by the back door hesitated, clearly wondering whether to try to stop her, by which time she'd slipped past him.

She followed Ben and the other man, staying behind them. If Ben missed, she'd be there to kill Thad instead. She wasn't going to let him hurt her sister.

The man with Ben glanced round once and saw her so she raised her gun to show him. The moon was out now and there was a gap in the clouds. Since her eyes had got used to the dim light, she supposed theirs had too. She had no trouble finding her way.

Ben didn't look round at her, so she continued to follow them, keeping her distance.

Ready.

Just in case.

Back at the house, men began to turn up from the village in response to the double shot. When told what had happened, some of them set off to follow Ben's tracks, while the others spread out round the house.

There was the sound of a car in the lane and two of the village men went to wait for it to stop.

Jonah got out and they told him the news. He looked at them in horror. 'Hutton's got my Leah? I'm going after her.'

Charlie held him back by the arm. 'You'll only slow them down, lad.'

Jonah stared at him, shook his head as if to deny his own weakness, then sighed and stopped trying to pull away.

'Get your gun. I'll follow them and take it with me,' Charlie said. 'I'm not a good shot but it'll frighten him.'

'Yes. But if he's killed her, I want you to promise to kill him.'

'Don't worry. If he's harmed her, he'll not live to hurt another person,' Charlie said grimly. 'Whatever I have to do.'

While Jonah was upstairs, Charlie told the two men not to allow Jonah to follow him. 'He's not strong enough.'

'We'll look after him,' one said. 'Good luck.'

Leah wriggled and fought, even tried to scratch Thad's eyes out. He stopped briefly to tie his handkerchief round her mouth to make sure she couldn't call out, then tied her hands with a bit of rope and upended her over his shoulder, before he continued walking.

The skin of his neck was burning hot to her touch and Leah began to wonder if he was feverish. He was wheezing as he breathed, too, as if his chest was congested. A bit like Jonah.

But he seemed to be paying no attention to himself and he continued to walk like a drunken man across the moors.

At one point he slowed down, panting, 'You can walk beside me from now on. If you don't keep up, I'll cut your throat and be done with you.'

She felt a bit dizzy after being carried with her head hanging down, and tried to pull the handkerchief out of her mouth.

He did it for her, letting it drop as if he'd forgotten its purpose.

'I'm feeling dizzy,' she said.

'So what? Shut up and keep up with me,' was all he said. 'If you make one squeak I'll kill you.'

Although there was a half-moon in the sky, the clouds were beginning to gather again and she couldn't work out where she was. She had no idea of the direction he'd taken her while he was carrying her, except that they seemed to have been walking uphill.

She trudged along beside him, trying to keep up so that she wouldn't upset him.

He stopped for a moment to listen and put out one hand to stop her moving. Then he shook his head and muttered, 'Must have been mistook.'

A short time later he stopped again to listen and this time he growled like an angry wasp. 'No. I weren't mistook.'

He yelled suddenly into the darkness behind them, making her jump in shock. 'If you try to take me, I'll strangle her. You might stop me but you won't get her back alive.' Then he laughed loudly.

Leah shivered at the malevolence in his voice. She was sure he wouldn't hesitate to kill her.

As they continued she tried to think what to do and pretended to stumble, after which she faked a slight limp.

'Stop pretending to limp.'

'I'm not pretending. I twisted my foot when I cruckled.'

'Then limp for all you're worth because I meant what I said: if you slow me down, I'll kill you quick as a flash.'

She limped on for about fifty yards, then pretended to trip and fall.

Almost immediately a shot rang out, and Hutton howled in anger, clutching his arm.

She rolled desperately away but he grabbed her by the foot and started hauling her back towards him. She realised she couldn't have rolled much further anyway because they were on the edge of a stony outcrop, which was like a small cliff, and she didn't want to fall over it, couldn't even see what was below them.

Figuring that if she didn't fight back, he'd kill her anyway, she continued to struggle.

He cursed and kicked out at her, then began tugging her by the feet again.

But she'd found a stone lodged deeply enough in the ground to cling to.

Another shot rang out, and it seemed to come from another direction. Was there more than one person trying to rescue her?

Thad dropped her feet and raised his head, turning it from side to side, as if looking for his pursuers.

Leah wriggled desperately backwards, away from the edge, still expecting at any moment that he would grab her again.

But he didn't. Instead he clutched his chest and staggered sideways to fall to the ground near the clifftop.

A third shot kicked into the ground beside him.

'Stay back, Rosa!' Ben yelled, then, 'Give yourself up, Hutton.'

'No!' he yelled. It sounded like an animal in distress. When he lifted himself into a half crouch, they waited for him to move towards them, but instead he threw himself towards the edge.

He misjudged, not managing to tumble right over it, but as men ran towards them, he deliberately rolled the final couple of feet and vanished abruptly from sight.

Leah bowed her head and wept in utter relief, unable to move, feeling as weak as a baby.

The thuds of the body bumping against rocks as it fell were dull, and would not have made anyone turn their head to see what it was if they hadn't known that a man was falling to his death.

After he went over the edge, there wasn't a single sound from Thad, though he'd been roaring threats only a few seconds previously.

At first none of the watchers moved, then two men ran to the edge to look over and see what had happened, while Ben came to kneel by Leah.

'Are you all right? Why were you limping? Did he hurt you?'

'I was pretending to limp to slow him down. And I pretended to trip and fall for the same reason. I thought he was going to kill me but we were so near the edge I had to do something or he might have pushed me over.'

'You helped save your own life, then, lass,' he said. 'I was frightened to fire at him before you did that, for fear of hitting you. Can you stand or do we need to carry you?'

Charlie, who'd been listening, moved forward and pulled her up. She clung to him, trembling all over in reaction.

'Who fired the second shot?' she asked as his solid body made her feel safer and the trembling eased.

'Your sister and I fired more or less at the same time. She had your gun. I had Jonah's. He wanted to come after you but I stopped him.'

He didn't need to explain why.

Rosa came up. 'Is that evil creature really dead?'

'Yes, lass. No one could fall down there and live. It's one of the steepest drops round here.'

'Did my shot hit him? It all seemed such a jumble, I didn't know what to do.'

'That's what it's like in war,' Charlie said. 'A mess. Everything confused. You don't know what you're doing

half the time. We can't always tell who fired a shot that
hit.'

'I hope I did hit him,' she said fiercely. 'He wanted to kill
my sister.'

'I don't know that any of us managed a fatal shot but we
definitely winged him,' Ben said. 'He threw himself over the
edge when he saw he couldn't get away.'

'Good. I won't have to worry about him or Sam Griggs
coming after me and my sister.'

Leah put her free arm round Rosa. She felt old and weary
but Jonah must be worried sick about them so she gathered
the last of her strength and turned to the men. 'I need to
get back to my husband and let him know we're safe.'

'There's an easier path down the hill just along there,' a
man said.

They followed him in single file along a little sheep path.
No one spoke. The moon came out as if to help them.

It seemed a long way to the house.

When they got near they saw Jonah standing in the doorway.
He called out his wife's name and ran to meet her, pulling
her into his arms and covering her face with kisses.

Charlie watched them fondly for a moment or two, then
he saw Rosa shiver. 'You can kiss your wife some more later,
Jonah,' he said loudly. 'We're all freezing to death here.'

They went inside and Leah's first action was to push the
kettle on to the hob.

At the sight of that, Rosa felt tears well in her eyes and
went to cling to her again, whispering, 'Is it really over?'

'Yes, love. We need to forget what happened and get on
with our lives. You're safe now.'

Rosa rested her head against her sister. She might not
forget it, but the fear had gone, the fear she'd lived with
since Thad first captured her.

EPILOGUE

There was a celebration in The Shepherd's Rest for the Ellindale folk the following Saturday, and it was Charlie who arranged it this time.

He came up to see his brother and Leah, to tell them what he intended to do. 'Some of the men came to your aid, risking their own lives. They didn't hesitate. They won't take money for it, so let's give them a treat, like you did last New Year's Eve.'

'Leah and I should be doing that,' Jonah said at once.

'No. Let me arrange it this time. I'm grateful that they—' he swallowed hard and blinked his eyes furiously for a moment before continuing, 'that the people from your village keep an eye on my family.'

It was as close to admitting aloud how much he loved his brother as he ever got, Leah thought. 'What are you thinking of doing, Charlie?'

'Well, actually, I remembered what you did, so I've seen Don and Izzy at the pub and they're happy to put the refreshments together for another village party.'

They would be, she thought. It would be a nice bonus for them, and any money that trickled into the village helped others, she was sure.

Jonah put a casual arm round his brother's shoulders. 'What exactly are you planning, lad?'

'Marion suggested an afternoon tea, with ham or cheese sandwiches and shop-bought cakes. And I chanced on a bargain, a sack of apples. They're last year's, but they're only a bit wrinkled and they're perfectly good to eat. There's enough to give one to each person as they leave.'

Leah smiled across the table at him. 'That sounds wonderful, Charlie.'

The following Saturday afternoon, people crowded into the village pub, talking and laughing at the prospect of a treat. Once again, the Willcoxes had the table of honour near the window. Once again, as oldest inhabitant, Simeon stood up to speak for his neighbours and friends.

'We're here to celebrate getting rid of them wicked devils. But I want to say that there's other things to celebrate. Since Mester Jonah and his wife have come to live here, things have getten a little better for us struggling folk at the top of the hill, because they spend their money here and hire our folk when they can. So we're pleased to have the Willcoxes in our village, we are that, and we're celebrating that today as well.'

His speech was interrupted by cheers and the banging of fists on tables.

Leah looked at the groups of people with happy faces and a lump came into her throat. She loved living here, never wanted to move away, was determined to go on helping her neighbours in every way possible.

When the noise had died down, Simeon continued, '*And* we're glad the little lass has done so well at school. Well done, Rosa love. No one from Ellindale has ever got an Esherwood Bequest before.'

More cheers and clapping.

Rosa blushed and bobbed her head as she smiled round at them all.

'Mr Charlie, we thank you for your generosity today but first, I want to offer a toast. My friends, raise your glasses or teacups and we'll drink to the family from Spring Cottage.'

When this was done, Jonah stood up to reply formally. 'I'd like to propose a toast to our village. It's at the heart of our lives.'

The old man nodded and called, 'To our village! Ellindale.'

Glasses were raised again, with another chorus of cheers, whistles and shouts.

When it had died down, Simeon nodded towards Izzy and Don, standing behind the bar, to say he'd finished.

Don called out, 'Food's ready. Mr Jonah, will you and your family please come and fill your plates first.'

As Leah set her plate down on their table she smiled at her sister-in-law, who was taking a seat next to her. Marion had been looking faintly uncomfortable ever since she came into the pub.

Leah guessed that Marion wasn't sure what to say or do, because she'd never been in such a situation before, so she said quietly, 'I'm glad you came today. I wanted the whole family to be here.'

'Oh. Yes. Well, I wasn't sure if I . . . but Charlie insisted . . . and of course, I'm glad to see you all safe and sound. I must say your neighbours seem very decent people.'

'There's another reason for you to be happy, Marion. Jonah and I love your sketches of labels for our bottles and we hope you'll carry on doing it and be part of the new business.'

For a moment, Marion just stared at her, open-mouthed. 'You really do like them?'

'Very much indeed. Simple but elegant. You're hired as our artist.'

Marion went bright pink and didn't seem able to put another sentence together, so Leah let her sister-in-law recover from the shock. Charlie winked at her and Jonah smiled gently round at his family.

For a moment, the group seemed alone in a little island of quietness. Other people chatted as they queued and filled their plates, but they left the Willcoxes alone.

'Well done, Marion love,' Charlie said to his wife. 'I'm proud of you.'

'Oh. Oh, my goodness!' Marion sniffed, then fumbled for her handkerchief and blew her nose.

Leah ate a little but mostly she sat lost in blissful dreams of the future. She had found something very important to do with her new life. She ended up holding Jonah's hand on one side, Rosa's on the other. No need for words with such dreams and hopes, and her own family around her.

After a while, when people had taken the edge off their appetites, the noise and laughter grew louder and she couldn't ignore her neighbours, some of whom stopped for a word. It was lovely to see so many smiling faces.

She and Jonah had, she hoped, given Ellindale folk a little more hope for the future than there had been before.

And if it was up to her, the little business would thrive, and the Youth Hostel too. Oh, she had so many plans and ideas.

Jonah nudged her with his elbow. 'Happy?'

'Oh, yes. Aren't you?'

'I've never been as happy in my whole life.'

CONTACT ANNA

Anna is always delighted to hear from readers and can be contacted via the internet.

Anna has her own web page, with details of her books, some behind-the-scenes information that is available nowhere else and the first chapters of her books to try out, as well as a picture gallery. You can also buy some of her ebooks from the 'shop' on the web page. Go to:
www.annajacobs.com

Anna can be contacted by email at
anna@annajacobs.com

You can also find Anna on Facebook at
www.facebook.com/AnnaJacobsBooks

If you'd like to receive an email newsletter about Anna and her books every month or two, you are cordially invited to join her announcements list. Just email her and ask to be added to the list, or follow the link from her web page.

My maternal grandfather, born in 1884, was both intelligent and highly eccentric, very much his own person, and always loved the outdoors.

A fun portrait of the Lords and partners. My paternal grandmother Sarah Alice is the one on the left, such a kind, loving woman!

A more formal family portrait of the Lords, with my grandmother on the right and my lively Auntie Peg on the left, their two brothers in between.